WHERE THE RIVER BENDS

WHERE THE RIVER BENDS

A novel by

RICHARD HADDAWAY

SOUTHERN METHODIST
UNIVERSITY PRESS
Dallas

This novel is a work of fiction. Names, characters, places, and incidents are either the product of the author's imagination or are used fictitiously.

• • •

Copyright © 2002 by Richard Haddaway
First edition, 2002

Requests for permission to reproduce material from this work should be sent to:
  Rights and Permissions
  Southern Methodist University Press
  PO Box 750415
  Dallas, Texas 75275-0415

Jacket art: *Steps, 1972,* © by Jamie Wyeth.
Design by Tom Dawson Graphic Design

This novel is an expanded version of *Our Island Home*, published by Lattitudes Press, 1990.

LIBRARY OF CONGRESS CATALOGING-IN-PUBLICATION DATA

Haddaway, Rich.
    Where the river bends : a novel / by Richard Haddaway.—1st ed.
        p. cm.
    "This novel is an expanded version of Our island home, published by Lattitudes
    Press, 1990"—T.p. verso.
    ISBN 0-87074-470-4 (acid-free paper)
1. Family owned business enterprises—Fiction. 2. Petroleum industry and trade—
Fiction. 3. Grandparent and child—Fiction. 4. Father and child—Fiction. 5. Texas—
Fiction. I. Haddaway, Rich. Our island home. II. Title.

PS3608.A27 W48 2002
813'.54—dc21   2002019375

Printed in the United States of America on acid-free paper

10 9 8 7 6 5 4 3 2 1

For James, my dearest boy; for Shannon, our newest gift; and for Kay, my one and all. Everything is for Kay. Everything.

ACKNOWLEDGMENT

My special gratitude to Kathryn Lang, Senior Editor at SMU Press, whose decade of hope and hoeing finally coaxed a bloom from this stubborn garden.

PART

Our Island Home
1958–1965

1

TOWERING, FORMIDABLE, GRIM AS STONE, GRANDDADDY ENTERED. His
hardwood steps shuddered across the grand dining hall as the ancient
grandfather clock in the foyer announced his arrival with two solemn
gongs. He strode across the room and, in one judicious movement, pulled
out his throne of a chair at the head of the table and sat.

First, as usual, he cleared his throat with a growlish clutter and took
a large and scowling look over his domain. We children, already silent,
stiffened within our starched Sunday clothes—the boys in slacks, white
shirts and clip-on bow ties, my sister in a puffed-out petticoated affair.

We knew what was next. We bowed our curled and tangled heads as
he clinked his butter knife against his water goblet, signifying that, by
God, the Almighty would have the floor in this house for one measly
minute and we had better give Him respectful silence or else we would
suffer His Representative's immediate and possibly everlasting wrath.

We did not breathe.

In a cathedral-size voice he prayed: "Lord bless this food for our use,
and us to thy service, in Christ's name. Amen."

"Amen," we exhaled.

The feast began. We called it Sunday Dinner.

• • •

3

The table, which was long enough to handle small aircraft, held the bounty of Granddaddy's garden: buttered yellow squash, glistening carrots, new potatoes bobbing in butter, sliced tomatoes, bacon-strewn black-eyed peas, corn-on-the-cob. Granddaddy pierced the piglet-size roast beef with a two-pronged sterling pitchfork and began slicing with his sword-length silver knife. The maids, Ethylene and Odessa, stood by, helping him get the roast to our plates, overseeing the gravy and bringing us new silverware when ours clunked to the floor.

We children sat at Granddaddy's left. There were five of us, all with various and occasionally violent shades of red hair. Granddaddy sometimes compared us to a brush fire, because we could get out of hand, or to an Irish rebellion. On bad days he compared us to the Flames of Hell.

I, Stephen, the oldest, sat next to Granddaddy. I was ten years old that summer. Next to me was my brother Endicott, who was nine. His hair was red enough and his curls shocking enough to make a clown jealous. Then Laura, his twin, who was red-blond like me. (Most people thought she and I were the twins.) John, six, was next. His hair was sandy red. The baby, Arthur, who was one, was in his highchair. His cobweb hair was peach-blond. Miss Godwin, the nurse, and my mother sat on opposite sides of Arthur. They took turns feeding him.

To Granddaddy's right were Aunt Kitty, my father's sister, and next to her was where Aunt Jew, Granddaddy's sister, had rolled up her wheelchair. After that were five empty chairs that were often occupied by guests, usually cousins—we were hardly ever at a loss for cousins.

At the opposing end of the table from Granddaddy was where my father always sat. He was gone again.

Our house was a three-story colonial castle. We had two libraries, two parlors, two conservatories—one for plants, the other for music. There were back stairs and front stairs and a dumb waiter that you could transport a cat in, which was always quite a surprise for Ethylene in the kitchen when you considered the state of mind of the cat by the time it was conveyed from the opening in the upstairs hallway through the creaking darkness downward.

The front stairway was designed for grand entrances—for debutantes and brides and such—but not, as we children were inclined, by way of the banister, which curved recklessly and precipitously and tended to spill one sprawling out onto the Persian rug-covered foyer. The dining room was big enough to feed an army in, which Granddaddy said we were as big as and ate like, and the kitchen was big enough to live in, which we did almost, near mealtimes.

Outside were porches and verandahs front and back and, holding it all up, four massive, muscular Greek Revival columns. Eaves and turns were everywhere, in which a civilization of pigeons and sparrows lived. All of it was white—a proper, authoritarian white; it took a painter six months to paint.

Although this was the 1950s, you couldn't tell it by the way we lived. Granddaddy had no use for the decade—nor, for that matter, for the Twentieth Century in general. He found it disagreeable. Granddaddy preferred the Eighteenth or, in a pinch, the Nineteenth. He had a large voice and lots of money. He was in charge. The Beckwith household lived in whatever century Granddaddy preferred.

We lived removed from time, remote from society (we were five miles west of the city limits of Fort Worth), protected from the razor heat of north-central Texas in the midst of giant trees. It was a green island of shade at the edge of the brown, outstretching numbness of West Texas—the last outpost of Southern civilization, as Granddaddy liked to describe it. The house sat in the middle of fifty acres of Trinity River bottomland, which had been cleared by a Confederate major just after the War; a grove of pecan trees had been planted around the house, which was built in the 1870s. With chickens, milk cows, and servants, with Granddaddy's big garden and all his investments, we were almost self-sufficient. We were almost happy.

"Endicott!" Granddaddy announced. Exclamation points came permanently attached to the natural boom of his voice.

Our forks halted. The small talk shrank.

We turned toward my pale pink, almost shivering brother, who squeaked, "Yes sir?"

Granddaddy was thoroughly pinched in his double-vested, charcoal

Sunday suit and Sunday shoes. (He should have bought a new suit ten years and twenty pounds ago, but he was waiting for a sale.) His voice rolled down over Endicott like the Red Sea over those wayward Egyptians: "There seems to be a spot of something red on your ear."

All eyes fell on the accused ear. Laura offered: "Toad blood, prob'ly."

John elaborated: "Endy was doing brain surgery on a toad."

"I see," Granddaddy said. I detected the slightest hint of amusement in the corner of his voice and eyes. "Go on."

Laura took over: "See, Endicott found this toad that was kind of cross-eyed, and he decided it might have a brain tumor."

"And did it?" Granddaddy asked Endicott.

"I don't know, sir," he said. "We never found it."

"The tumor?" Granddaddy asked.

"The brain," Endicott replied.

The surgery had been performed in Endy's and my room just before dinner. Endicott was the chief surgeon; the others assisted. Besides John and Laura were Ethylene's children, Whyvonne and Travis and Baby Midland, who were ten, nine, and three.

The surgical team—each had been assigned an appendage—stretched the toad, tying him face-up to a piece of plywood on a card table near Endicott's bed. Set out on the table were the operating instruments—a pocket knife, an ice pick, a bottle opener, and an electric drill. Odessa made surgeons' masks out of Arthur's old diapers.

I was at my desk across the room, looking over now and then. I had more important work to do.

They stood in a semicircle around the table, all except Baby Midland, who was off to the side, holding open an old pillowcase. Endicott called it the gut bag—"in case," he said, "there's any extra guts left over."

"Scalpel!" Endicott demanded with a muffled billow of breath through his mask.

Travis picked up the Cub Scout pocketknife and slapped it into John's hands. Then it began going down the row, around the card table, hand to small hand.

"Scapa!" Travis said, passing it over to John.

"Knife!" John said, slapping it over to Whyvonne.

"Scalpel!" Whyvonne said, slamming it into Laura's hand.

"Dammit, Whyvonne!" Laura shouted back at her, "you damn near cut my hand off!"

"You're supposed to do it that way so you won't drop stuff," Whyvonne said.

John said, "I'm gonna tell Mama you've been cussin' again."

"You little tattletale," Laura said.

"Shut up!" Endicott said.

He reached over and got the knife out of Laura's hand. His fingers were twice as long as they should have been, and rubbery. He was wearing Odessa's dishwashing gloves.

"X marks the spot," he said, cutting a small mark on the top of the toad's head. The toad had been chloroformed and was pretty much out of its misery already. "We'll drill about here. DRILL!"

"Drill!" Travis said, handing it to John.

"Drill! Drill! Drill!" they pronounced as it went down the line, each stepping out of the way of the attached extension cord.

The toad, with what awareness remained, was quaking.

Endicott held up the instrument for a final inspection. The flared bit was too wide—about the width of the toad's head. When I pointed that out he said it was the only one he could find in the shed. Endicott pulled the trigger, and the drill spun and hummed.

The toad, if memory serves, fainted.

Everyone leaned forward around the table. I got up from my desk and came closer. Baby Midland squeezed in. But then Endicott stopped the proceedings.

"Wipe!" he said. He was looking straight at Whyvonne.

"Wipe what?" she asked.

"My forehead. Look how much I'm sweatin'."

Whyvonne squinted up in anger. Her eyes were black beads. "Wipe ya own damn foe-head, fool!"

"That's tellin' him, Whyvonne," Laura said.

He returned her glare, then wiped his forehead with his upper arm. He turned back to the toad at hand.

The assistants and I leaned forward again. The drill whirled and whined. Carefully, Endicott pushed the end of the spinning bit into the top of the toad's head.

The bit almost immediately wedged itself in the pliant flesh, tearing the body from its moorings. Impaled, the toad twirled helplessly, a blur of dangling legs. Blood shot out across the room.

"Turn it off! Turn it off!" Laura shouted.

Endicott was hypnotized, but not the rest of us. We were being showered by toad blood, and we dived for cover.

"Shut it off, Endy!" Laura yelled from beneath the table.

Finally the screaming drill began dying with a long moan. Laura had pulled the plug. We stood up to see the toad spinning on the end of the drill bit in a slowing, dying, limp pirouette. Only a few, small tremblings of life appeared to be left in the creature.

"Gut bag!" said Endicott.

"Gut bag!" said Baby Midland, smiling big at finally being called into service. She toddled over and held open the pillowcase.

Endicott held the drill over the bag. He pushed the body off the drill bit as if it were the end piece of meat on a shish kebab. And with a philosophical sigh he said, "Well, you can't win 'em all."

Aunt Jew tried to speak but coughed instead and kept on laughing. She had finished eating and was smoking a cigarette the way she did everything, extravagantly. She was wrapped in smoke.

She nodded in Endicott's direction. "So what's happened to the patient?"

"We lost him," Endy said.

"Died, you mean? I figured as much."

"No. I looked in the gut bag later on and he wasn't there."

"Stephen dumped him out the window," John tattled.

"That toad was gonna stink up the place," I said.

"You're absolutely sure he was dead?" Aunt Jew asked me. "Some doctors go to extraordinary lengths to resuscitate a patient."

"No ma'am, I don't think there was any hope left," I said. "I think he was pretty well succumbed."

"He died of shock is what I figured," Endicott added.

"That's quite possible," Granddaddy surmised.

"The patient croaked, in other words," Aunt Jew said.

Her laughter billowed through the room like her smoke. She was hardly five feet tall, yet she laughed bigger per square inch than anybody I ever knew. She had poured herself a drink from the flask she kept in a leather pouch attached to her wheelchair.

"That poor thing," my mother said, trying for tenderness amid the torrents of laughter. She was our lone liberal, and she was ignored.

Even Granddaddy was overtly smiling now. Aunt Kitty was laughing because it seemed expected, and Ethylene was at the door in the back of the room, struggling to hold back her laughter.

Granddaddy said, "And did you learn anything from this operation, Endicott?"

"Yes sir," he said. He paused a minute, thinking. "If you're gonna operate on somebody, be sure you tie 'em down good first."

"A lesson worth remembering, I'm sure," Granddaddy said.

"Mama," John asked, "when do you think Daddy's gonna get here?" He had his linen napkin tucked up in his collar. Aunt Kitty had her napkin the same way, folded into the neck of her blouse, and Arthur had his bib tied on.

Mama said, "I just don't know, honey." Her voice slid away like a small wind.

"He hasn't called?" Laura asked.

"No, honey."

"But what about the ice cream," Endicott wanted to know.

"And the cake," John asked.

"I don't know," Mama said. "I just don't know."

This day was my father's thirty-fifth birthday, and Sunday Dinner was supposed to include a celebration. But he wasn't home yet. He was on a business trip.

Granddaddy was in the oil business (Beckwith Minerals), and Daddy worked for him. Daddy had been out in West Texas to look over some leased properties and to inspect some wells, and he should have been back. I figured he'd spent the night at our cabin on the Brazos River, about sixty miles to the west, but it had no phone, so Mama wasn't sure where he was.

"Since Daddy isn't here," Endicott said, "we might as well have the cake and ice cream now. You know, before it spoils."

"Daddy won't care," John said.

"Yeah," Laura said.

"I don't know," Mama said.

From the inside out, in a long breath, she slumped. Much of the Irish in her green-glinting eyes, dark-blush hair, and singing laughter was being worn away, and her weariness was worse some days than others, like now. My father had done that.I can remember the worry and the distance in her voice. She wasn't hiding it as well as usual, or maybe I was just getting older and starting to notice such things. She tried to be casual in her responses to my brothers and sister, but a ripple of hurt went across her voice.

Granddaddy noticed. "I think the ice cream and cake should wait until William returns," he said.

"Yes," she said. She gathered resolve from him.

"But Mama," Endicott said.

"We could save some cake for Daddy," John said.

"I wouldn't eat all the ice cream," Endicott said. "I promise."

Without realizing it, we had treaded into a deep and hidden place of family tension. I was barely old enough to know, but I heard it—something—a mumble of thunder on the far horizon. I was hearing the beginning of the end of an empire.

Granddaddy reentered the conversation in a deliberate and godly voice: "Didn't you children hear your mother? The *case* is *closed*."

"Yes sir," John said. Laura said the same thing. So did I, even though I'd stayed out of it. A moment of silence followed.

The curse of strong-willed people is that they produce strong-willed children and grandchildren. They create their own Hell. Endicott turned up the heat.

After what he hoped was an appropriate pause, he filed an appeal. "Mama," he said, "I was just thinking. What if Daddy . . ."

Endicott interrupted himself. He made the mistake of looking back over his shoulder at Granddaddy, to see if it was safe to proceed, and he was brought up short: He had stepped over that invisible line within Granddaddy that was most unwise to cross.

Overreacting, they call it nowadays. As an overreactor, Granddaddy was a thespian. Endicott shriveled down in his chair as the old man's ashen eyes darkened, then ignited into glowing lumps. Granddaddy leaned forward in his chair, expanding with a kind of steam, as my brother shrank back and down and down. Each of Granddaddy's words was flame-tipped: "Dammit. God *dammit. GOD DAMMIT!*"

Endicott was almost under the table by now.

"Can my voice not be heard? Is there something wrong with the acoustics in this room?"

Granddaddy's white puffs of hair seemed storm-frothed; his words rumbled down from on high where he and his righteous anger were enthroned: "Lawyers. God damn lawyers. All five of you, five God damn budding barristers, all in one house, all in my house.

"Well I won't have it. I will *not* permit you the license to grill your poor mother mercilessly. I will *not* allow you free rein in my house, to run roughshod over the rights of others. Is that understood?"

"Yes sir," we said, four very small voices.

"I may be old and I may be outnumbered," Granddaddy continued, "but I am still bigger than all of you put together. And until that changes, until further notice, my word will be law in this house. Is that understood?"

"Yes sir."

He concluded: "There will be no dessert period, not now, not this evening, not for *eternity* AND THEN SOME!"

Then he raised his arm—the long arm of the law—and pointed toward the stairs and the territory of damnation. "Now go to your rooms, every last one of you!"

"Yes sir," we said.

With heads drooping and without another word, we pushed back from the table and left the room in a ragged huddle. Even I, who had not been involved, and Arthur, who had only played with his carrots, were banished. Miss Godwin took Arthur back to the nursery, and we children walked slowly into the foyer and toward the stairs.

Granddaddy had spoken.

A small family could have stretched out and lived a full life in our foyer. The room was echo-wide and canyon-deep. Its Persian rugs were long enough to tell an epic. A pair of curly-wooded, doilied credenzas crouched against the wall. Several mirrors, a couple of coat racks, that sonorous grandfather clock, and a wobbly, embroidered settee filled out the room. Hanging on a gold cable from the shadowed ceiling two stories up was a chandelier as big as a Buick.

The stairs, set in a grand semicircular sweep, were wide enough to fit the four of us abreast, though it would have been a squeeze. So John went first, then Laura, then Endy and me side by side. Upward we trudged, downcast, beneath the portraits of hoary Beckwiths—Granddaddy's Virginia forebears. They were planters and congressmen and jurists and fine ladies, puffed and powdered, proud and sour. They no doubt would have been ashamed of this rough bunch of small Texans walking below them, headed toward a dessertless banishment.

Endicott, over the years, had acquired the job of chief spokesman and solicitor for us children. He had a facile tongue and more than enough charm, and he usually won his case, or at least a mitigated punishment. But not this time.

We were halfway up when Laura paused. In an ominous rustling of her petticoat, I saw what was coming. I stopped. Endicott continued, head down, absent-mindedly, until he was one step below her.

Laura wheeled around and let fly with a right undercut, low in his stomach, achingly low. Endy doubled over and lost all his air in a single, spurted thud of a cry. His clip-on bow tie popped off as his breath uncorked.

He was paralyzed, struggling for air, holding onto the banister with one hand and his gut with the other. Bent double, his red curls unfurled, dangling, trembling.

I walked around him. We went to our rooms. It was our way of saying that his services as our attorney would no longer be required.

The great heat of those days was staggering, even though we lived under all that shade, plus the secondary shade of the house with its twelve-foot ceilings, fans of all kinds, and tall, wide-open windows. We wore as few clothes as possible. For us older children that was cut-off, stringy jeans, T-shirts, and no shoes, and for the younger ones that was underwear alone. I stripped off my Sunday clothes and got into my summer uniform.

We children lived in a suite of rooms on the second floor, John in the first room to the left at the top of the stairs, Laura in the middle one, and Endicott and I in the biggest room. Across the hall was my parents' bedroom, which was formerly three bedrooms—the adjoining walls had been removed. It included my father's office. Next door was the children's library; at the end of the hall was the bathroom. Out from my parents' room was a private porch where my mother liked to go, alone, to lean against the balcony railing and look out into the tangle of trees.

Endy came in with his tie in his hand, his breath still stuttering. After he put on his other clothes, he went to his desk across the room and began working on a model airplane, the sleekest new fighter jet. I was at my own desk, and I paid him no mind. I had a possum to contend with.

I was an aspiring taxidermist. For the previous year or so, I had been enrolled in a correspondence course from the Lance Taylor School of Taxidermy in Birmingham, Alabama, having applied through a coupon in *Boys' Life* magazine. For $29.95 plus tax, the school admitted anybody. They sent instruction booklets, catalogues, and order blanks for supplies.

You started with small birds, then came small animals such as rats and rabbits, then fish, then frogs and snakes, larger birds such as hawks, and on to medium-size animals such as raccoons and possums. They sent a new booklet as you mastered each category.

After the possum category I would be moving on to tanning skins. I wanted to make my mother a mink coat for Christmas, but I didn't have any minks and I didn't know where I could get them. All I had so far was a jackrabbit pelt, which was drying on the ledge outside my bedroom window and which some ants had gotten into; it had gotten crinkly hard and wasn't very furry because in the summer rabbits shed, like everything else in Texas. I was thinking of making earmuffs out of it, but it smelled bad. I was hoping that by Christmas the smell would have abated enough that, considering the distance from ear to nose, Mama might be able to stand it. I was also worried about what to do with the tail—it was going to dangle from my mother's earmuffs like a lonely, puffy earring.

After skins was the last booklet, big animals such as deer and bears. I was thinking I might have to settle for a cow, if I could find a dead one, but then there was the problem of getting it up the stairs to my work area.

The supplies were expensive, even with the great discount I was getting from the school. It was amazing how much stuff you needed—a scalpel, needles and thread, preservatives, pliers, excelsior for the stuffing, string, various thicknesses of wires, paint, eyes. My savings were dwindling. The Super Deluxe Assortment of glass eyes, for instance, included everything from starling to alligator eyes and cost $17.95 plus shipping and handling.

But it wasn't just the expense. I was losing faith in my abilities.

I looked again at my specimens on the shelves above my desk, and what I saw left me crestfallen.

Rigor mortis sets in faster than one would think, especially in the heat of Texas. No matter how hard I tried to correct the problem, I could not seem to undo the pose into which my specimens were locked at the moment of their death. On their furry or feathered faces were expressions combining both agony and surprise. I had to admit they looked better freshly dead than after I got through with them.

My father and I had gone to a neighbor's farm to get my first specimen, a pigeon. Mr. Gregory had pigeons galore on the roof of his barn. He was glad to get rid of them, he said.

Daddy and I snuck up on them. He had his shotgun. When they flapped off the top of the barn, he blasted several out of the sky. I took the least damaged one.

Edna, I called her. I had mounted her on a pecan limb, upon which she staggered, her little pink feet clutching desperately to it. Her wings were out of kilter; her pink neon breast feathers slumped. Her beak was open and askance. Her eyes had a stricken look. The overall effect was a sort of wobbly frenzy.

But I loved her just the same. I got attached to my projects—I knew them intimately, from the inside out. They became something like very quiet pets.

Also on the shelf was a squirrel, which Aunt Jew had shot. She loved squirrel hunting. In the fall, Endy and I would roll her in her wheelchair out into the pecan grove and crouch behind her. She'd hunker under her brown shawl—her hunting shawl, she called it, a tweedy thing Aunt Kitty had knitted. She'd make her voice and false teeth chatter—a nervous, biting bark—and wait. As soon as a curious squirrel stuck his head from behind a limb, she'd blast him out of the tree with her .22 rifle. She hardly ever missed.

I named the squirrel Ludwig. His face was flattened, his front teeth bucked out, and his tail took several broken turns. One front paw dangled uselessly. I hadn't been able to find any squirrel glass eyes, so I had substituted owl eyes, which made poor Ludwig seem uncommonly amazed.

Among the other specimens was a black bass that was a garish, yellowish green because of my paint job. The rabbit's feet had drawn up; he looked like he was on tippy-toes. My two frogs grinned. The duck panted.

And now my latest project, Bess. The possum lay feet-up on my desk, and I was sewing the opening where the stuffing had been inserted. It wasn't going very well. There were gaps.

Her thin little paws splayed. Her tail drooped. She had a vacant stare; I hadn't put her eyes in yet. Her nose was turned up pertly and her lips curled churlishly. The overall effect? Roadkill.

But a smile rippled across my mind as I remembered the day Bess wandered into our lives.

We had two collies, Wilson and Woodrow, named for the president Granddaddy railed against most, even more than FDR. Alarmists, Granddaddy called the dogs with a sneer. Idealists. Nincompoops.

We worked on the dogs' education, forcing them to watch *Lassie* on Sunday nights, but it never did any good. "Go get help, Woody!" I'd shout, to see if they'd learned anything. "Go call the sheriff, Wilson!" Endicott would add. "I've been bit by a snake and I'm about to die!" They'd just sit and scratch.

One afternoon about a week before, Wilson and Woody had begun barking—squeal-high and curdlingly. I went around to the front yard.

The dogs had killed a possum. They were circling it, barking and lunging and biting at it.

I was overjoyed. I had just finished my rabbit and I was in need of a new specimen. The possum would be perfect. The dogs had hardly damaged it. If I could just get it up to my desk and start working on it before it froze up . . .

I grabbed the possum by its hairless white tail and took it up the front porch steps. I went into the foyer and yelled: "Hey, y'all! Come look at what the dogs got!" The dogs were barking and jumping and snapping at the possum, which I tried to hold out of their reach.

We had been rehearsing our play, *Robin Hood Meets the Little Rascals*. I was Spanky, Endicott was Robin, Laura was Darla, Whyvonne was Maid Marian, John was Alfalfa, Travis was Buckwheat, and Baby Midland was the stagehand. Odessa was making the costumes and Ethylene was Fry Tuck, as she called him, but she didn't have time to rehearse. She was cooking.

Laura and Whyvonne had been in Laura's room upstairs while the rest of us had been in the backyard. The girls were supposed to be locked in the castle, with the rest of us beneath their window. Endicott, as Robin, was going to climb the chinaberry tree to rescue them. Then came the barking.

"Cut!" I had yelled. Besides being the writer and a skinny Spanky, I was also the director.

So Laura and Whyvonne came back through the bedroom and down the upstairs hall and over to the landing to see what was going on. Endicott came in the front door behind me, followed by John, Travis, and Baby Midland.

Endicott had on his Robin Hood costume—underwear Odessa had dyed green and on which he had glued leaves. He was wearing a green baseball cap with a chicken feather sticking out of the top. Except for his freckles, that's all he had on. He had his bow and arrow with him.

Whyvonne had on a flowing dress made out of a sheet and a dunce cap with a scarf pinned to its peak. Baby Midland had on regular underwear, Travis's, which was her usual outfit, and John, Travis, Laura, and I had on our regular shorts and T-shirts, since we were Little Rascals. Laura wore a fetching bow in her hair, Whyvonne had ratted Travis's hair way out, and she'd gotten a sprig of John's hair to stand up with a shot of WD-40. "What-ho, y'all!" Endy Hood shouted as he ran into the foyer. He tried to make his voice deep and brave.

"What the hell!" Travis exclaimed.

"A possum!" John yelled.

Suddenly, the possum-playing possum roared awake. It snarled and reached up to try to bite me, and I let go of it, jumping back. Whyvonne screamed and so did I. The possum raced across the Persian rugs and crawled up on the banister, with Wilson and Woody right behind, barking and snapping. Whyvonne screamed again.

John, Travis, and Baby Midland began jumping and shouting, urging on the dogs: "Sic 'em! Sic 'em! Get that possum!"

The possum scurried up the banister, stopping to turn and hiss at the dogs. It was heading toward the girls. Whyvonne screamed so much that her dunce cap was listing.

"Hark!" cried Endicott. "Thou art safe, fair maidens! I shalt slay yon possum!"

He put his one arrow in his bow.

"Watch out for the dogs!" I yelled.

"Fear not!" Endicott pulled back and let fly with the arrow.

THWAP!

The arrow went high and stuck into the painting of Great-Great-Uncle Harrison Beckwith, a congressman, right through the middle of his three chins.

"Hark, dammit!" Endicott sighed. "Missed."

The possum was still climbing, the dogs were still barking, and Whyvonne was still screaming when Aunt Jew came rolling from the back hall into the foyer at top speed, her eyes blazing and her silver gray bun bouncing.

"Yankees!" she cried. "Where are they?"

Aunt Jew was a writer of historical romances. She loved history so much she lived in other epochs most of the time. When she'd fall off to sleep in the afternoons, one toddy too many, you never knew which era she might wake up in; it depended on the novel she was working on. This time it was the Civil War. Our noise had roused her into a belligerent state, as if General Sherman might be at the front gate.

Aunt Jew had her squirrel rifle with her, which she kept in the umbrella stand in the corner of her room. She was waving it around. It went off.

The foyer shook with the explosive crack and its echo. We screamed. The possum and the dogs, startled, went still. At the same time, several large chunks of crystal came crashing down from the chandelier. Aunt Jew had winged it.

Miss Godwin with Arthur, plus Aunt Kitty, my mother, Ethylene, Odessa, and finally Granddaddy came rushing into the foyer from all parts of the house and beyond. The possum resumed climbing, the dogs began barking again, and Whyvonne was screaming even louder. Baby Midland was crying. Endicott quit harking. Odessa came over to comfort Baby Midland. Arthur stayed asleep in Miss Godwin's arms. Aunt Kitty groaned, "My Lord, my Lord."

The gunfire made Aunt Jew snap out of it, back to the present. She began digging into the small pouch tied to the arm of her wheelchair. "I'll shoot that God damn possum," she said, "soon as I get another bullet in here."

"Please don't, Jew," my mother said. "You might hit a child."

"Or a dog," Aunt Kitty said.

Judge came puffing through the front door, shiny black from sweating.

"Hold your fire, Jew," Granddaddy said. He turned to the old man. "Judge, you think you could catch that possum for us?"

"Yessah. Maybe."

"Hold your fire!" Granddaddy announced, this time to the multitude, as Judge went toward the stairs.

Judge was our handyman, farm hand, and Odessa's husband. He was never one to hurry much or to get upset. He had the confidence of a fox, the same grace, intelligence. He went up the stairs two at a time as if they were nothing, although his left leg swiveled out with each step because of an old injury. He went in among the dogs. Without hesitating, he quickly reached behind the possum's neck and squeezed with his giant black hand until her tail went limp.

He took the possum down the stairs and out the front door. We all followed him, the dogs at his feet. Out in the yard he released his grasp, and the possum fell out on the grass, dead for sure. The dogs sniffed and pawed at her, still wary.

Ethylene cleaned up the chunks of crystal, Odessa removed the arrow from Uncle Harrison, and Whyvonne finally quit screaming.

I took that possum up to my room and began work immediately, hoping to get going on her before rigor mortis took hold.

And now, there lay Bess on my taxidermy table, feet up, tail dragging. Real, real dead. I sighed and went back to work.

Endicott and I, after a long afternoon of working on our crafts, watched from our window as Granddaddy walked back to his house. It was about six o'clock. Granddaddy lived in what had been designed as the servants' quarters. His little house, which was about a hundred yards out into the grove, was a replica of the Big House, white and roomy with a porch and two skinny columns, but it was only one story. He had exiled himself there about seven years before when we children began accumulating.

Soon Mama came up to check on us. She said if we were quiet we could come down and have supper on the back porch.

Ethylene had fixed a big pot of black-eyed peas and ham. She and her children, plus Odessa and Judge, ate with us on the screened-in porch. John and Baby Midland had on their coonskin Davy Crockett hats, which they had inherited from Endy and me. We were not allowed to wear fur at the regular dinner table.

Mama didn't eat anything. She smoked.

Since we were being so good, Mama finally said, she didn't see why we couldn't each have just a little cake and ice cream, as long as Granddaddy didn't find out. There wasn't going to be a party, she said. Daddy was probably coming in late again.

Odessa served dessert while Judge went out on the back porch steps as a lookout. If Granddaddy started toward the Big House, we were all supposed to pick up quick and move into the kitchen, and Judge would divert him till all the evidence was gathered into the sink and we kids were up the back stairs and gone.

Granddaddy never showed. He was probably lost in one of his ancient books; he spent hours each day in the easy chair beside his bed, buried up to his thatchy white eyebrows in the past.

We ate Daddy's birthday cake and ice cream. It didn't taste as good without the birthday song.

Back in our rooms we got ready for bed, which was just a matter of getting most of the rest of our clothes off. We slept in our underwear with not even a sheet over us. We needed every touch of air we could get.

First came the baths, though. Laura always went first. Just for being a girl she got the hottest, cleanest water in that deep, claw-foot tub. Endy and I, always last in line, got the leftover gritty, lukewarm water. We never got more than luke-clean.

As always, I sat in the gray-brown water looking at Endy's freckled back, waiting for the inevitable. He almost always saved one up, and sure enough . . . First came the carbonated little rumble, then his reddening laughter. That doofus. I kicked him when he did it, and he grabbed my foot and pulled up on it. Under I went.

Odessa and Judge lived in a little tarpaper-covered house at the other end of our property; Ethylene and her kids lived next door in a similar house, both up on concrete blocks. From our bedroom window, Endy and I could barely see their houses through the trees.

Travis, Endy, John, and I had a boys-only club; we'd send signals to each other with flashlights. After our bath, Endy waited in his underwear on the wide windowsill with the lights off; soon Travis sent three long flashes and a short one through the dark trees, meaning, "I'm all right, how you?" Endy flashed back, "Not much going on here either." Travis finished with "Goodnight, fart face."

Travis, Whyvonne, and Baby Midland were our best friends. They were better than siblings because we didn't have to live with them. But sometimes Whyvonne was like an older sister because she would try to boss us around, even though she was my age. She was bigger than us boys. She had legs as long and thick as a quarter horse's, or so it seemed, and she could run like one—she beat Endy in every footrace. When we were choosing sides for football or kick-the-can, Whyvonne was always first choice.

Her real name was Yvonne but her mama had always said it "Whyvonne," so that's how we said it, too. Ethylene had what Mama called "men friends." They'd come passing through. Then would come another baby; Baby Midland was the last one. Odessa and Judge, who never had kids, unofficially adopted Ethylene's. Midland was named in honor of Odessa, like a sister city. Two of Ethylene's babies died. Mama had to help her through some hard times.

Endy and I got into bed, turned on our lamps and read, I don't remember what, probably an adventure book from our library, like *We Were There at the Battle of Little Big Horn*. We waited for Mama, who was making her rounds. She always checked on Arthur first, then she'd come upstairs and say prayers with John, then Laura, and finally us. It took awhile.

When Mama came in, we laid our books aside. She got the chair from my desk and put it in the middle of the room between our beds. We turned out our lamps.

I can see her in my memory, in the small light of half a moon, bowed in her chair, listening. I think she was praying, too.

After the Lord's Prayer, Endy and I took turns God-blessing everybody we could think of, from the beasts of the field to cousins we had never met, from John's pet fish to President Eisenhower. It was something of a contest to see who could out-bless the other. It was a good stalling tactic, too.

Finally Mama rose and said gently, "And God bless everybody in the whole wide world. Amen," and that was that.

She went over and sat at the edge of Endy's bed, caressing him with a touch and a kiss. I heard her say, "Endy, for heaven's sake. You never got it off."

"What, Mama?"

"That spot."

I could tell what was happening. She fished through the pocket of her housedress and came up with a Kleenex. I heard her spit on it, a ladylike little spit. She went to work on Endy's ear.

"Hold still, dammit. It's really stuck on there." I don't know how she could see it in the dark.

I could hear him squirming. Endy could be dramatic.

"There," she said. "I think I got it."

"You almost pulled my ear off, Mama," he said with a whine.

"For God's sake, Endy. Your ear is perfectly fine. Now goodnight."

"Goodnight, Mama."

Then me, last. She sat on the edge of my bed and pushed her fingers through the front of my wayward, still-damp hair, then down across my forehead and my eyes. She bent over and kissed me, with her hand playing across my ear.

"I love you, Stephen," she said in a private whisper. "Goodnight."

"I love you too, Mama. Goodnight."

She rose and went through the door, down the hall, and down and down the turning stairs. I listened to every step.

Endy and I talked for a while in the darkness. He liked to hear himself chatter—did I think that toad had gone to Heaven, when did I think Daddy might be home, if you swallowed a lightning bug would your guts light up? I responded to him less and less until he gave up and fell away.

Even then I needed a quiet place. I was ten years old and I needed a place to go where I could hear my own voice inside and follow it to important things.

Endicott finally was quiet, and I had room to think. I thought about Daddy.

I knew where he was. I had been there dozens of times with him, at the cabin on the Brazos, next to where the river bends. He liked to sit on the porch with his cigarettes and his bottle and watch the night go deep.

I could hear it. In my bed, sixty miles away, I could hear the river my father was hearing, follow the same water he was following. The ceiling fan in my boyhood bedroom churned softly through the languid air. The bugs outside were singing a liquid song, beating and breathing and sighing, crickets mostly; and the frogs—there was a whole swirl of frogs. I went to where my father was, the porch at the cabin.

"We'll live here someday," he'd say. He said that every time.

He wanted us to move there. He wanted to tear down the old cabin and build a long ranch house with a huge porch and room for all of us kids. He was going to work for an oil company and not for Granddaddy anymore. We could have boats and rafts, he said, and fish every day and live like kings of the river.

I liked his dream. I went there.

I heard something.

I came awake. The noises reached into the deep of my dreams and brought me up.

That was him downstairs. Daddy was home. I must have been asleep for several hours.

My mother was waiting for him in the parlor because I heard her voice, too, but I couldn't make out any words. It was a low mumble. Sometimes their words slammed, but not this time.

They didn't stay long. They came up the long stairs together.

I could hear my father's footsteps separate from hers—heavier, worn down, unsteady.

2

DADDY HAD TO CHECK ON A BLOWOUT OF ONE OF BECKWITH MINERALS' gas wells, and he took me along. It was a couple of months after his birthday.

We left Fort Worth on a Saturday morning and drove about a hundred and fifty miles west, past Graham. By the time we got there, the well had been capped. Nobody had been hurt, but Daddy said Granddaddy wasn't going to be happy about losing all that gas.

"Hell, William, you might as well take a thousand-dollar bill and set a God damn match to it," Daddy said, talking like Granddaddy. "Don't the guys you hire know even basic engineering?"

He didn't say that directly to me. He was talking to the windshield. Sometimes he'd forget I was there and the contents of his mind came out like that, but mostly he'd go for hours quietly captured by his thoughts. I knew how to share his silence on those long trips. I turned away from him and went back to watching the landscape roll by, dreaming long dreams.

It was almost always me who went with Daddy on his trips. He'd tried to take Endicott or Laura (John was too young), but they'd get bored and beg to go home, and I think Endy talked more than Daddy could stand.

Daddy and I were a team. Out in the vacant wilds of West Texas we'd talk to ranchers and oilmen and county clerks about drilling leases or mineral rights, including all the gossip that went with oil talk—wildcats, dry holes, market conditions, politics.

You couldn't be pushy with the landowners. You had to talk about the weather and the cattle business and the weather some more, football and their kids and football some more. Then maybe you'd get down to business.

Daddy was friendly and well-liked. He knew his business and he knew his weather, both of which had been taught to him by an expert—Granddaddy. Leasing deals would be struck, usually without too much difficulty. Daddy said everybody loves a man with a red-headed kid along. They'd ruffle my hair, comment about my freckles, and laugh. Then they'd sign the papers.

It seemed to me he did a great job, but Granddaddy was usually unhappy. Although it was only a two-man company, Beckwith Minerals owned a vast number of oil properties. Mostly the company invested passively, teaming up with bigger partners. Granddaddy used the brothers Levy & Levy, a two-man accounting and law firm, but the rest of the work my father and grandfather could handle themselves—buying royalties, playing hunches, contracting with drillers.

It put a lot of pressure on Daddy. I'd overhear them arguing in Granddaddy's office. Our tree house was right above the Little House, and Granddaddy's windows were almost always open.

It wasn't really arguing, just Granddaddy and that congressional voice of his, stern and disappointed. He'd say Daddy should have gotten a quarter royalty instead of an eighth, leased the whole section, tried to get a working-interest override, terms I'd heard a thousand times but didn't really understand.

Daddy never said anything. He'd come out of Granddaddy's house and go back to the Big House, to his office upstairs. He'd go inside himself. And in a day or two he'd be on another business trip, sometimes with me but mostly by himself, and sometimes he'd forget things like birthdays.

From the highest hill on the highway looking down into the Brazos River valley, you could see an arching sliver of rich green water with bright green trees clinging to it. The rest was brown rangeland full of iron-red hills and bent bushes. It was fifteen more minutes curving down the highway before we got to the floor of the valley and the turnoff to our cabin.

From the paved state highway to the house was only about a mile more on a rutted road. I opened the gate and we bumped across the cattle guard. The rest of the way was hardly more than two tracks through beaten-down weeds. The road sagged and plummeted alongside the curving river, and Daddy's International seemed to regret every lurching step of the way. At the last was the familiar leaf-crunching of tires rolling under the live oaks, into the damp shade next to the cabin.

It was just one slouching room, about the size of a two-car garage, the color of old boards. It had been an old ranch hand's place, and he hadn't needed much. The kitchen was a shelf. The closet was one nail. The bedroom was everything else, which included one window and the front door and a sloppy rock fireplace. Two cots were by the fireplace. When it rained, we'd have to scoot our cots between the drips.

If you wanted running water, you had to run down to the river with a bucket. Need a bath? Back to the river. The outhouse was a one-holer that also served as a wasp battalion headquarters.

The best thing about that old shack was the porch. In the summers we'd put our cots out there at night because we could get more air. If it rained, we'd get about as wet as inside. And in the day, Daddy and I would sit up there in bottomed-out rocking chairs and look down the steep bank to the sleeping-green water and watch our lines. It was the easiest fishing in the world. If something moved, I could be at the bottom of that hill before Daddy could rise from his doze.

I went to the river's edge with four or five long, plunging, sandy steps. The frogs plopped into the water with a hiccup, the turtles rolled off their logs, and then all went back to quietness.

I faced upriver and watched the water turning down the way. It came to us in a graceful bend, a curving arm, creating a place of comfort and protection. Thirty-foot, floppy-leafed cottonwoods brought a fluttering shade. On the higher bank above, surrounding the cabin, grew well-muscled live oaks that brought more layers of shelter.

I could see far to the north, where the green river widened into soft blue. Directly across from us, a reach of sand bordered the river, and beyond were woods of pale green, feathery mesquites with tall grass underneath, its color fading toward fall. Cattle were coming from the grassy woods, trudging across the sandbar to the water for a drink.

It was late September and too early for any leaves to turn, but I could feel things breathing easier among the awkward hills. The first, small rush of coolness had invaded the land, and the ragged mesquites and the cluttered scrub oaks seemed to relax.

We kept the cane poles propped against one of the cottonwoods; the bait was in jars nearby. Nobody ever messed with our stuff, or if they did, they brought it back.

I baited the hooks (two with doughbait for carp, two with bloodbait for catfish), set out the lines, and positioned the poles on forked sticks Daddy had made. Then came the waiting.

Daddy stayed on the porch. He was always tired after those long drives. He fixed himself a big drink of bourbon and salty river water. ("Bourbon and branch," he called it. "Real branch.") He sat and drank—cringing with the first few tastes—and watched me fish.

My father had a strong, good face. His hair was the color of the light red sand that bordered our river, and in the waves of his hair were swirled grains of darker red, Endicott's color. He had a proper nose, a jutting chin, and patches of sun-baked freckles. If you took off his muddy boots and put him in an ascot, he would have looked at home at the country club, but he never liked going to such places. This was home for him.

The water was getting glassy, the way it usually did in the ending day when the wind sighed to almost nothing. The water stirred and swirled, but now it had no ruffles. The long shadows were settling over us. The locusts were making their last call. Evening was on the way.

I watched the water, waiting, watching. Hope dulled. Time spread. The day fell.

Soon a silent conversation was walking across my father's face. I looked back now and then at him sitting on the porch above and behind me, but I tried not to stare at his grimacing lips. I knew who he was talking to.

Second drink, third drink. I watched him in the fading light. He'd dip his jelly-jar glass in the bucket of river water beside him, then top it with bourbon from the bottle sitting beside his chair. The drinking went faster. Daddy was on the way to leaving.

• • •

With the last of the light I gave up on the fishing and came up the bank for supper. We heated canned beans and franks on the little propane stove, eating in our rocking chairs as the first of the night came down. We didn't say much. Daddy wasn't interested in eating. But he kept drinking.

I tried, though. I tried to keep things going.

"Daddy?"

"Yeah."

"This is where the porch is gonna be, isn't it?"

"Yeah."

"The longest porch in the history of mankind."

"Yep." I could feel him smile in the darkness.

That was Daddy's phrase, and that was his dream. That long, long ranch house he was going to build here, right on this spot, was going to have a porch all the way down it. And we were all going to sit out here and watch the river and be a family. Just us.

"Me and Endy'll be Huck and Tom. We'll be the kings of the river. Can Whyvonne and all them come visit?"

Daddy didn't say anything. He didn't want to talk. I figured he was going deep this time. Finally I went to my cot inside, and I don't think he even noticed.

Daddy stayed out on the porch with his bourbon and branch. Through the open door I watched the arc of his cigarette, rising and back, rising and back.

Daddy was always prickly in the mornings. I'd learned to be careful. I didn't say much.

He wanted his coffee and I left him alone with it. We'd brought a package of sweet rolls for breakfast, and I had some, plus some milk from the ice chest.

We always left the baited poles out all night, and most of the time the bait would be taken, a fish hooked—and maybe a pole would be pulled out into the river. Then you had to run down the bank looking for it, maybe swim out for it. You'd have a big fish if you could find it.

But not this time. Two hooks had the bait gone, two were still baited.

I pulled them all in and started over with new bait, then sat down on the bank. The Bermuda was damp, the air was new, the river was hushed. I leaned back, fishing, waiting.

"Dammit, Stephen!"

"Yes sir?"

My father's voice sliced through the morning. The car door slammed.

"Where the hell's my spinning rod? Didn't you get it? Didn't I . . . STEPHEN?"

Another door slammed. He was looking for the rod and reel he had asked me to get from the shed at home.

"I guess I forgot."

"God DAMMIT!"

He came over to the edge of the hill, looking down on me. He didn't have to shout.

"How many times did I tell you? Huh?" His voice was as big and biting as Granddaddy's. "Can't you do anything right, dammit? Anything?" He slammed one more car door and went back to the porch for more coffee.

I didn't want to hang around. I went far down the bank, out of sight of him, and turned up into the hills. I went up the incline above the cabin where the land jutted, ledge upon red-sandstone ledge, among the cactuses and weeds and stunted bushes, far from the cool greenness of the river.

I liked it there. I could look down on our tiny house and the twisting water. I could see miles of river, all the way up to the highway bridge and the dam beyond. The river turned softly down from the bridge, bent deeply in front of our cabin, and then arched back, almost touching itself on the other side of our mountain.

"Brazos de Dios" is what Daddy said was the river's full name. "The Arms of God."

"The Spanish conquistadors were the ones who named it," he told me in one of our evening talks on the cabin's porch.

"Arms of God?"

"Imagine them being up in those dry hills for days and days," Daddy said. "On horses. Pulling burros. Eating dust. For months.

"And they come over the last hill and there, spread out below, is this green valley, and running through it is our river, bending so gracefully like welcoming arms."

"Yeah."

Daddy made it easy for me to see it—he had gone to school to be a history teacher, and he would have been a good one, but then Granddaddy claimed him, and he became an oilman instead.

I looked out and saw it was just a twisting of things, tangled leaves and sandy water. Daddy was down there. I didn't want to go back.

I sat on the crumbly ground, then lay back with my hands locked beneath my head. I looked into the empty sky, down a long hallway of blue. I closed my eyes and made the blue go dark.

Hunger eventually pulled me toward the cabin. It was way past lunch; I could tell by the shadows.

When I came back, Daddy was sitting by the cane poles, watching beyond them, into the river and even deeper. He didn't hear me until I was almost on top of him.

"I made you a sandwich," he said. "Up on the porch."

"Thanks."

"Might be a little soggy," he said. "The bread got wet from the ice chest. Baloney, too. I was lettin' it sort of air out."

"It doesn't matter."

We fished for a few more hours and had a little luck. Daddy didn't say much. He didn't ask where I'd been. He kept his look buried in the water.

Finally he said we might as well give up on the fish and I said yeah, might as well. He said let's go to Dorthy's. I was hungry—that wet sandwich hadn't done much for me—and I said yes.

I helped him bring in the poles. By the time we hit the road, it was on the way to dark.

Daddy drove down our path of a road and turned onto the highway at the river bridge. Dorthy's was a couple of miles farther down the highway, toward Fort Worth. You could almost see the 's from the bridge.

Sportsman's Inn was really its name, but everybody called it Dorthy's, as if you were going to her house—which, in a way, you were. Even the old neon sign on the roof cooperated. Since the 1930s, Daddy said, Dorthy's sign had been burning out a letter at a time. Finally the *Inn* went out in 1946, all at once, with a pop loud enough to make everybody come outside and look. Now all that was left was 's, which to me stood for *Dorthy's*. It didn't give out enough yellow light to attract many June bugs, much less customers. Just the regulars, like my father and me, and we could have found Dorthy's in the darkest dark.

Her place, squatted beside the road at the back of a dust-flying parking area, was shaped something like a barracks. It was covered by asbestos siding stamped out to look like bricks. Its small windows were high up and filmed over from years of smoke- and grease-drenched air.

We went up the wooden steps. Daddy had to go first because of the door. It was warped. With his shoulders down, linebacker-style, he shoved. We barged in.

The air inside was thick enough to hug you. It was full of the sad-sliding music of fiddles and the beer-smeared voices of friends. And smells— that air was chicken-fried, sweat-stained, doused with witch hazel and Lilac Nights.

Because everyone had to barge in, each arrival was an event, a small surprise, a semi-polite break-in. Everybody but Hank Williams stopped and turned toward us. We were roundly greeted.

Voices came from shadowed booths and Formica tables. The only people I recognized were Roy and Dale, the county road workers who lived in adjoining trailers up the highway. A couple of other guys waved at us, but I couldn't recognize them in the dimness.

In the corner to the right was the jukebox, and in front of it was Dorthy in her blotchy white uniform, picking out music. Dorthy turned and grinned as big as a bear. "God damn, Will, where y'all been hidin' yourselves? God *damn!*"

Dorthy was as tall as my father—five feet ten—and outweighed him by maybe fifty pounds. But she was as packed in as a range cow. Her hair was steel-colored, chopped off at her neck. Her face was square, her nose flat. She had a whiskey voice—straight whiskey, no water, not even ice.

"You old sumbidge!" she said, coming up to us and putting her arms around my father. "Hell yes you been hidin'!"

"Naw," he said. "Just busy."

"And you, you little scamp!" she said, turning toward me and bending down. "How's my favorite little sumbidge?"

"Fine," I said from beneath her hug with what little breath she left me. I was forced to inhale her words, which were full of used smoke and old beer.

Although I was eleven, I was still her "little sumbidge," still a little kid to her, the way I had been for years.

"Y'all are hungry, I reckon," Dorthy said.

"Sure," Daddy said.

"ABERNATHY!" she yelled in a voice loud enough to wake up a dog two hills away. "TWO CHICKEN-FRIEDS!"

We were ushered over to our regular booth. And sure enough, just as I had feared, crouched and silent, sat Bert. It was his regular booth, too.

"Hidy, Bert," Daddy said.

"Hidy, Will," Bert said.

I tossed out my own little "hidy" as I scooted down the slick wooden seat across from him. I went all the way over to the wall; Daddy got in next to me.

Bert didn't say anything to me. He didn't even look at me.

"Scoot over, you old buzzard," Dorthy growled toward him. "I wanna talk to my friends here."

Still hunched and scowling worse, Bert worked his decrepit bones toward the wall one budge at a time.

"Lord God A-mighty, my mother moves faster than that," Dorthy said, standing there with her arms folded.

"I thought your mother was dead," Daddy said.

"She is, bless her soul," Dorthy said. "She *is*."

Bert almost smiled. Daddy laughed. I covered my mouth to hold back a grin.

"Ah, ta hell with it," Dorthy said. "This is gonna take all day." She picked up Bert's Pearl longneck and shook it. It was empty. She took it with her as she turned away.

After checking on a couple of other customers, Dorthy went around the bar and into the kitchen. Next to the door was a wide opening where food was passed forward from the kitchen, and through it I could see Miz Abernathy sitting beside the stove.

Her knobby arms were branched out with the *Fort Worth Star-Telegram* spread between them. She had a cigarette in one hand and her customary glass of gin in the other.

"ABERNATHY!"

The white hair nodded and stirred. The hands came down, and old Miz Abernathy stood. She looked toward Dorthy. She cocked her head, waiting for an order, and her silver-trimmed glasses flashed.

"TWO CHICKEN-FRIEDS!" Dorthy repeated into her face from a foot away. "Will and his boy are here!"

"Roy who?"

"Never mind," Dorthy said. "NEVER MIND!"

Miz Abernathy was an armful of kindling in a wrinkled sack. Her cloud of hair had gone past white to light blue. Her face was a colony of webs, rouged with the color of dawn, which was the result of her constant companion, her gin. She must have been past eighty.

She drew back her head, slugged down the rest of her gin, doused her cigarette, and tottered toward the refrigerator.

"Two chicken-frieds comin' right up!" she said. Her voice was tinkling pieces of glass.

In the booth, Bert had finally managed to make it over next to the wall, directly across from me. He was panting, sucking for air. His brown lips curled up to his gums, exposing brown stubs.

Everybody called him the old buzzard, with good reason, I thought. He was brown all over, except for the white stubble that dotted his face and tufted from his ears and the white twinings of hair that dangled from under his stomped-on, run-down, BERT'S BAIT cap. His fingernails were burned and battered claws, his crumpled ears were foldings of brown, and his beaked nose looked like he had been poking through the dirt with it, looking for grubs. His drab eyes were shot through with brown lines. His head perched tiltingly on a bent neck. All of him was permanently crouched into a snarl.

He'd already bummed a cigarette from Daddy. He bummed everything from Daddy—food, money, bourbon, time. Especially time.

Daddy took his flask out of his jacket pocket. He took a swig of bourbon, then passed it under the table to Bert.

Dorthy wasn't allowed to have hard liquor on the premises. She could only sell beer. Dorthy knew they drank the hard stuff; she just overlooked it.

Bert inhaled from the flask and exhaled a long, rattling wheeze. Then he squealed like a rabbit, thumped his fist against the Formica table, gritted his stubby teeth, curled his lips like an awning rolling up, and wheezed again.

"Damn, I needed that!" he said; his words were an unvoiced, all-whispered exhale.

When Dorthy came up, Bert fumble-closed the flask and quickly handed it back under the table to Daddy.

She set down a new Pearl for Bert and one for Daddy. She gave me my usual, a Grapette. She had a Lone Star for herself.

Dorthy shoved herself into the booth, using up most of the available space. Her rear end, once relaxed and sat upon, ballooned.

Away they went then with their talk. They all started cigarettes, which caused an uproar of smoke in the little booth. I sunk down and got quiet, drifting into my own thoughts.

Daddy, slowly, would be getting louder and more distant from me. That's the way it always happened, but first was his coming alive and blooming, which never lasted long. He was a rain-forest flower, a blue-dark violet, and he opened only in the most protected shade—here among his friends and far away from business and Granddaddy. But then, just like that, he'd fold again. Go underground. You had to be quick to see it.

I could count on Dorthy to watch out for me. When the folding started, she'd get slower in bringing my father his beers. She'd remind him it was time to get me home to bed. Maybe she'd take me across the room to help her pick out songs on the jukebox, or we'd play a quick game of shuffleboard on the sand-dusted wooden table.

Miz Abernathy came tottering out of the kitchen. She held two armfuls of food.

"Law sakes," she said, setting down those big oval, overburdened plates in front of Daddy and me. "Ain't seen y'all in a coon's age."

Miz Abernathy had no lips, only a pale pink line that went in the general direction of a smile, always. The gin did that. It kept her inner glow stoked.

"Evenin', Miz Abernathy!" my father shouted, aiming his words at her face. "Food looks good as always!"

"Same to you," she said. A fluttering occurred behind her steamed-over glasses. "Y'all catch any fish?"

"I almost caught a gar," I said. Just before we'd brought in the lines, a three-foot alligator gar had taken my hook, splashed once, and gotten away.

"A car?" Miz Abernathy asked.

"Yeah," Daddy said, looking over at Bert and me, "a '49 Oldsmobile and it fought like hell, didn't it, Stephen?"

Laughter broke out among us.

"A GAR! A GAR!" Dorthy shouted into Miz Abernathy's good ear, which wasn't much better than her bad one, which was dead.

"Oh," Miz Abernathy said. "Jimmy catch him?"

She'd always called me Jimmy. I don't know why. We'd never gotten her straight on that.

Daddy nodded and I said nothing.

"Good boy, Jimmy," she said to me. "Now you be sure and clean your plate."

I nodded. That wasn't going to be too hard.

A chicken-fried steak, brown as toast, was nestled next to a stack of limber, almost half-a-foot-long, grease-glistening French fries. In one corner of the plate was a slice of white bread, hanging off the side. In the other was a mound of salad under a heap of bright orange, cheek-piercing dressing. Everything floated on a lake of milk-white, peppered gravy, thick as oatmeal. Each bite of steak, each plank of potato could pick up a dollop of gravy; the bread would soak up the rest.

My mouth liquefied as the steam from the food trickled up into my face. My stomach purred. I plunged into the food.

Soon—sooner than I wished—fullness overtook me. All those wonderfully crisp tastes combined into a gray and heavy gravy. My eyelids felt the weight.

I pushed my mostly empty plate away. Daddy had crumpled his paper napkin on his well-scraped plate and pushed it aside, too. He was smoking. Bert was smoking. Daddy was on his third beer and Bert was on his no-telling-how-many. They'd had two or three slugs apiece from the flask. Their words were getting oozy. It was going to be a long night. I put my head down on my arms.

I loved the darkness there. I could spy on people. They thought I wasn't listening when really I was bringing in each of their words and examining them in private.

But they weren't worth having. Bert's words sloshed around and soon began to pass through the fingers of my brain like nonsense. I drifted beneath them.

In only a minute or two, or so it seemed, Daddy reached over and touched my shoulder. "Stevie," he asked, "you gettin' tired?"

I sat up. "A little," I said.

Daddy turned toward Bert. "Listen, maybe we oughta be goin'."

"God dammit, you just got here." Bert's eyes were loose and swinging like his words.

"I need to get the boy home, Bert. We gotta go to church in the mornin'. Stephen's got to be an acolyte."

"What the hell's an alco-lite?"

"They're the boys who assist the priest. They wear robes and light the candles and carry the cross. I was one."

"Your boy's too young to be playin' with fire."

Bert's lips curled up and a small laugh splattered out. Nobody joined him.

He tried to backtrack, covering his smile with his beer bottle. When he brought it back down, his lips had resumed their natural, ragged half-snarl.

He looked over at my father's watch. "Hell, it's only eight-thirty, Will. One more beer, all right? I'll buy."

"Naw, really, Bert. We better go." Daddy checked his watch himself.

"Well listen, then, how 'bout droppin' me by my place. My God damn pickup's busted."

I shouted "No! No!" inside my head. I tried to talk to my father through my whispered thoughts: "It's a trick, Daddy. Don't fall for it."

But Daddy said, "Yeah, I guess so, sure." He didn't even hear my elongated sigh. He said to Bert, "So how'd you get here?"

"Walked part ways. Got a ride in the rest. Cattle truck."

"So what you reckon's wrong with that old clunker of yours?"

"Same thing that's wrong with me. Just old and generally shot to hell."

"Know what you mean," Daddy said. He set down his beer bottle with some finality and pushed himself up from the booth.

I followed him to the cash register, which was at the end of the counter. Dorthy had some signs around it. One said: "Halitosis is better than no breath at all." Another said: "No shoes, no shirt, no service," and somebody'd added at the bottom, in a ballpoint scrawl, "No shit."

While she and Daddy chatted, I looked back at Bert, who had left the booth and struggled over to the door. He was leaning on the wall, gasping. The shortest walk did him in sometimes. All that smoking. And the booze didn't help, either.

Daddy finally wound things up with Dorthy, and the three of us headed toward the door. By now Bert was bent, his hand on the door's edge, his head languishing on his hand. His breath was heaving.

"Bert, you all right?" my father asked, coming up to him first.

"Breathin' . . . spell." Bert slipped in his croaking words between lunges of breath. "I'll be all . . . right I . . . reckon in a . . . minute."

"I'll bring up the car," Daddy said with a touch of urgency. "Stephen, you help him get down the steps."

"Don't need no . . . help."

Bert stepped aside and Daddy yanked on the door with two hands. It popped open. "Suit yourself," he told Bert.

The old man inched down the steps outside, holding on to the door facing. On the third step he let go and teetered. Each breath had become a convulsion; I was afraid he was going to wheeze himself off his feet. I kept close by.

Daddy didn't have far to go to get the station wagon—only a few yards across the weedy gravel of the parking lot. After he backed it around to us, he leaned over in the seat and pushed open the passenger door.

"Git on . . . in there, boy," Bert commanded. "I gotta . . . be by the . . . door. I . . . gotta have . . . the air from . . . the God damn . . . windah."

I slipped into the car and scooted over next to my father, as close as I could get.

Bert came over in small lurches to the car. He took hold of the open door with one hand and the metal edge above the door with the other. He twisted, breathing like an idling and uncertain outboard motor, and folded. Everything swiveled and fell into the car except his bum leg, the one that contained his World War I bullet. His bent leg got wedged between the door and the car.

"God DAMN!" His words were jagged, a broken bottle.

He reached down and took the dead and dangling leg by the cuff and hauled it into the car. "God DAMN!" He leaned toward me as he hoisted, showering his filthy, chunky breath down the back of my neck. "God DA-um!"

"What happened, Bert?" Daddy asked, leaning forward to look around me.

"My leg! My God damn leg!" Bert coiled up in the seat. The pain in his words was as clear as lightning. "I twisted it. God damn I think I twisted loose that bullet. God damn I know it. I can feel it! I can God damn FEEL it!"

"Bert, are you sure?" Daddy asked

"Here it comes, comin' up my leg!"

"Bert, you want me to get a doctor? Drive you to a doctor?"

Dorthy had stayed on the steps by the door. "What the hell is all this commotion?"

"Bert's havin' an attack!" I yelled through the open window.

Bert's words were gritted with strain and fear. "Oh God damn, God damn, it's comin' closer!" He was still grabbing his calf, trying to squeeze off the path of the piece of lead. "Right toward my God damn HEART!"

Dorthy came down the steps. As she tromped across the gravel of the parking lot, she said, sort of under her breath, "Not another God damn attack." She came up to the car and leaned through the window in front of Bert, thrusting in her head and one bosom. "Listen, you old fool, this is your third attack this week."

Bert leaned his head on my shoulder and clutched his chest and fluttered his eyes.

Dorthy continued: "You can't die now, you old jackass. You owe me fifty bucks."

The old man's breath halted in midgurgle. All of him went suddenly loose and quiet. He sort of slithered down against me.

Silence barged in. There was a very long ten seconds. The night noises came forward, rustling.

Bert's head lay propped against my shoulder. I had stiffened, but I could feel a trembling within my center. It spread outward and found its way into my voice. "Daddy, is he dead?"

A second, shorter span of silence followed. Daddy and Dorthy were perfectly still, wondering, waiting. Death stalked among us, taking everybody's breath away; I think even Dorthy had her doubts that he was faking.

But then came a whisper of hope, a trickle of movement, a twitch of breath. Yes, breathing. Bert was breathing through his words: "Hell, no,

I ain't dead." His voice was a low, slow growl, but on the rise. "At least not this time."

His eyes fluttered open, and he tensed and sat up. "One helluva close call, though." His voice was at full strength now—full-muddy. He turned toward Dorthy. "And what's this about fifty bucks, God dammit? I don't owe you one red cent."

"Just checkin'," Dorthy said with a snort. "Just checkin' to see if you was playin' possum, you old buzzard."

"Go to hell. I'm a sick man." He turned away from her. "Gimme the whiskey, Will."

My father took the flask from his jacket pocket and passed it over. Bert took it, untwisted the top and slugged down a chug-chug-chug with his throat. Then he lowered it and let out his usual long, pinched wheeze. He looked over at Dorthy, who had withdrawn her head. "Pain medicine. Doctor's orders."

"Doctor's orders my ass." Dorthy turned and started walking toward the slice of light from the front door. "You been drunk for twenty years solid. You don't know what pain is."

Bert leaned his head out the window. "I know what a pain you are, you old bat!"

She went inside without turning. Bert pulled his head back inside. "Let's go."

Bert needed the air, and, with all the windows down, he got gushings of it. The car rushed across the darkness, back toward the river. Bert leaned into the wind, sucking it in and moaning it out.

It took me a long time to calm down. I was sure Death had been but a nudge away, slumped against my shoulder. It made my boy's heart shiver, and I was trying to get warm again. All that dark wind wasn't helping.

We dipped into a tunnel of suddenly moist and cooler air, and that was the river. The air went *clickety-clickety-clickety*—something like the way Bert breathed—as we swept past the concrete pillars of the bridge.

Right after the bridge Daddy braked and turned onto Bert's road. It was just opposite the road to our place. Rocks popped under the tires and weeds scratched the underbelly of the car. I could smell the ticklish billows of dust behind us.

We went down and up and down, bending and bending. I counted the zigs and zags and hills. It was a way to count the time away. I wanted to be alone with Daddy, bound for home.

From maybe a mile away I could see a mound of light, and I heard a faint, familiar commotion, a low rumble of barks. Soon we pulled up to Bert's trailer, and here came his swarm of dogs spreading from around and beneath it. Before Bert could open the door and swivel his bad leg onto the ground, the dogs had surrounded us.

"God dammit!" he growled, pushing on the door and throwing his words at the dogs, who were crowding into the opening. "Git AWAY! Git away, God DAMMIT!"

There were at least forty dogs, of all makes and models, but most were brown or black and short-haired like a bird dog, mangy and ribbed. With yips and yaps, whines and wags, they jabbed their noses toward the car.

No rocks were in reach, so Bert threw his hands at them, pretending rocks, and some of the dogs flinched. As soon as he got his good leg over the side, he began kicking at them. They backed off.

Daddy went around and joined Bert, who, in a kind of a crippled jig, had kicked himself a good-size opening. A few dogs followed them as they went up the path in the weeds to the trailer, but the main crowd found me. As soon as I left the car and shut the door, they moved in.

A rolling ocean of dogs came at me, broke over me and quickly toppled me. They squirmed toward my face, nudging and whining and licking. I was lost in an exuberance of fur and a cloud of pungent air. I covered my face in my arms and blocked my nose and tucked myself into a lump. The dogs used their noses to try to pry me open. They tickled me. I giggled helplessly.

Eventually I collected myself. I pushed the dogs gently away, still laughing, and stood. I shuffled forward, not wanting to step on any paws. It was slow. I waded through the breaking waves of fur toward Bert's front door.

The dirt around the trailer, which had been padded to a crust by all those paws, was as smooth as a driveway. Tufts of Johnson grass as big as bushes provided landscaping. Yard art consisted of an old boat, a rusted barrel, and parts of outboard motors. Smashed and unsmashed cans were everywhere, all of them licked clean.

The bulging, rust-streaked trailer rested on uneven concrete blocks, and beneath it, in a small, unjunked corner, I could see dozens of cats' eyes blazing and blinking, yellow and green. The back side of the trailer leaned down the hill that fell to the river—a good wind or one of Bert's major coughs could have sent his abode tumbling back and over, down into the water.

At the screen door I scraped through sideways to keep the dogs from bounding in with me, and at last I was safe, though wet. I smelled like a damp doghouse.

My father was sitting across the main room on the brown, torn couch, holding a quarter of a jelly jar full of whiskey. I creaked across the bumpy floor and sat beside him. Bert sat at the kitchen table—a wobblier version of the Formica-topped ones at Dorthy's—on the other side of the room.

"One drink," my father said, slightly lifting the glass to point it out, "and then we'll go."

"Awright," I said. I slumped back and burrowed into my corner of the couch, adjusting myself among the spring-hard bulges.

I had heard that before—one drink. It was more likely they'd stay to the end of the bottle, which was on the table beside Bert and half full. This time it was Bert's bottle, Old Crow. It would be at least an hour. I wished I could lean back and sleep, but they'd only get louder.

"You see Stephen trying to get in here?" my father asked, turning toward Bert. "Every time we come out here, I think for sure he's gonna get licked to death." Daddy laughed.

"He's God damn lucky he wasn't eaten," Bert said. He had returned to his raspy, even-breathing grumble. "If I hadn'ta fed 'em this afternoon, he'da been eaten for sure. That God damn packa hounds. You know what it costs me ta feed 'em? Even with all those scraps Dorthy gives me, I still spend more on them dogs than I do on me." He sucked down a drink from his own jelly jar glass. "Hey, you wanna dog, Will? How 'bout a dozen?"

"Hell no."

"Free. Pick any one you want."

"You know somethin', Bert? Every time I leave here I always check my car—the back seat, the luggage rack, everywhere—to make sure you haven't slipped me a dog or two."

"Now Will, God *damn*. Me do a thing like that? To my best friend?" His mouth opened like a cellar door. He laughed like a horse coughs.

"I oughta check under the hood, too, see if you mighta tied a cat in there."

Daddy dropped his burning cigarette on the brown-scarred linoleum and smashed it with his shoe, then kicked it toward the middle of the room, where the other butts were scattered.

Bert was proud of his energy-saving housekeeping methods. Stamping out the cigarettes and pushing the butts to the middle of the floor not only saved him the bother of emptying ashtrays, but when it was time to clean house, all he had to do was open the front door, and, aided by the incline of the floor, the wind, eventually, would blow the ashes and butts out the back door. Of course you let in a few flies that way, but what the hell? They probably would have gotten in anyway.

Bert and Daddy wandered off into another long conversation. They talked about Daddy's outboard motor. He was always having trouble with it, and Bert was constantly working on it. He was a pretty good mechanic, but he did more talking than tinkering, more tinkering than fixing.

The trailer, which was smaller than our shed at home, was divided into two parts. We were in the combination kitchen–dining room–living room–den. In other words, you ate there and sat there. In the back was the bedroom, which was as small as a closet. Bert kept all his fishing rods, guns, and bullets there, plus his tools, towels, and tackle boxes, and somehow found room to sleep. He bathed in the river, shaved at the kitchen table, and peed out the back door (as long as the wind was right). He had an outhouse down the hill that leaned like the trailer did.

I walked to the back door and looked through the screen. The back, like the front yard, was well-lit by vapor lights on telephone poles. I could see scattered little hills of junk among a thicket of weeds.

Closer to the trailer, stretched high between two cottonwood trees, was a clothesline. Something was hanging from it, several somethings, swaying slightly in the small breeze. If it was underwear, it was furry.

I moved sideways to get a better look, and in the new angle of light I could see, attached with clothespins and hanging by their tails, three flat cats and a squashed armadillo. That meant Bert was starting a new batch of Bert's Bloodbait #2.

Daddy had told me how Bert made it: he always started with a base of Wheaties (about a dozen boxes), milk, raw oatmeal, several bottles of corn syrup, chopped raisins, and a heavy dash (one can) of nutmeg. All of this was mixed in the big iron pot out there under the clothesline. He'd build a fire under it, adding the ingredients a little at a time, continuing to stir. Let simmer. Go take a nap.

Then came the special ingredients: chopped-up, ripened dead things.

That's why those animals were hanging by their tails on the clothesline. They were ripening like large grapes, waiting for their blood to jell.

Once a week or so, when his truck was running, Bert went out "collecting." He rode along the highways, looking for run-over animals. When he found something that wasn't too long dead and hardened, he'd stop and pick it up and toss it into the back of his pickup. Sometimes, he liked to say, he'd have to wrestle his selection away from the buzzards.

He brought home the animals and hung them out on the line to "mature." He had to hang them pretty high to keep the dogs from jumping up and getting them. As they ripened, they swelled. And there was the rub: if you picked the animals off the line too soon, the bait would lack punch; if you waited too long, they'd explode. Bert had gotten the ripening process down to a fine art.

Catfish won't eat just anything; it's got to be the stinkiest, foulest thing around. Bert had learned, through trial and serious error, a sort of perfect awfulness, and that was Bert's Bloodbait #2. (Bloodbait #1 was a line that had been discontinued after a recipe miscue led to an unfortunate industrial accident involving a bloated Hereford.) We used Bert's #2 exclusively, as did many other fishermen in the area, and we could testify to its excellence.

When it was time to add the most important ingredients, Bert tied a kerchief over his face and took his animals down from the line. He had a big knife and a board. He skinned the animals and chopped them up. Then he tossed the curdled blood and bits of meat into the by-now boiling pot of cereal. Hundreds of buzzards would circle overhead, soaking up the waft. Bert's dogs would leave the area.

Bert stood and turned toward me. He lurched across the room.

"Hey, boy!" he said, coming inches away.

"Yes sir?" I turned toward him, then slunk down and back a little.

"I gotta sa-prise for you, boy." He was so close I could taste his words.

"Yes sir?" I said again.

"Didn't you hear me? I said a sa-*prise*, boy, a sa-*prise*!"

I was backed up all the way to the wall. I didn't know what I was supposed to say. "Yes?"

"Aren't you curious, dammit? Don't you want to know what the hell it is?"

"Yes sir. I guess so." I figured it might be one of those dead cats hanging on the line.

Bert said, "If I told ya what it was, it wouldn't be a saprise anymore." I turned my head away as the liquid in his voice left its banks and exploded into a thousand droplets of laughter.

He turned back toward the room. I breathed again.

"What?" I said. I didn't understand the joke.

Bert limped across the room. His laugh had turned into a cough, which seized him. He was at the front door now, bent over, fighting for air and still smiling. Finally he got control of the cough and gathered it in his throat. He opened the front screen door and spit. Several dogs came out from under the trailer to investigate.

"Come on, Bert, tell him," my father said.

"You really wanta know?" Bert asked me.

"Sure," I said.

"One more drink and I'll tell ya." Bert ended with a crackling cough, his medium-size laugh, which didn't require any spitting. He came back to his place at the table.

"Bert, do you have to string the boy along like that?" my father asked.

Bert poured another couple of inches of whiskey into his jelly jar. "Why Will, you sound like you're as anxious as the boy is to see what it is."

"Could be, I guess."

"How do you two ever make it to Christmas?"

Bert took a drink. His breath stammered. "All right. You win." He stood. "Y'all don't go away now."

Bert shuffled across the room to the wall near the front door. He leaned against it and pushed himself along, toward the back of the trailer.

I went back over to the couch and sat next to Daddy. Bert disappeared into his bedroom. It took a long time for him to find what he was looking for. I was crawling with curiosity.

I could hear the night bugs breathing outside. Or maybe it was all those dogs. And maybe it wasn't curiosity I was feeling, but fleas.

Bert came roaring into the room. "SaPRISE! SaPRISE!" He was almost running, the same way a three-legged rabbit can almost run.

In his hands was a shotgun. Its blue-black metal gleamed, its dark wood swirled. It took my breath away.

Bert was grinning as big as a jack-o-lantern. "It's yours, boy. Take it."

I reached up and took the shotgun. I was speechless.

The metal was cool and heavy. The wooden stock was smooth and warm. I fingered all the jutting, mysterious parts. My father leaned toward me, looking it over.

"What kind is it, Daddy?"

"Four hunnert 'n' ten," Bert said, blowing out a gush of smoke. "Single shot. Smith & Wesson." He had gone back to his chair.

We talked about the gun. Daddy showed me how to crack it open and where the shell went. We talked about safety, how I should never pull back the hammer until I was ready to shoot. Daddy showed me how to hold it into my shoulder, which was just like my BB gun. He said it was going to be just the same, except for the extra power. A tremendous power.

"Well, Bert, this is just mighty nice," Daddy said.

"It's what I always wanted," I said. I found it hard to look at Bert. I spoke quietly, like a prayer, toward the gun, which was lying in my lap.

Bert ignored me. "I figured it'd be good for the boy to learn on," he said to my father. "Single shots are about as safe as you can git."

"I been wantin' to get him somethin' like this. He's been beggin' for one. I guess he's old enough."

"You said he was eleven? Hell yes. Past time."

"Where'd you get it?" my father asked.

"Hell if I can remember. It's been years. I've had it back in that back closet for no tellin' how long. A spare, you know. Finally one day I remembered it, and I thought about your boy, so I fished it out of that closet and cleaned it up good. I think it oughta work okay."

While Daddy and Bert talked, I sat quietly, holding the gun in my lap, opening it, raising it to my shoulder, pointing it toward the front screen door, and pretending to fire it.

I wanted the power. You could rip a hole in the night and shake the heavens and end a life with one small touch of a finger. If I had only known the future contained in that blue-dark cylinder of steel—the churn of lives, the eclipse of days.

Bert turned his beaked and bleary face toward me. "You wanna shoot it?" His tone was crotchety again.

"Sure!" I said.

"Well, you got any bullets?"

I looked at Bert and could see that his eyes had gone sly again. It was another setup, another trap, and my voice fell along with everything else. "No," I said.

"Well," he grunted, pushing himself up, "I just might have some somewheres around here."

I watched him intently as he went behind the table to a cabinet above the stove. Another stupid joke? He shuffled some cans around.

"Well whataya know," he said into the echoing cabinet, "here's two boxes a four-ten shells, brand new, still in the sack."

He brought the paper sack back to the table and took a shell out of one of the boxes. He looked toward me. "Well, whataya waitin' for? Let's go see if it shoots."

Bert got an empty beer can off the table and headed out the back door. Daddy and I followed him. I was carrying the gun. Daddy stopped on the back steps, but I went on out into the yard with Bert.

The dogs poured out from under the trailer and surrounded us. "Git away, God dammit, git away!" Bert was holding the can up and kicking at the dogs with his good leg. "This ain't your supper, it's an empty can! Y'all been fed already today! Now git away!"

Bert limped and kicked and cussed in that familiar jig as we moved several yards down the hill toward the river. Most of the dogs followed him, keeping a kick-wide circle of bare ground around him. At the edge of the white pool from the vapor lights, he stopped and placed the can on a stump.

Bert yelled again at the dogs: "Now stay away from that God damn can, God dammit!"

We backed off a way. Several of the dogs slunk toward the can with their noses tentatively outstretched. "DAMN!" Bert yelled. He picked up a rock and threw it at the lead dog, a dark-furred shepherd, hitting him on the side. The dog flinched silently and bounded backward into the darkness, holding at that distance. The other dogs retreated with him.

"To hell with the can!" Bert shouted back toward my father. "We'll use these God damn dogs for targets! Movin' targets!"

But the dogs continued to stay safely away from the can as we moved back up the hill. About ten yards from the stump, we stopped.

"Load her up, boy," Bert said, handing me the shotgun and a shell.

My head was too energized with anticipation for complete thoughts. I did not clearly dread the kick of the blast nor the possibility of missing. I simply rode the bright energy.

Bert pointed with his bent finger as I went through each step of inserting the shell and closing the gun. My fingers were damp and jumpy but not tangling.

"That's it. That's right. That's good." Bert watched me like a bird of prey—a one-eyed, bent-winged, half-drunk hawk. I was his fuzzy chick, about to leap from the nest. "Now keep that finger away from the trigger till you're ready ta shoot."

I brought the gun up. Bert nudged the butt of it half an inch deeper into my shoulder. "Lookin' good, boy," he said. "You aimin' down the sight?"

"Yes sir," I said. My words were smudged by the side of the gun on my cheek.

"Well then, fire away!" Bert stepped away and behind me a little, and I was on my own.

My breathing and everything halted. The can was out there, a gleaming prize, and the rest was cold and gone, just background. Feeling was in my finger, a tingling, and everything else was held back in my breath. Words marched through my head, disembodied, something like multiplication tables: So what if it hurts? So what. So . . .

It was the sound more than anything that jerked into me as I pulled back my finger. A dark blast closed my eyes. Fire rolled through me, a bright metallic darkness. My suspended breath was punctured like a balloon. For an instant I was gone out with it, dispersed, vaporized.

Then a piece at a time the world came back, darkness and light and voices. Jagged pieces.

Bert's voice came bounding over the solid wall of whining noise that had come up in me and taken over. "Good shot!" he was saying. "Good shot!"

"Perfect!" my father said from behind me.

"Did I hit it?" I was asking. "Did I really hit it?"

"Sure, boy," Bert said.

I looked at the stump and nothing was on it. I let loose with a hoot of joy. "I hit it! I hit the God damn thing!"

I tucked the gun at my side and tried not to run as I went down the hill. I began pushing through the high weeds around the stump, waving them from side to side with the end of the gun.

Bert hobbled down the hill behind me. "I saw it hit. Farther down, boy. Nearly in the water."

I went on down the hill, and there, sure enough . . . a lump of silver lay in a bare spot next to the river. "Here it is, Bert!"

I turned and bounded back up the hill, and we met at the stump. "Lemme see . . . that thing," Bert said, wheezing from the walk. He sounded like a run-over bagpipe.

I handed him the gnarled piece of metal.

"Damn," he said, "not much . . . left."

My father was coming down the hill.

"Looky here . . . Will," Bert said. "One hell . . . of a good shot."

My father came up and took the can. "Mercy!" he said, turning it over in his hands, "you wouldn't know it was a can." His smile was solid and proud as he handed me the mangled tin.

We stood close. We three were a warm circle of smells, sweat and whiskey and burnt powder. I felt tightly a part of this circle of manliness, even if my smells weren't as strong.

We started up the hill in a loose knot. I was in the middle. We went slowly for Bert, who put his arm on my shoulder. That bum leg of his— he needed the support, I guess.

"I'm tellin' . . . ya, Will. That boy's . . . a natural," Bert said. "You see . . . him? Didn't hardly . . . shy a bit. Didn't flinch . . . hardly . . . a-tall. He's a natural . . . all right."

"You're right," my father said. "A natural."

We didn't stay much longer. It was getting late, and Daddy knew it. Back in the trailer, we didn't even sit down. Daddy finished his drink in a gulp or two.

Bert went with us to the car, working all the harder to breathe. He had to spit again.

I was full of nervous joy. I got in and shut the door and propped the shotgun on the front seat next to me. The barrel was still warm. I continued to hold the collapsed can.

Daddy started the car. Bert was leaning against my side with his head in the window just a little. His breath was a banking cloud of rankness.

"Y'all take care," he said.

"We will," my father said.

Then he stuck his head in a little farther. He was looking right at me. His bunched-up eyes were ragged and streaked with the night.

"Listen, boy," he said. "Tomorrow mornin', when you're alcolytin', light a candle for old Bert, wouldja?"

Then he whacked the side of the car the way you'd slap the flank of a horse to tell him to go. Daddy pulled out the clutch as Bert backed away and turned. We were off.

We turned around in the field and then found Bert's road, the dusty tracks, and headed toward the highway. On the first hill, I turned in the seat and looked back.

Bert was walking back toward his trailer through a surrounding of dogs. He was bent and slow. Each hand was out and down, playing with a dog's ear.

I kept watching. We went down into a gully, and by the time we reached the top of the second hill, Bert was opening his door and going in. The dogs were crowded around.

When we reached the third hill, which took a while, Bert was inside and the dogs had dispersed. His place was nothing more than a little island of light in the great bowl of darkness.

3

GRANDDADDY CALLED IT "ASSEMBLING THE MULTITUDES." THAT WAS my job.

As the oldest male grandchild, I had inherited the title of Assistant Patriarch, and it was part of my duties as shepherd-in-training to round up the family for certain occasions such as birthdays, Sunday Dinners, and visits from the rector. On the first Sunday of December 1959, Christmas Card Day rolled around again. All of the family was required to attend. I was dispatched.

The day arrived, wide and blue. A norther had blown in, wiping the sky clean of clouds, taking the last of the leaves from our great company of pecan trees. The central furnace was on, the fires were going in the fireplaces, and hot chocolate was planned for later in the afternoon, once we got this dreaded work under way. Maybe afterward, toward evening, we'd be set free to dive into the winter freedom outside. It was still football season for us, and we children played the game in every spare hour. Granddaddy's garden was one boundary, trees were the others, and certain limbs were the goal posts. Hills of leaves turned tackles into splashes.

I came down the back stairs toward the kitchen, passing through the arch-windowed conservatory. Here, among the hanging twists of ivy and a forest of ferns, the jungled summer never ceased. I took a deep, wet breath and thought of the second play among my body of work, *The Little*

Rascals Meet Tarzan. This room would be perfect for a winter performance. I hadn't decided whether to cast Endy as Tarzan or as Cheetah.

On the other side of the kitchen, across an expanse of checkerboard
floor, Odessa was cleaning the last of the Sunday Dinner dishes. She had
her back to me. Her sleeves were rolled, her arms elbow-deep in the
soapy water.

She was a black version of Miz Abernathy. She wasn't quite as old or
white-headed, but she was as bent and bony. She had bad bouts with
arthritis; her movements were rickety and unoiled.

"You seen Mama, Odessa?"

She didn't turn around. "In the dinin' room, honey. Gettin' the cards
together."

"Okay."

That's the thing about living in a house as big as the Ritz. Finding
people. I always went first to headquarters, the kitchen. Odessa usually
knew where everybody was and how they were feeling. Then I had to
locate the boss, Mama, and get my instructions before I could set out on
my flock-gathering mission. And just because I found everybody didn't
mean they'd do what I asked. We usually had a lot of missing-in-action
sheep, and I'd have to go back for the strays.

But not this time. Christmas Card Day was important to Granddaddy, and what was a big deal to Granddaddy was a big deal to everyone
in his vicinity. I was not expecting any resistance.

Mama was stacking boxes of cards on the dining room table, along
with long, ink-spotted lists of names, rolls of stamps, ink pads, and return
address stamps. Around the table were china cups for tea, apple cider, or
hot chocolate; a plateful of sparkling sugar cookies sat in the middle of the
table, just out of reach. We'd have to build up a stack of finished cards
before we'd get to grab for the cookies.

A sweep of her burnt-red hair had come loose from its gathering
place at the top of her head and fallen to the corner of her sea-green eyes,
and she was mindlessly pushing it away with each of her leanings over the
table. She worked with the cards.

"Granddaddy wants us at four o'clock," she said. "Can you go ahead
and get everybody down here, honey?"

"Okay, Mama. Everybody?"

"Yep, everybody. Granddaddy says we must all share the suffering."

Mama had trained to be a history teacher, just like Daddy; they had met at the University of Texas. But before their dreams had time to develop, Granddaddy called my father back home to be his assistant. Daddy's two older brothers had wisely chosen separate careers in law and medicine, and Kitty was Kitty. That left Daddy. Soon the grand space around them filled with red-headed kids and a thousand responsibilities. Her dreams got folded up and put away, like the good linen, just as Daddy's had. The drawbridge came up on Granddaddy's fortress island of shade, and there they were, in the compounding gloom of generations, which for the Beckwiths went all the way back to the fog-bound, Druid hills of England. Too often, her Irish sunshine couldn't push through.

The less able-bodied among us lived downstairs in the set of bedrooms between the parlor and the music room, just off the foyer behind the sweep of stairs. The nursery was there—a two-bedroom suite in which Miss Godwin and Arthur lived. Aunt Jew's bedroom was on one side of the nursery and Aunt Kitty's on the other.

"Aunt Kitty?" I called out, knocking on her half-opened door. The knocking opened it wider.

She was lying across her well-made bed, on her stomach, reaching down between the bed and the wall. About all I could see were her house-slippered feet.

"I think I see it," she said. Her cat-screech voice was muffled. It went where her dangling arm went, into a blanketed cavern.

"Maybe I can get it from here," I said. I got down on my hands and knees, then all the way to my chest, and scooted forward. I reached under the bed the best I could.

"I got it," I said. My voice was as cave-deep as hers. "Two of 'em. Maybe three."

"Good boy. Good boy."

I pulled myself out from under the bed and stood. Aunt Kitty had turned and was sitting on the bed when I handed her the three flyswatters.

"Just what I was lookin' for," she said. She took her favorite one from me and snapped it in the air. "Got one!" she said with a wide-open smile, rows of ungainly teeth showing.

She'd lie in bed at night and swat the darkness. It helped her get to sleep, and it was how the flyswatters got lost. They'd fall as she nodded off.

Two of the flyswatters were nice new ones, but she wanted the third one, the one Judge had made for her. He had bent a coat hanger for the handle and used a piece of screen for the swatter, which was bigger than normal and limber and deadly. She never missed with it.

Aunt Kitty was "special," as Mama liked to say. She was five years older than my father, or about forty then. Her age had finally surpassed her IQ. She was thick in body, dense in mind, stubby all over. Her hair was rabbit-brown, parted in the middle and brushed down straight over her ears and neck, then chopped. Her forehead was narrow; her eyes were Asian thin. Her face was drab from a lack of makeup and an absence of animation (except when a fly entered her purview). Her eyes were spots of mud.

Aunt Kitty was in charge of killing flies. It was the central drama of her life. If anyone anywhere in the house spotted a fly, Aunt Kitty was called to the scene. She'd grab a swatter from her arsenal and come running. With the livestock and Granddaddy's garden (he believed in manure) and the crumbs we children let get away from us at mealtime, we had a God's plenty of flies. She earned her keep.

For flies, however, this was off-season, although we children did our best to keep her busy and in practice. Periodically, a delegation of us would come rushing into the front parlor and surround her in her Queen Anne chair, where she was needlepointing or knitting and watching TV.

"Aunt Kitty!" our spokesman would say, breathlessly. "There's a great big fly on the dining room table!"

"Ohmagosh!" she'd say, lurching upward with the help of all those small hands. One of us would hand her the flyswatter as we loped across the foyer and into the vaulted dining room.

We'd halt, our voices becoming high-blown whispers.

"Down at the other end, Aunt Kitty!" one of us would say.

"By the butter dish!" would say another.

"Wait!" Aunt Kitty would say. "I think I see him!"

The crowd would separate—Aunt Kitty needed room. We'd let her sneak ahead of us.

Once in striking distance, Aunt Kitty would squinch up her nose, her eyes, and all of her forehead, which lifted her inch-thick glasses. And slowly, slowly, she'd rear back with the flyswatter in a stance as good as Mickey Mantle's.

WHAM!

The crystal glasses on the table would shudder. Anybody nearby and unaware would jump.

"Got him!" she'd say jubilantly.

And Travis or John or Whyvonne would chime in, "Good shot, Aunt Kitty!"

When the dust settled, Endicott would get on the floor under the table. He'd crawl around until he found the fly. "Yep!" he'd announce, "this fly's deader'n hell!"

Aunt Kitty would beam. Then, after she'd wandered back to the television, Endy would get the tweezers and the pill bottle from his pocket, and put the dead fly back in with the others.

In a week or so, when life began to get too quiet, we'd take out another dead fly from the bottle and set it out on the dining room table-cloth and play the game all over again. Aunt Kitty killed hundreds of dead flies in her lifetime.

After reminding her it was time for Christmas cards, I went next door. I quietly knocked and went on in.

Arthur was sitting in the middle of the carpeted floor of the nursery with a book in his lap, pushing the crumpled pages with his stubby fingers.

"Hi, Miss Godwin," I said.

She was where I expected, in the rocker just beyond the baby, using the light from the big window for her Bible reading. Today was Sunday, Bible Day for her, because the next day was Monday night Bible Class and her Baptist church gave pop quizzes. She told Endy and me that's how God worked, too; He just might snatch you up out of this life anytime He felt like it, just like a pop quiz, to see how good you'd been, and if you failed *that* test, boy, you were a goner for sure.

As she looked up, she pulled her glasses down to the tip of her pinched nose. "Hello, Stephen."

"Gaa!" Arthur said, which was his word for *go*. He held his arms up. He wanted me to come pick him up.

I loved the feel of him, the pillow pudge of his cheeks, his cottony shirt, and his billowy blond hair. It was good to get a drooly smile. I picked him up and we exchanged honks. Endy taught him that. When Arthur pulled on your nose, you had to honk, then we'd pull on his and you'd get a honk from him. Miss Godwin didn't approve.

"Christmas Card Day's at four," I said. "Granddaddy wants everybody."

"Oh, that's right." She looked out into the room and pinched her eyes shut. "I remember last year."

Miss Godwin had been with our family since right after Arthur was born, which made this her second Christmas Card Day. She was learning. Christmas Card Day could get kind of tense.

I got a real good hug from Arthur. His shirtfront was soggy from the drool. The book he had, the one about Babar the elephant, was wrinkly from it; it was bent, torn, chewed on, and marked with crayons from years of drooling and doodling Beckwith children. Babar had survived a lot.

Miss Godwin said she'd get Arthur changed and be in the dining room directly.

I would have knocked, but it wouldn't have done any good. Aunt Jew was too far gone to hear me. She was buried in her writing. I eased into her room.

She was at the far end, in her wheelchair, rolled up in front of the Underwood on her rolltop desk, a bourbon and branch on one side of her and a burning cigarillo in the ashtray on the other. She was a hundred years deep.

Aunt Jew was working on what turned out to be her most successful novel, *The Wind in the Magnolias*. It was also her most salacious.

She stood out from the crowd of historical romance writers by pushing her romantic scenes to the limit. Her depictions would be considered tame today, but in those days a proper lady kept her Jewel Beckwith books buried in her credenza, beneath the Christmas tablecloths.

Aunt Jew was bent over her typewriter. One hand clutched her drab-white, disorganized hair. She was chuckling to herself, reading what she'd just written, and that could mean only one thing.

"Aunt Jew?" I said. I was pretty loud.

"Hot damn," she said to herself. "Hot damn."

Yep, this scene had to be good.

"Aunt Jew?" I was louder.

"Yeah, yeah, yeah." She didn't look up or around. She had brought her hands back to the keys and was typing as she talked.

I remembered the beginning of the love scene from the week previous. Endy and I had pushed Aunt Jew out deep into the pecan grove for her usual "morning roll," out behind Granddaddy's house, and left her there with her rifle and her coffee. It was a cool, crisp morning, perfect for squirrels. As soon as we got her set up behind one of the bigger trees, with her brakes locked and her bullets within reach, we raced back to her room and to the Grand Mystery.

Endicott and I were ten and a half and eleven and a half, old enough to be experiencing vague stirrings, a sort of deep itch. We had such a reaction as he and I leaned over her desk, reading aloud our separate parts from pages stacked beside the typewriter. Endy was the buxom maiden.

" 'Oh, Colonel!' "

" 'Dahlia, my love!' "

" 'Colonel, no!' "

" 'Oh, yes, my darling, yes! Now! Now!' "

I went to the next page, but it was empty.

"Now what?" Endy wanted to know.

"Now's when the old goat moves in for the kill," I said.

"You mean the colonel?"

"Yep, bet you a dollar to a doughnut Miss Dahlia's about to get deflowered. Then she'll be a fallen woman."

"So what's the big deal about a fallen woman?" Endy asked.

"It's kind of hard to explain."

"I wonder if I'll ever meet a girl like Miss Dahlia," Endy said.

"Yeah. Maybe. Gonna ask her out on a date?"

"I don't know. Maybe. But first I'd have to help her up, I guess."

What a doofus.

Aunt Jew was still paying me no mind. She laughed to herself again—something of a horse laugh containing small snortings—and said, once more, "Hot damn!"

I got up on my toes again and this time read her last sentence: "The old colonel set down his glass of bourbon and *lunged* at Miss Dahlia!"

Yep, this had to be it, the official deflowering. Page 440. I couldn't wait to tell Endy.

"It's Christmas Card Day," I bellowed. I was running out of time. "Four o'clock."

"Oh God damn," she said. She looked up from her rolled-over paper. Her old eyes pulled away and scrolled through the years, forward and forward, approaching the present, and finally focusing on my presence and the clock on the wall behind me. "Christmas Card Day. God damn." Her ridged forehead gathered into a scowl, like rumpled leather. "I just hope to hell nobody gets shot this year."

"You'll be there?"

"Yeah. God. Sure."

I was hoping things upstairs were going to be pretty much as I had left them. Everybody had been in Endy's and my room playing board games, being quiet, with orders to stay unscruffed in preparation for an afternoon with Granddaddy. They were also aware that Daddy was upstairs in his office across the hall, and if there was too much noise he could explode as spectacularly as Granddaddy.

My taxidermy table had been moved into the middle of the room with chairs put around it, and everyone had been playing quietly when I left, but when I came into the room I realized something terrible had happened. Monopoly money was scattered over the table and under it, and the Monopoly board was upended on the floor. The girls were on one side of the room, the boys on the other. Muffled sobs came from the boys' side. Somebody, I was soon able to determine, had been bitten.

John helped me piece the story together. Endicott, he said, had amassed a raft of rental units on one of his properties—he had turned Park Place into a giant housing project—and was collecting exorbitant amounts of money from whoever fell into his clutches.

That happened to be Whyvonne. As soon as she reluctantly hopped her game piece into his lair, he reached over to her pile of money and began grabbing with a Scrooge-like chuckle of glee. She bit him on the hand. Hard.

Now Endy was over on his bed, balled up in agony and red with stifled crying. Not much of a mogul. Normally he would have been choking out shrieks, but our father's proximity had put a damper on his dramatics.

"That greedy bastard," Whyvonne said. She had expropriated some of his money and at least half his houses in the spirit of moral outrage, and that had led to the overturning of the board and more hissed threats. There were political overtones, and I wanted to stay out of it.

"Endy deserved it," Laura said.

"He did not," Travis said. "He *earned* that money."

"He didn't have to be so grabby," Laura said.

I went over to Endy. "You all right?"

I sat on the edge of the bed. He was facing away, all scrunched up. "No!" he yelled into his pillow. His word was strangled.

What a baby, I was thinking. But then I looked over at Whyvonne. Those were pretty big teeth. This was when I most hated being the oldest, and assistant patriarch to boot.

"Look y'all, we gotta go down in a minute for Christmas Card Day," I said.

"Already?" John asked. He had moved over to Endicott's desk, with Travis, and they were checking out the new model Endy was working on, a B-58. The real ones were being built in Fort Worth. We'd seen a couple flying over, and they'd scared the heck out of our three cows. Grand-daddy had called the base to complain.

Ethylene's kids began to withdraw. They'd have to go to their own house now, but that was fine with them. They knew we were heading to the front lines of scrutiny, whereas they were going to the small comforts of their warm little house. Baby Midland put Laura's doll on my bed, Travis handed the jet to John, and Whyvonne got their coats (she was assistant matriarch). Endicott was down to a whimper.

"What a baby," Laura said, filing past him.

"I don't see no blood," Whyvonne said, next in line.

"Yeah," Baby Midland said in solidarity.

As the girls were heading out the door, Endy jerked up on the bed and held out the aggrieved hand. I could see a red, ridged semicircle, on either end of which were two deeper dents where the canines had left their mark.

"Internal bleeding!" he yelled. "Look how red it is underneath!"

The girls stopped and looked back.

"Big deal," Laura said.

"You always red," Whyvonne said. "Ain't nothin' new."

"Yeah," Baby Midland said.

"I bet I get hydrophobia!" Endy moaned, falling back to the bed. "Just like Old Yeller!" He began to bubble some spit out from his lips. You couldn't really call it foam.

"We'll have to shoot you, then," Laura said.

"*I* wanna shoot him," Whyvonne said.

"Let me! Let me!" Baby Midland said, jumping up at her sister's side.

They left the room, arguing.

After I did the last of my patchwork grooming, which consisted of a quick straightening of my tie and a futile swipe of the hairbrush through the random swirls, I left my room. Endy was working at the mirror of his own dresser—chin up, tongue out—to reattach his clip-on tie. He was no longer foaming.

I went across the hall. My father was last on my list.

Daddy was in his office. From the hall, looking through my parents' living-room-size bedroom, I could see him at his desk in his office beyond. He was leaning back in his wood-slatted office chair, staring through the frost-edged window into the leafless trees that spread beyond the portico. A winter chill had settled into his face, a pale distance.

This was the hunkering down season for Daddy, when he spent most of his time bookkeeping. At the end of the calendar year taxes were figured, income surveyed, and he'd present next year's proposed budget to Granddaddy, estimating how much more property could be leased, mineral rights acquired, wells contracted.

This always brought up a review of the past year. Every mistake Daddy might have made—every dry hole or near miss or failed deal—was gone over, hashed and rehashed as only Granddaddy could do, with his blunt tongue, grinding logic, and sneering wit.

"Daddy?"

I came across the bedroom. It was best not to get too close to him before I said something. He was easily startled. He could be so deeply lost.

"Daddy?"

His desk was like Aunt Jew's, a bronze-brown mahogany rolltop—heaped in papers, notes, and maps that overflowed on the library table next to it. A typewriter was under there, and the office telephone. All of the cubbyhole slots on the desk were stuffed. A cigarette was burning in a burrowed place. He was holding an empty coffee cup.

He turned away from his inner space and looked at me as I came up to the doorway and leaned against the jamb. His look was barren.

"Time for those God damned Christmas cards?"

"Yeah, Daddy."

"I figured."

His voice was as dry as winter weeds. "I'll be there in a minute," he said. He turned away, back to the frosted window.

I looked down and up the long dining room table at my restless, mostly red-headed herd. We were assembled. A miracle.

Aunt Jew was the last straggler—I figured she was seeing to the removal of the last petal from poor Miss Dahlia. A minute later, Grand-daddy came striding in.

"All right, let's get this show on the road," he said, his parliamentary voice rolling over us from behind.

As he eased into his chairman-of-the-board chair at the head of the table, he reached for the top page of the Christmas card list. He slipped on his tortoise-shell glasses, arched his snow-capped eyebrows, and, in no mood to dally, asked: "So who's dead and who's not?"

"For God sakes, Thaddeus, hold your goddamn horses," Aunt Jew said. She snatched the page out of his hand and put it on top with the others. "I haven't even gotten a chance to open the Death Box yet."

"Well let's get on with it, Jew," he said.

"Tea, Mistah Beckwith?"

Odessa had come in with the sterling teapot. She wobbled up to him. "Why yes, Odie, thanks," he said. Her calming voice and easy presence always disarmed him, if only for seconds. He waited while the tea steamed into his china cup.

"Miss Jewel?"

"Yes, Odessa, that would be nice."

Odessa was like the Red Cross. When she came onto the battlefield, the shooting stopped, if only for a lull.

A shoebox was at Aunt Jew's side, and she took the top off. Inside, collected over the past year, were clippings from the Beckwiths' North-ern Virginia hometown newspaper, the weekly *Sommersville Democrat*. She removed a foot-thick wad of paper, all of which pertained to the comings and goings and unions of a passel of Beckwiths—once-removed, twice-removed, but for Granddaddy, never quite removed enough. Sometimes it was my job to scour the paper for Beckwiths and scissor them out; sometimes others got the task, usually my mother.

Although Granddaddy called it the Death Box, that was a misnomer, since most of the news was about births. For him, the term was a sign of hope. He seemed to get a kind of satisfaction every time he got to cross another aging Beckwith off the Christmas card list, pare it down, make it more manageable, so he could get on to more important things, like reading the *Wall Street Journal* or planning next year's garden.

Now Aunt Jew looked back to the original list in her other hand, preparing to make comparisons with the newspaper clippings. She went filtering through the pages. "Well looky here," she said, peering down through her half-rimmed glasses, "here's old Aunt Willa. I wonder if we've got an obit on her this year." She went back to the Death Box. "Funny, I don't remember getting one." She looked over at her brother, her eyes bulging up over the rims of her glasses. "My God, Thaddeus, if Aunt Willa isn't dead by now, she oughta be. The poor dear must be a hunnert 'n' ten if she's a day."

"Shall we cross her off the list?" Granddaddy asked hopefully. He pulled the cap off his fountain pen.

"Better not," Aunt Jew said, still looking but not coming upon an Aunt Willa death notice. "The poor thing. She's probably just hangin' on by a thread."

We were arranged differently on Christmas Card Day. In the interest of efficiency, Aunt Jew was rolled up to Granddaddy's right, and next to her was my mother, then my father. They each had boxes of cards in front of them, and their separate lists—my mother's contained her own bushy family tree; my father's was full of the names of the investors and clients of Beckwith Minerals.

We kids and Aunt Kitty were on the other side, functioning as secretaries and dealing with cards from three sources—Mama, Daddy, and Granddaddy/Aunt Jew. All of us signed all but Daddy's cards, and wrote small comments on cards to people we knew. Aunt Kitty licked stamps, Endicott stamped on return addresses, Laura and I licked envelopes, John stacked the finished products—all in a kind of production line. Baby Arthur and Miss Godwin, across the table next to Mama, just added to the spirit of things, which I wouldn't call festive.

"Who's Aunt Willa?" John asked.

And away we went. The annual family history lesson began—not the only family history discussion of the year, but the main one.

"Well let's see," Aunt Jew said, retracting her pen from Aunt Willa's card and pointing it skyward as her other hand went under her chin. "She is your grandfather's father's oldest brother's second wife. Is that right, Thad?"

"Yes."

Granddaddy was already disgusted. The door had been opened and now, in a jumbled group tour, we were all going in—into the dust-covered, dark-cornered, Byzantine world of the Southern Family. I knew what Granddaddy was thinking: we'll never get these damn Christmas cards done.

He was right.

"Is she really our aunt, then?" Laura asked. She was already, in her own tomboy way, beginning to go the way of Southern women—absorbing, making sense of, and becoming fascinated by the family web, which was as intricate as lace and as tough as steel. It took a mathematician to diagram it, a novelist to comprehend it, and, eventually, a wholehearted, thoroughly humbled person to accept it, forgive it, and live with it.

"Technically, no," Aunt Jew said, sinking away into history. Sinking took her awhile, and we waited. Mama got one card done, Daddy got two, and Granddaddy rummaged impatiently through the lists he took back from his sister as Aunt Jew drifted downward, her wadded lids closing over her eyes for a minute. "But you've got to remember," she said on the way down, "that any older female who gets associated with a family and hangs around long enough is going to get called Aunt Something or Other. Even black ones."

"And Aunt Willa," I said, trying to help Granddaddy out a little, to push things along.

"Yes. Aunt Willa."

"I wish you wouldn't," my mother said. "The children."

"Oh, piffle," Aunt Jew said. "Aunt Willa ran a boarding house."

"What's so bad about that?" Endicott asked.

"Some of the guests didn't stay very long at a time," she said with a wicked-coughing laugh. "The men, I mean. They were pretty temporary."

"For God's sake, Jew," Granddaddy said.

"Your Great-Great-Uncle Endicott, however, was one of her regular, er, gentleman callers. He finally married her. How old was he, Thad? Eighty-something by then?"

"I believe. Yes." Granddaddy shifted his tone proudly. "The Beckwith men have always been known for their fortitude."

"The poor old coot," Aunt Jew said with a dentured grin. "I think Willa was in her early thirties, maybe her twenties. Great-Uncle Endy blew out his aorta about six months after the wedding."

"He held off the entire Northern Army with just a handful of men, or at least that was the story," Granddaddy said. "The Yankees never entered Sommersville, although they did occupy the family plantation just outside of town."

"But Aunt Willa defeated him," Aunt Jew said.

"At least he died with his boots on, so to speak," Granddaddy said.

"He died?" Endy asked. "The uncle I was named for?"

"Don't worry about your Great-Great-Uncle Endicott," she said. She turned back to Granddaddy: "He died happy. From what I heard, even the undertaker couldn't wipe the smile off the old geezer's face."

Daddy was laughing and Granddaddy was trying to hide a smile with his hand.

"And what about Aunt Willa?" I asked.

"Oh, she's smilin' too, honey—every time she goes to the bank with another one of Uncle Endy's farm checks. Aunt Willa's in high cotton, my dear."

Granddaddy had every intention of making a clean break when he left that Virginia backwater town in 1918. That's how Aunt Jew related the story to us children in times past, when it was just her and Mama and us on the front porch on a summer's evening.

He had a new law degree from the University of Virginia, a new wife named Eleanor, and sparkling dreams. He had a job offer from the First National Bank of Fort Worth, Texas—a town that was the front gate to a wide-open, dry-skied land of promise. That's what he wanted.

Except . . . Eleanor wanted to pack a few things.

"Just Mother's credenzas," she said so sweetly. (Aunt Jew would perfume her voice with a lilt when she talked like Eleanor.) "Please Tad?" He was young and robust, Aunt Jew said, and he would have done anything for her. "It's Mother's wedding gift to us, plus everything inside—the family silver, what the Yankees didn't find, and the linen napkins from Dublin, and the tea service from London. Please Tad? Please?"

"I suppose we could have it shipped out."

"And Odessa?"

"Odessa?"

She was Eleanor's favorite Negro. They had grown up together. Her name, before she married Judge, was Odessa Beckwith. A handful of decades before then, our family had owned her family.

"She wants to go with us, honey. She could be such a help to us and she's such a dear. I'm going to have babies one of these days, you know, and Odie would be so good with them. Please?"

"I reckon."

"Oh my darling. My sweet man."

The poor sap. That's what Aunt Jew said.

He thought he was starting over, she said. He thought he was getting on that train and heading toward a brand new life in the fresh-aired West.

Almost at once Granddaddy became immersed in the drive to succeed, to make his own way separate from his Virginia circle of influence. A few years after his arrival in Fort Worth he eased out of the banking business and went out on his own—real estate, oil, the stock market. There were more ups than downs. He got through the Depression with a minimum of discomfort. He accumulated a fortune.

But before he knew it, with most of his attention on his career, Virginia resprouted around him. He agreed to the big house out in the country. (Yes, it looked suspiciously like the old home place; it had been built by another homesick Southerner.) But by moving beyond the edge of the city, he was hoping to discourage civilization from getting out to him.

That, however, didn't stop the women, Eleanor's society friends, most of whom were fellow Southern expatriates. They were organizing, they were driving automobiles, and they found Eleanor—the Shakespeare Society and the Daughters of the Confederacy; sugar cookies and parliamentary haggling; World War I bandages and World War II war bonds. Those good ladies soon overran the place.

Eleanor had to have the yardboy take out all of the dirt from the front beds and replace it with peat moss, but she got her azaleas planted. They had four children. Odessa got married, some of her cousins moved out from Virginia, and before long there were twice as many black children as white ones on the Beckwith place. By 1935 it was all looking suspiciously like a plantation community.

The South had risen again. The South had risen around him. The pecan grove grew up, the shade thickened, and a familiar sort of swamp-scented, drawling air accumulated and settled over everything. And Christmas Card Day, which Eleanor had begun in 1919, grew quickly into a major family tradition.

It took on a life of its own, as most traditions do. It couldn't be stopped. It had become, to Granddaddy, a symbol of his defeat, and he was not fond of such symbols.

"I've got a *P* here beside Aunt Willa's name," Aunt Jew said, peering down at the top page again. "She gets shelled, right?"

"Unshelled," Granddaddy said. He had the other pages of the list, and he was continuing to shuffle through them.

"For God's sake, Thaddeus, how is Aunt Willa supposed to crack her own pecans?" Aunt Jew asked. "With her God damned dentures? Send her shelled, Stephen."

"Yes ma'am," I said.

That was another thing that went out along with the Christmas cards—pecans. They came from the fifty giant trees around us. Every fall, with the help of Judge and some men and boys that he would collect from the colored side of town, we'd harvest the pecans. Endy, Travis, and I, along with the hired boys, would climb high in the trees and jump on the branches. The men had long poles they'd poke with, rustling the yellow-tinted leaves. That was one day, and for a week afterward, we'd go out with baskets and pick up the nuts. We'd get bushels.

Half the pecans were taken into town to a company that shelled them. That cost a pretty penny, as Granddaddy said, and he was miserly with pennies. Granddaddy's sweet-meat, shelled pecans were prized by Southern cooks; the pecan pies you could make from them were unsurpassed in cream and crunch. Only the most special got them; others got unshelled ones; the rest got only a card.

Aunt Jew at last signed the card the way she usually did—"Merry Christmas from the Texas Bunch"—that's how we were known in Sommersville—and signed her name, "Love, Jewel." She handed the card to Granddaddy and took the list from him so she could get the address. He made a kind of slashing signature and handed the card to me. Aunt Jew handed me the addressed envelope. I signed the card and handed it down to Endy. While he was signing it, I wrote Aunt Willa's address on one of the prewrapped boxes of shelled pecans. Endy handed the card down to Laura, and down the line it went—John, Daddy, Mama, and back across the table to me. I put the card into the envelope, Laura licked and sealed it, Aunt Kitty put on the postage, Endy stamped on our return address, and then it was handed to John, who put it in the "done pile," together with the brown-wrapped, string-tied box of pecans.

All this, and Aunt Willa might have been dead.

4

IN THE SUMMER OF MY TWELFTH YEAR, LIKE SO MANY OTHER SUMMERS, we went to the ocean.

We traveled in two station wagons, the old International and a new Oldsmobile, a woody, and still I could hardly breathe for eight hours. Squashed in—besides clothes and food, rods and reels and crab nets, tackle boxes and buckets and the outboard motor—were Laura, Endy, John, Baby Arthur, who was three then and needed Miss Godwin to keep up with him, so she went, plus Aunt Kitty, Ethylene, Whyvonne, Travis, Baby Midland, and me. We also took the collies, one per car. They barked at one another, car to car whenever we passed each other, and at every cow.

It was Granddaddy's vacation to stay at home and soak up the quiet. Aunt Jew couldn't go because her wheelchair would bog down in the sand. Odessa and Judge stayed to take care of them.

Mama drove one car and Daddy the other. We had to stop at least once an hour to re-sort children because of fights. We were in the back seats, lined up, in shorts, white knees, black knees, scratched knees. We were supposed to be still, reading comic books or watching for cows, which were about the only scenery.

With that much boredom, somebody's going to get slugged. They did. We'd stop. Re-sort.

Our boredom also got us to stop at scenic attractions, such as the Hi-Way Snake Farm near Waco. Mama was worried that, with so many unleashed kids, somebody might get bitten. I think the snake man was more worried about his snakes.

For fifty cents you got to see lots of snakes, mostly rattlers in enclosed rocky areas. On each display was a sign that said DO NOT AGGRAVATE THE SNAKES.

Most of the snakes were asleep in tangled gobs. Who wants to see a bunch of sleeping snakes? We wanted some aggravation. We specialized in aggravation. John tapped on the glass, Endy spit his bubblegum at them, Whyvonne screamed.

Because we were such a crowd just on our own and because he knew we were going to wake up his snakes one way or another anyway, the snake man agreed to let loose a rat—a snake snack. As much as Mama hated rats, she still felt sorry for it. The critter went nuts, hot-footing it among the slumbering coils. Sure enough, there was one snake half awake. The rat didn't last long—about as long as the cornbread lasted at our dining room table. The rat got gulped, we all got root beers, and away we went, two down and six more ungodly hours to go.

We went in July and stayed two weeks, like always. Daddy rented this big house at Port Aransas, which is at the upper tip of Mustang Island on the Gulf of Mexico. It had a huge, wood-paneled room with beds lining the walls—that's where all us children stayed—a separate room Mama and Daddy stayed in, another for Miss Godwin and Arthur, and a third for Aunt Kitty and Ethylene. The house was on stilts with windows everywhere, open except when it rained, so the Gulf breeze rushed across us day and night. When I salted my eggs at breakfast, Endy's got more than mine did.

Every morning, almost, we children got up when the dawn was no more than a shadow, rushed down the stairs (we slept in our dry bathing suits) and down the shell-graveled street. It went about a block, with houses like ours among the grass-tufted dunes, and then the road opened out into the beach. We ran out across the cool sand, whooping like black and white Indians, Wilson and Woody racing ahead. We charged into the warm foam, leaping across the waves. We dived for shells, raced the waves, and played King of the Mountain with our innertubes until our muscles were as floppy as seaweed. Then we sat in the wet sand at the edge of the water, building castles and forts and stomping them before the tide got there first.

My mother came with us but lagged behind. She gave us our freedom, but she was available in case of trouble. After all, the ocean was full of varmints, and Baby Midland couldn't swim. Mama stayed in sight, wandering across the sand, looking for shells. She found the most beautiful things—olives, sand dollars, shark's teeth, little pink conchs. She was a jeweler, bringing treasures into focus. In her hands, under her careful eyes, the sand glittered.

"Look what I just found!" she said, coming up to us where we were circled around a mound of sand growing jagged with spires and turrets.

By now, with the morning fully present, the wind had come back with full gustiness. I can remember my mother's red-mahogany hair loose and fluttering, her dress billowing around her ankles. Her sandals were full of sand. Her tired eyes were glinting.

We abandoned our castle. We crowded around her. Baby Midland was hopping: "Lemme see! Lemme see!"

"Look at this," Mama said.

"A starfish!" Laura said.

"A perfect one!" Whyvonne said.

"Lemme see! Lemme see!" Baby Midland chanted.

My mother bent down and then we all bent down so that we were all level with Baby Midland.

"Law! Law!" Baby Midland said, all breathless, sounding like her mother. "A star's come down from heaven and landed in our ocean!"

"It's an echinoderm," Laura said. She was already becoming a biologist. She was becoming a pain. "It eats mollusks."

"I coulda told you that," Endicott said.

"You mean it's alive?" Mid asked. "A star that's alive?"

"This one's deader'n hell," Travis said.

"Stiff as a board," Whyvonne said.

"It's still a star," Mid said. She held it. "A star."

My mother spread her treasures on the sand, and we began to pick through them. We tried to divide up everything equally, except in the case of Baby Midland. We made sure she got the best and most. She kept her treasures in a shoebox under her bed, and in the evenings she'd take out the box, dump out her shells on her bedspread, and go over them. My mother would sit on the edge of the bed and help her, exclaiming over everything.

We ran back to the house for breakfast in the middle of these mornings, and then we ran back to the waves. The adults came to the beach to visit us off and on, sitting in lawn chairs and watching us. My mother read, Aunt Kitty needlepointed, Ethylene took a nap, and Miss Godwin, looking up from her Bible, watched Arthur, who splashed about in the shallows or dug sand into his pail.

My father came a few times, too. He wore a ragged shirt, khaki pants, old shoes, and a brown cap. He waded out into the waves with his rod and reel. He never caught much, except a small shark once, and Whyvonne didn't go swimming after that for three days, even though we assured her the shark wasn't big enough to have eaten more than one of her toes at a time.

We were forced to go in at noon. "Y'all'll be cooked clean through to the bone if you don't come in outta that hot sun," Ethylene said. She meant us white ones. We were the color of toast—cinnamon toast because of all our freckles. And because of the salted wind, all seven of us had Afros. Ethylene liked to say we all looked like cousins. My mother laughed and agreed. But it wasn't true when we boys got into the shower. Nature hadn't touched our private selves. We had racially divided bottoms, shiny black and powder-puff white.

After lunch and a nap, late in the afternoon, we went fishing on the jetty. My father was in charge of unsnarling lines, baiting hooks, and tying on new hooks when the old ones got hung on the rocks and had to be broken off. He sometimes screamed at us. He often stayed clenched quiet for long periods. But sometimes he caught fire with laughter, and his lost-blue eyes came home.

All of us but Arthur were equipped with a cane pole. We walked down the concrete path of the jetty—as far away from other people as we could get—for safety reasons; theirs—and clambered down among the giant granite blocks that tumbled to the water. Our prey was piggies.

Piggy perch are small, spiny fish that croak when caught. (Endy could do a pretty good imitation, an airy burp.) We caught them by the hundreds. Ethylene was in charge of unhooking them. She sat in a spot on the edge of the concrete walk and took the fish off as we swung them over to her. She put them in a wet tow sack. In a while it sounded like a barnyard.

"Got one, Mama!" Baby Midland said.

"Here's another one, Ethylene!" John said.

"Look, Mama!" Whyvonne said. "I just hooked one in the tail!"

"Hold it, y'all! Hold it!" Ethylene kept saying. The concrete path was hopping with piggies. "Y'all are gonna cover me up with fish!"

My father and I went fishing alone once that summer. He'd brought his outboard motor from the river cabin, thinking if we could just get out a little ways we might catch something big.

I woke up in darkness when I heard the alarm go off in Daddy's room. I heard him walk across the big room. He came up to my bed, not even a shadow, touched my shoulder and said, "Stephen," in a low, smoky voice that broke apart.

"Yeah," I whispered, and I swiveled out of bed.

I put on my blue jeans and T-shirt, socks and tennis shoes. A touch of sleepy wind came across and ruffled my shirt and hair. I loved the breathing of that house.

We ate cereal. Daddy drank coffee. We didn't say anything.

The car was already loaded. We didn't have to drive very far to get to the bay side of our skinny little island. From breakfast to dock was only ten minutes.

The sign that said ROY'S BOATS in crumbling orange letters was one wall of a shack. Roy came out from behind his name.

He was grumbly and mussed. His spilling gut waddled like a separate being as he moved. He grunted toward the boats tied up at the dock at the bottom of a slight hill. "Six bucks," he said. "All day." My father gave him the money.

All the boats were aluminum, V-bottomed sixteen-footers. We drove down to the dock and loaded the closest one.

My father pull-started the motor and backed the boat away from the dock. The old outboard, a seven-and-a-half-horsepower Evinrude, sounded good, uncluttered, like it had been given a new set of lungs. Bert had finally gotten it working good.

The whine of the motor geared upward as we buzz-sawed across the ripple-coated bay water toward the jetties. We moved against a small wind. The damp air waved chills across my bare arms.

To our right a row of bony brown docks protruded where people were loading their boats. To our left was a gray table of water a mile wide. Several seal-backed porpoises were rolling and snorting. Above, here and there, like something torn and blown about, seagulls dived and shrieked.

Our island, years ago, had been sliced open by a trench. Big ships came through the opening, across the front of the bay to the tall docks of the port within. On either side of the cut were jetties, south and north, jutting into the Gulf. The deep opening between was about a quarter mile wide. The south jetty was where we did our piggy fishing.

At the base of the jetties we turned into the opening that led to the open ocean. The waves increased into long and steady rolls. The wind, no longer dissuaded by the island, came free and full, bringing a chop to the water. My father slowed the motor.

The gray swelling in the east had grown across the dome of darkness. I could see a great distance now. Soon the first of the sun hunched up out of the white-tipped waves in the Gulf, and the sky splintered into pink.

Daddy was convinced some very big fish moved just out from the jetties, feeding on the little fish that were attracted to the hiding places of the rocks. He thought if we trolled our jigs along the edge of the rocks, we might come upon something big.

He got one of the jigs from his tackle box and tossed it forward to me. He'd made it himself, melting the lead in the kitchen at home and pouring it into molds around the hooks. After the lead cooled, he put the jigs in a vice and tied a fluff of white underfeathers to the end, hiding the hook. (I was in charge of stealing feathers from the chickens.) He painted the eyes an alarming red and added a gash of wounded red at the base of the body, covering the thread.

He'd tied the jigs the previous winter in his office, read lots of *Field & Stream* magazines, and made saltwater rods from kits for the two of us. We practiced casting in the open place between the gravel driveway and the arbor. He was supposed to be reading drilling maps and seismic reports. I don't know if Granddaddy noticed. He probably did.

I put my rod together and strung it, which was maddeningly hard to do among the bouncings of the boat. I tied on a steel leader and clipped on the jig. Daddy did the same. We cast out at about the same time, let some line out, and locked the reels. We began to troll.

Daddy turned up the speed just enough. We needed the boat to go about as fast as a darting, wary minnow. We'd jerk the rods every few seconds to give liveliness to the baits.

Now it was a matter of wandering into the path of a fish. We hugged the south jetty, moving toward the split sun.

The big party boats went speeding past, heading out to the sapphire water where the big fish lived. Daddy had to watch out for their wake, which came glancing in on us, while the waves from the open ocean came in bulges from the opposite direction. Our little boat tilted and swayed.

His plan was to troll up and down the jetties and across the mouth between them, close to the rocks and then farther out, until we wore out or until the wind got too high.

In thirty minutes we rounded the south jetty and came down its other side, the Gulf side. The swells ballooned and subsided in the easy rhythm of a rocking chair. We moved down the jetty until we got to the edge of the breaking surf near the shore, then retraced our path in the waves.

The sun burned off the memory of the earlier chill. A hushed breeze built up. I imagined the jig beneath the waves, lurching along like something crippled.

"Stephen, help me keep an eye out for the birds," my father said.

I turned back to look at him. It was the first thing he'd said to me since he woke me up. Daddy didn't think talking and fishing went together.

He had his left hand on the handle of the motor, the other on his spinning rod. He was squinting toward the open ocean, looking for the birds through the strings of smoke that came up from his cigarette. His face was deep brown and darkly lined. His brown cap was edged with old sweat stains. It wasn't hot yet, but it would be. The sun was low but enormous, and the color of the waves was changing from the green calm of morning to the fiery blue of day.

I turned away to the horizon. I knew what to look for because I had seen them before from the jetty, a swarm of little sharp-angled birds climbing, turning, collapsing into a chopped-up circle of feeding fish. But now only a few birds strolled across the sky. Far off, near the horizon, the bumpy water was dotted with shrimp boats, and beyond I could see the tiny, jagged tops of oil platforms.

Daddy and I were wide open to the sky and the breezy ocean. He was fully present, quietly happy, free. We were as close as we would ever be.

• • •

Soon we came back to the end of the south jetty, to the disjointed waves where the fast boats were still coming through. I watched the veering waves to prepare my balance.

I could see the fishermen on the jetty, casting from the moss-streaked, granite blocks. I waved to one, and the man waved back. He cupped his mouth and yelled, "Y'all doin' any good?" I shook my head no. "Y'all be careful them waves!" he yelled again. My father nodded his head yes.

We bucked across the channel's mouth, a half mile, to the north jetty. Behind it, the waves evened out. We trolled to the verge of the surf, then returned, like before.

The sun went from orange to white. The air thinned and warmed and dried, and the wind came up. The blue of the sky was emptier. No birds gathered. No clouds. Not many other boats.

My father took the boat a hundred yards out from the end of the south jetty before we turned to cross the mouth again. I no longer took notice of the steeper rise and tilt in the unprotected channel.

We had been fishing at least two hours. My expectation was becoming blunted, and my concentration began to thin. My thoughts, unanchored, began to sway.

Then, suddenly, I sprang alert. A sound came from my father, tugged out of him as he reared back on his rod.

"You got one, Daddy? A strike?"

I had turned in my seat to face him. He was reeling in, jerking the rod at twice the beat in case the fish might strike again.

"Hell," he said.

"Was it a strike?"

My father finished reeling in and swung the jig into his hand. He looked at it. "Hard to tell. I coulda hit bottom. Hell, I prob'ly did."

He cast out. I turned and faced the ocean. The day stretched out again.

The motor droned, the heat got saltier because of the sweat that came with it; we loped across the waves. Another hour passed. We went back and forth and back around the rocks.

Cumulus thoughts came up in me, lifting me into a drift of time. I don't know where my father went; probably the same place. Time dozed, then slumbered, then suddenly recoiled into a knot.

I was yanked back to earth as my rod lunged forward. I rocked back against the sudden weight, then turned in my seat just as the ocean opened. From the white cut rose a silver thing, dragon-big, thrashing the air and walloping against the water with a tremendous slap.

"Lord God Almighty damn, Stephen!" My father's eyes were leaping. "God *damn!*"

"Oh *Daddy!*"

My father was reeling in madly to prevent a tangle. He had shifted the motor into neutral. "God Almighty, did you see that thing jump? That's the biggest God damn tarpon I've ever seen in my life!"

"Daddy, what should I *do*?"

The line was streaming from my reel. We were out from the end of the south jetty and the fish was moving into the open ocean. My blood was burning.

"Daddy, all my line's goin' away! I can't hold him, Daddy!" My voice crackled between its old high and its brand-new adolescent low.

My father moved unsteadily, crouched toward me, kneeling on the middle seat and reaching with one hand. The other was gripping the edge of the boat. He pulled on the line next to my reel.

"Drag's about right. Any tighter and the line might snap."

"But Daddy, all my line's . . ."

"You got plenty left."

My father eased backward, bent and balancing, to his seat. The line continued to whine in surges from my reel.

The quickened blood roared through my head. I was awash with adrenaline. I was instinct. I was muscle and amazement.

Then the line lessened and I felt it coming.

"Look!" I had time to say.

The waves parted white and silver. The fish arced five feet and not all of him cleared in his flight away from the boat. He flashed like a broad sword in the big sun.

"God damn, Stephen, what are we gonna do with that thing?"

"Daddy, my line. I can't gain any. He keeps goin' out."

My father leaned forward and took another look at the spool. "Yeah, it's gettin' pretty low. Maybe I can ease up toward him with the motor. You can gain back some line. But keep the pressure on him. You gotta keep slack out of the line."

He shifted the motor into forward and we moved slowly away from the end of the jetty. I reeled in, keeping the heaviness in the rod.

"Too fast?" my father asked.

"Okay."

"You gotta keep him fightin' the drag as much as you can or we'll never wear him down."

We glided toward the fish and I slowly took in line. The sun was noon-sharp. My skin pinkened with the growing heat. The blood thumped in my neck and ears. My arms ached. But as the reel began to fill with line again, a feeling of control began to grow.

"We better not get too close," my father said.

"Maybe that's enough, then."

"If he jumped in the boat he'd sink us."

The motor stopped but the fish continued. The weight tightened through the rod and then the reel began to sing again. Against the new pressure the fish rebelled and rose, a slashing animal agonized. My feeling of control splintered at the sight of the fish, its mouth gaping, its eyes white and wide.

"Daddy, look at the line go. I haven't worn him down a bit."

"It's gonna take a while, Stephen. We got a big fight on our hands."

"And what if I *do* wear him down. Then what?"

"Hell if I know. I guess we'll thinka something."

"He won't even fit in the boat."

"I sure as hell wouldn't try. If there was any life left in him he could knock us outta here. We'll tie him to the side maybe. But there's no use worrying about that now."

"Maybe you better start after him again, Daddy. My line."

"Here we go."

My father put his cigarette in his mouth and turned, pulled the rope and started the motor. We began to move again, and I began to crank the reel.

I tried to remain mechanical and concentrated, keeping the daydreams locked out. I held back on my thoughts like I did with the rod, keeping pressure.

"Whoa!"

"Close enough?" my father asked, twisting the handle and choking off the motor.

"Yeah, Daddy."

As the boat slid into an easy stop, I quit reeling and tightened my fingers around the rod. The fish moved into the resistance of the weight of the boat. The line strained as before and I steadied my breath, ready for the maddened leap.

It didn't come. At the point of full strain the line held. The fish didn't overcome the drag.

"Daddy, it's . . . he's not . . . I think I'm wearing him down."

My father looked into the water where the line entered. Beyond, between the waves, a few feet under, we could see the white shadow. It glimmered. It was enormous.

"Stevie, maybe you are."

The fish and I had been attached for half an hour. The motor was silent, the wind had fallen, the slow waves slapped against the boat. The fish tugged us along. We glided into the open sea.

The enormous strain against the line kept me from gaining any back. It would have been dangerous to use the motor to get any closer to the fish.

I watched him. He was strolling. His great silver fan of a tail stroked widely, languidly, sometimes quietly breaking the surface.

"Looks like we're bein' taken for a ride, Stephen."

"Yeah."

"Wonder how long he can keep it up."

"How far is it to Mexico?"

I heard the smile in my father's voice. "Now don't get discouraged, Stephen. That fish can't last forever."

"Neither can I."

"You really gettin' tired?"

"Yeah, Daddy."

Strings of pain began at my wrists and pushed through my forearms, bent sharply at my elbows, shot into my shoulders, and tied a knot in my back below my neck. Pain bulged low in my stomach where the butt of the rod was buried. The pain was bunched in my legs, which were buckled against the aluminum seat. My skin was stinging from the sun. The glare of the waves heated my eyes. I stretched everything the best I could, trying to loosen the pain and squirm out of it.

I turned and looked back. The jetty was a brown ridge that seemed to bob in the water. Beyond, the beach was a line on a map. I turned again. Ahead, everything was waves and sky—two shades of blue, deep and deeper, divided by a bumpy line.

My eyes kept returning to the fish. In the troughs of the waves, the dorsal fin and the top of the tail were exposed. That's when I got a good look at him. But most of the time he was nothing but a vague form, a glimmer beneath a blanketing of blue, the dim light of a dream.

A trickle of sweat fell splintering into my eye; I wiped it with the end of my T-shirt. The sunlight glanced harshly off the sea's shattering mirror. Everything glared.

I was too worn to think. My brain was clenched and dull, like all my muscles and every connecting fiber. The only thing I contained was one numbing desire: for it all to be over with, somehow, soon.

My father stirred in his seat. He lit another cigarette and looked over his shoulder at the diminishing shoreline. I saw a flutter of uneasiness in his eyes, but he said nothing.

"We're gettin' far," I said, bending my head into my shoulder to wipe the sweat from my forehead.

"Yeah."

"What if we get out of sight of land?"

"I don't know. That'll be a while yet."

"Then what?"

My father took in and out an extended sigh with his cigarette. "Maybe . . . maybe the fish'll make his move before then."

"His move?"

"He can't go on like this forever. He'll make one last struggle, I bet. It'll be rough. He'll go wilder than ever. It'll make or break us."

"But when?"

"Listen, you want me to hold the rod for a while? Let you stretch? That fish isn't doing anything anyway."

I thought about it. To stand up, to shake my arms and legs and loosen the coiled pain. But what if the fish suddenly surged? There would be confusion handing the rod back. And besides, it was my fish. All of it, the pain and the fish.

"I'm okay."

I looked at the fish again. The tarpon was at least six feet long, at least a hundred and fifty pounds of silver-scaled muscle, twice my size. He seemed to be swimming unconcerned, hardly inconvenienced. I thought my chances of landing a tugboat were about as good.

The fish was pulling us into boundlessness. At some point, engulfed in distance, we would have to cut the line and turn back. It was hours away but it was coming. The fish was winning.

I held on.

I closed my eyes but I was still watching the fish. He was there too, deep in me, a glimmer in the self-made dark. He was hope, just out of reach.

Time congealed. The waves rocked us, the fish pulled us, and it was a long, long time.

It broke. Time. Everything.

The fish surged and I was pulling back and my father was shouting and so was I.

"Hold on! Hold on!" Daddy was saying.

"Oh God!" I was saying. "Oh God!"

The arc in the rod had doubled and I was rearing back on it. The line was whirling out of the reel. The fish was gone into the deep.

"He's diving!" I shouted.

"Hold on!" my father shouted back. "Just hold on!"

I couldn't do anything else. The line peeled out in spurts. The end of the rod pointed straight down, almost directly below the boat.

Then as sudden as a jerk the line fell dead. I fell back in the seat, but I caught myself.

"Daddy, something . . . the line! I think the line broke!"

"Maybe not!" he shouted back. "Reel in! Reel in!"

I began turning the reel handle like an egg beater. There was nothing and more nothing and then came the explosion. Five yards from the boat the tarpon broke.

We drew our breaths and leaned away, our eyes bulging, as the fish leapt toward us. Fins and muscles wrenched in his long, arching dive into the sky. His gaping eyes flashed dark pinpoints of terror. His gills were wide open, as red as new blood. His torn mouth gulped wide.

The hook hung loose in the torn place, and in the jump and twitch it was flung away, falling separately from the great crash of the body near the boat. We were splattered with spray; the boat lurched. And then the waves softened, and silence came roaring in.

My face was limp, my jaw dangling. My fingers were as stiff as claws, curled around a useless stick. I shuddered and blinked and stared. I watched the water heal.

A seashell sound swayed inside, and that was my exhaustion. I listened to it for a long time.

My father moved. I broke out of the stare and looked over.

"Here," he said. "Some water."

I reached with palsied hands, blinking, and took the full lid of the water jug. Only grating air came out when I tried to say thanks.

The icy water slapped down my throat. I nodded yes when my father asked if I wanted more, and my lubricated voice was able to say thanks this time. As I drank I watched the waves, and there was nothing.

"I was afraid of that," my father said. "I was afraid he'd do that."

"What."

"Dive like that. Circle back on us."

"I wish I'da reeled in faster."

"Maybe. You could have maybe reeled in that fast but I'm not sure. I'm not sure I could have done it, either."

"I just wish I'da known what he was doing. I could have reeled in fast right when he turned back toward us."

"That was a smart fish, Stephen. Real smart."

I began slowly reeling in the line. The pain cranked through my wrists.

"It happened so fast," I said.

"I know."

The jig came out of the water. I swung it toward me and took it in my hand.

"Not much left of it," I said.

"Lemme see."

I swung the bait over to him.

"All the feathers are gone," I said.

"Most of the paint, too."

My father broke off the line from the twisted leader.

"Can we save it, Daddy?"

"Sure." He opened his tackle box and put it in.

We drifted for a time. I stood and stretched and pulled against my cramped muscles. The blood came in and pushed out much of the pain. I locked my knees and held on to the side of the boat with one hand and peed over the side.

I sat down again and looked across the sun-glazed waves. Daddy peed into a can and washed it out. He drank some coffee from his thermos and smoked a cigarette. I drank some more water.

And then he said, "There's one thing I know for sure."

"Yeah?"

"You fought like hell. You did as well as anyone could have done, anyone, a man twice as big."

I looked at my father, and a chill sprinkled across my back, down my arms and through my eyes. His eyes were sharp glass, sharp blue.

"You've grown up a bunch since the last time I looked, Stephen."

Daddy turned in his seat and started the motor. We started the long, slow trip toward shore.

For one applauding moment I was a hero. Laura, Whyvonne, Endicott, John, Travis, Baby Midland, even Arthur—they all were impressed. I had to tell the story of the fish a hundred times, and each time it was an inch longer, a pound heavier; the fight a minute longer, a trickle sweatier.

Now everybody wanted to go out with Daddy and catch a tarpon, too. Endy thought he might catch one from the jetty with a jig like I'd used. And of course I wanted to go with Daddy and try again.

To each of these appeals Daddy said, "We'll see."

The problem was the weather. On the day after the big fish, white clouds bubbled up over the ocean and rolled in. They crowded together into dark-shouldered piles. By that afternoon, showers came. On the third day the overcast solidified, and the rain, with darker patches of thunder and downpour, was steady.

What else could we children do? We turned into caged beasts.

My mother tried to tame us. She got coloring books for the younger ones and tried to get us older ones channeled into something civilized, such as Chinese checkers.

Arthur ate Baby Midland's burnt orange crayon and half the lime green one. Whyvonne accused Endicott of hiding her marbles down his pants. She wanted me to frisk him, and I wouldn't. He bristled at the accusation, but when he did, he clicked.

My father was caged in with us. He sat at the kitchen table, in the corner by the window, watching the rain drizzle down the windowpanes.

He was bunched up inside, pacing. In the middle of the morning on the third day of rain, he began to drink.

My father plus alcohol and loud children equaled gasoline and fire. Mama tried to keep the ingredients apart. In the afternoon she took us for a long drive along the puddled beach. My father stayed put at the kitchen table with his bourbon.

The trip into the rain was bleak. We children were quiet. My mother was gloomy. Aunt Kitty, steadfast in her vacancy, looked out on the gray roll of waves with a manufactured smile.

When we got back, my father was in an expansive mood. He wanted to take us out to eat.

Somehow we all fit into one station wagon. We drove down the beach to the Chicken Coop. We ordered from the carhop and stayed parked in the rain. We had to eat in the car because Ethylene and her children were with us.

Soon the car was full of chicken bones and sticky with spilled Cokes and fogged from all those piercing voices. Daddy's glow wore off. He mixed some bourbon in his Coke. We drove back to the house.

We took our showers and got into our nightclothes. My father stayed at the kitchen table and drank. He was deathly quiet.

As we were getting settled into bed, which usually took at least an hour, my father told my mother he was going to take a drive. He went out into the rain.

In our beds, we drifted into silence, one at a time, the youngest to the oldest—John quit bouncing his leg against the mattress, Whyvonne and Laura quit whispering, Endy ran out of speculations about the next day's weather.

The adults were quiet, too. Daddy didn't come back.

For a long time I listened to the slow rain and the slower breathing of the other children in the line of beds beside mine. I wanted to go down with them to the swimming dark, but something held me back.

I left my bed and went into the kitchen for some milk and a handful of cookies and took them to the table. My mother was playing solitaire.

I watched as she bent over her cards. The light from the lamp on the ledge above the table was shaded and pooled. We were the only ones awake.

Her forehead was jagged, her eyebrows tangled, her eyes an emerald density; a green-dark, overshaded sea.

"You couldn't sleep, honey?" Her voice was worn like the wind at the end of a long day.

"Not very tired, I guess."

"We haven't done much today."

"Yeah. Maybe that's it. What time is it?"

"Honey, I don't know. Around midnight, I guess. My watch is in the bedroom."

"I don't guess Daddy's home yet."

"No."

I knew that. I wanted Mama to think I'd been sleeping. She didn't need to worry about me, too.

I figured Daddy had gone to the liquor store for another bottle. He probably drove to the beach and parked at the edge of the surf, drinking, watching the dark water, listening to the dark waves.

Mama said, "Maybe he'll be home soon."

We sat for a long time. Mama gave up on her hand of solitaire and we played a few games of gin rummy. We almost laughed once or twice.

In the middle of our third game—I was winning that one, too, but Mama was only half playing—we heard a car drive up. We set our cards down, and I followed my mother across the main room.

She opened the glass-fronted door and stood in front of the closed screen door. We looked down on Daddy's car from our second-story perch.

The engine was turned off but the headlights stayed on. He didn't come out.

Mama went down the long stretch of wooden stairs. I went behind her. The rain was slow and cold.

She opened the car door. I stood behind her. Daddy had his hand on the steering wheel. His head was leaning back.

"Will?"

"Daddy?"

She jostled him.

"Wake up!"

I joined her from behind. "Wake up, Daddy!"

My mother shook him again at his shoulder, and then the muscles showed up in his neck. His head came out of the nod, his muddied eyes came open and his mouth said, "Huh?"

"You gotta wake up, Will, and get to bed."

"Huh?"

"C'mon, Will, wake up! We're getting soaked out here."

"Huh?"

"Help me, Stephen. We gotta get him inside."

We pulled with four arms and he toppled toward us. The rain splattered over his face, and his eyes began to flutter. "Huh?" he said.

His muscles came alive and he pulled up, pushing on the steering wheel and the back of the seat. We were pulling on him. We got his arms over our shoulders and pulled some more. He pushed out with his legs until he was free of the car.

Daddy was between us. His legs were slumping but they held half his weight. Our shoulders did the rest. As we moved away from the car, I reached in and turned off the headlights, then pushed the door to with my foot.

We took half steps, heaving with the weight. A whiskey cloud blew across us.

It was a long way up the stairs. Mama angled in first between the railings, pulling, and I came in behind, pushing. We were all sideways.

My father got stronger as we went, taking more of his own weight. The rain helped wake him.

When we got into the house my mother whispered, "Stephen, we've got to get him back to the bedroom."

"Okay."

We went across the main room, through the kitchen area, and into their bedroom. When we got close to the bed, we turned. Daddy let go. We helped him swivel his legs up and around.

He turned away from me on the bed. My mother began untying his shoes.

"You oughta get on to bed now, honey," she said to me, still whispering.

"You don't need any more help, Mama?"

"I think we'll be all right now, honey. You go on and get those wet clothes off."

"Okay, Mama." She didn't look at me.

I got some dry clothes from the dresser. I was drying off in the bathroom when Mama knocked softly.

"Stephen honey, would you bring the mop out of there when you get through?"

As soon as I came out, I knew why Mama needed it. I took the mop to her and tried not to look at what was splashed across the wooden floor.

"Thank you, darlin'," she said. "Now could you go get me a wet washrag?"

When I got back, the smell was still there and it made chilly burning memories in my throat. Mama was sitting on the bed beside my father and the mess was gone. "Thank you," she said when I handed her the damp washcloth.

I stood there for a while. I didn't know what to say. Mama put the cool cloth on my father's forehead, reaching over him because he was turned away, touching him with such care. He was one of her sick children.

"Goodnight, darlin'," she said to me. "Thank you, honey."

I came down the row of beds in the half darkness. I got into my bed and brought the sheet and the light cover over me. I nestled in and turned my head toward Endicott, who was in the next bed.

He was an unkempt nest of red-dark curls; the rest of him was covered. I could hardly hear him because of the wind and the slow rain and the far-off sighing of the surf. But there was a slow, sweet rise and fall of breath from him.

I wanted him to stay asleep. I wanted all of them to stay there. They didn't need to know.

5

BERT HADN'T SHOWED UP AT THE CAFE FOR LUNCH, DORTHY TOLD
Daddy over the phone, so she left Miz Abernathy in charge and drove out
to his place.

He should have come up to the door because of all the dog racket,
but he didn't. After she fought her way through that swarm of dogs, she
went on through the screen door. It was unlocked like always. She yelled
for him but nobody answered.

The place looked ransacked inside, but that wasn't anything new. She
called out for him again and went on back to the bedroom and there he was.

He was covered with a blanket, and it was tucked under his chin. He
was facing the wall, she said, and he was all scrunched up like a baby. His
eyes were closed. He was gone.

"God damn," Dorthy said, "it just broke my God damn heart."

Daddy said he asked Dorthy if she thought it was that World War I
bullet that had worked loose and finally got him.

"Hell," Dorthy said, "maybe. But maybe the poor old buzzard just
finally ran out of gas."

Daddy let me drive from just past Weatherford on in to Dorthy's place. I
was fourteen, and I had my learner's permit. I would be taking driver's ed
in the summer and get my real license after that. I could barely peek over

that big steering wheel and sometimes I looked under it, using it as a semicircular periscope.

I remember bays and inlets and whole oceans of bluebonnets. Among the blue, like pools of sunlight, were intrusions of Indian paintbrushes and black-eyed Susans. The meadowlarks were so loud—"Chee-er! Chee-er!"—I could hear them at seventy miles per hour through the open windows.

Houston's warm soupy weather had come for a visit. Fat white clouds with drooping gray underbellies filled the sky. Daddy and I were drooping, too. Our white shirts were wet and sagging. Our dark Sunday suit coats and ties lay across the back seat

In the rearview mirror I could see that my hair had sprung loose from its grip of hair oil, and the heavy curls wobbled in the wind. My face was a constellation of pimples. A boy was in that mirror, and parts of a man— a solid jaw and a rounded nose, a sharp Adam's apple and soft brown, boy-long eyelashes. I was too thin and too shy, and my eyes were green fire.

Daddy and I didn't say much. I glanced at him now and then. He was looking beyond the landscape, out over the jagged horizon.

He hadn't been outdoors much lately, and his face had a wintered look, a gray distance. Here was spring all around us, in all its piercing newness, and my father was a season behind.

About once every thirty minutes Daddy would reach to the back seat and take out the silver-plated flask from the pocket of his suit coat and drink a swallow or two of bourbon. He was pacing himself. I knew the pace. It wouldn't last.

Finally we went around the last cedar-scraggly hill and came down the shaded valley to Dorthy's. I hadn't been there since fall. Nothing had changed.

The little building was the same, forlorn but friendly. I could hear the valiant, erratic crackling of the 's as I drove beneath the sign and across the weedy parking lot.

Cars and pickups were everywhere. Most of them were dust-caked, feeble, and wrinkled, and our two-toned '56 Ford (one tone dusty, the other dustier, a coating of blue somewhere below), fit right in. I had to park beside the bar ditch.

Daddy reached back and got the flask, took a solid drink, then twisted the lid back and cleared his breath. "You ready?"

"Yeah," I said.

Daddy went up the wooden steps first, as usual. He shoved, the door groaned and gave, and we barged in like always.

"Stevie honey! Will!" Dorthy tromped over and pulled me face-forward into her bosoms. I had just enough time to take in a breath before everything got cut off in the squeeze.

Dorthy hugged my father, too. She had a bottle of beer and a lit cigarette in one hand, and a fried chicken leg in the other; still she managed to squeeze most of the air out of us.

She was wrapped tight in a shiny black dress; all of her bulges appeared to have been inhaled and captured. Her black-beaded hat was as big as a sombrero.

She and my father talked quietly for a moment, her voice at the edge of tears. She'd already had several too many beers.

One long table had been made out of the short ones, and it stretched down the middle of the room, heaped with food—cheese-crusted casseroles, big bowls of orange-dressed salad and mysteriously chunked gelatin salads, red pies and blue pies, cross-hatched or creamed, frosted cakes, pink-shouldered hams, and a mountain of grease-glinting fried chicken.

People were standing around in groups. The men wore western suits, cowboy hats, and Sunday boots, and the ladies were dressed up darkly, many with small, feathered Mamie Eisenhower hats (Jackie hadn't caught on here yet). Most everyone was smoking. Everybody had a beer. Two old ladies on the other side of the room played shuffleboard.

One of the big metal coolers, overflowing with ice and bottles, had been moved from behind the counter to the center of the room. Dorthy went over to get us a drink.

She had been talking with a priest when we came in. He walked over to us.

"I'm Father Tom," he said, shaking my father's hand.

"Yes. Glad to meet ya," Daddy said. "I'm Will Beckwith. I spoke with you on the phone yesterday."

"Why yes. Of course."

"And this is my son Stephen."

His handshake was firm and dry. He was young, thin, round-faced, with thinning blond hair and an educated drawl. He was all in black except for his white collar, which was as stiff as steel and too wide for his neck, so his head seemed to rattle around in it.

Dorthy came up with handfuls of bottles. She passed them out.

"Here you go, Revernd," she said. "Pearl, wasn't it?"

"Why yes. Thanks." He took one of the bottles.

Dorthy handed me a Dr Pepper, and Daddy got a Lone Star. Dorthy kept hold of her own longneck, plus her cigarette and the chicken leg.

"Look at that," Dorthy said to my father. "That's the Revernd's second beer, and it ain't even noon yet. And I always thought beer and such was supposed to be the work of the Devil."

"I don't know about that," Father Tom said, holding up his bottle and looking at it. "This one here says it's the work of the Pearl Brewing Company, San Antonio, Texas."

Dorthy guffawed and whacked her thigh with the hand that held the chicken leg. "Hot damn, that settles it! I'm becomin' an Episcopal. Where do I sign up?"

"Episcopalians never have been too hot for the hellfire talk," my father said.

"All I know is to hell with the holy bastards in this neck of the woods." Then Dorthy turned toward the priest and said, "Pardon my language, Revernd." She turned to me: "But Stevie honey, I tried all day yesterday to find a preacher around here to come and say a few words over the body of a harmless old man, and ever' damn one of 'em says he was busy. Truth is, not a one of 'em wanted to be caught walkin' into a tavern, at least in the daylight. Your Daddy had to call all the way over to Graham to get the Revernd here."

Dorthy took a drag from her cigarette, a bite from her chicken, and a swig from her bottle, all without missing a beat.

"I'm just glad I could help," Father Tom said.

"Where's Miz Abernathy?" I asked.

"Back in the kitchen," Dorthy said, "fussin' over some more food. As if we didn't have enough already to feed an army. Sugar, you can have some now if you want, but I was plannin' on ever'body eatin' after the funeral. I had to have this one little leg here to tide me over. You want one?" She wagged it at me like it was a finger. Some crust crumbled off.

"I can wait, I think," I told her.

Dorthy turned toward my father and Father Tom, who were both smoking now. She was nervous, wound up, not taking many breaths. "I'm ready to get this thing over with," she said. "It's Bert that's holdin' us up. You'd think the old bastard could be on time for his own funeral. (Pardon my language, Revernd.)

"Funeral home in Graham's takin' care of him, and I bet that undertaker's kid has gotten lost. See, what's happened is, I talked to the undertaker over the phone and he asked me if his son could handle ever'thing. The kid's eighteen, he said. Nice, quiet boy. Needs the practice, his daddy said. They've given me half price on account of him being so new and all. I told him that was fine. You gotta start someplace, I said. I don't think Bert'll mind. But God damn, you can't hardly have a funeral without a body.

"Homer!" she yelled out, "come over here a minute!"

A rugged-faced man in a crumpled brown suit, carrying a beer and holding a cigarette in his teeth, got up from his place in one of the booths and came over. He was one of Dorthy's regulars.

"Yeah, honey," he said.

"Homer, I want you to go outside and look for Bert."

"Bert? You mean you invited that old so-and-so to the party?"

"All right, Homer, all right. This kid's bringin' the body over from Graham. He's prob'ly lost. You go out and flag him down."

"Yes'm."

"That God damn Homer, ain't he a sight," Dorthy said as Homer yanked at the front door and went out.

Old Miz Abernathy emerged from the kitchen, taking another heaping plate of fried chicken to the long table. She tottered and swayed. The plate was tucked against her waist, held up by the long bones in one arm. In her other hand was her small glass of gin. A cigarette dangled from her thin lips, the smoke boiling across her wilted face.

After delivering the platter, Miz Abernathy came toward us. She was wearing a long, flapper-style dress, black with swirls of black beads sewn across the front, which matched Dorthy's hat. Her hat was a small black bowl with black feathers sweeping across it. She had a matching, beaded evening bag tucked under her arm. Her darkness spoke of mourning and yet the beads, even in the smoky dimness of the tavern, sparkled. She was festively somber. She set the tone.

"Hidy, ever'body," she said in her brittle little voice. "Hidy, Jimmy." I smiled.

"You're lookin' good," my father said.

"Enh?"

"I said you're lookin' good!" he said louder. Others in the room looked around to see what the shouting was about.

"Pardon?" she said.

"I SAID YOU'RE LOOKIN' GOOD!" All conversation in the cafe stopped.

"Thanks," Miz Abernathy said. "I'm feelin' good."

She transferred her gin glass from her cigarette hand to her free hand. As she did, a long, dangling ash fell down the front of Dorthy's dress.

"God *damn*!" Dorthy shot out. "God damn you, Martha Abernathy, and your God damn ashes!" Dorthy brushed at them with her hand, producing a gray smear across the black material. "Oh God damn if I ain't makin' it worse! (Pardon my language, Revernd.)" She turned to Miz Abernathy. Her tone was piercing, which was what it took. "BRING ME A WET RAG, GOD DAMMIT!"

"Sorry," the old woman said, turning and hobbling toward the kitchen.

"You'd think after all these years she'd learn to flick her ashes in the God damn ashtray like most folks," Dorthy said. "No tellin' how many of her ashes drop in the food back there."

"It's what gives it that special flavor," my father said.

Then Father Tom said, "The poor dear seems to be hard of hearing."

"Are you kiddin', Revernd?" Dorthy said. "That old woman ain't heard a God damn thing I've said since 1937. And she can't read lips, 'cause hell, half the time she's too drunk to see 'em.

"But guess what," Dorthy continued, turning to me. "Guess what that old Bert has done."

"What's that?"

"I found his will out there in the trailer yesterday when I was cleanin' up, handwrit on the back of one of my menus. The old buzzard had some savings stashed away. Bloodbait money, I guess. Hell, I always thought he was flat broke, the way he'd complain to me, ask for credit and all. Anyway, he said for me to take out enough from that to get Miz Abernathy fixed up with a hearin' aid.

"Now all I gotta do is talk her into going to Fort Worth to get fixed up. You ever tried to talk a mule into anything? Well, try a *deaf* mule. That's what I'm dealin' with."

"What all did Bert's will say?" I asked.

"Well, he left me his place, and the rest of the savings he said was to go against his tab here, and the funeral, and feedin' his dogs till I find 'em all a good home. That place of his is paid for. He had about twenty acres. Your Daddy said he thought I could get a pretty nice bundle for it, since it's right on the river and so pretty.

"But I ain't gonna sell it. I just might move out there when I get tired of Sportsman's Inn. And by the way, he left you and your daddy all his fishin' and huntin' stuff."

"We'll help you go through it all tomorrow," my father said.

"But you know," Dorthy said, "still it makes me sad he didn't have any relatives to leave all that to. Sure I'm happy to have come into all this, but still it makes me sad to think of him all alone out there, at the end of his bloodline, all alone."

A hush came among us as Dorthy's voice quivered to a whisper. Her big square head turned downward.

Homer barged open the door and stuck his head through. "Bert's here!" he yelled.

"Hell, it's about time," Dorthy said, coming across the big room from the kitchen. "Let's get it in gear, folks! Grab your beers and let's go!"

People started heading for the door. Many of them stopped by the big beer cooler to get themselves one for the road. Dorthy was there. She was putting some ice and a few beers in a small cooler she could take with her to the gravesite. I stopped and got another Dr Pepper, then filed out with the others.

Even though the clouds were piled up in cumulus crowds, plenty of light got through. The bright heat attacked us.

Everybody stood by their cars, waiting for instructions, sweltering. I went to our car and got our coats and ties. Daddy and I stood at the bottom of the steps.

Miz Abernathy was one of the last to come out. She had a new cigarette going, and her gin had been freshened up to the top of her glass. A little of it spilled as she tottered down the steps. My father stood by with his hand out, and she accepted it lightly. With the bottom of her dress hugging her ankles, she took tinier steps than usual. She was wearing precipitous heels. She walked like an aged and unbalanced ballerina.

At last Dorthy came out holding the beer cooler, a handle in each hand. A burning cigarette was wedged in her fingers, her purse was sitting on the cooler, and she was holding her beer bottle in her teeth. The chicken leg was gone.

Daddy took the cooler from her. She turned and slammed the door, got out her key, and locked it. With Scotch tape she put up a small sign on the door, written on one sheet from an order pad. It said: "Gone to Bert's funeral. Back when over. D."

Dorthy came down the steps and weaved among the rows of cars, some of which had pulled out and were trying to line up. My father followed her with the beer cooler. I came next. Miz Abernathy was last. Our new shoes were extra-crunchy on the gravel.

"Y'all are immediate family," Dorthy said to Daddy, looking back at him. "Why don't you and Stephen go with us in the hearse."

"Okay," he said.

"Just look at that sumbidge," she said as we came up to the car where it was parked on the shoulder of the road. "We got plenty of room. Hell, we got room for a whole choir in there."

The hearse was huge. It was a stretch Cadillac, shiny black like Miz Abernathy's black beads and Dorthy's platter of a hat. The Caddy had missile-headed silver bosoms on the front.

Daddy and I got in the back seat, with Miz Abernathy between us. Dorthy could have got back there with us, on the seat facing toward us, with room left over for the beer cooler and half the buffet, but she took the cooler from my father and got in the front seat with it.

"Hidy," she said to the driver. "I'm Dorthy. And you must be Dwane."

"Y-y-yes'm," he said.

Dorthy introduced the rest of us around. "Hidy," we said, leaning forward. He turned backward, smiling self-effacingly at each of us through the Plexiglas barrier Dorthy had slid open.

Dwane was tall and pole-thin and cream-skinned, but his cheeks and neck were clawed purple from acne. His brown hair was plastered with oil. He looked just a little older than me.

"I brung ya a beer," Dorthy said to him. She opened the cooler and brought out a bottle. "Here, honey, you're gonna need it, wearin' that dark suit and all on a day like this. Lone Star all right?" She opened it with a church key, which she had on a chain around her neck, one of those chains people wear for their glasses. "My God, it's hotter'n hell in here. Let's get this car movin' so we can get us a breeze." She was waving her hand in front of her face and giving out an exaggerated panting sound.

"I d-d-don't think I oughta d-drink this," Dwane said.

Dorthy was holding the bottle out toward him. "Why the hell not?" she asked.

"Ba-Baptist," he said. "I'm Baptist."

"Oh God damn," Dorthy said. "We ain't gonna tell anybody. Here." She shoved it up against his chest.

"Yes'm," Dwane said, taking the bottle reluctantly. He brought it up to his trembling lips and drank down a quarter of it.

"That's more like it," Dorthy said.

Then she looked back at us in the back seat. "Y'all in?" Daddy and I nodded yes. Miz Abernathy took a sip from her gin. "Then I reckon we're ready, Dwane honey," Dorthy said. She stuck her head out the window and whistled into her fingers like a football coach. The people were in their cars, running their engines. "Follow us!" she yelled, and gave a windmill-size wave toward the river.

Dwane shifted the gears with a long, tearing grind. He jerked his foot off the clutch and we thump-thump-thumped backward. Daddy and I were tying our ties, and Dwane wasn't making it easy.

"Lordy mercy, I spilled my gin!" Miz Abernathy croaked.

"Damn, boy, don't you know how to drive this thing?" Dorthy asked.

"I-I never dri-driven it m-m-much before," Dwane said.

"Honey, we wanna go *forward*," she said. "Right here's the middle of the H," she said, holding his hand, which was holding the gearshift. "In and up is first." She guided his hand. "That's it. Now smooth, smooth, pull out your foot on the clutch."

The gears clamored again and the hearse hopped forward this time, turning out onto the pavement of the highway. A pickup coming down the highway from behind us had to swerve into the other lane to miss us. It let out a long, complaining honk.

"God almighty!" Dorthy shouted. "Holy shit!"

Dwane flinched as if Dorthy were going to whack him with her bottle. But she guided his hand down to second and then pulled away and pointed down the highway toward the river. "That's right, this way. I'll tell ya when to turn. It's just up the road a little, just past the bridge. It ain't that far. God I hope we make it there in one piece." She went back to his hand. "Now third, up, and fourth, straight down." The ride smoothed out. "Now, honey, you're cookin' with gas."

When Dwane had lurched forward, Miz Abernathy spilled a good part of her gin down the front of her dress, in among the beads. She was brushing at it with the back of her hand. "I'm stinkin' of gin," she said. "Just stinkin'."

Dorthy turned back in her seat toward us. "You're always stinkin' of gin, Martha Abernathy," she said.

"Enh?"

"Never mind," Dorthy said, handing Miz Abernathy a handkerchief. "NEVER MIND!"

The road curved and fell quickly toward the river. There were deep green cedars among the pale mesquites, scatterings of bluebonnets among the weeds, and juttings of quartz-sparkling sandstone in the shallow, pink soil. A hundred shades of smells, all green, wafted across us.

Dwane drove slowly and nervously, and the hearse stammered when he hit the little hills. I looked back. A ragtag procession of beaten cars and bent-up pickups followed, most with their lights on. A cattle truck approached from the opposite direction, stopping on the shoulder until we passed by. The driver removed his cowboy hat, and Dorthy gave a small wave to him in acknowledgment.

The casket was right behind my seat, resting on a track. It looked huge and barren. Bert must have had a lot more room in there than he needed.

I wondered what he looked like. I hoped he was wearing something comfortable, along with his greasy cap and his pipe, but I bet he was dressed in some ill-fitting Sunday clothes, a coat and tie that had him all choked up like we were. I bet the funeral home insisted.

The road made a final, deepening drop to the river, and Dwane let his speed build up. The air went hollow and moist as we moved across the bridge, clicking with little rushings as we passed each concrete column. I took a quick look. The water was foam-streaked and noisy. Water was being released from the dam.

"Whoa! Whoa!" Dorthy insisted. "Right here! Take a right!"

We all suddenly leaned to the left, including Bert, as the hearse turned sharply to the right—sharp enough to bend, it seemed—and this time Miz Abernathy's gin spilled on me. It went all down my pants leg. The gears ground as Dwane searched for second on Bert's rocky road.

He found it too late. He should have been in first as we went up that first steep hill. We almost made it, but the engine shuddered and died, and we drifted back to the bottom, nudging the priest's car behind us.

Dorthy leaned out the window. "Sorry, Reverend!" she yelled, waving a sort of apology. Then she turned back toward Dwane. "Ya gonna hafta put her in first and keep her there, boy."

"Yes'm," Dwane said. His lower lip was quivering, and he was staring down at the beer bottle between his legs. He looked as if he were going to cry.

My father leaned forward in his seat. "Dwane," he said, "I know this thing must be like drivin' a house. Now don't feel bad. We understand. But I'd suggest you giver a little more gas this time, too."

"That's right, Dwane honey," Dorthy said. "You're doin' just fine." She patted him on the thigh. "Don't let all my cussin' bother you none. It don't mean nothin'. So let's give 'er the gas and go." Then she looked out the window, speaking to herself: "I bet Roy and Dale is wonderin' where the hell we are."

Dwane seemed to recover somewhat. He started the engine and immediately floored it. He popped the clutch and we roared upward, over the hill and then down like a roller coaster.

"God damn God damn God damn!" Dorthy shouted, pushing her foot on an imaginary brake and holding on to the back of her seat.

There were two more hills, and Dwane didn't slow down. He wanted to get it over with, I guess. Dorthy shrieked and cussed all the way.

Finally she shouted, "Hold it, God dammit, hold it!" We squealed to a halt as a big billow of dust rolled over us from behind. We were fifty yards from Bert's trailer. There was no gin left in Miz Abernathy's glass.

"Thank God that's over," Dorthy said.

"Me, too," Dwane said, turning off the engine.

"Here comes the greetin' committee," my father said.

Like the dust cloud that came at us from behind, a dust-rustling, rushing river of about forty dogs came at us from ahead, racing out from under the shade of the trailer. They ringed the hearse, wagging and lolling and barking, jumping up with their paws resting on the open windows to look inside. I reached out and petted one or two.

"These God damn dogs," Dorthy said. "What am I gonna do with 'em all?"

She turned sideways in her seat. "Dwane? Did you know you was takin' at least two dogs back with you to Graham?" She winked at my father.

"I am?"

"Yep. It's part of the deal I made with your father. Half price on the funeral and two dogs took off my hands."

"I guess we can use 'em."

"Good. That leaves just thirty-eight more to get shed of. And then there's the cats."

A second, slower group of dogs had left the shade and joined the others. We were engulfed.

We left the hearse and entered the flood of dogs, all but Dwane. I began petting as many as I could, but that began a panic of envy, and I was coming close to being overpowered.

"Swat 'em off ya, Stephen," Dorthy said. "It's the only thing you can do."

I spoke loudly to reach over the onrushing barks and yelps: "How ya gonna have a funeral with all these dogs?"

"I got that figured out," Dorthy said. "When the funeral's about to start, I'm gonna feed 'em a coupla sacks of dog food. That oughta keep 'em busy, and maybe they'll leave us in peace for a while."

As the rest of the cars drove up, the dogs were dispersed by curiosity and I was set free. I followed Dorthy.

Another hill stretched above Bert's trailer, a second slope above the river. It was long and grassy, with tufts of yellow and white wildflowers here and there. At the rounded top was a small grove of live oaks.

Dorthy and I walked up the hill. Roy and Dale were coming down. They were the two county road workers who lived in matching trailers up the road from Dorthy's place. She had assigned them as the gravediggers. We all met in the center of the meadow.

"How's my hole comin'?" Dorthy asked.

"*Your* hole," Roy said. "I thought it was *Bert's* hole."

"Lord, it was almost mine and several others'. We had one helluva ride over here."

Roy and Dale were almost twins, both in their forties, both with dark, scar-laced hands and bony faces, stained teeth and grease-backed, bumpy hair. They had their shirts off. Their white chests and backs were caked with wet-pink, hairy dirt.

I remember them being at Sportsman's Inn almost every time I came in. They had matching wives, matching kids, and matching tattoos, plus matching pickups named Trigger and Buttercup. They'd sing "Happy Trails to You" when they had enough beer in them. That was often.

"You remember Will's boy Stephen, don'tcha?" Dorthy asked.

"Why sure," Roy said. "Hidy."

"Hidy," I said.

"Hidy," Dale said.

I didn't say any names because I was never sure which was which.

"So how about the grave," Dorthy said. "You got 'er dug?"

"Fixin' to be," Dale said. At least I think it was Dale.

"Dorthy, God damn," Roy said. "We been pickin' and shovelin' on that hole for a good three hours now. She's about three foot deep."

"Three foot?" Dorthy said. "Roy, God damn, the buzzards can dig down that deep. Hell, that's nothin' to a buzzard."

"I know, Dorthy. Now let me finish." Roy leaned back on the handle of his pick. "I'll tell ya, if we'd a known we were gonna be diggin' in solid rock up here, I'd a brought the Cat along. Now it'd take me all afternoon to get that thing up from the county barn. But Dale remembered he had some dynamite in his truck. We got it all set up. We was just fixin' ta set it off when y'all drove up."

"*Dynamite?*" Dorthy asked. "Roy, you ain't fixin' to blow us *all* to kingdom come, are ya?"

"Naw, he knows what he's doin'," Dale said.

"Yeah, it'll work out okay," Roy said. "All I need you ta do, Dorthy, is go on back down there and tell the others to take cover for a little bit. Tell 'em to get behind their cars and scrunch down. There might be some flyin' rocks."

"All right," Dorthy said, turning away. "I'll tell 'em."

"I appreciate it," Roy said.

We broke apart. Dorthy and I came back down the hill together and went to the others, who had congregated near the hearse.

"Listen, y'all," Dorthy said to the crowd, "Roy and Dale are gonna have to blast. You'll need to take cover."

The news was taken in stride. The people wandered back to their cars and hunkered behind them. Dorthy, Miz Abernathy, Father Tom, Dwane, and Daddy and I squatted behind the hearse. We had plenty of room. There was even room for a few dogs, one of which overpowered Miz Abernathy and lapped up half the gin from her glass, which she had just refilled.

"God damn dawg!" she said. "Git away! Git away!"

While Miz Abernathy was busy fighting off the dog, Dorthy had removed her big black hat. She began to wave it toward the hill.

"READY!" she yelled out in a voice as big as Broadway.

"READY!" came back the reply. I couldn't tell if it was Roy or Dale.

Dorthy ducked down with the rest of us. Then she whispered, "Revernd, you ever been to a funeral like this one?"

"I don't believe I have," he said.

I don't know why we all got so quiet. Expectation, I suppose. We held everything back except our breath. Even the dogs seemed to know something was coming. Most had gone to the shadowed dust beneath the cars, where they waited with mouths closed, ears stiff.

The explosion was deep and stubby. I could feel the ground stutter a little. I was peeking through the windows of the hearse, and I saw the big trees at the top of the hill tremble. Rock pellets showered, and the canyons echoed. The dogs cringed and whimpered.

"Is that it?" my father asked.

"I guess so," Dorthy said, brushing some tiny rocks off her hat.

Dust came last, settling over the hill. We were tinged with a pink powder.

Everybody began to stand and stretch. My father helped Miz Abernathy up. I went with Dorthy across the field and up the hill. Roy and Dale were coming toward us.

"How's it look?" Dorthy asked.

"Pretty good," Roy said. "A little wide but plenty deep."

"Good," she said.

"I told you Roy knows how to handle dynamite," Dale said. "Hardly a rock flew."

"Not any big ones," Dorthy said.

"But you never can really tell with dynamite," Roy said. "It's always best to take cover."

Roy and Dale had brought their shirts with them. They were putting them on and buttoning them up. They didn't even try to brush off the dirt.

"Listen, I appreciate all this, boys," Dorthy said. "There's some beer down there in the front seat of the hearse. Why don't y'all go down and get you one."

"Thanks, Dorthy," Dale said.

"Stephen," she said, "I'm gonna go feed the dogs. Why don't y'all go ahead and bring the casket up. I'll be with ya in a minute."

"Okay," I said.

Roy, Dale, and I went down the hill together, and Dorthy veered off and went toward the trailer. "C'mon, dogs!" she yelled out. "Supper time!"

Daddy and I and four other men took the handles of the casket, and Dwane helped guide it out of the hearse. We quietly turned and began a deliberate walk into the tall grass of the long hill. The crowd fell in behind us

The dust had settled out of the air. The sound of the explosion had echoed out of the memory of the hills. The birds came back. Their songs came back. Meadowlarks were in the field with us, and a mockingbird was in the live oaks at the top of the hill, where we were headed. It was spring and the birds couldn't help it.

A hush came across the crowd like a fall of wind, and the hush came into me as well. It came like breath. I breathed in whispers. My breathing was a prayer.

With six of us carrying it, the casket wasn't so heavy. The problem was trying to keep the weight balanced. There were rocks and small gullies, and we stumbled and paused and went crooked, trying to get around things.

The worst part was the heat. It was so dense the small wind could hardly stir it. The clouds just hung there, drooping and full. The sweat collected on us.

I glanced back once. We were a ragged and uncertain procession. Almost everybody was old. Most of them held to each other as they moved up the hill, pausing and struggling the way we did.

The priest was right behind us. Over his black clothes, draped from his neck, was a white stole, the color of Easter. In one hand was his Book of Common Prayer, and he was reading quietly from it. Miz Abernathy was holding his arm, steadying herself against him. She had left her gin glass on the hood of the hearse.

Finally we came up under the wide and welcome shade of the stooping oaks. The air was moister, rich with the smell of the upturned earth.

We set the casket down beside the deep, uneven hole, among the chunks of sandstone, and then we stepped to the side. We waited as the others gathered around.

Dorthy came up from the other side of the hill, without a single dog following her, and settled in beside my father. Miz Abernathy moved over next to me. She put her bony arm through mine and leaned against me just a little.

After he gave me the shotgun, I'd started spending more time with Bert. I was remembering how I used to go to his trailer in the mornings, before my father got up. Bert was less than a half hour's walk away.

The road just past our cabin went upriver on the high bluff. I'd throw rocks into the chasm, and I could never hear them splash. The air was always new, the birds happy, all but the mourning doves. The soft dust of the ranch road was warm pillows to my bare feet.

Then, at the highway, I had to put on my boots because the asphalt was like melted gum and because Bert's road, on the other side, was jagged with big and little rocks.

Just past the first hill the dogs sensed my approach. It began with a single yip from a younger sentry dog. The others waited for more evidence, then joined. In a minute, the yips cascaded into a warning chorus.

On the second hill they recognized me and came running—an onrushing, tumbling herd—and on the last hill they surrounded me, inundating me in a gulf of fur and a gush of barks. I waded on in to the trailer from there.

Bert was always up, the coffee ready. I had milk and sugar with a splash of coffee, and the old man had double-black, oil-slicked coffee with a splash of whiskey.

He was best in the mornings, as clear-headed as he ever got. His voice was always mellow-low and full of cobwebs, which took half a morning to get spit out.

After coffee, we'd row out into the river in his johnboat across the glassy water and check his trotlines. I'd grab the main line and pull the boat along. You had to be careful when you got to the smaller lines that dangled from the main one. That's where the hooks were.

It was fun to feel something wiggling down the line and try to guess what it was. Usually it was a catfish but sometimes a bass, a carp, a turtle. Once it was a water moccasin. Bert was going too fast and he pulled that snake right into the boat, nearly into his lap. With a whoop and a holler, the old man pitched that line overboard and abandoned ship. His dead leg was suddenly reborn. He sprang, sideways, from the boat to the bank, in one almost-graceful, gazelle-like bound.

Besides checking the trotlines, we fed the dogs, did a little target practice, and then retired to the shaded riverbank below the trailer and fished. Bert would tell stories, fishing and hunting stories, war and love stories. He had done hand-to-hand combat with countless ladies in "bood-wars" (the process did sound something like war to me). When he talked about it, his voice got ticklish and sly, and I recoiled, sensing sin, however vaguely, and yet I was drawn to it, fearful and curious. Bert gave few details. My imagination billowed. If I asked too many questions, Bert changed the subject—to war wounds, maybe, of which he had many—so many, in fact, I thought he must be one entire, connective scar tissue.

My father usually drove up around noon, and we'd all go to Dorthy's for lunch. We'd split up after that and then regroup at suppertime, again at Dorthy's. The men drank and smoked, throwing scraps of conversation my way.

In the fall of my eleventh year Bert took me squirrel hunting. I spent the night at the trailer, sleeping on the couch, and Bert woke me early, before the first hint of pink. We fed the dogs to keep them at home. Then, among the giant pecan trees, Bert walked like an Indian, silently, and breathed like a frog, gasping. He had to point out both squirrels, but I shot them cleanly. By noon, when my father got to the trailer, the squirrels were being fried and the whiskey was being poured. Soon I was spotting the squirrels on my own and walking like an Indian, too, and less croaky than Bert. I saw a lot more squirrels.

Singing almost, deep and plain and deliberate, the priest read: *Man, that is born of a woman, hath but a short time to live, and is full of misery. He cometh*

up, and is cut down, like a flower; he fleeth as it were a shadow, and never contin-
ueth in one stay. . . .

At the end of each part of the prayer, Father Tom trailed into a deeper pause. The words opened me. I was fourteen years old and I was coming open to many things.

In the midst of life we are in death; of whom may we seek for succor, but of
thee, O Lord, who for our sins art justly displeased? . . .

Again I remembered walking up to Bert's. Because of the racket from all those dogs, he'd go out on his little porch to see who they'd surrounded. When I came into view, he'd wave. I'd wave back. His old brown lips would unsnarl into a half smile. "Hidy, boy!" he'd yell out across the hills. "Come on in!"

Yet, O Lord God most holy, O Lord most mighty, O holy and most merciful
Savior, deliver us not into the bitter pains of eternal death. . . .

Bert would go slide-slipping down the hill behind his trailer, his eyes bunched up with wrinkles, his face bristling with gray, the cold pipe clenched in his brown teeth and a flat whiskey bottle in his back pocket. "You comin', boy? We got lines to check. Hop on your toes and you won't git stickers." And so I'd hop down the hill to the river's edge.

Thou knowest, Lord, the secrets of our hearts; shut not thy merciful ears to
our prayer; but spare us, Lord most holy, O God most mighty, O holy and merci-
ful Savior, thou most worthy Judge eternal, suffer us not, at our last hour, for
any pains of death, to fall from thee. . . .

We'd paddle out into the river. The water was swirling glass. I'd help him put new bait on the trotlines, that nose-curdling bloodbait of his, and take the catfish off. The morning air was perfectly still. Bert's rattling breath echoed into the tall hills. He'd sell those catfish to Dorthy and to some of the other restaurants around the lake, and then he'd drink up the profits.

The priest directed that the casket be lowered into the grave. It was done, carefully, with ropes Dwane had brought up.

Unto Almighty God we commend the soul of our brother departed, and we
commit his body to the ground. . . .

Sometimes we walked long into the woods. A lot of times we would-n't even take the gun. Bert had a way of being the quietest person I ever knew, when he wanted to, when his emphysema wasn't acting up. He could breathe the way the woods breathed and move as softly as young branches. He taught me how to accept the rhythm of the woods and become it and disappear.

Earth to earth, ashes to ashes, dust to dust. . . .

Bert and I, open to the quiet, walked into the hush of morning, eased across the bending river, on foot, in boats, in spirit. . . .

The priest continued to read. There was a little soft crying, some from back in the crowd and some from Miz Abernathy and Dorthy.

I looked down the hill, all the way down to the river, and I could hear the silver water rustling. A trickle of wind came among us, waving through the high grass and the bunches of wildflowers.

"Look who's comin'," I said.

It was the dogs, swarms of them, out from around Bert's trailer and up the hill and charging.

"Oh Lord," Dorthy said.

"They must have finished eatin'," my father said.

The priest had finished his prayers, and it was a good thing, too. He would have never been heard—perhaps not even celestially—above the grand chorus of barkings and yelps and whines that rose across the canyons. The great stampede of dogs mounted the hill and spread through the crowd.

The dogs were young and old, small and middle-size and as big as skinny sheep, light and dark and swirled and spotted, short-haired and long-, all scraggly and all scruffy and all loving.

They were insistent. They jumped up on us and nuzzled their way into us. There was nothing else you could do but abandon your sad thoughts and bend down and hug a dog. Miz Abernathy got knocked over by a black Labrador, but she was the only casualty. My father helped her up, and she was laughing.

"All y'all get you a dog or two!" Dorthy yelled out over the crowd. "And then let's go back to the cafe and eat!"

One of the many times he thought he was dying, Bert had made Dorthy promise she'd find each of his dogs a good home. She made good on it now, standing among the crowd, assigning dogs to folks. Mostly it was the dogs who assigned themselves to the people, and there was a lot of unassigning and reassigning.

We left the grave in a great wagging tumult and went down the hill to our cars. Everybody was loaded down with dogs. There was much coaxing and whistling and lifting, car doors slamming and reslamming, hats knocked off and hats left behind.

We got six dogs in the back of the hearse where the casket had been, and we only had two dogfights on the way back to the cafe. Dwane drove pretty fast.

While several men stayed behind to fill up the hole and set up the tombstone, the rest of us made a frontal assault on the long table of food back at the cafe. Dorthy put the jukebox on free play. A few people danced but mostly they just ate. A bunch of dogs were under the table, ready for whatever dropped. Soon the men came back from the gravesite, and the party got rolling.

My father and Dorthy were in rare form. They were the centerpiece of the main table, where the most and best reminiscing went on. People crowded around our table just to listen.

Dorthy knew stories about Bert that went back to the beginning, when he came to settle down beside the Brazos during the Depression. He was an itinerant knife-sharpener, just passing through, and he came by Sportsman's Inn to sharpen their knives in exchange for something to eat. Dorthy was just a waitress back then.

Bert had been through World War I, and his limp was bad even then, before the dramatic flourishes he developed later. He had come from Arkansas—the pine mountains near Mena—and he had learned how to make a living out of nothing, she said, like everybody else up in those hills and hollows.

Bert stayed. He got into the bloodbait business, selling it through the baitshops on the lake. Dorthy became the owner of the cafe. Their friendship prospered, but in its own, indirect way. She was an old bat, he was an old buzzard. That's when Dorthy put her hand to her face to try to hide the tears.

She got up to get a round of beer for everyone, and when she came back, several of the men, including my father, were arguing over which was Bert's finest near-death performance.

Father Tom left after about an hour, with two puppies for his young children. It was two hours later before Dwane left. He'd had several beers—maybe more than several—and lost most of his shyness, all of his stuttering, and his tie. Dorthy talked him into taking four dogs, two small ones for his house and two big ones to stay at the funeral parlor as full-time guard dogs.

When he backed out of the parking lot, Dwane was even driving better, too. He would have done just fine except that the two biggest dogs were standing on his lap and slobbering on the rearview mirror. He scraped Dale's pickup. Dale didn't care.

The sun went down and the food disappeared. I wish Daddy would have eaten more. His talk and movements got slower and dimmer, and sad, too. Dorthy and I talked him into leaving before things got worse.

We said our long good-byes to Miz Abernathy and the few stragglers, then Dorthy went out to the car with us.

Our car was at the far corner of the lot. I was between my father and Dorthy, sort of holding them up. They were weighed down with beer and memories.

We made it to the car, and she hugged us longer than ever. Dorthy clouded up with sniffles again, but it wasn't too bad.

At last she let us go and turned back toward the cafe. Daddy said he was tired and handed me the keys. We got into the car and I started the engine.

In the hovering dark, among the red-orange light of the 's and the smoke-strewn slice of light from the cafe, I watched Dorthy walking away. She was bent and worn. She stopped at the bottom of the steps, leaned her head back, and—raising the bottle to her lips like a royal-court trumpeter—a final salute to Bert—she polished off her beer.

Almost before I could back the car onto the highway, my father left me.

He left the world. He let go of it—he'd been barely hanging on for the last couple of hours anyway—and down he went. He pulled a dark blanket over himself, and curled up, and that was it.

Nothing. Not a word.

I was not used to driving at night, but there were no cars and so it didn't matter. I was extra careful anyway. I worked hard to keep the car on the right side of the lines. I hadn't had anything to drink, but it was still hard to get the car in the right spot. The headlights made things look different. We were floating on a searching little island of carlight, and all around was this great ocean of night and small waves of wind.

I had to get the gate myself. I didn't even ask Daddy.

As I drove down the rutted road to the cabin, I could hear my father moving a little, moving darkly. He took the whiskey flask out of his back pocket. I could tell from his mouth sounds that he had come to the end of it.

The first thing he did when we got to the cabin was to pour himself a tall drink of solid bourbon from one of the bottles he kept there. His tie was wadded up in his coat pocket, and he hung up the coat on the nail behind the door. He went out on the back porch.

I changed clothes. I put on blue jeans and a T-shirt, and took off my shoes and socks. I had a nail, too, over on my side of the room beside my cot, and I hung up my funeral suit the best I could.

I went out on the porch. Daddy was in the chair farthest from the door. He had his feet up on the porch railing. About all I could see of his face were deep shadows and the glow of his cigarette. I sat next to him and put my feet up, too.

The night was sticky warm, moonless, almost windless. I couldn't see the river, and I could barely hear it. I could hear the frogs and the night bugs, though, chirping in the tall grass along the bank, and every now and then I could hear a carp jumping with a flat splash.

I looked into the darkness my father was looking into. You could throw something in there and it would maybe never hit bottom.

Daddy's snoring woke me when the first light of morning was angling in. The noise was severe and slimy.

I lay on my cot for as long as I could, but I couldn't stand it. I got on my clothes fast. I wanted to get out of there. I could hardly breathe because his breath was everywhere, clouding up the room.

Daddy lay on the cot next to mine, on top of his sleeping bag, which was all bunched up. He was still wearing his white shirt and his suit pants and his good shoes. His shirt was halfway open. A blotched stain was on the front of it.

His face was roughened with burnt-red stubble. The waves were loose in his scattered hair. The red had died out of it, and the brown was too brown, like dirt. His lidded eyes were restless.

I went out on the porch. Flattened cigarette butts were everywhere on the wooden floor, and there were burned places where some of them hadn't gone out. His glass was tumped over by his chair. An empty bottle lay beside it.

I went down the road. I didn't know what else to do. At least I could breathe out there, away from the crowded air of the cabin.

The morning was coming on strong. I walked through the canopied sections of the road, then out into the open where the shade ends and the highway crosses. When I got there, I put on my tennis shoes.

The morning was retreating. The sun was already bearing down. I was sweating by the time I got over the first hill on Bert's road. The dogs should have started barking by then, but they had all gone to their new homes.

At the bottom of the last hill I took off my shoes and plunged my feet into the rippling deep dust of Bert's driveway. It was just like always. I went on up to the trailer, hopping among the broken things and the jagged cans, and sat down on the railroad ties that were Bert's front stoop.

I looked up and across the wide field, up the slope to the family of live oaks where Bert was lying. Everything was bright. Everything was silent. I waited a long time.

I heard somebody coming and I looked up. It was Dorthy. She was driving Bert's old pickup, and the back was full of dogs. They were already barking. I could hear them over the rickety engine.

Dorthy came roaring up as if she were being chased. She was. A ten-foot-high wall of dust followed her, and it came boiling up over everything.

We were choking, even some of the dogs, but it didn't slow them down. They leaped out of the bed of the truck, all in a tangle, and came running up to me and over me. Down I went off that stoop. They had me penned in the dust for a second or two.

"Hey, Stevie!" Dorthy said, sliding out of the truck as the door squealed open. "Whatcha doin' here?"

I couldn't answer. I was overcome. I was laughing.

Dorthy was laughing, too, looking at me. She got a big sack of dog food out from the cab, and that was enough to rescue me. The dogs turned tail and charged toward Dorthy.

"Whoa, dogs, whoa!" she yelled out. "Hold your God damn horses, God dammit!"

I pulled myself up and dusted myself off, slapping my jeans and shirt. A dog had picked up one of my shoes, then dropped it on his way to the food. I went over and got it.

Dorthy took the sack over to the three feed buckets Bert kept out. She poured some into each bucket, and the dogs spread out in a somewhat orderly fashion, as if they knew who belonged to which bucket, about four dogs to each. Dorthy asked me to get them some water, so I went over and turned on the hose into a fourth bucket. She went back to the truck and got a smaller sack, this one of cat food, and took it over to the pan just underneath the trailer.

Soon we were through. We went over to the front stoop and sat down next to each other. Dorthy started a cigarette.

"Those God damn dogs," she said. "I kep' 'em penned up in that little yard behind my trailer and they raised hell all night. I didn't sleep a God damn bit. And they ate all my God damn bushes and part of my back porch and God knows what all."

"So what are you gonna do?" I asked.

"I was thinkin' I might just leave 'em out here. They can keep the place guarded, and I can come out here every day and feed 'em. I need to check on things out here anyway."

"The dogs'll be happier out here," I said. "It's home."

"Yeah."

We sat quietly for a while. Dorthy smoked and I looked out over the bright pasture. "Where's your daddy?" Dorthy asked. Her morning voice was silky and husky at the same time.

"Asleep," I said.

"This late? Lord, child, it must be ten o'clock by now."

We were quiet again for a minute, a long and empty minute.

Then it broke. I broke. Without warning, there it was, rolling from the center of me, overflowing in high, sharp sobs.

"Oh, honey."

Dorthy put one big arm around me. She pulled me close to her and held me tight.

"Lord, child," she said. "Lord have mercy."

It kept coming. For Bert and for my father and for everything that was lost and buried and gone. Dorthy held on to me for a long time.

6

THEY LET SCHOOL OUT EARLY AND MAMA HAD TO PICK US UP—ME IN high school, Endy and Laura in junior high, the others in elementary. Ethylene came with Mama and we went to the black schools to get Whyvonne, Travis, and Midland. It was a bright day in November 1963.

During the next few days we all gathered in the front parlor around our little black-and-white set and watched the hearse and the horses, heard the trumpets and the guns. Ethylene's great black hulk shook and swayed, a wash of tears polished her cheeks, and my mother held her. A secret, abiding hope had been slain in Ethylene, and we didn't understand.

Granddaddy, watching silently from his blue velvet armchair at the back of the room, said with his steely demeanor that white people weren't supposed to cry over a Democrat. We followed his instructions.

But the world was reeling, it was changing, and it was knocking on our front gate. Granddaddy had managed to repulse every assault on his island domain so far, but not anymore. The world was about to overtake him.

The next summer Ethylene fell for a man named Alexander Jones. Odessa, who was like Ethylene's mother whether Ethylene liked it or not, didn't like him. She said he was too slick; maybe worse, maybe slippery.

He had a gold tooth and hair that glistened like silver in the sun; "but he ain't no treasure, sistah, I'm tellin' ya." He'd come up to our back door and call up to Ethylene in the kitchen. She'd come down with a plate of food, sit on the back porch, and talk to him while he ate.

He was involved in dog racing. He'd flash around a lot of money, his shiny shoes, and that gold tooth. Travis said it was solid gold and worth at least two hundred dollars, but Whyvonne said it was probably only dipped. Whyvonne hated Alexander Jones. She knew he was moving in on her mother, and that meant the rest of them were going to get squeezed out.

Whyvonne was like me. She was old enough to see things happening but she wasn't old enough to know what to do about them. You were supposed to be a sort of leader among the younger kids, but you knew deep down you had to be just another follower of your parents, even if where they were going was over a cliff.

President Johnson was making a Great Society, Ethylene wanted her share, and Alexander Jones said he could arrange it. He had a friend of a friend who said he could get Ethylene a job in Los Angeles. Lots better money, working in a restaurant, he said.

"All those movie stars!" Travis said.

"We'll be rich!" Mid said.

Whyvonne and Laura rode their horses, Ozzie and Harriet, every day that summer, mornings and evenings. They didn't have much time left.

I watched the girls from my bedroom. They galloped around the horse path through the spotted shade of the giant trees, sometimes together and sometimes single-filing by, jumping the dried irrigation ditches and following the barbed wire fence around the edge of the estate, up the front and past the honeysuckled entrance, down the side next to the Windhams' property, and around behind Whyvonne's house and across the back, behind the stock tank and Granddaddy's garden.

I remember the heave of the horses' breath, the beat of the hooves, the squeak of the saddles. I could feel the power of the horses bouncing into them from below, between their legs. On their last morning together, at the other end of the grove beside the garden, I watched them come together and stop, horse to horse. And touch, black to white, arm in arm, a leaned-in hug. It was goodbye. And a kiss. Each reached for the other, and both had tears.

That summer of my fifteenth year was the summer of leaving. It had started the year before with Bert, then John Kennedy, and now the rest in a summer cluster.

Ethylene and her brood left on a July morning in 1964. Mama had given them the old station wagon, the one we always took to the coast. It had held up pretty well, considering how many kids had learned to drive with it. Whyvonne, Travis, Laura, Endicott, and I—we'd all hit a tree or two, parallel parking between pecan trees out in the grove, and so the car had its pits and scrapes and, on the bumpers, vestiges of bark. Mama thought it would hold together long enough to get them to Los Angeles.

They had emptied the best of their stuff from their little house into the car, and it was packed to the roof in the back when Ethylene pulled up next to the front porch, where we were waiting. Most of us were on the steps, the Beckwith kids, Mama and Odessa, plus Aunt Jew and Aunt Kitty and Miss Godwin behind us, with Judge and Granddaddy hanging back around the giant columns. My father was gone again.

Everybody was trying to hold back, especially Ethylene. I think she was afraid of what she might do, that she might just fall in a faint right out of the car and onto the driveway like people did at her church, usually at funerals, when the Lord got hold of them. Endicott had laid a bet with me that she would, but I said no, I didn't think so, I thought Ethylene was too determined to make a better life for herself and her kids and he said maybe so but that didn't mean she wouldn't fall out.

I was right. Everybody pretty much behaved themselves. Ethylene and Odessa had said their good-byes privately beforehand, and Midland had hugged us all already, so everybody stayed in the car. My mother went up to Ethylene and reached herself through the window and she and Ethylene had one last dab of tears.

I knew that would happen. I knew how strongly my mother felt about her, because together they had worked so hard to keep all eight of us alive, well-fed, and whole, and up to that point, except for Travis falling out of a tree and breaking his arm in two places, had succeeded.

They cried some but nobody wailed. Ethylene's tears streamed down her pooched cheeks, but she had a handkerchief ready. My mother wiped her own eyes with the back of her hand, then gave Ethylene a second hug and then an envelope. There must have been a lot of money in it, because it was enough for Ethylene to lose her breath over in a big moaning sucking sound—enough to live on for maybe a year, Endicott speculated, and I said yeah, it'd last long enough unless Alexander Jones got wind of it.

Endy and I hadn't said much to Travis. We hadn't in a long time, a couple of years. He pulled away from us and stayed to himself, and Ethylene was on him all the time and had grounded him a lot. He'd just run away—he kept going back to his cousin's house in town, Charles's, and they got into some trouble with the police. Ethylene didn't say much about it, but Midland blabbed. Travis flunked sixth grade.

He'd had one friend here, Woody. The collie spent all his time hanging around Ethylene's little house, mostly because he got some choice scraps, like fatback. He'd been lonely since his brother Wilson had got bitten by a snake and died.

So there was Travis, an orphan among all those women, sitting glumly out on his little front stoop, grounded, Woody out there with him, and they gradually fell in together.

Travis was in the back seat now, leaning his head on his arm, which was propped on the edge of the open window. Woody kept his eye on him.

My mother stepped back and the engine started. There was a lot of waving—"Good luck!"—"Take care!"—"Bye, y'all!"

One world was waving to another. As the car took off, I had a little envy for them because they were going to the very real world, the hip-hopping Twentieth Century, and we were staying back in the mint-juleped Nineteenth, if not the well-reasoned Eighteenth, where Granddaddy was determined to keep us.

With Ethylene and her kids, the good cheer and easy hugs and peach pies were leaving. They were the kind of people who touched each other and they had touched us and now it was going to be a lot quieter. Endy leaned over to me and said in a whisper, "I bet Travis gets laid before either one of us does."

The gravel was deep and that loaded-down car made a racket getting through it. Everybody was waving except Travis, who kept his head down, but then he raised it when Woody took out after him.

"Woody! Woody!" John yelled, but the collie kept following the car, down the driveway between the long rows of magnolias.

"Woody! Come back!" Endy yelled. "You can't go with 'em!"

Travis finally waved. He waved at Woody, just a little one, a sad one, and that's maybe all Woody wanted.

The dog stopped. The car chugged on out through the honeysuckle archway and onto the road and to the west, to the Promised Land. Woody sat in the gravel and watched them go. His big blond, white-tipped bush of a tail was as still as it could be.

The rest of the summer, just another month of it, was spent packing. Endicott was going to military school in New Mexico, and Laura was going to boarding school in Dallas. It was Granddaddy's decision. My parents went along with it.

Laura was a whiz at math and was showing a strong interest in biology and chemistry. Granddaddy didn't think the Fort Worth public schools offered enough for her. Besides, I think he was concerned that Laura was tending too much in the unpolished direction of her great-aunt Jewel. Granddaddy thought Laura might be better off in the company of refined women, and he was sending her to the Hockaday School for Girls in Dallas.

Endy showed a tendency for leadership, mischief, and unfocused bravura, in equal quantities, and not much of an intellectual spark; lawyer material, in other words. Granddaddy didn't think the public schools could handle him, either.

He thought Endy might have a military career in his future—something more honorable than the law, Granddaddy believed—and so Endy was going to the New Mexico Military Institute, in the desert, where Granddaddy was hoping they might sweat some sense into him.

At fourteen, Endicott had caught up with me in height. He'd gotten angles and left his pudginess behind. He was going to be taller than me, I figured, because he was growing so fast and because I seemed to have quit. I was five-six and still skinny, and Endy was fuller, better muscled. He excelled in every sport.

He was leaving the next day, and they were going to make him an officer and a gentleman. I wondered if they knew just how much work they had ahead of them. I knew the real Endicott Philip George Beckwith.

I would remain at home, Granddaddy decreed, I think because I was so average. I had neither a special spark to be developed, like Laura, nor a special shortcoming that needed work, like Endy. Granddaddy thought the public schools were good enough for me.

And they didn't say it, but I think they needed me at home. Mama needed somebody to hang on to. I was just a kid, but I was all she had.

As always, the family kept quiet about Daddy. We walked on tiptoes. We whispered. At the breakfast table, maybe, somebody—probably innocent Arthur—would ask, "Where's Daddy?"

My mother would say, "He's on a business trip, honey. Checkin' wells."

And maybe that was true. Daddy might have to go to Ranger or Abilene or Breckenridge to see an engineer or a pipeline company or a lawyer. But it shouldn't have taken so long. One day, maybe two. Instead, he'd be gone for four days or five or a week. He'd stay in some desolate motel or go back to the cabin on the river.

I knew what he was doing. Mama knew.

Daddy had hit a new low shortly after Bert died, and the absences got longer and more frequent. It had become obvious to everyone, even to Daddy, that he had a problem.

"He needs to get hold of himself," I overheard Granddaddy telling my mother. "No ifs, ands, or buts. I'll fire him from the family business if I have to."

I'm sure Granddaddy told my father the same thing. Granddaddy was never one to hold back when he thought his counsel was needed. Threats and lectures were his idea of counsel.

And late in the spring Daddy seemed to get control. He quit going to the river so often, and to Dorthy's. He'd try not to stay overnight on his business trips. He remained at home and went to church and looked miserable.

He had little patience. He'd snap at us, then withdraw. He'd stay up in his office or take long, long walks. He paced—inside himself and out. You could see he was caged.

Sometimes in my restless nights of that summer, between all the good-byes, I'd sneak out to the tree house. I always waited until Endy sagged into sleep, which never took more than an hour. I'd climb out our bedroom window, down the chinaberry tree, and walk across the grove. I didn't need a flashlight. I knew the way by heart.

The tree house was in one of the big pecan trees, maybe fifty yards out and twenty feet up. Boards nailed to the tree were our steps. On the August night I'm remembering, I came out in my usual summer uniform, barefooted, in T-shirt and cut-off jeans.

A few months before, I had stolen some cigarettes and matches from my parents. It was easy. They bought cigarettes by the carton and kept them in the pantry. Nobody missed anything. I kept the cigarettes in a nook on the side of the tree where the boards joined. Nobody ever found out.

I struck one of the matches and pulled a glow onto the end of an L&M. The smoke choked me on the way down and came spewing out. But two more puffs and I was used to it.

I watched the blinking woods where the lightning bugs were darting. I was not far from the servants' quarters where Granddaddy was, almost directly above him. His light was on in his bedroom, and I could see just an angle of him, his arm and shoulder and his pajama sleeve. He was reading in bed. That's the way he always went to sleep, in the middle of a Montaigne essay.

In the Big House, most of the lights in the bedrooms were off. The Beckwiths and their retainers had retired to their separateness.

The world was calling. It was taking us away, one at a time. Whyvonne and JFK and Bert. Now Laura and Endy. And Daddy. Was I the only one who could see it?

Endy didn't understand, and the little ones, John and Arthur, were too young. Aunt Kitty fluttered from thing to thing. Aunt Jew was encased in a bygone era. Granddaddy stood firm, with a solid scowl, behind the battlements.

Laura might have known. She'd look up from her microscope and I could see a hint of something, and I wondered if it was more than fatigue. I think she knew the separateness, the drift, the danger.

My parents' room was on the other side of the house, so I couldn't see it now, even though I was up as high as their balcony.

Mama was probably out there. She was through with the children for the night and she always went to the bedroom balcony for a last cigarette, maybe two. She liked to stand and look down into the chasm of dark leaves. She knew.

Daddy was gone. Later that summer his trips started getting longer again, more often. This time he'd been away three or four days.

The real world was knocking at the Beckwith fortress. Soon it would be pounding.

7

"SOCIALISTS!" GRANDDADDY ANNOUNCED.

The passing of bowls, the clink of spoons, the exchange of pleasantries—all suddenly ceased as Granddaddy launched into the topic of the afternoon, *The Decline of Western Civilization as We Knew It.* I'd heard it before.

We were each in our proper places, each in our separate selves, dressed in our Sunday best. Nothing had changed about Sunday Dinner. There were simply fewer of us.

It was the middle of September. Endicott and Laura had been gone only a few weeks, but it seemed longer.

Endy's letters were brave and braggy. He'd already gotten into trouble—talking too much, late for formation, boots unbuffed, unauthorized candy wrappers—and he'd had KP three times. He said he was getting good at "pealing patattoes," was shooting well, had been elected platoon leader, and made the football team. There was this one boy who kept wetting the bed, he wrote, and the guys called him Lake.

Laura's letters were more proper, less sprawling. She wasn't happy about being in a school full of giggling pre-debutantes, but she'd already found a friend, a classmate who shared her love of horses. She'd found a good riding coach and at least one good teacher, and said she hated Sunday dress-up day but that it was a lot like Sunday Dinner. She asked about Ozzie and wondered if we had heard from Whyvonne.

I missed them both, Endy especially. Lying in my bed at night, I had only my own breathing to listen to. I could hear the wind too much.

"The socialists have taken over the country!" Granddaddy continued.

"Damn right!" said Aunt Jew, who usually only mumbled but now and again could form words, especially when Western civilization was at stake. Several bits of fried okra came out with her volley, and she almost lost her upper plate.

"Who are the socialists?" Arthur wanted to know. He must have been asleep during the last ninety-nine lectures Granddaddy had conducted on this topic.

"Democrats," John said, turning toward Arthur. "Granddaddy's talking about Democrats."

"Lyndon Johnson Democrats," Granddaddy corrected. "I'm not referring to *real* Democrats."

Granddaddy slashed into his roast beef, and his sterling knife flashed in the crystal light from above. It was one of the same knives Great-Great-Grandmother Beckwith had hidden from the Yankees, buried under the third oak tree on your left when you faced out from the north portico at the family home, Hidden Oaks, in northern Virginia.

"Generous! Yes, by God, the socialists are generous!" Granddaddy paused to take a grinding bite of beef. He chewed on his next several words: "They're so God damn generous they'd give you your shirt right off your own back!"

"I don't get it," John whispered across to me. (There was a gap on my side of two places, Endy's and Laura's. It would have made sense for everybody to scoot up a couple of spaces, but that would have broken tradition.)

"He means they're generous with other people's money," I whispered back.

Granddaddy heard me. "Exactly! Generous to a fault! They will raise the downtrodden by threading over the backs of us few remaining taxpayers until we have been trampled into the mud of penury!"

"What's penury?" Arthur asked, from the other side of John.

"Dead broke," I said.

"Damn right!" Aunt Jew said again to Granddaddy's last assertion. This time she dribbled some of her water across her chin, and Miss Godwin was quick with her napkin.

Granddaddy was erect in his high-backed chair, unbent by the years, certain as ever. His words were fortified and towering. Not a bit of the dark fire had gone out of his gray-black eyes.

"What the liberals discount—and I presume it is out of simple ignorance—is the fact that Man is a fallen creature. Man is encumbered by Original Sin." Granddaddy turned toward us. "John," he said, "define for us the doctrine of Original Sin."

John, in midbite, gulped. He set his fork down and brought his napkin to his lips. He pretended to chew a bit more. He was stalling, panicked. Increasing levels of redness bloomed across his face.

"Adam and Eve!" I whispered at him.

And Mama whispered at him from the other direction: "The apple!"

"And that damn snake!" Aunt Kitty shot out.

"Damn right!" Aunt Jew said.

"Yes," Granddaddy said. "They're giving you good hints, John—Adam and Eve, the apple, and, as Kitty so pungently put it, 'that damn snake.' "

Aunt Kitty blushed. My mother laughed into her napkin. Granddaddy smiled as he took several bites of beef and black-eyed peas in quick succession. He took a deep drink from his goblet of water. He was arming himself.

The younger boys were being brought into the conversations these days, and they were unpracticed. Granddaddy, nevertheless, seemed pleased enough with John. He believed the boy showed evidence of gumption.

He had always been Granddaddy's favorite. The boy was a natural capitalist. The summer before he had set up a booth at the side of the road in front of our house.

"WORMS!" his sign said. "25 for 25 cents!" He reeled in the customers with the steeply discounted price—bait and switch, literally—then informed them they'd have to dig their own. He'd point them toward the woods and offer to rent them a shovel for a dollar an hour.

Last fall John had gone into the fur coat business. He'd taken his worm profits, purchased a brood pair of chinchillas, and then seen his empire collapse overnight after the little critters chewed their way out of their cage in his bedroom and escaped into our labyrinthine house.

The idea of extra rodents in the house upset Mama. Granddaddy declared he'd do something about it, but he didn't say what. Two days later, Aunt Jew, in an unprecedented moment of alertness, spied the chinchillas, retrieved her .22 rifle from her umbrella stand, and bagged one of them, leaving a small bullet hole just above the baseboard in the front hall.

John lost all hope for his fur business, Aunt Jew lost her shooting privileges, permanently, and Mama remained apprehensive about coming upon the surviving chinchilla, although it was never heard from again.

John was the fair-haired one, the blondest and handsomest. He was blessed with smoothness, a second sense that life could be played like an instrument. He was learning the notes, playing the game, manipulating the strings. He was ten years old going on twenty-five, a cynic-in-the-making who had gotten down the basics; he just needed work on the package, more polish, a warmer sizzle. I figured he'd be selling commodities over the phone before he was sixteen.

Arthur, however, seemed so much younger. Whereas John was already standing apart, looking things over, calculating the price, Arthur remained tightly within the family circle, which was mostly made up of older women. He thrived on the easy comfort there. He cooked, he cleaned, he loved to help out.

God knows my mother needed him. She relished him, every inch of his unburdened soul. He got the best of her hugs, the most of her laughter, the last of her hope.

She was fading, the way red hair goes to age; not graying, just quieting. I remember her sitting there on the other side of Arthur, at the end of the line, next to my father's empty place. As always she was mostly hidden, mostly quiet; a small, weary laugh.

Daddy had been gone two weeks this time. Two weeks—and this should have been no more than a three- or four-day trip, like the others.

He'd called only once, a week ago, saying he was having trouble tracking down a mineral deed at the Bennett County Courthouse. I'd heard Granddaddy and Mama talking about it in down-turned voices at the edge of the parlor.

"Laziness," Granddaddy said around the last few bites of a forkful of okra. "Pure-D laziness. That's the Original Sin. Man is born with a tendency toward indolence, and it has been this way from the beginning, since we first crawled from the muck, wagging our tails behind us."

Granddaddy had dabbled a bit in modern thought—mid- to late-nineteenth century, which he termed modern. He'd read *On the Origin of Species* and had found it reasonable.

He stabbed at more okra and continued. "Hell, I imagine the first thing our earliest varmint relatives did when they crawled out on dry land was to lie back and work on their suntan."

"Did we used to have tails, Granddaddy?" John asked.

"And long, long tongues?" Arthur asked. He stuck his pointy little tongue out toward some black-eyed peas that he had shish-kebabed on his fork.

"Yes," Granddaddy said, "and before that, fins. We were not formed whole and complete and fully equipped, the way the Bible says Adam appeared. That's a fairy tale. The real truth is much more stunning. We began in the mud in the midst of a swamp and evolved. We became fish, then lizards, and eventually monkeys. And from the very beginning we have relished the mud from whence we emerged."

Granddaddy glanced slyly toward Miss Godwin. He had just baited a hook—several hooks, in fact—and cast toward her. She did not believe the Bible contained any fairy tales.

She offered no response, however. Miss Godwin nestled her fundamentally stiff neck down behind her high collar and pinched her lips together. Her job depended on the maintenance of household harmony, and she elected to keep it. She continued with the feeding of Aunt Jew, pushing the food through the old woman's sagging lips.

Miss Godwin, as always, lived narrowly, from duty to duty. She'd take Miss Jewel out to the front porch for a cigarette—Miss Godwin had to hold the cigarette for her—or it was time for Miss Jewel's lunch, bath, nap, or evening cocktail.

My great-aunt wasn't much more than bones and shadows then. She was eighty-seven, and old for her age. Her face was gathered folds of skin, her hair a lump of gray strands, her nose grown to hefty proportions. She may have been almost buried under all that age, but she wasn't gone. She could hardly talk, but she could give out some spirited moan-words when things weren't going her way. And late in the evening when she was allowed a single nightcap through a straw, she could mumble joyfully.

Aunt Kitty, too, puttered right along, knitting, swatting, sleeping, watching television. She loved the westerns: *Gunsmoke*, especially, but also *Wagon Train*, *The Rifleman*, and *Bonanza*. She loved seeing the bad guys crumple the way those flies fell to her ferocious swatting.

Aunt Kitty was fifty-two then, nine years older than my father, but she looked half his age; she had lived like a flower in a hothouse.

The phone rang, and Odessa went across the room to the foyer to answer it. The phone call was for my mother, and she left the room. Granddaddy continued with the topic of the day.

Mama returned as Granddaddy was calling Adam "the world's original wild-eyed liberal—looking for a short-cut to wisdom—that lazy, misguided son of a bitch." She walked toward him and waited, standing behind Aunt Jew, resting her hands on the handles of the wheelchair.

She was trying not to be noticed. Usually it worked—she had this special way of hiding behind her own quietness—but there was a broken look about her, and it stood out. It disrupted our concentration.

Granddaddy hurried with his last few words. Mama came over, bent, and whispered something to him. He stood. She motioned to me, and the three of us went into the foyer, beyond the hearing of the others.

That was the Bennett County sheriff on the phone, she said. He'd been called out to the tourist court where my father was staying. Daddy had locked himself in his room, and they could hear him crying and carrying on in there.

They got another key and went in. It took two deputies, which was all they had, to hold him down and get him to the hospital. He thought bugs were crawling all over him. He must have been drinking for days.

Mama was leaning against the wall next to the telephone table. It was hard for her to get her breath, but she wasn't crying. The sheriff said Daddy was in the hospital, finally quiet. She asked if I would drive and if Granddaddy would go with us to see what needed to be done.

While I went to the shed to bring the car around, Granddaddy returned to the Little House to get more tobacco for his pipe. Mama went back into the dining room to tell the others where we were going, and why. I don't know what she said, but when I came back in to tell her we were ready, everybody was very quiet.

It was eighty-five due-west miles to the hospital. The small highway was narrow and unlighted and almost empty. Most of it was the same way we took to the cabin on the Brazos; I knew it well.

Mama had a new car, a Mercury sedan with a husky engine and an instrument panel that lit up like Las Vegas, according to Granddaddy, who had thought the old car was still perfectly fine. It was a gift from my father. Granddaddy probably berated him for his extravagance.

Mama was in the front seat, Granddaddy in the back. He smoked his pipe and cursed the small ashtray. Mama was silent. The radio was off, the windows were down, and the last of the day blew through the car.

The people at the little hospital were kind. They had few patients and lots of time. The building—one story, ranch-style, on a tree-starved hill—contained only twelve beds, most of which were empty. It took the doctor only a few minutes to walk over from his home next door. He took us back to his office behind the waiting room.

Dr. McFarland was as rumpled as his desk, which was scattered with patients' charts and papers, books and pictures of grandchildren. Despite his seventy years, he was precise, steady, direct. The doctor took off his wire-rim glasses, leaned a hard look at Granddaddy, and said in a gravelly twang: "Mr. Beckwith is an alcoholic. I suppose you know that."

Granddaddy didn't flinch. "Yes," he said.

But I did, inside. I had never heard that word before—*alcoholic*—except from a distance. We didn't talk about such things in our Eighteenth Century household. Granddaddy had no use for psychology. "Warmed-over air," he called it. He believed in character, principles, moral fiber, which you either had or you didn't. And Daddy, I suppose, didn't measure up.

"A person doesn't get into Mr. Beckwith's shape in a day, over a weekend," the doctor said. "It's obvious to me that he's been doing damage to himself for a long time."

Mama was sitting in the chair next to me, and I could feel the tension rise in her. Her words were rushed and breathless. "But we were hoping . . ."

Granddaddy interrupted: "I just don't understand why William can't help himself. Why he can't stop."

"He tries, Granddaddy," my mother said. "He tries real hard."

"He can quit. I've seen him," Granddaddy said.

"Will was doing so much better earlier this summer," she said. "Then . . . then this."

They were talking too quickly, each trampling on the last words of the other. It was our family's version of panic.

Granddaddy was almost tentative. I had never seen him that way before. It frightened me to think that something could tame the enormous fierceness out of him, even for a moment. It had never occurred to me that anything in life was bigger than Granddaddy.

The doctor took control of the conversation. He called alcoholism an affliction. Certain people, he said—and he said he didn't know why some and not others—don't drink like normal people. They take a drink and it sets off a compulsion. They won't stop until they can't bring the glass to their mouths. And over time, if something isn't done, they won't stop until they're dead.

"I've seen many a man—good men, prominent men—brought down to degradation by the stuff."

The doctor said he knew about a sanitarium in Minnesota that had a good reputation. They would send a male attendant down and take Daddy back on the train. He'd stay for two months. It might be better if he were far away for a while, the doctor said. He needs to face himself and change, he said, without interference from anybody.

"Yes," Granddaddy said, returning to steadiness. He asked my mother and she said yes, too, but I could tell she was confused. Granddaddy called Minnesota from the doctor's office while Mama and I went to the waiting room.

"Everything is happening so fast," Mama said.

We sat in the small room, three chairs on each side of a bare room, except for a picture of a hill of bluebonnets. Paint by numbers, with dabs out of alignment. I think the doctor's wife might have done it. It was signed "Marge."

We were quiet. Mama smoked too much. I really wanted one of her cigarettes.

Granddaddy came in after a while. He confirmed what the doctor had told us about the sanitarium, except for one thing. No visitors. We could write letters, but that was all.

"Two months," Mama said. "That's a long time."

"Yes," Granddaddy said. "But I don't think we have a choice."

"What about Will? Do you think he'll go along with this?"

"The doctor's talking to him now."

We waited again. Mama and Granddaddy talked about some of the bad signs they'd seen in Daddy, the hope and the dashed hope; the good days, the bad days, the missing days. In a minute, without much effort, they put together a picture of deterioration, a chart with zigs and zags that trended down and down. It was suddenly obvious.

Granddaddy worked with his pipe and I got another Coke. The nurse got them more coffee. Dr. McFarland came back in.

"I told Mr. Beckwith about the sanitarium," he said. "I don't know how much he's understanding, but I think I got through to him, and he's agreed to go."

"Well then," Granddaddy said, "I'll call them back and accept. They said they could have somebody down here to pick him up by tomorrow evening."

"I'm going to stay here with Will," my mother said. "I'll stay until he leaves tomorrow."

"We can find you a motel room," Granddaddy said.

"No," she said. "I'll stay here. I'll stay in his room."

"Don't you want Stephen and me to stay with you?"

"No, Granddaddy. You all go back tonight. Stephen needs to get back to school tomorrow. I'll drive Will's car back."

"Very well," Granddaddy said. "If you think so. I suppose it makes the most sense."

"I don't want him to feel alone anymore," Mama said.

Daddy's room was a vacant white all over. There was a small, dark window with the blinds shut, a chair, and his bed. A low lamp made mountains of shadows. Mama went into the room, but I stayed at the door.

Daddy was sleeping, or at least his eyes were closed. He was crouched sideways under the covers, facing the door. He looked cold.

"Will?" my mother said gently.

His arms were at his sides, tied to the bed railing by cloth ropes.

"Will, honey?"

He was so small and so gray—a washed-away, milky gray, worse than winter. His skin was stubbled and loose on his face. There were broken lines I had never seen before. His hair was swirled into tangles and clumped from unwashed oil.

"Will?"

His eyes flitted beneath the crumpled lids, struggled, and then flew open. The pupils were globes. His eyes were black and wide and vacant and wild with darkness.

He didn't know where he was. He didn't know who we were. His eyes were flailing.

I stepped back from the sight of him.

8

THE TEXAS & PACIFIC TERMINAL WAS AS BIG AS A CATHEDRAL. THE HIGH windows were stained with dust, diffusing the winter light. Sparrows nested in the ceiling's lacework of steel beams, cheeping as they blew about in leaflike sweeps.

We straggled across an expanse of marbled floor, huddled behind Granddaddy. He seemed to know where he was going.

Aunt Jew was just behind him in her wheelchair, pushed by Miss Godwin, who was wearing her whitest, stiffest nurse's dress and a crisp cap pinned to her graying bun. Aunt Jew was wrapped in a shawl, with a blanket across her lap. She mumbled about wanting a cigarette, and Miss Godwin said, "Not now, honey. Not now."

It was Sunday, a week before Christmas, the air was brisk and new, and Christmas Card Day was behind us. We had just been to church and were still in our Sunday clothes. It was almost noon.

Laura, John, Endicott, and I surrounded the wheelchair. Mama was behind, holding Arthur by the hand. Odessa and Judge, also in their Sunday best, brought up the rear. Odessa was wearing her biggest, featheriest Sunday hat; it looked like round three of a cockfight. Judge limped along.

We had come to welcome my father home.

• • •

Daddy had stayed through the full two-month course at the Minnesota sanitarium. None of us had seen him, but we'd all written him. We children had gotten just one letter from him, but Mama had gotten more— private ones, plus others from the doctors.

The sanitarium had a buddy system. People who went through treatment were given a partner in their hometown to help them reenter society, somebody who had been through the sanitarium themselves and had been successful in their recovery. Al Heath had been assigned as Daddy's partner.

Al came to our house three times while Daddy was away. He talked about the kind of treatment Daddy was undergoing and how he'd be when he got out. We liked him, most of us. Granddaddy kept his distance.

Al was a Fort Worth lawyer. He looked to be about my father's age, with some of the same markings, as if he had been to some of the same dark stretches at the end of the line. He was too-soon gray, and his eyes were half hidden above darkened puffs. Everything about him seemed bunched into knots—the muscles of his face, the words, the handshake.

He tried to explain how Daddy was going to be different—that he would probably be a little quieter at first, shy and uneasy, maybe moody or depressed.

He didn't know Daddy very well, I thought. That's the way he already was, on his best days. It was hard for me to believe he was going to be able to come roaring back, better than ever.

Al said Daddy would be going to a lot of meetings of Alcoholics Anonymous, where people like him got together and helped each other by talking about their problems. He was especially good with the younger children, explaining things with simplicity and care. He said alcoholism was a disease, like diabetes, and it could never be cured but it could be arrested: as long as Daddy never took another drink for as long as he lived, he could live a normal and happy life. Eventually, Al said, we could almost forget Daddy ever had a problem.

He told us all this at several Sunday Dinners. He was articulate, but he'd get tangled in his words sometimes. It was those knots.

I think part of the reason for the nerves was Granddaddy. He was always gracious and gentlemanly, and he welcomed Al to our table, but I knew, and I think Al knew, how much Granddaddy was holding back, like an unconvinced juror. He was suspicious of this whole thing—that you can go to a meeting and talk about your problems, and that's all it takes to make everything fine and forgiven. I watched Granddaddy, with his head resting on his hand, holding a handful of jowls, and I could almost hear him harrumphing inside.

Once, as Al was leaving, I overheard him tell my mother that he and his wife were divorcing, and that she'd moved back to Atlanta. "My drinking destroyed my family," he said. His cracking voice dimmed. "I hope it's not too late for this family."

Mama jolted inside. I could hear it, a stutter in her breath.

The one letter from Daddy came around Thanksgiving. Mama read it to us at breakfast. Endicott and Laura were home for the holiday then, too.

> *Dear Children:*
>
> *I am doing well, and I hope you are the same.*
>
> *They gave us a little time after breakfast to write letters, and I'm sitting at a desk in the rec room looking out at the Minnesota woods. Fall had already arrived by the time I got here, and soon the leaves were gone and the woods were filling up with snow.*
>
> *Now it snows almost every day here, a little, and sometimes much more. There will be three or four feet of it in the middle of winter, they say, but I will be home by then. I will be home before Xmas. That's what they promise.*
>
> *I wish you all were here with me. We could go walking in the woods.*
>
> *I love you all and can't wait to see you.*
>
> *Daddy*

The others seemed reassured, but something didn't sound right to me. It didn't sound much like Daddy. It was like it was from an ordinary person who didn't know us very well but who was being very nice.

Endicott led the others outside, to play touch football like the old days—he and John versus me and Laura and Arthur. He thought he was hot stuff, just needing two on his side. I said we'd see about that. I said I'd be right out.

I stayed. I told Mama I wanted to see that letter. "It doesn't sound like Daddy," I said.

"Honey, okay, I . . ."

She handed it to me. She didn't want to.

It was written on the sanitarium's stationery, in pencil. The words were shaky and erased and misspelled and slanted the wrong way.

"What . . ."

"Stephen, I didn't want to tell the others," Mama said. "I didn't want them to see this. They wouldn't understand."

"Daddy's in trouble," I said. "It's real bad, isn't it?"

I looked hard at her. I was looking for the truth and she was tired of holding it in and she let go of it with just that one look from me.

"Honey, it's the treatment. He's getting . . . they're giving him what they call electroshock therapy."

"I've heard of it. To the brain."

"Electrical charges, yes. The idea is to wipe out these bad memories he has, this compulsion to drink, depression. That's how the doctors explained it to me. And Al said the same thing."

"Daddy's mind is wiped out?"

"It comes back. That's the idea. His memory, not just the bad things but everything, spelling and everything. But it comes back a little at a time, and you learn to accept things and deal with the bad things as they come back. Al had it."

"He did?"

"Not as much as Will, but almost. That's what he told me."

"He seems pretty normal to me."

"It's reassured me."

"Does Daddy even know who we are anymore?"

"It's coming back. They tell me it's coming back, almost all of his memory. By Christmas he should be all right."

"I hope it's coming back, Mama. I hope he's coming back."

"He's coming back, honey. He is."

Aunt Jew and Miss Godwin used the elevator, but the rest of us went up the stairs to the open area where the trains came in. Al was already there.

We assembled around him. Al said he'd talked to a conductor who said Daddy's train was going to be on time. We stood there, shoulders hunched inward, hands pocketed or folded under arms, exchanging pieces of sentences with each other in the sharp north wind.

We kept looking down the tracks. Aunt Jew asked for a cigarette, and

Miss Godwin had trouble lighting it. Aunt Kitty stared and smiled. She loved trains.

Granddaddy stood apart, dignified, solid, unbent. He was wearing his gray winter's suit and his gray felt Stetson. The wind went around him.

Daddy came in on thunder, in a wash of wind. The engines pushed passed us, rattling the concrete platform and pushing the diesel-coated air over us. We stepped back from the force, all of us but Granddaddy. He met everything, including trains, head on.

It was a short train. The cars eased to a stop in front of us, and the one we wanted was only a little ways down. The Beckwith multitude picked up stakes and moved down two cars.

We waited beside the steps, with the younger ones in front, Al off to the side, and Granddaddy in the rear. Two old ladies got off first, then a mother with three children, several more small groupings of people, and then Daddy.

He was radiant. He was all-over new. My mother lost her breath and all of us were locked in hesitation, staring at him.

Daddy looked like an older version of a combination of Endicott and me; an older brother. He was golden and tall. Except for the lines around his eyes that went down and deep, he was repaired. He came down the steps. A smile overtook his face

Arthur broke the spell of propriety and broke free. He came running up to him. "Daddy! Daddy!"

My father set down his small suitcase and bent down and scooped up the blond bundle. "Arthur!" Daddy said. "Arthur!"

I had never seen my father cry before. His face crumpled into a child's pained face, but a smile was in the middle of it. Tears were everywhere. Daddy buried his face into Arthur's scruffy nest of hair.

Then most of the rest of us rushed in, Mama first, then Laura, Endy, John, and I. We surrounded him and covered him in hugs. Mama was crying all over. My face was wet. You couldn't even see Daddy anymore because of all of us.

Then we slowly separated in order to give the others a chance. Al stepped in and hugged my father, patting his back. They were already close, even through Al had only seen him once in Minnesota. They had been writing.

Daddy went around to the others, bending down to kiss Aunt Jew and then reaching over to give Aunt Kitty a peck on the cheek. She smiled. Odessa marched right up and gave my father a man-handling hug, saying "Come 'ere, boy! Gimme some sugar!" Judge and Miss Godwin stood back, and Daddy gave them each a little wave.

Granddaddy stood back the farthest, unmoved. My father went up to him. They stood separate from each other for a moment. Then Granddaddy reached out his hand and my father shook it with both of his.

"Welcome home, William," Granddaddy said with corporate firmness.

"Thanks, Dad," my father said.

Then Daddy turned back toward us. Tears still covered his face, filling some of the worry lines, the many worries.

9

LIFE FELL BACK INTO A PATTERN. IT WAS GOOD. DADDY WAS DOING reasonably well, I thought. At least I tried hard to believe it.

I know my mother did. I watched her, almost every evening, wading out into the drifts of winter leaves in the grove. She folded her arms around herself in a hard hug and walked out beyond my seeing. That was the way she prayed.

Endicott and Laura went back to school. John and Arthur weren't paying much attention. Granddaddy, I could tell, had his doubts.

But Daddy tried. Every inch of him tried.

Attentive. Careful. Quiet. Nice.

He was at every meal, at church, at every school function, up in our rooms at homework time to see if we needed any help—which I think made things worse for him, because a lot of times he couldn't remember the simplest things, like spelling and multiplication.

Or he was up in his office, working, sweating, working. From my bedroom I could hear that old adding machine going. He was punching in the numbers of Beckwith Minerals and pulling the crank down—punch-punch, pull; punch-punch-punch, pull—or that old Underwood was going, the letters splatting against the paper and then the ding.

He was going to be perfect. Granddaddy was going to be proud.

I went out to the tree house now and then, at night, even in the cold, just to breathe. Daddy was around so much, hovering, trying. I'd lean on the railing of that high-perched platform with a cigarette, pulling in the winter air along with the smoke. I could breathe in that private place.

Daddy went to AA meetings nearly every night with Al. One night, about two months after he'd been home from the sanitarium, Daddy took me with him. It was sometime in February 1965. I was sixteen.

The group met in an old mansion in a ratty neighborhood near downtown. Mostly it was men, plus a few older women. I expected to see more bums; there were a few, but most looked ordinary, like car salesmen or repairmen, and some looked like Al and Daddy, like they had just left a meeting of the board of directors of some company.

A guy got up and asked for a moment of silence, they all said a prayer for serenity, and then, one at a time, people talked about their problems. They asked Daddy to talk for a minute, but he passed. I guess he was shy because I was there.

At the end everyone formed a big circle around the room. Young and old, handsome and worn down, dressed up and bedraggled—they held hands with each other. They bowed their heads, closed their eyes, and said the Lord's Prayer.

People were holding hands and a low current of warmth passed between them, hand to wobbly hand. I felt it.

I opened my eyes for a second and looked at my father next to me. His eyes were squinted shut. He was bearing down. He was trying so hard. I wondered if he felt it.

It was good to come home to the river after so long, even in February. The grasses were brown and the flowers were gone, but there was the green of the live oaks and cedars, and the sunny-blue water of the river. The warming air held some promise—that maybe spring was at least in the planning stage.

We stopped at Dorthy's first. It had been six months since she'd seen Daddy, longer since she'd seen me. She didn't know about the sanitarium; in fact, she brought Daddy a beer when we sat down, and he had to tell her to take it back. He explained things just a little, that he had to give it up for health reasons.

"It was killing me," Daddy said with a laugh.

"Hell, that sounds like a health reason to me," Dorthy said.

She brought my father some coffee and me a Dr Pepper and then sat down and drank the beer that had been for my father; she said it seemed a shame to see a good beer go to waste.

Daddy told her a little more about where he'd been and what had happened.

"Lord, honey, I know what you mean about that drinkin'," Dorthy said with that sly smile, signaling a joke was on the way. "Hell, I've got to watch it myself. I try to never have more'n a couple a six-packs a day, except on special occasions."

"Like what," I asked.

"Weekends."

Dorthy said she thought Miz Abernathy might have a drinking problem, too, but she'd never gotten the old lady sober enough long enough to talk to her about it.

"Hell, at this late date," Dorthy said, "the poor dear might as well drink herself to death. She's pretty well bit the dust as it is."

Miz Abernathy came tottering out with our chicken-fried steaks. She sat next to Dorthy, sipping her gin and smoking a cigarette. As usual, she didn't hear any of the conversation. Dorthy hadn't been able to talk her into getting the hearing aid Bert had mentioned in his will. She just smiled that pasted-on, gin-inspired, sweet-pickle smile.

It was dark by the time we got to the cabin. The first thing we did was work on a fire in the fireplace. It wasn't terribly cold, but a little heat felt good.

I brought in the logs and Daddy assembled crumpled newspaper, sticks—a fire was billowing in no time. We took our coats off and situated ourselves around the fire in the rocking chairs from the front porch.

We sat facing the swaying flames. It was our only light.

For a long time we said nothing. Now and then Daddy would throw a log on the fire, then go back to rocking. I rocked and waited.

He finally said, "Stephen."

"Yes," I said.

But he waited again. He started another cigarette. He smoked.

"Stephen, one of the things . . . In AA we have these steps we have to take. Twelve steps. To get your life back in order and be healthy again."

Daddy paused again. I waited.

"I'm supposed to make a list of all the people I've harmed because of my drinking, and make amends. I've made that list, and you're up there at the top of it. You and your mother."

"Yes," I said. I didn't know what else to say.

I looked over at him, across the struggling light. He was looking down and away.

"God," he said finally. "God almighty damn. I don't deserve you all. I don't. I'm so sorry, Stephen. For all of it. A lifetime. Gone."

We sat and rocked a long time. Finally I took off my boots and got in my sleeping bag. I lay on my cot and watched the fire some more. I watched the fire die.

Something flared; a piece of a dream, maybe. Something woke me.

I hadn't been asleep very long, maybe a couple of hours. When I woke the room had darkened and cooled; the fire was an orange smudge in the corner. My father was not on his cot. His chair was gone.

I got up and went across the room to the window.

I could see just an outline of him. He was sitting on the porch, in his coat, smoking a cigarette. He was wrapped in the night, staring, captured.

10

I ANSWERED THE PHONE.

"Stevie?"

"Yes?"

"Stevie, it's Dorthy. Out at Sportsman's Inn."

I moved around the little table in the foyer to get away from the talk in the dining room. "Dorthy. Yes. What's . . ."

"Honey, it's your daddy." Her words were small, afraid, and all of her fear went straight into me. It was a couple of weeks after my weekend with Daddy at the Brazos. Now he was on another business trip to West Texas, but he was supposed to have been back the day before.

"Daddy?"

"He's all right. He's all right. Don't get so worried, honey."

"What about Daddy? He was supposed to call."

"I talked to him last night. He was out here."

"So why . . ."

"Stevie, you know somethin', I usually don't call like this, call folks, talk about folks. I hear a lot of stuff out here. Beer talk, I call it. Lot of horseshit really is all it is. I don't pay it much mind, certainly don't repeat it to a man's family."

"Is Daddy drinking again, Dorthy?"

"No, honey. Not a drop."

Mama came up to me in the foyer and stood listening. It was right before breakfast and we were getting ready for church. She stood close.

"I don't understand, Dor . . ."

"Honey, he's in terrible bad shape. We talked some last night."

"Depressed."

"Real down, honey, yes. Downer than anybody I ever heard. Tears in his eyes. Didn't eat hardly a bit of his chicken-fried. Real down."

"Tell me . . ."

"I tried it all, Stevie. Jokes. Some music. Some pie. Some talk about the good times, Bert, you, all his family, all the good things I could think of. Nothin'."

"And then what?"

"He said he was real tired. Said he was goin' to the cabin. It wasn't all that late."

"I wish he'd call."

"I thought about it all night. I couldn't sleep. I've never heard somebody be so down on himself. That's all he talked about, how bad he'd treated you all, how he hadn't been able to break away from his father, start over with an oil company out here, build that big house for you all like he's always dreamed about. I'm worried."

"You think somebody should come out there?"

"That's why I was callin', honey. Yeah, I do. I told him last night I thought he ought to go on home, talk to somebody, get some help, but he said he needed to stay out at the cabin and think things through. I don't think it's good for him to be out there by himself so much."

"I guess I better come out there."

"Stevie, I'd go out to the cabin and talk to him some more, but I didn't figure I could do him any good. Didn't seem to help much last night. I figure maybe one of you all was what was needed."

"I'm gonna talk to his friend Al."

"The AA guy."

"He'll know what to do."

"Then y'all are comin' on out?"

"Yeah, as soon as we can."

"Good. I'll fix you lunch."

"I can't promise anything, Dorthy. We probably ought to go on out to the cabin first."

"That makes sense. Y'all do what you need to. Then come on by and we'll have lunch."

"Okay. If we can. Bye, Dorothy. And thank you so much for calling."

"Sure, honey. Bye."

Mama hardly waited for me to put down the receiver. "He hasn't been drinking?" she asked.

"No, Mama. Depressed, Dorthy said. Real depressed."

"I figured that. I knew that. I can't talk him out of it."

"It's pretty bad, Dorthy said."

"He needs more help, Stephen. Some kind of help. Somebody else."

"We need to talk to Al."

"Yes. Absolutely. I'll call him, honey. I better call him."

"I'll go get dressed. He'll help, I know. He'll want to go out to the river with us."

I got dressed, first out of my Sunday pants and shirt, then into what I would have worn when I got home, blue jeans and sweatshirt and tennis shoes. It was a little cool outside, but I wouldn't need a coat.

I finished with my bathroom chores, and I went down to breakfast.

On Sundays it was just cereal. Odessa was off on Sunday mornings so she could go to church. As soon as she got back she'd go to work on Sunday Dinner.

Mama had called Al. He was on his way, she said.

I poured myself come cornflakes, the sugared kind. I was a kid in little ways like that, but mostly I wasn't a kid anymore at all.

"Is Daddy sick again?" Arthur asked.

"Yes, honey," Mama said.

Granddaddy was sunk into himself. Mama must have talked to him. His eyebrows were pinched into one long bumpy ridge.

Mama and I talked some more. We decided it would be best for just Al and me to go. She needed to stay with the younger kids, get them to church. Besides, Al would know best what to do.

He had all kinds of resources. First, he told her on the phone, he and Daddy would talk a lot, all the way back to Fort Worth. Then he'd know better what to recommend. Maybe Daddy needed to go back to Minnesota, or maybe to a psychiatrist here. He told her not to give up hope. Yes, this was dangerous but it was not uncommon, he said. Delayed reactions to things, things that had piled up.

But Al was coming right over. And before I could finish my cereal he was in the driveway, honking.

Al drove. I directed.

We had interrupted his morning preparations. His beard was coming in—the same steel color as his hair—across the sharp corners of his jaw and into the little valleys of his cheeks.

Al and I didn't speak for thirty minutes, except for the first pleasantries and me giving him general directions. I watched the March wind whipping the leafless mesquites and sending last fall's oak leaves tumbling across the road. It was a southern wind, moist from the Gulf, warming. We had the windows open. The breeze filled and fluffed my wayward hair, all that was left of the boy in me. The rest was sharpening, maturing, darkening, drooping. I had sunken places, like Al. For sixteen, I had a lot of geography in my face.

I was thinking about the night before. Saturday nights had been major bath nights for us since I could remember, and slowly they evolved into evaluation nights for me.

On these Saturday nights, sunk into the steaming water of that old clawfoot tub, I could soak and dream and examine and play. Endicott was gone. I didn't have to stare at his ugly red back. I didn't have to hide my own stretching and growing, and those hormonal seizures. I could stretch out. I could sink into myself.

I got up to my knees and bent and washed my hair. Then I dried off and went to the sink and cleared the mirror with my towel and began the looking over.

I had to step back from the cabinet-size mirror to see myself—or at least most of me, from the knees up. I was pitiful, skinny, boy-muscled. I had a ways to go to get where I thought I should be, to a minimum acceptable standard. A long ways.

At least I was shaving. Although it was only once a week, there was legitimate red-brown fuzz that needed attention. I came back close to the mirror and started the close-ups. When I scraped the shaving cream with each pass of the razor, the red bumps reappeared. I could see which were growing and which were waning, and fret over each of the fresh ones. After shaving I worked on them with more soap and water and, at the end, applied the brown medicine that hid them for an hour before it started flaking off.

I was one of the smallest guys in my class—eleventh grade. I was a shy, half-Irish boy with almost red hair that didn't quite curl—just waved and frizzed—and eyes as green-dark as the shaded river. I had never had a date. I could not speak to a girl.

Part of my problem was my glasses. I needed glasses, I had glasses, but I couldn't bear to wear them. I thought glasses would put me officially into loserhood.

I wore them to see the blackboard or the freeway, but I wouldn't wear them in the hall between classes. So I couldn't see anybody coming. I was as friendly as I could be to each long-haired person who passed me (in those days, that was girls only). Some would call me by name while others were probably wondering about my goofy friendliness. Anybody who might have been interested went by me in a blur. I made no connection.

My home life was getting my focus. It was Daddy. It was starting again.

I don't mean the drinking. It was the hollowed-out place inside him where the drinking had been, the blackened crater left after the electricity had jolted through. He was pulled by it, into it, deeper by the day. It was almost the same thing as drinking, the same absence.

I saw it in his sunken glances at the dinner table, in a pause of conversation. I saw it in his unfocused walks in our spring-greening forest, in his fitful reading of a book in the parlor. I'd seen it a month ago at the river, in the middle of the night on the porch. It called to him. He had always been in love with oblivion.

"This isn't going to be easy, Stephen," Al finally said.

It had been maybe an hour. We were way past Weatherford.

"I know."

"From what I can tell, he's probably in pretty bad shape."

"Yeah."

"The worst part. This is the very worst part. I've been there."

"Not the hospital?"

"Nope. You've got help there. You've got people all around you, telling you over and over you're gonna make it. It's safe and secure.

"Then comes the real world, and I mean real, very real, because you don't have your friend with you anymore, your best friend, Old Reliable, to protect and comfort you."

"You mean drinking."

"Precisely. You are unarmed, for the first time in years. That's when the regrets come, and you are defenseless. They've been sleeping for a long time, and now they're alive and vicious. You've got nothing to drown them in. They've got free rein."

We came down the last long hill and, in the middle of the wide Brazos valley, went past Sportsman's Inn. I pointed it out, but we didn't stop. The first of the lunch crowd had arrived, three or four pickups. Dorthy couldn't sell beer on Sundays, which cut into her business considerably. She always threatened to close down, take Sundays off, but she never did.

Spring was making inroads. Some early, small wildflowers had popped up along the highway, and the trees beside the river were sprinkled with pale green buds. I pointed out our turnoff to Al, and we lurched onto the ranch road just past the bridge. The car thumped over the cattle guard after I got the gate.

The road to the cabin was overhung with branches, making a cave of quietness from which the cardinals spoke. To the left, down the sharp hill, I could see a glint of green, the bending river. I wished I was alone and walking there, and that everything was the same.

The cabin slouched as comfortably as ever in the spotty shade among the live oaks. This was their time of shedding. The leaves, like brown droplets, were twisting down the air and piling up in rivulets against the door and across the roof.

My father's car was parked at the side where it belonged. It was the old fishing car, the tired blue Ford. We pulled up beside it in the little clearing.

First I wanted to know that Daddy was all right, but I wasn't looking forward to the rest of it, the awkwardness of him seeing us, and then the long drive back. At least I wouldn't have to hear his broken voice all the way home. I'd be driving the Ford back, and Daddy would go with Al. That would be good. Daddy could get some good listening from a good friend. Somebody who understood.

Al got out first and went around on the river side, up on the porch. "Will?" he yelled out. "You in there? It's Al!"

There was no answer, only our breathing and the labored breathing of the woods. I bet he was sleeping. He'd probably stayed up into the darkness, almost all night.

"Will?" Al yelled again.

"Daddy?"

He rapped on the door.

"Will? It's Al and Stephen! You in there?"

I pushed in on the unlocked door and started in. Al knew somehow, he knew not to let me go first, and he pushed in ahead of me and held me back at the same time. "Oh God, Stephen!" He kept his arm out, holding me back. "Dear God!"

It was too late. I was right with him and I was seeing what he was seeing—part of my father lying behind the cot across the room, the shotgun on the floor beside him, the shotgun Bert had given me; a bunched-up river of blood on the wooden floor beneath the gun; and one of his legs lying outward, the cuff too high and a patch of sick gray skin.

It was everything all at once that made my breath stop—the seeing, the blurred force of it, and Al, who came over to me, covering me with his body and pulling me away to the porch. As soon as I got my first breath it came out as a cry.

11

THE SERVICE WAS AT TWO O'CLOCK AT OUR EPISCOPAL CHURCH; THE limousines were at the house by one-thirty. Aunts and uncles, cousins and friends had gathered at our house, including Dorthy and Miz Abernathy. We were on our way to the cars when Aunt Jew brought it all to a halt. She'd lost her teeth.

Everybody—family, guests, limousine drivers—went looking for those dentures. Aunt Jew refused to budge without them. She sat in her wheelchair on the front porch, arms crossed, wheels locked, mouth crumpled.

We looked everywhere, in all her old forgetful places where they had turned up before, from the oven to the fish bowl. No luck. Time ticked away. Granddaddy went from grim to grimmer.

At ten minutes till two, Granddaddy exploded. "God damn it, Jew, can't you borrow some teeth? We've got to get moving!"

Aunt Jew's caved-in face caved in further. I had never seen her cry before. I didn't know she could. I think, in her buried way, in the way my family grieved, those tears were for my father. They were for my strangled family.

Several women, with Miss Godwin in charge, rushed in to comfort her. Aunt Kitty stood by awkwardly. Granddaddy stormed away.

We hunted some more. No luck. Miss Godwin kept talking to her, sympathizing, cajoling, and at last Aunt Jew agreed to go without her teeth.

We went to the cars, all in a jumble, and it took a while to sort out everyone. We were thirty minutes late.

The words of the church service were an empty wind over me. At the grave, the words were of dust and ashes. I was already ashes.

There was a hug or two, but mostly we were each alone. Nobody knew what to say, and so they didn't say anything.

Daddy was buried at the main cemetery in west Fort Worth, on the side of a hill under live oaks. The clouds pushed along, the bulging clouds of springtime. It was like Bert's resting place—the same kind of tree-topped hill—but without the dogs.

Dorthy and Miz Abernathy had driven in that morning and had to leave right after the service. "The cafe never hardly sleeps, you know," Dorthy liked to say. "'Course I'm not countin' Abernathy."

Dorthy had been quiet and uneasy all day. The house, the important people, and the big cars made her nervous.

But Miz Abernathy was never one to hold back. She came right out with it as soon as she stepped through our front door: "Son of a bitch, Dorthy, this place is bigger'n a God damn barn."

"Yes," Dorthy said coldly, signaling her to hush. Miz Abernathy wasn't good with signals.

"Lordy, this front hall is bigger than our whole damn cafe," she continued. Her sunken eyes sprang wide and her mouth hung open even wider. She stood in the middle of the foyer and looked up the turning stairway and into the brilliant, wounded, Buick-size chandelier. "Now don't that beat all?"

The five of us children were together again, the old gang, broken. We didn't have much to say. We were all sad, but Laura's grief was encased in a dark-eyed despondency. I don't think she was happy at the girls' school. At home she stayed in her room most of the time.

John was uncharacteristically quiet, putting his dreams and schemes on hold. He had recently taken over my taxidermy equipment and hand-books with my blessing, and was considering a plan to market more exotic products, such as (patent pending) Moccasin Moccasins, house shoes made of water moccasin skins. I thought the idea had potential.

From day to evening Arthur was busy helping Odessa in the kitchen and Aunt Kitty with her nerves. He helped Miss Godwin help Aunt Jew negotiate her wheelchair across the Persian rugs to greet the guests and catch her occasional drool. Arthur was my mother's child. He wanted to comfort the world.

Endy wore his dress blues to the funeral. The academy's uniforms were fair copies of real military dress, and he even had a medal or two, for sharpshooting and platoon leading. Firm angles of manhood were coming along in him, sharpening his chin and jaw and Adam's apple; even his hair, always exasperatingly untamed, was cropped into submission. But Mama wasn't fooled by any of it.

"Oh, Lord, Endy," she said, right after lunch and just before the funeral, just before Aunt Jew's teeth crisis. "Come here."

And right there in the parlor, in front of an army of Beckwiths—uncles and aunts and cousins, a judge and a doctor and an Air Force colonel, all darkly and sedately uniformed and Republican grim—Mama got a Kleenex out of her purse and gave it a motherly spit and attacked a smear of peanut butter on Endy's cheek.

"Gosh, Mama." He tried to pull back. "I can get it off myself."

But she had him in her grip, and she wouldn't let up until it was gone. Satisfied, she pulled him close and I heard her whisper, "You will always be my little boy, Endy. You're just gonna have to put up with it."

You put on a tie and a brave face, and you greet everyone. Then it's over. That's how the Beckwiths did funerals.

It wasn't over until the last of the relatives and distinguished guests left that night, through the last cup of coffee and the last piece of pie, one more cigarette, one final hug from the last sniffling aunt. It was like church all day and into the night.

Mama cleaned up a little and told Odessa to leave the dishes till tomorrow, and we went to bed.

The five of us children went up the stairs in a group. We didn't say anything. We went to our rooms and we closed our doors and that was it.

Endy got off his clothes and lumped them on the chair. When he was down to his underwear he got into the bed.

I turned off the last lamp and got into my bed. I was in my underwear, too, and with the wind through the windows it was like the old days, like a summer night.

I heard the back porch screen door pull closed. I got out of bed and went over to the window. Endy didn't stir.

I watched Granddaddy striding across the pebbled driveway, then on across the side yard and to the path in the trees to his house. The only thing I could see clearly was the spot of white that was his hair. He was still draped in the darkness of his suit.

Nothing had changed. Sunday evening after Al brought me home I heard Granddaddy talking on the phone to his friend at the newspaper, the publisher, and the next day there appeared no "Prominent man found shot" story on the front page. Just a regular obituary back in the back pages, William Arthur Beckwith, age forty-three, president of Beckwith Minerals; his school and the war and us; services, no cause, no reason. That's how Granddaddy wanted it. Clean.

And through the week he never cracked nor wavered. Granddaddy's handshake was as firm as always. Women touched him, touched his shoulder, wives of friends and daughters-in-law, tears in their eyes. He let them touch him and he moved on, to others, to handshakes, to whispered talk and coffee.

I watched him now as he walked. He didn't pause to look or wonder at the night.

I saw the lamp come on in his bedroom. I knew the routine. He would get into bed, reach over for his reading glasses and one of his ancient books, the solid thoughts of learned men of ages past. Eventually the light would go off and Granddaddy would enter the steel-vaulted night that he had prepared for himself, untouched, unchanged, secure.

I went back to bed. I already knew it was going to take a long time to get to sleep.

Endy came awake. It must have been about an hour.

"I wonder where Daddy is right now," he said. His voice was young and soft and far away. He was speaking toward the ceiling.

"I don't know, Endy."

"Do you think he can see us right now?"

"I don't know. Maybe."

"Remember how he'd come up the stairs and give us a good-night kiss?"

"Yeah."

"He always thought I was asleep, but I wasn't."

"I wasn't either."

"I thought I heard him on the stairs, Stephen. That's why I woke up."

"I don't think it was anything."

"But maybe it was. Maybe it was him coming up the stairs in my dreams."

"Yeah, in your dreams, maybe. And maybe he'll say goodnight in your dreams, too, Endy. Why don't you try to sleep?"

"Yeah."

With the great waves of March wind coming across the room, I remembered the ocean again, and that helped some. I remembered that big house at the forefront of the beach, and those nights, those windy island nights.

I turned toward Endicott, listening, waiting, and soon I heard the familiar slow, sweet rise and fall of breath from him.

I let the soft night come between us. I wish it could have stayed.

PART

Merry Christmas
1984

12

I REACHED INTO THE CABINET AND GRASPED THE TUMBLER, TURNING IT right-side up as I brought it out.

"Merry Christmas," the glass said gothically, in red, with sprigs of holly between the *Merry* and the *Christmas* and between the *Christmas* and the *Merry*. I set the glass on my palm and twirled it with my other hand. *Merry Christmas Merry Christmas Merry Christmas*. A Christmas merry-go-round. A festive touch.

It was July 26, 1984, another brain-baking Austin summer. I was thirty-six years old and I needed a little off-season cheer.

The tumbler was perfect, mostly because it was big. Big enough for six, seven cubes of ice. Big enough to make your hand stretch to get around it. And all that helped to cut down on the number of refills, which brought more cheer that much faster.

Fa la la la la.

La la.

La.

La.

The ice cubes went from a clink to a click as I dropped them into the glass. I piled them in, above the rim.

Pouring the stuff wasn't easy. The bottle had a glass-loop handle near the top I could reach two fingers into. Those gallon jugs were heavy, and this one was almost full. It took two hands, one to lift and one to guide.

I knew the right spot to pour to, just to the top of the *M* or the *C*, the capital letters. That was about three-fourths up, which might sound like a stiff drink, even when you topped it off with water, but really it wasn't. Not when you considered the ice.

The bourbon had teeth. The ice cracked and chattered when the alcohol hit it, and I liked the potent sound the two made. The ice slid down to a comfortable level that would be below my lips, providing more room for water, which was proper for the perfect bourbon and branch. No cheating, half and half. Simple mathematics.

I had come home from the newspaper a little after midnight—insert key in side door, turn, enter, turn, flip dead bolt—step by step, locking the world away. Let the dog in, go to the kitchen, a few more steps and—Merry Christmas.

It was Thursday, and although the night hadn't been awful, the week had been wearing. Ronnie and Fritz, Fritz and Ronnie. Election crap. But it was over for another week. My days off were Fridays and Saturdays. Hark the herald bourbon.

I brought the drink into the den, settled into our high-backed nest of a couch, slipped off my shoes, propped my feet on the coffee table, and reached over to give our border collie, Romeo, his expected ear-rub. I got out the cigarettes and put one to my lips. I flicked the lighter. The flame added to the circle of low light in the enormous room, flickering at the edges of the cave of darkness.

I pulled in, bending the flame toward me. The tobacco sizzled. The smoke curled down into me, moving across my word-burned brain like an April-wide cloud, bringing shaded comfort.

I liked the warming way the smoke went down, hot at first. Soon a glow began from deep inside. A radiance. With each puff the smoke came through and flowed out, and it was a lifting, a lightening.

Everything down to the capillaries was open and beating and cozy. It was as good as a wind coming through, the best of a day at the river.

I brought the stingingly cold tumbler toward my lips as slowly as I could, giving myself time to bring in the smell. The inhalation of the bourbon was as good as oxygen. The air of it was as enriched as its mahogany color, and that was the taste, too. It came in with a tinge, a bitter familiarity, hitting my empty stomach with a joyful splash.

A sip at a time my blood took it in, a chemical hug, pumping it up from my stomach in a rich red, sugared fountain. Up and through and up it went, trickling, finally, across the cracked crust of my desert self.

Third swallow, fourth swallow, dripping through the parched cells of my honeycombed brain, cooling them, engorging them, seeping into the deepest folds.

I was alive again. I could breathe.

I walked back to the couch with my second drink and settled into the routine: dog ears, cigarette, the bright cold refreshment. Everything was easier. The air inside had mellowed.

I was looking for the quiet. That's what I needed, and I went through my litany of places. Peace was in those places.

I remembered the big bedroom of my growing up and those wide-open windows and the night flowing through. I remembered the times on the porch of the cabin, the fallen night, all that soft darkness and the mumbling crickets down by the river and the way the water turned. If you listened carefully, you could hear the water brushing against the bank below, bending out.

This was the best part, the slow unfurling inside at the end of a long night of words. The clenched hours were behind me. The drought was over.

I was the flowering of a leaf, and then leaves, and the wind came fluttering through the branches of myself as I took in the liquid and blew out the smoke.

I let go, and I was a leaf on the wind, taken about, floating. I went back.

That first view of the Big House, just after turning off the farm-to-market road through the honeysuckled arch, was always spectacular. It stood proud and white and Thomas-Jefferson-solid at the far bend of the quarter-mile-long horseshoe driveway. On either side were rows of magnolias, which this day—the day I was bringing Liz home to meet the Beckwith clan for the first time—were dotted with bulges of white. The house was set back against the grove of pecan trees, which were just coming into leaf. A sweep of Bermuda in the middle of the horseshoe was greening and shiny, making a sort of reflecting pool.

We crackled across the gravel, down and down the driveway in the citrusy magnolia shade, in Liz's beaten-down '57 Ford Fairlane, which she affectionately called White Trash. I was driving.

"Holy shit, Stephen," she said, "you weren't exaggerating. It looks like the United God Damn States Supreme Court Building. Holy *shit*."

"Yeah, well, this is where Granddaddy laid down the law. Still does, too."

I turned the car into the parking area just off the end of the U and killed the engine. A wave of cold dread rose in me.

"Lizzie, I . . . I'm scared shitless."

"I wish . . . well, you know what I wish, Stephen. We talked about it enough. That you'd have at least written them."

"I know."

"Stephen, look, I know you're scared." Her fierce green eyes locked in on me, and I felt comfort there, a touch of solidarity from my fellow rebel. "I'm right here with you. It's going to be all right. They're your *family*, for God's sake. They're not going to hurt you."

I wished I could believe her. All I knew for sure was that I was almost twenty and I had given my life to her.

God, the distance—in time, in place. In one giant leap I had gone, at age seventeen, from the middle of Granddaddy's version of the Eighteenth Century to the frenzied forefront of the Twentieth. In fact, arriving at the University of Texas three years earlier—1966—I had immediately gravitated to the fringes of Austin's version of the avant-garde. Its leader was Leon Ross, a seventh-year philosophy major, an artist and son of prominent ranchers, black-headed and Rasputin-bearded and probably psychotic. He took me under his great, dark wing.

Leon called the mid-1960s the Second Great Ice Age. He believed society was frozen to the core by its bourgeois morality, and that the only way to freedom and joy was what he called the Great Thaw.

"Burn your bridges, burn everything!" he liked to say. "Break free!"

He said the world's only hope was to tear down Western civilization one psyche at a time, then build back something magnificent and free. To hell with picking it apart with tweezers, as in Freudian analysis. Leon believed in the wrecking-ball approach. His tool was a concoction he called Leon's One-Two Punch—One was vodka, Two was Everclear, and the rest, which wasn't much, was grapefruit juice with a touch of grenadine. He'd make up big batches before his Friday night, all-weekend bacchanals, which he called Freudian Flips. That's what you did after you had two or three punches—psychiatric acrobatics, except without nets, and with nobody to catch you because everybody else was already on their backs, breathless.

I loved the whole dark dive into this brave new world. People—most of them older than I—would sit in a circle in Leon's dim-lighted carpeted den, slinging around such names as Reich and Rilke and Rimbaud, Picasso and Klee and Sartre, accompanied by the high-wattage sound of Big Brother & the Holding Company. One of my fellow travelers was an "older" woman—all of nineteen then—with an Endy-colored Afro, a Kool-drenched voice, and a wet laugh. Her name was Liz.

Leon had three bedrooms in his once-elegant, lake-view, modern-sloping house, each with sheeted mattresses on the floor, candles in wine bottles to light the way, and piped-in music—Dylan and the Stones and the blues—that came in not through wires in each room, but hammered whole through the walls from huge speakers in the den.

All the walls in Leon's house overflowed with his psycho-body art—bespattered sheets tacked to the walls. Their markings were mostly boy stains, yellowish and vanilla, or the brown, periodic stains of girls. There was an occasional pink blob—somebody spilling his punch, his guts, both—or the burned holes made after a poorly rolled marijuana cigarette crumbled into bits of flame. One grouping—*Three Sheets to the Wind*—was a series containing evidence of a party that got out of hand. The last sheet on the right, in addition to the usual orgiastic traces, was torn and tear-stained and had an arrest warrant stapled to it.

"The Rorschach tests of life," Leon said. "See? If you look hard enough, you can see the deepest yearnings of humanity upon these sheets."

It was, to Leon, true life—the divine mess. Liz and I had left our mark.

We walked past the mounding bunches of pink-blooming azaleas and up the concrete steps onto the wide-boarded front porch between the two middle columns. The long length of plywood for Aunt Jew's wheelchair was at the side by the banister, and the wicker furniture was out.

As I opened the beveled front door and walked into the foyer, the first thing I saw was that creaking, clicking giant of a grandfather clock. A second, colder wave hit me. It said twenty minutes after two, GST—Granddaddy Standard Time.

I glanced across the foyer and into the dining room at the set table, shiny with silver.

"Oh shit," I said, and my voice, crimped in fear, reverted to an adolescent crackle.

Before Liz had time to say anything, Granddaddy appeared. With solid certainty and stern vigor, with steps as sure as a lesser man's stomps, he moved across the foyer with his hand held out to her.

"Welcome, my dear," he said, taking her hand gently as he turned to me with the old, familiar scorn and said, "You're late, boy." He turned back to the front parlor, where the others must have been waiting, and said, in the usual boom, "Somebody tell Odessa dinner's served!" All of that was one breath, one movement, and he bounded away toward the dining room. Liz was left with her hand still out and a dangling smile.

"That was Granddaddy," I said.

"I gathered," Liz replied.

She and I were immediately inundated. People came from three directions—the parlor, the back hall, and the kitchen via the dining room. My mother came first with Aunt Kitty, followed by John and Laura and Endicott (the latter two were home for spring break). Miss Godwin rolled in Aunt Jew from their rooms in the back of the house. Arthur, who had been helping out in the kitchen, came through the dining room with Odessa and Judge.

Hugs and handshakes came from all directions, too. Introductions and pleasantries were started and interrupted. Nervous jokes were tossed in. Usually dogs would have stirred through the forest of legs, but the Beckwiths were down to only one dog, Woody, who had been in the parlor and came wobbling up to me stilt-legged and squinty. I bent down to him for a furry, dry-nosed hug. It was my only calming moment.

"Let's eat!" Granddaddy announced from the dining room, and that was the end of the greeting period.

Over the last three years in college I had been coming home less and less. I stayed in Austin through summer terms, and was planning on doing so this summer, although it wasn't helping much to advance my progress toward a degree.

I was branching out hopelessly toward a Bachelor's of Electives. Astronomy, Russian history, geology—I loved it all. Granddaddy didn't seem to mind much. He liked the idea of a broad education; it fit his ideal of the well-rounded gentleman. Once or twice he suggested I try some business courses, and I quietly refused. I knew what he was planning for his Assistant Patriarch. No way was I going to take my father's place in the giant, cold shadow of my grandfather.

I found I could stay away without much homesickness, as long as my mother's letters kept coming. Every two weeks or so she'd send a chatty newsletter of family events. Endicott and Laura got copies, but Mama always added a personal note to each of us.

Laura was at Rice University, majoring in biology and planning on medical school. Endy had gone from military school to the Air Force Academy in Colorado. John was in high school, Mister Everything, dating every weekend, playing the guitar, and dreaming of a life as a surfer. Arthur was in sixth grade, shy and sweet and helpful.

My mother was working harder than ever. Odessa was becoming increasingly decrepit like most of the rest of the household, but she wanted to keep working so my mother did her best to help Odessa keep her dignity. Besides taking over most of the paperwork my father had done for Granddaddy in the oil business, my mother worked alongside Odessa, cleaning half the house and cooking half the meals.

Miss Godwin couldn't help much, since Aunt Jew was demanding more of her time. My great-aunt was ensconced in a previous era most of the time, still smoking and drinking and occasionally sending for her squirrel rifle, which was safely hidden in the basement. Aunt Kitty puttered along, crocheting potholders and watching westerns and swatting dead flies. (With two boys remaining in the house, the tradition continued.)

My letters home tended toward the philosophical and political. I was stretching, testing, rebelling—enraging Granddaddy at every turn. I announced my opposition to the war in Vietnam, a newfound agnosticism, a Buddhist bent.

Granddaddy would fire back with his brittle, condescending wit in a fountain-penned scrawl on the back of a corporate letter to shareholders, quoting from Montaigne or Dr. Johnson or Sir Thomas Browne, maybe enclosing a clipping or a cartoon from the *Wall Street Journal*. Sometimes he could be surprising.

> *Stephen: Enclosed please find a check for $50.00, payable to you, outside of your monthly stipend. No reason. Think of it as a St. Swithin's Day gift.*
>
> *I have no doubt that you can find a use for it; something prodigal, I imagine. I have never doubted your prodigality. It runs in the family, unfortunately, showing itself in the Beckwith males at around sixteen and oftentimes not running out until the late thirties or thereabouts.*
>
> *Yours, Granddaddy*

He had no idea how prodigal I had been. He was about to find out. I was praying for courage.

Tradition's iron grip on the family had not loosened. Granddaddy saw to that.

After delivering his usual commanding blessing, he went to work on a brown and glistening side of roast beef, using the familiar sword-size sterling knife. The slabs of meat were forked over to the passing plates, and the steaming vegetables were spooned on as the plates circled the table. Butter-crusted rolls were sent around in cloth-covered baskets. Small plates of sliced tomatoes were at each place. There followed a low murmur of conversation amid a period of serious eating. Odessa passed in and out with resupplies.

Everybody was trying not to watch Aunt Jew's tremored eating, but we couldn't help ourselves, just as you can't pass a car crash without ogling. Soon there accumulated on the table in front of her a pool of gravy and iced tea, a pileup of beef and beans and corn. Then came a small avalanche of peas rolling down her bib and across the tablecloth in all directions, like little hubcaps, followed by Aunt Jew's quivering lament: "God *dammit.*"

Granddaddy broke in, hoping to divert attention from the disaster at hand.

"So tell me, Elizabeth," he said with that sharp little downturn in his thin lips that always signaled a slice of wit, "I've lately been thinking Stephen looked something like a cross between Lassie and Isaiah. What do you think?"

My hair was collar-long and heaped about, ringleted and redder than ever—it seemed to get redder the longer it got. My beard still struggled for thickness. It had a boy's silkiness and scraggliness, but it was enough to be a sure aggravation to Granddaddy. In a one of his letters to me he'd referred to hippies as "odd birds, red-knotted whippersnappers, and not near rare enough as far as I'm concerned." He was referring both to the hue of my hair and to my political leanings.

The comment caused more than the usual titter. Endicott, Republican-shorn and Republican-straight, thought it was hilarious and not only snickered effusively but threw in a couple of Lassie-like barks. My mother smiled. Aunt Jew didn't hear Granddaddy's remark. Miss Godwin didn't understand it. Aunt Kitty laughed blankly, in a genial show of support.

My mother tried to move the conversation along. "So tell us about law school, Liz," she said.

"You sued anybody yet?" John asked.

"We need more women lawyers," Laura said. "Heck, we need more women *everything*." Granddaddy uncharacteristically let this comment pass.

I had told them only a few things about her in my letters—that she was a second-year law student, that we were dating each other, that I was quite fond of her, and that I wanted to bring her home to meet them, a sure sign of a serious relationship. Liz had toned down her appearance considerably since we'd first met, probably as a byproduct of law school. The electrified Jimi hair had calmed down to easy, left-leaning waves.

Voices were coming from all sides, and Liz, after waiting through each one, turned back to the original, to my mother. "Well, Mrs. Beckwith, I've . . . "

"Mama, Granddaddy . . . " I jumped in. I put my hand out, on hers, to apologize for interrupting and tacitly to ask for reassurance. "I wanted to tell you all . . . Liz and I have some news."

You could have heard a pea drop. One did, in fact, from Aunt Jew's fork. It rolled off the table.

"I . . . Liz and I got married."

Everyone halted in midbite. Odessa, standing beside me and about to set a new basket of rolls on the table, froze. There was not a word from anyone, hardly a breath.

I stammered onward, into the breach. "Last weekend. The justice of the peace. It just seemed like a good idea. We . . . "

"You're nineteen years old, for God sakes," my mother said.

"Almost twenty, Mama," I said. "And Liz's almost twenty-two, if that helps."

"Well . . ."

"I just want to know one thing," Granddaddy said. He spoke up sternly, clearly, pushing my wavering voice out of the way.

We waited, suspended, as Granddaddy gathered gravity in the pause. He set his fork down, his knife, and leaned out and almost over me. His eyes narrowed and darkened. "So when can we expect the baby?" The sarcasm curled from his words like a stench of smoke.

"Granddaddy, no. That's not true." He had left me with hardly any breath at all, but I tried. "We just love each other and we . . ."

"Granddaddy, how dare you!"

It was my mother, of all people. My sweet mother. With anger and conviction, bayonet-sharp, she marched forward, defending us. I watched the old man's jaw loosen and drop.

"How dare you say such an awful thing," she continued, "so personal, so cruel, so terribly, terribly rude. I am ashamed of you! ASHAMED!" Tears and redness rose in her voice, which she flung at him, phrase after rising phrase, and all the familiar sweetness of her presence was subsumed.

Now Granddaddy stood up and back from the rising force of it, speechless and, yes, perhaps, ashamed.

He didn't look at us. He didn't excuse himself. He simply stood and turned and stalked off. All forks and words and breaths were silent as Granddaddy's footsteps retreated into the kitchen and away.

13

I PICKED UP THE TUMBLER, BREAKING MY REVERIE. THE DRINK WAS gone out of it already, the second time, and a rattling of ice was left, half a glass.

I used to finish a drink at about the same time as the ice disappeared; I'd take it down to emptiness just as the cold was going out of it. But not this time. Not the first drink, either.

It had been that way lately, the last few weeks. It was getting worse.

But the week had been a bad one. I needed a knock-out punch, a quick end to it, a clear dividing line, and then the weekend.

A weekend of uncomfortable silence from her, of crap.

Maybe I should stop for a minute. One cigarette, at least, and let it settle. Let my thoughts settle. Breathe a little. Slow it down. Slow, now. Steady. Steady.

Still, I wanted to keep holding the glass. I liked the cold of it, the weight of it, the feeling there was something there, waiting for me. The ice would melt and I would take sips. Always a little of the bourbon was absorbed by the ice, and then the ice would release a hint of the prize.

I started a cigarette and kept hold of the glass. That's what I needed. That sliding, slowing, into the breathable past.

● ● ●

"We're in love," I told my mother in the parlor, after dinner.

"That's the *only* reason we got married," Liz said. "We wanted to be together. I'm not pregnant."

Mama leaned out from her wingchair, looking with care at each of us. "You took my breath away, Stephen. I'm sorry, really truly sorry, that you kept this a secret and didn't at least tell me what you were planning, but I suppose I can understand, considering how Granddaddy handles things.

"Anyway, I want the best for you both. You need to know that."

"Thank you, Mrs. Beckwith," Liz said, and they touched, hand to hand, with an exchange of little squeezes.

The three of us had some private time from the rest of the family after Sunday Dinner. Others were napping, some were reading. Granddaddy was in hiding.

Mama leaned back, smiled broadly, and said, "I think you better call me Ellen, Liz honey. We're gonna need to be on a first-name basis, what with all we've got ahead of us."

"Sure," Liz said.

Mama reached over for her cigarettes. Liz and I were smoking, too.

Mama smiled. "Well, for better and for worse, you've married this family, too, honey—lock, stock, and crazy aunt—and Granddaddy, too. You're a Beckwith now, Liz, and all I can say is God help you."

My mother was coming into her own. Slowly, slowly, brick by brick and aunt by aunt, she was digging her way out from under an avalanche of Beckwiths—which included hundreds of years of history and ten bedrooms to clean and fifty acres to care for and two hundred oil wells to oversee. Although the red glint in her curls was dulling to gray, the sharp line in her jaw had filled in, and the puffs under her eyes had darkened and sagged, a quiet strength was building in her.

But now her confidence was retreating. She told us she was worried about starting some kind of war with Granddaddy. She was sorry about the public display of it all.

"It's all right, Ellen," Liz said. "I really think it'll be all right."

"I don't know," Mama said. "You don't know Granddaddy. He can hold a grudge till kingdom come."

"I was proud of you, Mama," I said. "Not many people can stand up to Granddaddy. Daddy never did."

She didn't seem to hear me. She was locked into her train of thought.

• • •

"Granddaddy had no right. No matter what the truth was, he had no right to ask something like that. You two are adults. It was a major invasion of privacy."

"Yes," Liz said.

"But I'm glad y'all aren't pregnant. It's too early. You need to get to know each other first."

Mama turned to me. "Your father and I never did—get to know each other, I mean. Not really. Almost as soon as we married, we started having babies. I became so terribly busy. And then one day I looked up and he was gone. He was a stranger. He never came back."

Later that night we were at a pizza place in Fort Worth—Liz, Endy, Laura, and I. We needed to get away from the Big House. After that conversation with my mother, the four of us had escaped.

"God, Laura, I can't believe it," Endicott said. "Do you have any idea how it happened? Travis was drafted, right?"

"Whyvonne said it was a land mine," Laura said. "She didn't know where or how. Just a land mine."

A swell of tears came up in me, and a glance of memory with them. I saw that old station wagon puttering down our long driveway, away, Travis with his head on his arms and Woody running after them. They were going to the Promised Land.

"God, I wish we could have known about this," I said. "We could have done something, sent flowers, even gone out there."

"I just got the letter yesterday," Laura said. "The funeral was a month ago. I haven't had the heart to tell Mama yet. Then we'll have to tell Odessa. She's gonna be so upset. She loved that boy."

"Damn," I said. "I'll write Ethylene."

"Those bastards," Endy said. "Those gook bastards."

"You don't think our government might have had something to do with his death?" Liz asked in a prosecutorial tone.

"And what about the guys who set the trap and buried it in the jungle?" Endy asked.

"Just defending their homeland," Laura said.

"Policy goons in Washington," Liz said. "That's who's to blame."

I was pouring more beer from the pitcher. I hated the war as much as anybody, but I couldn't stand any more fighting, this war on the home front, all of it.

"How often does Whyvonne write you?" I asked Laura. She was looking as weary as the rest of us—all but Endy. We were buried so deeply in our studies. Laura had an extra layer of darkness under her eyes from all those hours peering into a microscope.

"Every few months. And guess what else."

"What?" Liz asked. She knew all about these people, from the stories I'd been telling her for the last two years.

"Baby Midland. She's had a baby herself."

"Laura," I said, "how could . . ."

"Twelve years old."

"WHAT?"

"Twelve. Yeah. Almost thirteen. Some older kid in the neighborhood, might as well have been rape. And they're keeping the baby and Whyvonne said Ethylene's gonna help raise him. You know she's taking in all those other kids, running some kind of little day-care center in her apartment in Watts. Whyvonne said one more wouldn't make much difference. Anyway, Mid's dropped out of school."

"Dammit," I said. "Is Whyvonne at least doing okay?"

"She's fine. Working full time at a bookstore, keeping up at UCLA. She wants to get into coaching sports, maybe track."

"Perfect," I said. "Bet she can still shut you down, Endy."

The pizza arrived, and he went diving for it. He was that same starving kid he'd always been, always the first to reach for the cornbread or a second piece of Odessa's pecan pie.

"Maybe," he said. He turned to Laura. "Tell her I've been in training, mountain climbing, through the mud. Tell her I'm ready for her," he said, chewing. "Grudge match."

"Yeah, I'll tell her."

That night Liz and I moved Endicott's bed across the room next to mine, turning the two singles into a double—Endy was spending the night with a friend.

Liz went on a museum tour of my room, looking for the pieces of me that remained. She cackled as she took each taxidermied specimen from the shelves.

"Oh my God, Stephen, what the hell happened to this one? And this?"

She asked about the squirrel, the duck, the frogs playing poker—Ludwig, Lucky, the Bobbsey Brothers. There had been deterioration over the years—mildew and mold and moths, and some kind of small mealy bugs. One withered webbed foot fell off Lucky when Liz picked her up.

Then she saw Bess, the possum. Liz reached for her, holding her at arm's length—then knotted up with laughter. She leaned back against my desk, her free hand pushing at her tears. Piqued, I reached down and put Bess back on the shelf, waiting for Liz's laughter to subside.

"Taxidermy is an art," I said. "It's not that easy."

Liz had collected herself. "It's an art, I'm afraid, that has eluded you."

She already sounded like a God damn lawyer. "Screw you," I said. "I suffered over that possum and I don't care what you say. I'm proud of her."

She came over to me. She guided me over to my bed, and we sat.

"I love you, Stephen," she said. She reached over and smoothed my eyebrows with a finger, trying to take away the frown. It was working.

"I think Bess is lovely," she said. "She belongs in the Louvre. Really. I'm surprised they haven't called."

I was smiling. We leaned back together on the bed.

"I love you, Stephen Beckwith."

The next day, on our way to Jacksboro to visit Liz's parents, I drove out of our way to show her the Brazos. I was ready to show her—I thought I was—but when we got close everything went cold in me.

"There," I said. I slowed the car. Nobody was behind us. "The turnoff. The cabin."

"Can we . . ."

"No," I said. I was surprised at how firm my resolve was, how suddenly it came up. "I haven't been back and I don't want to go back." Liz didn't push it.

"Over there's the road to Bert's."

I turned back. No, I wasn't ready, not anywhere near ready. I wanted the memories to stay where they were.

The main thing was Dorthy's. I wanted Liz to meet her. Mama had talked to her a couple of times since Daddy died, and I had talked to her once from Austin when I heard about Miz Abernathy.

There was only one pickup in the front of Sportsman's Inn, and it looked like Bert's. It was lunchtime and there should have been more customers. It looked seedier, dustier, more forlorn than usual.

But the 's hadn't given up. It sputtered still. Liz and I walked up the steps together, and I stepped forward and shoved my way in.

It was echo-empty inside. No music, no shuffling shuffleboard, no low talk or smoke or clinking beer bottles or frying.

"DORTHY?"

I heard some rustling in the back, deep into the kitchen. "Be with ya in a minute!"

Footsteps. The kitchen door swung open. And she froze, staring at me with her big arms folded under her copious bosoms.

"Sorry. We don't serve hippies in here," she said.

"Dorthy? It's me, Stephen."

Her worn face bunched up into a smile. "Stevie? That you? My favorite little sumbidge?"

She was tromping over to me as she said it, and a tear had time to get started in one eye by the time she got to me and took my breath away in one of her man-handling hugs. "What's that hair all over your face? You little sumbidge, God it's good to see ya!"

As soon as I could get enough breath back, I said, "Dorthy, this is Liz. My wife."

"Holy shit, you're married?" She turned toward Liz. "Welcome to the family, honey."

I smiled at Liz and she smiled back weakly as she fell under that avalanche of Dorthy's hug. "You got yourself a good boy there, Liz."

"I know it," she said. She was released. "Get him to a barbershop and you'll have yourself a prize." Liz just smiled. "Y'all hungry? 'Course you are! Come on back to the kitchen."

We followed her through the swinging door. "Where's everybody?" I asked.

"Guess you hadn't heard," she said. "I had to close down for a week. Crime scene and all. You know, like on *Dragnet*."

"What?"

"Cheeseburgers all right? That's all I got. Run out of chicken-frieds."

"Sure."

She switched on the griddle, got some beef patties out of the big refrigerator, and then went to the cooler to get us each a Lone Star.

"Yeah, right in the middle of my God damn floor. Roy was sittin' at that middle table out yonder—yeah, cattin' around, as if it was a secret—I don't even remember with who—some young thing from up around Olney—and Shirleen—that's his wife—walks in, pulls a .38 out of her purse, and empties it in his gut—BANG! BANG! BANG! She says to Miss Suzie Q, 'You little bitch, I'd shoot you too but I'm plumb out of bullets'—and she throws the gun at her and hot-foots it home to their trailer."

"Damn," I said.

"Blood all over the place, Stevie. It was a mess. I figured I oughta close down for a few days anyway—crime scene or not—sort of as a memorial—plus I needed some time to get that blood cleaned up—took a shitload of elbow grease, I'm tellin' ya. And it hadn't been hardly a month since Miz Abernathy croaked—fell out right there where you're sittin', Liz honey—right by the stove, gin in her hand like always—just fell out. So I had Dwane come out here and do the funeral—it was quieter than Bert's, not near the dogs and dynamite and all—and then I had to turn around and get Dwane out here again to get Roy planted. You know Dale had moved to Abilene, cattin' around himself, left Billie Faye for some stray, so we tried to track him down but couldn't. Anyway, it's been one damn funeral after another around here.

"Can you hand me a couple of those potatoes, honey?" she asked Liz. "Behind ya there, under the counter. So anyway, Dwane's finally gettin' pretty good at drivin' that big old hearse."

Liz had worked hard to prepare the way for me with her family. She had talked to them about me, about how I made her feel cherished, and she'd broken the news that we were married.

"That's the main thing, honey," her daddy had said, "that he's good to you. Otherwise I'd have to kill the little bastard."

The Flanagans were solid, work-weathered ranchers. They were Irish Texans like my mother's family, but the redness in them had been bronzed. A lifetime of wind had washed away all false pretenses; their words went straight, their laughter came easily, and, day or night, you could count on finding a good piece of pie in the kitchen. Nobody went hungry or unloved.

We arrived in time for supper. It was a democratic, maid-free situation. Mama cooked, the boys set the table, nobody presided, and the kids took turns with the blessing. Same with the dishes: the boys did them, and Daddy was one of the boys.

Liz called her brothers Billy Fred, Willy Ed, and Silly Ted. Bill was seventeen, Ed was fifteen, and Teddy was eleven. I could see sunny Endicott in them, and maybe they could see something worthy in me, a guy too small to be much good with ranching chores and pasty from too much reading, but okay anyway. If their sister liked me, that was good enough for them. And her parents, knowing their daughter and her strange ways, were probably grateful I wasn't a one-eyed Muslim vegetarian. At least I wasn't a Yankee.

"Hell, I remember Liz's first county fair," her daddy said as he reached for another biscuit to sop up his homemade beef stew. "She was nine years old. Everybody else picked a rabbit or a pig or something to show. Lizzie wanted to show a llama."

"Where'd you find one?" I asked.

"Hank found a guy with some in the Hill Country," her mother said. "Cutest, woolliest little things."

"I named my llama Ding-Dong," Liz said.

"Named her after that song," said Bill.

"What song?" I asked.

"You know, llama-llama-ding-dong," Liz said. "Or at least that's what I thought they were singing."

"Won a blue ribbon," her daddy said. "Best of Show. It's been more than ten years now. Our little llama lady has grown up."

"Please pass the potatoes."

"And the biscuits?"

"Whatever happened to that llama?" I asked.

"Sold it to a neighbor," her daddy said. "The guy's got a herd of 'em now. He makes pretty good money with 'em."

"Liz started a trend," her mama said.

"Damnedest thing you ever saw," her father said.

Liz and I stayed up with the Flanagans out on the front porch, all except the oldest brother, Bill, who took off in his pickup to do homework with his girlfriend. Liz and her father and I smoked, and the four of us had several beers.

We talked about law school and my plans and my family. Her father said he wanted to meet my grandfather—he had heard of him; Granddaddy was a presence in the oil business just as he was a presence wherever he went, and Liz's father wanted to talk about rumors of leasing and drilling in the area. I knew just enough about farming and cattle to ask a few good questions, and such talk continued, pleasant as the breeze. After a round of good nights, Liz and I went to her room.

Her bedroom was a portrait of her growing-up years, the way mine was. On her bureau she had several rag dolls and baby dolls, but her favorite was a Dale Evans doll. On top of the dollhouse was a baseball glove. Next to the cheerleader pompon was a football helmet with LIZ hand-lettered on the side. The closet had petticoats, a bridle, and a fishing pole. In the bookshelves *Winnie the Pooh* jostled *Waiting for Godot*.

We got ready for bed. We were up late, past the brothers, and took our baths after them.

I was in the daintily embroidered double bed, waiting for her, when she came in. Only the lamp was on, and it was low. She was in a pair of her old shortie pajamas, which she must have gotten from the bottom of the drawer, a leftover from her slumber party days. She slipped into bed beside me.

"Tell me a story, Stephen."

"Sure."

I smiled. I remembered. Stories were the story of our love.

After a steady period of almost-weekly psych parties, Liz and I had slowly separated ourselves from Leon. We'd meet at the school cafeteria or the library and talk about our lives and our dreams.

She loved the stories of my family. We spent hours looking at the Beckwith clan as if it were a Russian novel, sprawled out over a serf-ridden estate. We'd take it a piece at a time—a brother, an aunt, my father, or grandfather—and I'd tell her a story about them. Or I'd guide her on a tour through the Big House, and I'd tell her stories room by room, from fluted column to column—with Granddaddy, always Granddaddy, as the central, unbending beam that held the whole thing up.

She was enthralled. It was a refreshing change from the gray bulges of words in her law books and from the interminable philosophical rants from Leon and his friends. She couldn't get enough of my stories and was always making time for me in her cramped schedule.

Then one evening we were at her kitchen table in her ratty little hippie house in Austin, drinking coffee, and she got up from her place and came over to me.

"Tell me a story, Stephen." She touched my shoulder and then my hair. She let her hands go into my wayward curls and across one ear.

"All right," I said.

I had loved her deeply but from a silent distance ever since those first entangled nights on Leon's mattresses, marooned as I was in my shyness yet encouraged by Leon's punch. I loved her bold laughter and incisive opinions and radical smile.

"Let's see," I continued, "once upon a time . . ."

"Wait a minute, Stephen. You can't tell a good bedtime story unless you're in bed."

"Okay."

I stood and followed her, the ragged young Russian prince with the Dostoyevski droop in his eyes. Everything, suddenly, was changing. She wanted me, the real me.

She took my hand. I let her lead the way into her little bedroom. Bob Dylan was revisiting Highway 61 on her scratchy stereo and evening was falling and a candle was the only light, wavering like Dylan's voice.

Liz reached for me. She pulled me down to the bed.

"Stephen," she said, pulling me in. "Stephen." And I went and I was whole.

That night and more nights, day after night, I told her a story and more stories, and she pulled me into her and into life, and then a year later I said what about being part of my story forever and she said yes. "We'll start our own story," she said.

We went down to the courthouse and got a license and here we were.

"Stephen? The story you promised?"

My mind came back to her, to the ranch-house bedroom, and I scooted in closer and put my arms around her.

"Oh yeah. Let's see. Once upon a time?"

"That's the one."

She turned off the lamp and the moon came in, shy and pale.

"Once upon a time there were seven children, two dogs, a very scared possum, and an aunt with a loaded gun . . ."

"Stephen," she interrupted, "there's something you need to know."

"What's that?"

She touched my forehead with her hand. "I love being part of your story."

14

I STOOD AT THE SINK. ICE, BOURBON, WATER. I DIDN'T HAVE TO THINK about the process, but it was involving enough to interrupt my memories. That was okay.

I had smoothed out, gone fluid. Two drinks did that. The anticipation, the edge, was gone. Now it was just a matter of dealing with the liquids, getting them together and making drink No. 3. Sliding, gliding, free.

Not enough ice? No problem. I could have gotten out another tray but what was the point? Next time I'd crack open a new tray.

So half a glass of ice. Then bourbon. Oops. Too much. Way up over the big letters.

You can't really pour it back into the bottle. Spilling and all. So just live with it. Drink it down some. Come back in later and get more ice before the drink is half gone. More water. That's what you need. Just drink it down a little first.

Now there wasn't much room for water. Just a tad. I was careful to get just enough.

The ice in the drink was melting fast. It didn't have a chance. All that hard liquid pouring down on it, crackling, huddling down into the glass, and the result was a drink as brown as dirt this time, hard as rust. Before I could get the drink to the couch the ice was just a drift of slivers on top of the dark water.

And burning fast. Hardly enough to cool things. I'd have to go ahead and drink this one down, hurry up and get it to half at least so I could go back and get more ice.

Maybe no more water. If I got enough ice on the next trip to the kitchen, that would take care of it. Yeah, that would take care of it.

Liz and I got out of college at the same time. That would have been '71. She got her law degree and I got one in journalism. She got her two degrees in seven years and I got my bachelor's in five.

Life was good. We moved to a little rock house in a tree-dense neighborhood in south Austin. I went to work as a reporter for the *Austin Alternative*, the smaller of the two newspapers in town, the one most likely to tell the truth. Liz started as a staff attorney for the Department of Housing and Urban Development, working to break down barriers for the poor and the wrong-colored. Neither of us made much money. We didn't care. What we cared about was the Truth. We were on a mission.

We lived in the shadow of Texas's Capitol of Ignorance, which attracted all variety of wheeler-dealer blowhards when the yahoos of the Texas legislature met every two years. Truth was not listed in their lexicon of values.

"Let's see," somebody said at a party once, "if the legislature meets every two years for six months, and pushes the state back ten years deeper into the Dark Ages each time, by the time we retire Texas'll be back in the Stone Age."

"Not if I can help it," Liz said.

"Nor I," I said.

"I think we're already there," said my boss, Langdon Stenson.

I covered the legislature, and when that wasn't in session, the city council, the school board, this committee, and that commission. If nobody had gathered, I might take a run by the cop shop to check for bloodshed, and if I came up empty there, I'd drive back to the office and knock out a few obits. If we were short on reporters, and we always were, I might cover a concert or a movie and review a restaurant on the way.

Liz, besides working overtime to help her understaffed law office, did pro bono work with neighborhood activist groups on weekends and evenings.

A Dairy Queen anchored the end of our block, fronting the main drag of Lamar Boulevard, and we were regulars. I'd walk there late in the evening and bring food home. We'd eat, watching the ten o'clock news. We'd pour bourbon into our half-full cups of Dr Pepper or root beer, knock it back, and finally call it a night somewhere in the middle of *The Tonight Show*. The next day, we'd do it all over again.

Granddaddy was relieved to see us out of school and working. Not only was he glad to see the tuition bills stop and our income begin, but he told me he was afraid if I had stayed in school one more minute, I would have gotten so liberal that my bleeding heart would have burst like an overripe pumpkin.

You wouldn't want to call it softening, but I could see evidence of Granddaddy trying to make up for that unseemly Sunday Dinner. As we returned for visits in months following, he increasingly appeared to enjoy Liz's company. They'd trade wit the way circus performers toss knives, slicing the air with stringent remarks about history, philosophy, Richard Nixon, and the media.

A year after that infamous dinner, he sent us a letter belatedly congratulating us on our marriage and ending it thus:

> *As for a wedding gift, I admit to knowing little about china patterns or silverware (except that good food tastes just as good on the cheap stuff), but I do know what works otherwise. I do know what young people need, which is the same as what old people need. See enclosed.*
> *Enjoy it. Blow it.*
>
> > Lovingly,
> > Granddaddy

It was a check for one thousand dollars. This was the early 1970s, and it was a fortune.

We followed his advice. A year after our careers began, we took a delayed honeymoon in Hawaii that included a seventy-two-hour drunken private luau in our hotel room in which I ended up wearing a grass skirt and nothing else. I swayed my hips for her, and Liz was delighted with what came peeking through the shrubbery. She pounced.

• • •

Back to work. Year two. Year three.

Our hard-driving weekends were the only interruption in this blur of burgers and work. Newspaper people. Lawyers. Somebody's house. A bar after work. Chips and dip from the grocery store. Peanuts in a bowl. Bourbon. Gin. Ashtrays. Shop talk. Shop talk. Shop talk. Until the world went blank.

Then Monday, and we churned it out all over again.

Liz and I talked a lot about time, or the lack of it. Every Monday morning began at the kitchen table with opened pocket calendars, searching for an hour we might share—lunch maybe? an evening out?

Not often.

A scandal, a new apartment development. Charges, lawsuits. A legislator caught with his pants down at the YMCA boys' camp. Another HUD housing grant going to a sleazy builder. I covered it, she sued hell out of 'em.

By the end of our third year in the real word, Liz was chief litigator and I was assistant managing editor for news. We were exhausted.

Langdon Stenson, executive editor of the *Austin Alternative*, walked into my shabby cubicle of an office. He flopped into the chair across from me and propped his feet on my desk, shuffling some papers around with his scuffed loafers to make a bare spot. He lounged back into his usual position, with his hands behind his head, and I was expecting the usual—a complaint about his golf score, a second-guess about a story, a headline that wasn't quite right.

Langdon was a grumpy, rumpled, brown-haired bear, a literary linebacker gone to seed, six and a half feet and two hundred and fifty pounds of rough-and-tumble ability to take on the powers that be—in a rotunda or a courtroom or in the advertising offices upstairs. He was a West Texas farm boy who could talk the talk and walk the amble, and all those good-old-boy politicians and deal makers were taken in. He came at them with a spillover gut and a tie that had never been tightened and that showed a pretty good selection of most of the menu items of every roadside barbecue joint between Austin and San Angelo. He'd seduce them with an Aggie joke or speculation on who was going to be the next state football champs among such titans as the Dime Box Diamondbacks or the

Tomball Turkeys. They were charmed, at least until the truth of the story he managed to wrest from them came out all over the front pages of the *Alternative*.

I didn't see anything ominous in the boss's crumpled forehead and worried eyes. It was a newsman's usual visage.

"Hey, kid, bad news," Langdon said.

"Yeah? Another off-day on the links? Gonna blame that bad shoulder of yours again?"

Langdon always called me "kid," which, in a way, I still was—boy genius at twenty-six, youngest assistant managing editor the *Alternative* ever had—although the boy in me was wearing down fast. And so, in fact, was the genius. I hadn't had a fresh idea in months. But I loved my job and felt propelled, like I could go on forever, weary or not.

Here came the wall. It was 1974.

"Listen, kid—seriously. We're outta here," Langdon said.

"Huh?"

"Closed. Finished. Kaput. Screwed."

"What?"

"That rumor about the paper being for sale—yeah, turns out it was true," Langdon said. "But our esteemed owner couldn't find anybody who wanted to lose money like he was. Then when the Puckett lawsuit deal came along, the red-ink bleeding really got going—red-ink arterial bleeding, you might call it—so they decided to pull the plug. Bankruptcy."

I was stunned.

"Get Jack in my office," Langdon continued, bringing his feet down and sitting up. "He can do the story. It'll be the lead for today, of course. I've got a statement from the publisher and the owner.

"Let's go ahead and get a staff meeting together. Get Sherry to call as many folks as she can, at home, in the bars, wherever. Get 'em in here. Staff meeting at two this afternoon. Last paychecks will be ready for everybody then—everybody gets a couple of weeks' severance. And that's it."

I stood as Langdon got ready to leave. "Look at the bright side, kid. We don't have to come up with a lead story for Sunday."

I followed him out of the office. "And one more thing. That royal asshole publisher of ours is sending a bunch of security guards up here to 'supervise' the move. In other words, they don't want anybody stealing any pencils or typewriters or anything. They're gonna sell all this stuff at auction."

As he was walking away, he looked back over his shoulder at me. "What a load of crap."

Langdon dropped the bomb at noon, and by the time Liz got home that evening I was well on my way to being bombed myself. I was down to my third martini—I'd stopped for a bottle of Tanqueray on my way home. I wanted something special. Celebration, you know.

We'd drunk up all the bourbon in my desk right after the staff meeting. Everybody was drinking openly in the newsroom among that sea of typewriters and ashtrays and crumpled paper and coffee-stained carpet, crying, toasting, sloshing, loading up their plaques and pictures in cardboard boxes thoughtfully provided by management.

Sitting on the couch and waiting for Liz to come home, I kept going over and over it, what went wrong, where I was to blame.

That God damn Puckett. I told him. How many times did I tell him? I told him to watch out for that guy, that lobbyist guy, whatsizname, Albert, Albertson. Don't trust that guy, I said.

That's the first thing you learn as a reporter. It's a game; every story is a negotiation. Nobody gives you something for nothing. They want to manipulate you, and that's fine, as long as you understand the game and know it's your objective to get something back from them. The truth. The story.

What did you get from this guy, Puckett? All you got was his line of bullshit. He got what he wanted, but what did you get? You got a line of crap. You got just one angle on the story, Albertson's angle, not enough. Hell, this newspaper might as well save some money, just run press releases, cut out the middleman, and guess who that is, Puckett? That's *you.*

That's when the paper got sued. Puckett was right in the middle of it. And so was I.

This Albertson, this slimeball, was making charges about kickbacks to the purchasing agent for the schools, and I said Puckett, are you sure? Albertson has no ax to grind? He just wants *the* truth to come out? And you've checked all kinds of sources and seen the paperwork and you're sure and you want us to go with this story?

I wanted to go with it. I can't deny that. This thing was big—not just the schools, but the state was involved, the state education agency and a couple of legislators and maybe even the governor. We got the lead spot on the six o'clock news: "The *Austin Alternative* reported today that . . ."

I even thought we had a chance—a bare chance, but still a chance—for a Pulitzer.

Poof.

Charges unfounded. Paperwork forged. Albertson was the guy we should have nailed, and we did, but a little late. So Tate from the schools filed suit against us and that afternoon the newspaper's lawyer calls us into a meeting—the publisher and everybody was there—and he began: "Look, guys, I don't know for sure yet, I gotta study some more stuff, but I think we're up shit creek here."

Liz got home from work and joined me in my misery. I fixed her a martini, and we drank to the *Alternative*; to truth, justice, and the American way; to existentialism; to unemployment insurance.

Liz loved the paper and all its characters. She wanted to know how everybody had reacted and wondered how they would handle it financially and said, "Don't worry, Stephen, as long as I've got a job we won't starve."

I got smashed. Liz got semi-smashed. She made it to bed. I passed out on the couch.

The next day I had some friends over from work and we hashed it out all over again. Went over all the rumors and tried to pull them into a coherent whole. Shit, why didn't we see such-and-such? Those Gucci guys in the publisher's office. Remember? A week ago, wasn't it?

We watched the television news. By Day Two we were the third item on the ten o'clock news—one more Watergate casualty, five hundred more in Vietnam—and they went with the "impact" angle: What would a political town like Austin be like with only one major daily?

We reread the stories in the Other Paper, which had a straight-news treatment, ho-hum, plus a feature on the sad good-byes of the workers. How magnanimous of them. We made fun of their typos. I passed out again.

Next night, another cry-in-our-beer party. This one at Langdon's. We cried in our margaritas. Liz had to wrestle the keys from me in order to drive us home. She was pissed.

The next night and the next, more of the same, at home, with friends. Liz had to go to work, but I didn't. She stayed home after work. I partied.

I was living on bourbon and onion dip. One hangover bled into another.

I kept telling her, "Look, I need to clear my mind of this. Erase the misery. You know, excise the anger and all the other bad stuff, flush out the wound."

"Yeah, right," she said. "It's not brain surgery you're doing here, Stephen. If you're not careful, you're gonna flush the whole son of a bitch down the toilet."

For some reason that toad flashed through my mind, the one Endy had operated on when we were kids. I remembered the disposition of that toad.

"That son of a bitch you're talking about," I said. "The one down the toilet. That would be me?"

"Yep, that would be you."

By the middle of Week Two, I hadn't left the couch except to go to a couple of parties, or to the store to get cigarettes, more onion dip, more bourbon in the gallon size. I called my cut-rate brand Old Yeller—it makes you old and it makes you yell and it turns you into a no-account, sagging, sleeping-under-the-pickup yeller dog. The stuff even had a yellow tinge to it.

"Shit, kid, that's right up my alley," Langdon said when I told him about Old Yeller back when we were working together. I took the bottle out of my desk. It was coming on midnight, we were working on some kind of tear-your-guts-out child abuse story and he leaned back in his chair in my office and took a swig and howled to the recessed fluorescent moon on the ceiling. Old Yeller.

A month or so after the paper closed, my complexion was sallow, reflecting the dingy bilge that had become my blood. My brain was gummy with the buildup. My breath spoke it. My eyes were smudged with it. Old Yeller.

Liz and I had always been liberal with alcohol. That's how we met at those psych out parties. That's how we opened the door so quickly with each other. It oiled the hinges.

Booze had helped me slam out of my Eighteenth Century past, out of my shyness and my marooned family, had fueled my vaulting into the new age, and helped me in the continuing reinvention of myself, based on honesty and independence and fearlessness. Screw the past. Bury it. Deep.

After that, alcohol became my chief management tool. Just enough, and I could open up at parties. Just enough in the evenings, and I could change from a slavering thirteen-year-old into a suave, slow lover. Just enough, too, and I could sleep sweetly, and all my memories of long ago would not go bump in the night.

"And what about another job?" Liz asked.

"I'm working on my game plan."

Two months later I went to the Other Paper for an interview. It was humiliating.

I—the great boy wonder Stephen Beckwith—assistant managing editor—had to take a basic reporting and editing test?

Yep.

And how did I do? I don't know. They wouldn't say.

They wore suits. They didn't smoke. They smiled. They could have been bankers.

We'll call you, they said. We'll be in touch.

Month Three. Month Four.

They offered me a job as a copy editor. Lowest of the low. Nights. I would work weekends, too. Weekend nights. Prove yourself and work your way up, they said.

Horseshit.

I took the job.

Month Six. Month Ten.

Night after night, grinding it out. The word factory. The place looked like an insurance company and ran like the Bureau of Engraving, no smoking, no tobacco chewing, no eating tacos at your desk. Everybody wore ties and polite smiles. The top editors looked like publishers and the publisher looked like a Methodist minister.

You sit at a desk, you stare at a computer screen, the stories are fed to you in assembly-line fashion down the computer conveyor belt. You read, you edit, you write a headline. Bang, bang, bang. Next.

I'd write a clever headline now and again. I'd make an important catch of a reporting error—especially those errors in people's names. Hell, I'd been around Austin long enough to know the middle names and nicknames of every muckety-muck in town.

But that was it. I made a few friends. We'd go out for a drink after work—we got off at midnight and had an hour before the bars closed. We drank fast.

I didn't crash and burn like Liz was afraid I might. I cut back and regained control.

15

I was having a tough time getting drink No. 3 down. Thick as tar, warm. I couldn't push it. Shit. With each tilt of the tumbler I braced for the dense sourness. It hit my stomach with a thud.

I should get up from the couch, go to the kitchen for more ice, more water, something. This wasn't the way it was supposed to be. I might as well be drinking straight from the bottle.

Going in easily, a long sliding sip—that was the best way. Like the best of breaths in the woods, pulling it all in—the smoke, the bourbon—with long inhalations.

Finishing it was all wrong. But I kept drinking, pushing ahead, down. I didn't feel like making my way to the kitchen.

So where was I?—still 1974—the descent. I was in Year One in my new job on the copy desk. It was midmorning and I was at home when the phone rang. It was Mama. She couldn't speak.

I knew her broken breath. I'd heard it before.

Odessa had to get on the line. "Oh honey," she said. "Oh honey, come quick."

In less than an hour, Liz and I were on the road headed for Fort Worth. We arrived in the early afternoon. We were up all night.

It took half the night for Mama to put together the whole story for us. She cried and she had to rest. We had to string the story together from her ragged little beads.

Aunt Kitty, she said, was the one who answered the door. It was just after noon. She invited the young men into the front parlor, got them situated, and went into the kitchen to make them some lemonade.

My mother was upstairs taking a nap and everybody else was napping or gone. Aunt Kitty decided the young men should have some cookies, too, so she began baking them.

The young men were stranded in the parlor and they must have wondered what was going on. They finally wandered back until they found the kitchen. They talked to Aunt Kitty and convinced her they had to talk to Mrs. Beckwith. If she'd go find her, they said, they wouldn't let the cookies burn.

So Aunt Kitty went upstairs and woke up my mother, telling her they had two gentlemen callers downstairs who were dressed up like Endicott.

Like Endy?

The gentlemen callers were back in the parlor chatting with Aunt Kitty and drinking their lemonade and eating the cookies when Mama came down the stairs, awake after she had washed her face and combed out her hair. Aunt Kitty was telling them they reminded her of "her boy" Endicott and they were trying to explain that they were in the Air Force, too, and when Mama came in Aunt Kitty was saying what a coincidence, so was Endicott and he flew jets and he was in a war someplace and he had quite a number of freckles.

They stood, tucking their hats under their left arms gently and applying grimness to their baby faces, a government-issued grimness that was as well pressed as their uniforms. Mama understood before she got across the room.

It took a week for the body to get from Vietnam to the Haroldson & Parsley Funeral Home in Fort Worth. Liz and I stayed the weekend, but we went back to Austin for a few days—she was in the midst of several big lawsuits—and returned to Fort Worth the next Thursday. The funeral was Saturday.

All of the siblings came, John from college in New Orleans and Laura from postdoctoral studies in Houston and Arthur from upstairs (he was a senior in high school). We showed up and suited up, like good soldiers. Mama, too. She was elegant in her public grief, gracious, merely damp at her eyes.

That's the way Granddaddy wanted it. It was our duty to stand tall.

He led by example, as always. Grim as stone—that was Granddaddy, and despite the added years, the whiter hair and slightly loosening jowls, he was a mightier fortress than ever.

"Congressman, General, hello. Please come in." He was at the door, greeting people. He walked in with them, across the foyer to the crowded parlor, and Odessa was ready with coffee. She was in her black uniform with the white collar and so were two of her friends whom she had recruited. There were three big coffee urns in the kitchen, which the ladies from church had brought in, and boxes of cookies from the bakery and all kinds of food from friends.

"I'm so sorry for your loss, Mr. Beckwith," the congressman said.

"We're looking into the incident, sir," the general said. "We are assuming enemy fire at this point, but there apparently was no transmission from Captain Beckwith's plane before the incident."

"I'll want to know," Granddaddy said. "His mother will want to know."

"Of course," the general said.

"You can be assured," the congressman said.

"Those bastards," Langdon whispered to me.

He was running the paper in Abilene, and he'd driven into town to be with me. He'd seen the item on the Associated Press wire. Not many sons of such prominent people were killed in the war—mostly it was boys like Travis—and that's why it was news.

"So where are the sons of all the bigwigs around here?" he asked me. "I'll tell you where they are, they're at a frat party at Yale. The bastards."

We buried Endy next to my father, on the slope of the hill above the Trinity River in the main cemetery in Fort Worth. He went out with a great clatter of patriotism. They played taps and fired rifles; the politicians teared up and the news cameras rolled. Endy would have loved it.

I shut down and kept quiet politically. This was my mother's time. She needed to hear that lonely trumpet and feel that folded flag, which they handed to her at the end. Her boy's life, folded up and put away. I put my arm around her.

I was still the Assistant Patriarch, and here were all my sheep, or what was left of them, a little more worn, a little more lost. We were lined up on that front row of folded chairs under a canopy beside the grave.

Aunt Kitty, next to Granddaddy, was as serenely vacant as ever. Mama was next, and I was between her and Liz. Sometimes it seemed as if they were holding *me* up. Liz, especially. Her life and career were going from strength to strength, as mine were fading.

Laura was grimmer, drab, sullen. She paid no attention to her appearance; that was part of it. Whatever was easy—brown clothes, square haircut, nun shoes. Work was her world, the world in miniature. The life of microorganisms was the focus of her life.

John was drinking away his college days. Mama was distressed about him and had written to us about it. He'd dropped out of Tulane several times and was currently working as a waiter. He'd spent time in the drunk tank. He had a girlfriend as wild as he was. All of it was etched in the broken lines of his eyes and was settling into the dreary blond waves of his hair.

Arthur had found a life of perfect service. He went to church every Sunday with Mama, dutifully, willingly, and almost every Sunday served as an acolyte, carrying the crucifix and tending to the needs of the priests like a butler.

Miss Godwin was pleased with him. Godly devotion warmed her dutiful heart. As Aunt Jew dwindled into an emptying past, Miss Godwin's job became easier, and she and Arthur had more time to talk about the Bible.

The buglers and riflemen and news crews were packing up, and many of the onlookers had gone, when I looked up from our small herd of stragglers and saw her moving over the far hill. She came striding toward us just as always, close-cropped, well-muscled, sleek as a deer.

"Oh my God!" I said.

"Whyvonne!" Laura yelled, springing to life.

And we were running, my sister and I, like the old days, like all those races and games of our childhood. We ran to her, across the wooded hill of the cemetery and into her widespread arms.

"Oh God," she said. "I got here as fast as I could."

"Whyvonne," Laura said. "Whyvonne."

"That poor little red-headed son of a bitch," Whyvonne said. "I loved him so much."

"I know," I said, wiping at my cheeks.

"They got Travis and then they got Endy," Whyvonne said. "This fucking war."

By evening almost everyone had dispersed. Liz had gone to Jacksboro to see her folks. Laura, Whyvonne, my mother, and Odessa had gone to a restaurant to reminisce. I didn't feel like going anywhere.

I stayed at home, but I couldn't stand another minute in the Big House. I needed to walk.

I knew our woods by heart and didn't use the flashlight, though I brought one. The tree wasn't hard to find, just across from Granddaddy's house. I walked to it without a doubt or stumble.

I tested each of the steps nailed to the tree. At least fifteen years old now, they were solid and steady.

I climbed some twenty feet, to the side of the main floor, and then had to swing over. There was an extra board to hang on to. It was easy, even in the dark.

The floor was solid, but I could feel leaves and little branches with my feet. Arthur probably hadn't been there in a while.

I was barefooted, in my cut-off jeans and T-shirt, the old uniform of boyhood. It felt good to shed civilization. Endy and I, that's what we always did, first chance, as soon as Sunday school or Sunday Dinner was over.

There was moon enough for me to see that nothing had changed. The deer horns, the goat horns, the rabbit pelt were nailed up on the tree in their usual spot. I brought my cigarettes.

I remembered a thousand nights of long ago—Endy across the room from me, in his bed, in the dark, yak-yak-yakking about model airplanes and what our motto should be for our club and how itchy his Robin Hood underwear was and did I think Granddaddy might actually lock us in our rooms and throw away the key like he said and where was Daddy and where did the wind go at night and did God ever sleep and Danny said his big brother's weenie was so long he could pee back over his own shoulder until I said please. Please, Endy. Please, for God's sake, shut up and go to sleep.

I had my own stuff to think about, my own night to find a place in, down to the quiet. I had Daddy to think about and figure out and make better and make everybody better. I needed some quiet.

Now I had it, except it wasn't the quiet. It was silence.

I heard the back screen door creech open and fall closed. I figured it was Granddaddy coming home to the Little House, and I was right. I was perfectly quiet. I put my cigarette out.

Glances of moonlight came through the leaves, just enough to light his way and to let me see him here and there, mostly just the white inklings of his hair since he was still in his funeral clothes. I could hear his steps on the gravel of the parking area, and then they changed.

His steps shuffled into the old leaves, and then he left the path to his house and came into the darkness of the woods. He came to my tree.

He leaned against the trunk just below me. I could see him through the cracks in the boards of the floor. I didn't breathe.

He rested his bent body against the tree as if a great weight were upon him. He put his hand to his forehead.

His breathing heaved just once. The sound of his sigh went all through me.

16

I WAS BACK IN THE KITCHEN NOW. AND WHEN I WENT TO GET THE ICE I remembered I hadn't gotten any before and that I had planned to put some into that last drink, the mud-colored one that didn't have any ice and hardly any water. But I hadn't and now it was gone.

I got out a couple of ice trays. Plenty of ice this time, this next drink, slow it down a little, not like that last one.

This was No. 4. Already? Yeah, way over the limit of two, okay, but this was a weekend. Hell of a week. Like all of 'em. Shit. A measly four drinks.

We had good ice trays, the kind with the rough metal the ice won't stick to. I let the tap water crackle over the back of the first one, pulled the handle, popped it out. I only dropped a few cubes onto the counter.

And a few more getting them into the ice container, and a couple more from the container to the tumbler.

Everything was loose. It made for a flow of thoughts, a kind of sway within, but the muscles sometimes didn't go in the direction they were aimed. So there was a little spillage. The bourbon didn't all go in the glass and what dribbled down the side I wiped off with my finger and licked. Even the dab of water I added spilled over the side a little.

The sway. A breathing flow. I was loose all the way down—to my feet, to my heart and mind. That was good.

• • •

My life of nights. After Endy's funeral my life went back to its daily grind of nights at the newspaper. Year One became years and years.

Slowly I developed a secret life. I had the perfect setup.

I'd get off work at midnight; home was only twenty minutes away on the empty streets.

I'd come to the couch of that same little south Austin house, nestling into the quiet. I took in the quiet along with the first sip, the first pull of smoke. Easing, easing. Locking the world away. A world of words was what I wanted to get away from.

By the third year in my new job I was promoted to copy desk chief, and that meant all the stories—the live and developing news of Austin and Texas, the nation and the world—came through my purview, across my computer screen. I punched the final button that sent those stories to the typesetter, and from there they went on the makeup pages that were burned into plates that went on the press that turned and turned into the morning paper. I was the last stop, the final word, so to speak.

Every night was a madhouse because stories developed and changed at the last minute. They'd crowd up on the screens of a dozen copy editors and come to me in a colliding rush minutes before the deadline. And it was my ass if we didn't make the deadline, and every mistake that made it into the paper was mine.

But I was so cool. That's what everybody said. That guy Beckwith is so cool under pressure.

And I was. Throw anything at me—a war, an assassination, the Second Coming—and I could get it in, trimmed and shaped and decorated with the perfect headline, seconds to spare.

Wham, bam, done. That God damn Beckwith can do anything.

Control, man. Control.

One drink had been fine at first, way back then. A simple easing. Clear the head and good night.

After Endy died I was drinking three a night, four, thinking, remembering. Year Three. Year Seven. From Jimmy malaise to Ronnie Reaganomics. For me, it was all a long muddle of nights.

It was easy to hide things from Liz because of our separate shifts and all her extra work. I could stay up for hours if I wanted—three in the morning, four—drink as much as I wanted. Then I could stay in bed as late as I needed to, sleeping off the damage. Because I didn't have to go to work until four in the afternoon, I was always able to recover.

Liz didn't say anything but I could sense I crossed the line with her now and then, especially when we were in bed. I could feel her discomfort. She'd turn away from my ninety-proof kisses.

So I'd back off the booze, and she'd be all right. I was as careful as I could be around her. Then everything changed.

"There's something . . . Stephen, I think something's happening to me."

"Yeah?" It was a Friday night, reunion night for us. I propped up on one elbow and pulled the covers up under my arm.

"I'm late."

"How late?"

"Real late. Two months late."

"That's late all right. That's real late. Do you think . . . ?"

"Yeah, Stephen. I think. I really think so."

"Oh my God, Lizzie." I leaned over to her. I kissed her. "Oh my God."

That's it, I finally said one night after the inevitability hit me. I had a talk with myself. That's enough, Stephen. Knock it off. Cut back. You've got a baby on the way. You can't keep doing this, not this much.

So I cut down to one drink, and I did all right for a while, except at home, at bedtime, with Liz on reunion nights. I wanted that same coolness under pressure that I showed at work. I wanted to stroll in. I wanted just the right move, the suave smile, a cigarette for the lady. With just the right number of drinks, I could have it. Timing. Control.

Shall we dance? I will swirl you beneath the stars, out here on the terrace, and we will dance and swirl and dance and arrive, deeply, together. And I will hardly ruffle my tux.

Have a drink, my dear. We will have a drink and then we shall dance.

Debonair I wasn't. Not with just one drink to hold me back after a long, empty week. One flick of the pelvis, mine, hers, and I was a goner, a sprawling boy. The two-step.

And sleep. One drink just wasn't enough, either. I'd close my eyes and the conveyered words of my long night of work kept rolling.

So wait a minute, I thought. Maybe we're being a little hasty with this cutback. Maybe there's a compromise here.

What was the harm in a little chemical nudge to move me into the necessary blankness, where I could be repaired and refueled for the next day's breathless pursuit of whatever needed pursuing—the wars, the political intrigues, the cranberry sauce recipes?

Two drinks, three drinks, a flip of the light switch, good night. A flip of the switch, too, and you could put the brakes on the boy in bed. It takes at least two. No big deal.

Okay, sometimes four. Sometimes it took a little extra time to sort things out. And Liz, the bigger she got, became too tired for me at all. So I'd stay up with Old Yeller on reunion nights after she went to bed. My pal Yeller.

Gradually I stayed up a little later during the week, too. Two in the morning, three. Just like before. Three drinks, four drinks. I was going to be a father and my freedom was about to be taken away forever.

Then on a Thursday morning at five it was time, and I didn't even know it. Liz had to push me out of bed with her feet to get me going to take her to the hospital.

They said "Push!" and I was pushing.

Yeah. Me. The dad. Pushing right along with her and straining and sweating and saying "Push!" And through our masks—the nurses, the doctor, and I, surrounding her—it sounded like something out of a huddle on the football field. Hut! Hut! Push! All of it was enough to push my buzzing brain back into focus.

Her sweat glistened in those high-beam lights above us. Her hair was a red mop and the muscles showed up everywhere down her face and arms and thighs. I think if we had asked her to, Liz would have pushed her heart right out along with that baby.

I kept running back to the waiting room to give progress reports. Mama and Odessa and Aunt Kitty had come down from Fort Worth. Liz's parents and grandmother had made it in from Jacksboro. It was late that afternoon by the time things started really moving, so everybody had plenty of time to get there.

Mama was excited and happy, but this wasn't new for her. She was already a grandmother. John, less than a year before, was the first to produce a grandchild.

Cherise, his girlfriend, was a Creole debutante. The wedding was subdued—no rice, no music, just a few sniffles and the sound of shotguns being pumped. Six months later we'd welcomed Dylan John Beckwith.

Granddaddy went into a month-long rage about the name. "A travesty! A God damn Welsh peasant name!" Mama ignored him and fell in love with the child.

Now Granddaddy was going to be a great-grandfather again, and I told Mama to tell him it could be worse, that we were considering naming ours Che Leonid Beckwith.

When I went back into the birthing room, William Endicott Beckwith—named for my father and my brother—entered the world head first, shoulders out, the way you had to barge into Dorthy's. I was already smitten before he was snipped free.

17

DRINK NO. 4 WAS ALMOST GONE NOW. THE HOUSE WAS TICK-TOCK quiet. The lamp at the end of the couch was dim, hiding the two-story expanse of space above me.

I looked up the stairs. I could see Will's room from the couch. The door was open, and there was the smallest light there, his nightlight.

Most nights after work I'd go up to his room. I liked to check on him, to find him there, under his Snoopy blanket with his lips pooched against the pillow. I always touched his frothy, red-blond curls and kissed his creamy cheek.

I remembered lying in my own bed and listening for my father's footsteps on the stairs. I remembered the uncertain steps, and I wondered how my own steps would sound this night. I better not.

Four months earlier, in March, a Saturday afternoon, and I was just getting up. Liz hit me with it first thing. "What the fuck is wrong with you, Stephen?"

She was noticing, finally. I'd been wondering when this conversation was coming.

"How late are you staying up during the week?" she asked. "How much are you drinking?"

"God, not now. Can I have some coffee first, please?"

We were sitting in our places on the couch, me by the lamp, she at the other end. I had gotten coffee but she hadn't given me time to light my first cigarette or take a drink from the mug.

Will was a little over a year old then. I could tell from the kitchen mess that she'd already fed him lunch, and I figured he was in his crib now, down for his nap.

Liz backed off a minute while I had my first few sips of coffee. Then she bore down.

"Let me see your hand, Stephen." I didn't want to give it to her. I knew what she was noticing. "Let me see it."

I shifted my cigarette and gave her my free right hand, reaching across to her. She held it, then let go, leaving it suspended.

"God dammit, Stephen. Can't you see that?"

My hand was a frail, shy thing, a dying butterfly. We were looking at my trembling heart.

"Yeah," I said.

"How much are you drinking, Stephen? Your hand shakes like my grandfather's. Shit, Stephen. This is bullshit."

It wasn't the only sign. I had gone from one-hundred-forty-five pounds to one-twenty-seven. I no longer saw a red-blond boy in the mirror, but a soft gray man. My eyes and spirit were going drab, my hair unraveling, mouth drying, stomach frothing, lungs fogging, blood stiffening. All of my appetites—mental, physical, sexual—were dying. A great, slow poisoning was taking place, and it was all there in my palsied hand.

How many times had I tried now to get control?

Let's see. First time, right after I found out Will was on the way. That didn't last long. I cut back again just after he arrived, and again it worked for a while.

Liz stayed home for three months, after which we worked out a system where she would take the baby to the sitter's house on her way to work and I would pick him up midmorning when I got up, then take him back to Mrs. Applewhite's on my way to work in the afternoon. Liz would pick him up on her way home. We called it the baby shuffle.

And my secret system of control worked, too. One drink for me at night, quickly to bed, and by ten in the morning I was up and fresh and ready to see Will.

I kept him in the cradle in front of the couch. I could sit and read and rock him with my foot. Will looked a lot like Arthur had, with that same blond cobweb hair and soft roundness. Mama sent us the Babar book, and I started reading it to him before he could even follow the pictures.

Lots of mornings we'd go for a walk. I'd put him in the stroller and off we'd go, with Romeo prancing beside us. Our neighborhood was overhung with live oaks. The baby would reach up with his pudgy hand for the sparkles of light that came dancing down between the leaves.

I told him he and I would go to the Brazos someday. I was going to see about buying the property from my family and building a cabin there. A big one, all new logs, and he and I would sit on that porch in the sun-spangled shade and look down the bank at our fishing poles. I told him it was the easiest fishing in the world.

"Gaa!" he said, like Arthur.

Those were good days. I was doing fine with one long bourbon and branch after work—just one—and I learned again to stretch it out into three or four cigarettes. Those feelings of sweet relief would last an hour, and that was enough, and the peace came until it was the vague heaviness of sleep, and I could go to bed and be carried and gone.

But it changed again, not many months later, gradually. Another drink—another little compromise—and maybe another.

Worse. Slowly worse again. After three drinks, compromises are as easy as breathing. Nothing to hang on to—internal controls melt like sand under the surf—and there you go. Slipping.

I tried to keep things propped up, to answer the phone midmorning when Liz called to wake me up to get the baby from the sitter. I put the empty bottles of Old Yeller at the bottom of the garbage. I paid for every other bottle with cash, to keep her from seeing it in the checkbook. I stayed bathed and shaved and kept my breath scrubbed clean. I drank as little as I could around her.

In the spring of '83, we'd moved to this grand house with its soaringly high-ceilinged den and correspondingly huge mortgage, which was no problem thanks to Liz's dynamite career. It had a back window as big as a movie screen that looked out over an acre of gangly live oaks bordering a wandering creek.

I loved the house. Will had more sparkling shade to play in, and I could sit out back and imagine—especially at night—that our creek was the Brazos.

We had four bedrooms and three bathrooms, which meant we had plenty of relatives coming to stay with us. We had lots of closets now, too, and Mama got a moving van to send us stuff from the Big House, lots of antiques and a set of china and some things of Daddy's she thought I ought to have—his tackle boxes and spinning rods and his old twelve-gauge shotgun. She sent the rod I'd caught the tarpon with and Bess, which we perched in Will's room. I was bringing him into the fold. We even pretended he was sliding down our slick new banister as I held him.

I should have been so happy.

But things were worse. Slowly worse. And now she wanted to see my hand.

We talked a long time that Saturday. Liz was afraid, tearfully afraid, and I listened. I had never seen her afraid before. She insisted I go to a doctor, and I agreed.

At the doctor's office I stripped, I bent, I coughed. I got weighed and measured, felt up and peered at, and I answered a hundred questions.

"You drink too much," Dr. Allison said, writing in his chart at the conclusion of things as I sat on the papered edge of the examining table. "Cut back." If he only knew how many times I'd tried that already. I didn't say anything.

Dr. Allison's father had been Liz's family's doctor. The son was raised in Jacksboro, moved to Austin, and started a family practice of his own. He was a compact, young-looking, hardly-gray fifty.

"I'm not telling you to quit drinking altogether, Stephen. Just don't let the stuff run your life."

"All right."

"You can do it, Stephen. Take charge of your life."

"Yes sir."

Dr. Allison was of the old school—the West Texas, no-nonsense, get-a-grip school. He put me on vitamins, told me to cut back on smoking, to get some exercise and to start eating a good breakfast, and he gave me a prescription for some mild sleeping pills. He blamed most of it on the stress of my job.

Liz seemed heartened by the report from the doctor and my reaction to it. She admitted she'd halfway thought the doctor might want to hospitalize me. This meant things weren't as bad as she'd feared.

I made resolutions, all of them aloud to her. First, no more drinking during the week, and especially not on Friday nights when she and I had time together. She admitted it was bothering her, so I said, that's it, it's over.

We agreed parties could be an exception. I'd let myself have two spread-out drinks, mostly for show. I didn't want to look out of place.

I was going to start cooking breakfast for myself, taking more walks with Will, reading at night. I promised I'd start on that long list of chores she had for me—raking leaves, weeding the garden, painting the dog house.

I was just as heartened as Liz. It sounded like control, and that sounded good to me. Yes. Control. For sure this time.

"For God sakes, look what booze did to my father," I told her a couple of weeks after the exam.

"I know."

"Daddy's problem was he didn't get a grip soon enough."

"Maybe so."

18

It had been four months since my most recent get-a-grip change of heart brought on by the doctor's exam. Everything went great for the first two.

I did everything I promised—everything the doctor ordered—and my health came roaring back. By drinking less, eating better, and sleeping regularly, I saw a difference almost immediately.

And then Aunt Jew died. She slumped into the past and never came back.

It wasn't sadness. It was her raucous funeral that got me in trouble.

She'd had quite a career in journalism—"the old, *old* school," she called it, working for UPI in Washington during the Roosevelt years—had spent some time on the women's professional golfing circuit, lost the use of her legs to diabetes, then started writing novels. She'd met some interesting people along the way.

In one of her last lucid moments, she handed me a list of some of her old pals. "Honey, if they're still standing, invite 'em to my funeral," she said. "Make it an open bar. I want a hell of a sendoff."

She got it. Everybody who was still kicking was invited, and they all brought extra bottles. I had come to Fort Worth by myself—Liz was overwhelmed with work—and in three days I never made it upstairs to my room. People kept filling my glass.

The parlor, by two each morning, looked like a nursing home battle-field. Bodies sprawled about, false teeth, hearing aids, a wooden leg.

One guy talked about the Roosevelts' dog, Fala. "That dog got good press, but don't believe it," he said. "Hell of a vicious mutt. I remember this one state dinner, I got fed up with him pulling on my God damn shoelaces and I crawled under the table and bit him on his furry little leg. Tit for tat, don't you know. I was drunk as a skunk, of course. Eleanor never invited me back."

Somebody else, an agent, said she was considering a proposal to turn *The Wind in the Magnolias* into a musical. "Bob Fosse does hoop skirts," she said. "I think it's got promise."

"I don't know," somebody else said. "It might take the old colonel all of Act Two just to get into Miss Dahlia's drawers. I'm telling you, the skirts in those days were fortresses, and Jewel understood that. Hell, it took her a hundred pages just to get the poor dear unbuttoned."

We buried Aunt Jew with her squirrel rifle and her Underwood. It took a week for Granddaddy to get the last guest out of the house. It was a week before my head cleared.

That's when John showed up in Austin. He was a mess. I couldn't turn him away, could I? After three days I wished I had.

He was bleary, sniffly, with a personality as sparkling as the occupation circumstance had chosen for him—he was now an oyster shucker. That's what he'd been doing since dropping out of culinary school, which he'd tried after Tulane kicked him out. That and washing dishes, then sniffing up his profits and whatever he could hustle from Bourbon Street.

His bright-blond hair had gone soap-scum gray. His smile had yellowed, his blue-hot eyes gone dull.

He'd been in Fort Worth, visiting Dylan. The boy was staying with Mama now, and it looked like that would be a permanent arrangement. Cherise had crumpled her Mustang into a telephone pole and was now in a deep coma, at a hospital known locally as the Vegetable Bin. John couldn't take care of the boy, and his in-laws, who had moved to Phoenix for a life of retirement and golf, weren't interested.

John stayed up late, drinking my booze and waiting for me to get home from work. I had no choice but to join him. Right?

"I was thinking about Daddy," he said, one word smearing into the next.

"Yeah."

"I don't remember much, really. It was like he was always hiding."

"Yeah," I said. "Aren't we all?"

Summer 1984—the meltdown continued. A copy desk get-together. We were celebrating successfully upgrading the newspaper to a less primitive computer system. It had been a nightmare of glitches and crashes and the mysterious disappearances of stories.

I had made myself a gut-level promise to do exactly what I said I would at parties, which was no more than two drinks, spread out over the evening. Just enough for comfort. Liz and I had agreed to that.

Yes, I'd screwed up at Aunt Jew's funeral, and then with John, but now, in the presence of Liz, I was going to do it. Control. Two drinks.

Despite my hidden bitterness at being left behind in the race to the top of the heap because of the folding of the other paper, I liked my colleagues. There was an us-against-the-world mentality. We copy editors were a lost and lonely battalion of word warriors, and I was their platoon leader.

The going was always tough—the sweaty slogging through the mud of the day, the obituaries, and city council meetings. But then there was the occasional thrill of breaking news, which broke like bombs over us— the botched hostage raid, the sudden death of a newly elected pope. Some nights I came home bloodied and revved and feeling victorious, but most workdays were just another night at the word factory, the assembly line that got faster and faster as the night came to a conclusion. I came home drained. One way or another, the newspaper got most of my blood.

There were maybe ten people at Frank's. They all brought stuff, booze and beer and chips. Liz seemed to be having a good time.

We smoked. We drank. We expounded. We gossiped. A good and easy evening.

But one drink extra, just one, and everything went wrong. I crossed that invisible line inside where the incline gets suddenly steeper, rocky, and darkening. One minute I was dancing, twirling my conversational partners with wit and good humor, and the next I was tumbling into darkness—slurred, lost, dazed—and a couple of guys had to help me. Liz drove me home.

I remembered the overheated air in that car. Her anger was a volatile vapor. All it would have taken was a spark.

It didn't happen. She fumed. I sank into the sloshing darkness.

A week later it happened again—at Liz's big party.

She'd been offered a Washington appointment—the Justice Department, deputy assistant to the assistant attorney general, something like that—but she turned it down and that's what everybody was celebrating. They loved her, and she was staying. She was promoted to regional director of the whole damn Southwest, Department of Housing and Urban Development. Big new office and a secretary. It was a big deal, really big. She was moving up fast, Washington or not. I was so proud of her.

The party for Liz was at the U.S. attorney's house, and in attendance were judges, lobbyists, the lieutenant governor—the kind of people we used to hate. They all knew that Liz was a comer, a star ascending, and they wanted to curry favor with her. Where might she go from here—to be mayor of Austin? a U.S. rep? maybe a cabinet position?

A guy circulated with champagne on trays, and just as I finished one drink, here he came again. "Champagne, sir?"

I wanted to celebrate with her. But I blew it again, just like the newspaper party. Once you cross that line inside . . .

Liz figured it out in time, while I was still just sloppy and lurchy. She offered excuses (a headache) and she held onto me tight. I leaned against her, smiling, thanking hosts, and I got to the car without a major stumble.

The party had just gotten started. This was her moment and I made her miss most of it.

Same fuming air in the car as she drove me home, and this time she didn't speak to me all week. We went back to work—I on Sunday night, she on Monday, our separate routines—and she didn't call me at work and wouldn't return my calls. Yes, she'd call to make sure I got up to go get Will and to see that he had a good lunch. She reminded me again about the closet and I promised her again I'd get to it. She wanted a lock installed on the closet upstairs in the guest bedroom where I kept Daddy's fishing stuff and his twelve-gauge. Will was toddling now and she didn't want him getting into any of that.

Yes, I said, I'll get to it. Mr. Step-and-Fetch-It at your service, I was thinking.

I went back to my nightly drinks. What the hell difference did it make anymore?

I knew what was coming in the building silence. It had been building in her all week. I was sure of it. She was secretly looking at my hands again. She could see it coming back. Fast.

In her mind she was building her case like the prosecutor she was. For what? the hospital? a divorce? some kind of ultimatum?

It could happen any day now. Tomorrow? Yeah, maybe tomorrow. Maybe this day—July 26, 1984—was the end.

That's what I was thinking as I started another cigarette. The smoke went in and out of me and the drink went down. No. 4. Or was it No. 5? Yeah, five, and look how thick I'd made it. Everything was coming loose. The end of things.

Fuck her and the horse she rode in on. I don't need her. I need the quiet. I need to breathe. It'll all blow over.

A guy gets a little drunk. So what? I made a mistake at that party. You can't make mistakes? Everybody makes mistakes except Ms. Perfect.

What the hell.

One more drink already. That doesn't count. Who's counting? One for the road, right?

Fuck you, bitch. I can do any God damn thing I want to.

The drink went down defiantly. I drank it faster than it took to smoke one cigarette.

This drink. This was the one. Over the line and down. My brain was tipping like a sphere cut loose from its axis. It wobbled as it slowed, worse the more it slowed, nodding, falling into a broken circle, shit.

The chemical was overpowering my blood, upending the structure of balance. It was rushing in, closing in on me. I was tumbling under the flood.

I needed to get out of there. I couldn't breathe.

One more. Make one more drink and get out of here. Pass out, pass away, gone. I got back to the kitchen somehow, sloshed another drink together. You've gotta get out of here. Shit.

The counter. The kitchen table. Back of the couch. Edge of the fireplace. Back door. I held on, the lurched walk, and went out and I could breathe. God, yes, finally.

I had a place in the back yard, my private place, and that's what I was thinking of. I had set up an old beach chair in the back yard, at the edge of the slope that fell a few feet to our creek; beside it was a wobbly little table.

Romeo went with me. In a wave-tilting boat we went across the patio and out across a bay of grass. I found the chair, and—I don't know how—I brought the bottle.

Merry Christmas. Merry Christmas. Merry Christmas.

I could just make out the letters. The bottom of the tumbler was resting on the palm of my left hand. With my right hand I turned it, slowly. The red Gothic letters went around in a blur, but I knew what they were supposed to say.

Merry Christmas.

I had smoked another cigarette and was working on the next drink. No. 6? It was down to half, straight bourbon, and the bitter warmth of it knocked on the door of nausea every time it went in.

Everything around me was shallow and dim. The dog was asleep. I turned the tumbler in my hand. My head was nodding and my eyes were trying to close. There was a sloshing silence inside me—a manufactured, chemical peace—flat, empty.

"Stephen?"

Was that him? I thought I heard him. Sometimes I thought I heard my father.

Inside me, at the edge of things, below, with a caverned voice. "Stephen?"

I looked back at the house. Our bedroom was dark. Liz was probably in her usual sound sleep.

Above was Will's room, also dark. I supposed he was safely deep in dreams, but he could be at the window and I'd never know. He could be watching me, watching the red point of my cigarette rise to my mouth and back, rise and back.

"Stephen?"

It wasn't hard to put myself on that old porch by the river. The yard sloped into darkness and the darkened trees were the right shelter. With the stirring of bugs, I could hear the water turning below.

I remembered lying on my cot and looking through the door of the cabin when Daddy was on the porch. He was a lump of darkness, bent in his chair, smoking, nodding. Going down. I watched the red point of his cigarette, rising and back.

My shirt was sticking to me now in the wet heat of the Austin night. Breathing was a chore. The blanketed air, the layered darkness, that's how a Texas summer night comes down.

I poured some more. Enough of it went in the tumbler. I drank.

"Stephen?"

Daddy called to me and I went out. I sat beside him. We watched the night go down, from deep to deeper. He wanted to say something. But he didn't, he couldn't, and we drank. The tears were all over the place now, all over me, but there wasn't any noise. I didn't say anything and Daddy didn't say anything and that's how he left.

I heard the blast. Bert was beside me, helping me hold the gun up and aim right at the can on the stump and very slowly I squeezed the trigger.

The night catches fire.

Daddy?

The last thing Daddy saw. Fire.

Into his eyes. That would have to be it, the last thing, the way the blast goes in, the way it went into him. Even with your eyes closed the fire comes crashing in.

You blast away the darkness. That's the only way to get rid of it.

I had his other shotgun. It was in the upstairs closet.

I tried to stand. I wanted to find the gun. But a great, crushing weight pushed me back into the chair.

Now I tried again and stood momentarily, but the weight was too much and down I went the other way, all the way to the grass.

After an incredible effort, from hands and knees to a crouch, pushing, I stood. I found a forward motion and began to stumble toward the light, the house, a lunging walk.

The patio. The back door. I opened it, staggered, and fell to the side, and that's when the blast hit me. A burn of lights, the edge of the fireplace. My face in the carpet, and I was swimming through the pain.

A tumbled swimming. That was it. Waves. Reaching out with my arms to pull myself above the waves and pulling down and crying and turning down.

"Oh, Stephen."

All the lights were on. I tried to get up. Something was in my eyes, a burning, this God damn barking dog and light and swimming.

I touched my head and came back with a handful of blood and she was there with her hands over my shoulders trying to pull me away and turn me to see and my breath was heaving.

"God, Stephen, God, don't move. I've got to get a towel. Something."

"Daddy?" I was asking. "Where are you, Daddy?"

"Oh my God, Stephen. A huge gash. God the blood."

I was vomiting, there was blood, there were tears. My head was on the carpet and my eyes were closed. The side of my nose and my mouth were lying in the puddle. Some of the blood and the vomit were flowing into the side of my mouth. I was breathing it in.

Liz pressed a towel to my forehead.

"Hold the towel here, Stephen. Keep pressure on it. I'm gonna get help."

I could hear my little boy at the top of the stairs, crying. "Daddy?" he was saying. "Daddy?"

Liz went into the kitchen to call an ambulance.

19

HERE CAME THIS NAKED GUY, FALLING BACK ACROSS THE ROOM IN A reverse weave. Down he went, beside my bed, face up.

He was a heap of kindling on the floor—a ripple of ribs and a jutting of jaw. His hair was as wispy-thin as a baby's.

"Hey, you ah ight?" I asked. The drugs had turned my lips to oatmeal.

The guy moved a little. He moaned. He mumbled.

He could have been eighty because of his feebleness, but there were no wrinkles. I noticed a patch of reddish pubic hair, but nothing nested there, or not much. He was worn down to nubs, all over.

I'd seen him before, old pictures in books. Bergen-Belsen, 1945. But there was no way I could be there.

I struggled for reality, got pieces for my efforts, enough pieces to realize that the ambulance had taken me one place, for stitches, then here, for what?

I thought about getting up and helping him, but I couldn't. I was plastered to the bed by the centrifugal force of Valium.

"God dammit, Troy."

A nurse came in. She must have heard the commotion. She went over and grabbed the guy's arm and pulled him up to a dangling position as if he were a stick-figure puppet. She was a small woman, but she could handle him. She danced the floppy scarecrow backward toward his bed, across from mine. After a tango dip, she let him drop. He sprawled across the bed.

"You want me to tie you in this bed again?" she asked him.

He moaned something.

"Let's get this gown on ya again, buddy boy."

Apparently he'd been trying to go to the bathroom, which was on the other side of the room, and that's when he fell. Along the way he must have slid out of his hospital gown. The nurse pulled him up, pushed the gown back on him and tied it. She let him flop back on the pillow.

She began taking his vitals. All the while she talked toward the wall, over Troy. I realized she was talking to me.

"Can you believe this guy? Troy's been with us before, you know, several times. He's a union man, works for the railroad, they got great insurance and job protection. His family comes in, dumps old Troy on us, and skedaddles. We clean him up and sober him up the best we can, fatten him up a little and try to get the message across.

"No luck. Couple a months, Troy's back, a little worse off than the time before."

Then it was my turn. She got the thermometer from my nightstand and pushed it under my tongue. She squeezed down on my wrist and peered down at her watch and never quit talking.

"Can you believe Troy's been in here two weeks already? Yep. Two weeks this time, and he's been eating pretty good and resting all the time and this is as good as he's gotten.

"Not a drop of booze in two weeks and he's still this loaded. Can you believe it? He's still on a God damn ship, rocking all over the damn place, can't even take a piss without falling all over himself.

"Two weeks. Dead drunk. Can't walk, can't talk. That's the thing about booze. Drink enough of it and it kinda soaks in permanently. Wet brain, they call it. That's Troy.

"He hasn't got another drunk in him. We told him that last time and it didn't do any good; the shrink had him write his own obituary, plan his own funeral.

"This time it's for sure. He goes out with the boys one more time and he's comin' back in a God damn casket.

"The poor son of a bitch."

I looked at her name tag, but I couldn't make it out. About all I saw was a blur of brown hair and fiery fingernails. Since the middle of the night before, when I was brought here—I thought it was the night before, but it might have been two nights ago—the nurses had been giving me shots every few hours, and everything—my eyelids, my mind, my vision—was drooping.

The nurse let go of my wrist and it flopped down to the bed. She pulled out the thermometer and looked at it, then shook it down. She pushed back the bandage on my forehead to see how the stitched-up gash was healing.

"So anyway, welcome to the real world, buddy boy," she said. She turned and headed out of the room. "Welcome to Detox."

20

"Lizzie?"

"Hey, Stephen."

"Lizzie."

I could hardly push up my eyelids. It was Monday evening and I was still in Detox, still in a chemical muck, but it was different. They weren't giving me any more shots. This was my own muck—a soupy, humid, unbright swamp of despair.

I didn't want to see that freckled sunrise of a face of hers. I looked up at the ceiling and my eyes closed again. She sat on the edge of the bed and took my hand.

"I've really fucked up bad, Liz," I finally said.

"You ain't shittin', Bucko."

"You're gonna leave me, aren't you?"

She plopped a plastic grocery bag on my chest.

"Yeah, right, and when you get to the bottom of these cookies you'll find the divorce decree. Oh, and your toothbrush and stuff is in here, too."

When I opened my eyes and turned to her, a buildup of tears came out. "Fresh out of the oven?"

"Yep."

I sniffled and smiled.

"Your oven, Lizzie? Confession time."

"Mrs. Wiggly's oven."

"As in Piggly Wiggly?"

"That's the one. And I got you a bunch. Figure you'll need 'em for bribing all these nurses."

I sat up on my elbow. "Especially the night nurse. I call her Nurse Hatchet."

"As in Ratched? I think I know who you're talking about. Rose something, Rosie, a real thorny bitch, yeah, but kind of likable." She reached over and helped me brush a tear away. "She was the admitting nurse on duty when we brought you over here from the emergency room the other night. God you were a mess."

"I know."

"Blood everywhere. Vomit. God knows. I just threw that shirt of yours away."

"She's really a pretty good old gal. Nurse Hatchet. The drug lady. We've had some nice chats."

"I know. She's the one I've been talking to. Not the damn doctors. I've called her up at midnight the last few nights to get the real poop on you. Not that I couldn't sleep or anything."

"What'd she say?"

"You're fucked up, Stephen. That's what she said. Just like everybody else in here."

Liz went out into the waiting room and got coffee for us. She wasn't gone long. I got us a couple of cookies out of the box and handed her one when she got back.

"I've talked to just about everybody," she said.

I sat up on the edge of the bed, and she sat next to me. My bunk buddy, Troy, was across the room in his bed, snoozing. Our talking didn't rouse him.

"At work?"

"Yeah."

"Mama?"

"Yeah. Talked to her, too. Several times."

"God. What did they say? What did Mama say?"

"I don't think your mother was all that surprised. She mentioned Aunt Jew's funeral. You must have really gone on a toot that weekend."

"Yeah. It was pretty bad. I bet she's really worried."

"She's worried, yeah. But she says she's praying like hell, and that's a direct quote."

I smiled. I knew Mama meant it. I could feel her strength across the miles.

We started cigarettes.

"And work. Tell me about what they said, Lizzie."

"Surprised. That was mostly it."

"I surprised a lot of people, I guess. Yeah. Mr. Cool blows it big time."

"Whatsizname. Mike," she said. "I talked to him."

"The assistant managing editor. Yeah. He's a good guy. Drinks a lot, though. Almost everybody up at that paper drinks a lot."

"I know."

"Any of those guys could be here. Bunch of them probably oughta be."

"But it's you, Stephen."

"Yeah, it's me."

"It's your turn to face the music, Stephen."

In the pause of our conversation we could hear Troy across the room, semi-awake, humming "The Eyes of Texas Are upon You." A bar song—way, way off key.

"*That's* the music I'm facing now, Lizzie. Troy sings that same damn song night and day."

"God help you."

We laughed. It had been so long.

"So Mike was surprised?"

"He was surprised. Yeah. And real sympathetic. Really, Stephen. I told him about how long you were gonna be here—six weeks—and he said don't worry about it. Get better. Get with the program. That's how he put it."

"Shit. We've got an election coming up. Reagan's gonna stomp the hell out of Mondale. I need to be there. God I love elections."

"You need to be here, Stephen. You need to get well."

"Yeah. I know. Yeah. I guess they can do it without me."

"Sure they can. They'll have to."

"Yeah."

"God, you don't know, Lizzie. Holding it back, holding it back with you and everybody. For so long, sweating inside. I tried so hard, get a hold, slip. Then again. Then those parties. Shit."

"It's all over, Stephen." She reached over and took my hand. "It's all out in the open now."

"The bottom dropped out. All of a sudden. There it goes. Control. Everything."

"Yeah."

"The past. All this built-up stuff."

"You were asking for your father that night. It didn't really make much sense."

"Yeah. He just sorta showed up. And after all this time. Why now, I wonder?"

"Maybe you needed him, Stephen."

"Yeah. Maybe. I haven't wanted to think about it."

"Maybe it's time."

"Da-da?"

I didn't know Will had come, too. Liz must have handed him off to a nurse before she came in to see me, and now the nurse walked in, holding him. He reached out his tottering little arms to me.

"Will." Tears came up and across my voice. I could hardly say his name.

He brought his arms around my neck, and I got a wet smear of a kiss on the side of my face. "Da-da."

I held him. He looked at me and touched my bandaged forehead and hugged me again. His puffed cheek pressed against mine.

Liz came into the hug. "I'm not leaving, Stephen," she whispered to me. "Just keep trying, try your best to make this hospital thing work, that's all I ask, and Will and I'll hang in there with you."

I couldn't let them go. "Yes," I said. "Yes."

21

"I NEED A VOLUNTEER," LOU SAID AS HE WALKED INTO THE CLASSROOM. "Stephen, I think you'd do nicely. Come on up here."

Everybody laughed, of course. Lou always got laughs when he yanked "volunteers" out of the reluctant assemblage—victims he had in mind before he walked in. The laughs were exhales of relief—they weren't the ones picked.

We were in Group. That's what people called group therapy at Willow Ridge Hospital. We sat around a big table with a dozen other patients and did things like write an imaginary letter to the person we'd hurt most by our drinking or drugging. Then we'd read it to the group. Almost always there was an emotional meltdown by somebody, followed by hugs and support.

I hated it. I couldn't melt in public. There was more of my granite grandfather in me than I cared to admit

But with those counseling sessions and private ones, the staff had been uncovering my secret self. They'd opened the stone box, rifled through the trinkets, compared notes. Lou had been listening.

He was head of counseling, stubby and intense, with sweaty-dark hair. He was so fast and so sharp with his insights—some people called him a munchkin on speed—that he could cut you off at the knees before you knew what hit you. And he didn't even have to bend over to do it.

I was standing on the small stage in front of the classroom, next to Lou, who had his arm up and over my shoulder, using me as a prop. Denial, pride, faulty thinking—it didn't matter, he could zero in on it with his infrared analysis. I could feel him warming up.

I was two weeks into the program, and I had moved out of Detox and into a regular room. My roommate was Mike, an airline pilot. He was orderly, quiet, and pleasant. He liked to tell me about flights he didn't remember. Blackouts. "Yeah, thank God for autopilot."

I was looking better. My dirty-rust hair, washed regularly now, had become a lively, waving red blond again. Tones of peach and pink were rising out of the sallow skin of my face. I remember looking in the mirror a lot at the hospital. I kept looking for who might be coming forward out of the swamp.

But I had a good distance still to go. Lumpy bruises spread out from beneath my still-bandaged forehead. My eyes rested on dark hills of skin; I slept little, and what I could remember of my nights was running from the center of my dreams.

"And here we have Stephen Beckwith, the classic oldest child. Call him Mr. Responsible."

Lou paused, waiting for a response. "Hey, are you all awake out there? I said CALL HIM MR. RESPONSIBLE!"

The audience answered in a sleepy jumble, "Hello, Mr. Responsible."

Lou smiled his satanic, schoolmarm smile. "Thank you, class."

He walked back to his place at the head of the table and took a drink from his Dr Pepper, hardly pausing. I was alone for the moment on that small stage.

"So, like I said, here we have Stephen. Saint Stephen. The oldest child. Mr. Responsible." He came back to me, circled me, paced the stage, and returned, speaking all the while. "The leader. The rock. Old reliable Stephen. Always on time, never screws up, and then suddenly, BAM! He fucks up big time. He takes a dive. He winds up—say it together now, class . . ."

They knew the response. They said in raucous unison, and I joined them with a smile—"OVER THE HILL!"

"That's right, kiddos, over the hill at good old Willow Ridge Hospital for Drunks and Druggies and Assorted Wackos." Lou stepped away from me again, back to the table, quickly checking his notes as he continued to address the class. "And so, from the looks of things, old Stevie boy here took a pretty mean dive." From out in the room he pointed to my forehead. "Right into the fireplace, wasn't it?"

"Yeah."

"You tryin' to barbecue yourself or what, guy? Kind of a slow suicide on a turning spit? Or maybe you just wanted to join the Fires of Hell, since that's how you already felt on the inside?"

I smiled uncomfortably, and Lou moved in for the kill.

"Kinda like the old man, huh, Stephen? Same song, second verse. Same hell your father knew. Same guilt, same regret. He wrote the script, you followed the directions."

Sharp tears broke out like sweat across my eyes, but I just stood there.

"BAM! Right in the old forehead. BAM!" The counselor's words were explosive. He slammed the heel of his hand into his forehead.

Lou went back to his place at the table and came back with a rectangular package wrapped in brown paper.

"Know what this is, class?"

He ripped off the paper and held it in front of my face.

"Austin and Vicinity phone book?" someone said.

"That's just what it says on the cover, my friends. What it actually is is a script. Pretend it is, Stephen. A script that is the story of your life. Your future."

"Okay," I said.

Lou pushed it into my stomach and I lost some breath. "Tear it up," he said.

I stood there, confused.

"Tear it up, dammit. This is your life we're talking about here, old boy. Tear it up, God dammit. Start over. Write your own life. YOU ARE NOT YOUR FATHER!"

Did he mean for me to start now, in front of the class?

"God dammit, didn't you hear me? *Tear it up*, I said. TEAR IT UP, RIP IT APART, GET RID OF IT!"

He was screaming into my face, and my tears had returned. I opened the book and starting pulling out the pages, ripping and wadding, faster and faster.

I was crying. Lou put his arm around me. I kept pulling the pages away.

22

MAMA CAME ON THE SECOND MORNING OF THE THIRD WEEK. SHE JUST showed up. I wasn't ready.

I had showered and dressed and was heading for breakfast. There she was, in the waiting room.

I saw her before she saw me. I stopped in the hallway, just before the full turn into the room. She was looking away, toward the wrong hall, looking for me, I guess, or just looking away into her own thoughts. I had a chance to watch her, to catch my breath, and a great sweep of memories washed over me.

I remembered that big house by the ocean, Daddy coming in, she and I getting him across the room so quietly, then me bringing her that washrag and the mop. I remembered my boyhood nights in my room at home, Daddy's unsteady footsteps on the stairs, and hers with his, helping. I thought about the little waiting room in that country hospital where they had taken Daddy. I remembered the paint-by-number bluebonnets that the doctor's wife had done. We were all so afraid. But Mama had just gone right on into Daddy's room, into his broken interior. Each time, she did what she could.

She was smoking, and the smoke added to the gray of her swept-up cherrywood hair. Somebody had brought her a Styrofoam cup of coffee.

"Mama?"

Startled, she turned around. She saw me, all of me, all at once. She saw all the way in. I could feel it.

"Stephen honey."

Just the seeing of me was so much—the way she had seen my father. I couldn't say anything. She came up to me.

"Stevie honey, are you all right?"

And then I said the bravest thing I've ever said in my life. I was holding her in an all-over hug and my face was buried in her neck and the first stuttering breaths had already begun.

"No, Mama," I said.

I was sobbing, but I got it out: "No Mama, I'm not all right at all."

Mama wasn't one to philosophize or analyze or speculate, so we didn't go into what had been happening at the hospital, or what had led me there. She didn't like reaching across other people's boundaries, even her children's. It was one of the main rules in our house. Keep the door closed.

"Have you talked to Granddaddy about what's happened?" I asked.

"Honey, yes, we've talked," Mama said.

After we finished our coffee and dried our tears in the waiting room, we went to the hospital cafeteria for breakfast.

She didn't want anything—she'd already been to breakfast—but she went through the line with me. I introduced her to a couple of other patients and to one of the counselors as we went along, and then we went to a table in the corner.

"So what did Granddaddy say?"

"Not much. You know how Granddaddy is. He never says much about anything except how the government is bleeding us to death and civilization is about to collapse. Sometimes I think he's not even aware that a family has grown up around him."

"I know."

"I told him what had happened. I told him you were here. He seemed to listen, but it's hard to tell. You know how he is. He just doesn't respond. He just kind of fades off into the blue. I don't know if he's thinking about the stock market or oil prices or what. I don't know if anything I'm saying gets through to him."

"Yeah."

"So yesterday afternoon I told him I was coming to Austin to see you and he said he wanted to come, too. To keep me company, he said. Surprised the heck out of me."

"Granddaddy's *here*?"

"Yeah. He's back at the motel."

"Oh God. But why . . . How come he didn't come with you now?"

"He's been in one of his rages, Stephen. A big one."

"Oh God. What now?"

"Dear Lord, he's been on a tear ever since we left yesterday. He complained about all the traffic on the interstate—he never travels anymore, hardly leaves the house, I can't remember when's the last time he left town.

"Anyway, once we got to Austin, he had a fit about the price of the motel—thirty-nine dollars a night, which I thought was pretty reasonable but Granddaddy called it highway robbery. He kept saying, 'A bed, a lamp, a commode is all you're gettin', and they're charging this much?' Of course he remembers the days when you could get all that for a quarter at a boarding house."

I was smiling. "He's so far behind the times it's pitiful."

"Then he couldn't sleep last night. He said he tossed and turned all night, thinking about the price of everything and fighting with what he called his rubber pillow and feeling the lumps in the bed—I didn't feel any lumps."

"Y'all have adjoining rooms?"

"Yeah. And he was pounding on my door at five this morning, all agitated, so we went to breakfast and he got pancakes and he raised a stink about not getting enough syrup and why didn't they give you a pourer instead of those little God damn plastic containers that you have to open with your teeth and then they charge you a dollar ninety-nine for all that with hidden charges for the quote unquote free syrup. It was quite a commotion he made. They gave him his breakfast free. So now he's napping. I don't know what he's going to do."

"Is he going to try to come see me?"

"Honey, I don't know what Granddaddy has in mind. He never tells me anything."

23

Six of us were at a table eating lunch in the hospital cafeteria. We were talking about what was planned for us that afternoon and who was getting a pass for that weekend and about this new kid who'd been admitted the night before. "Spray paint, that's his deal," Arlene said. "What I heard, the kid came in with a red nose, you know, from getting too close to the paint."

"Sniffing his God damn brains out," Marie said.

"I hear Nurse Hatchet's already got a pet name for him," Arlene said. "Bozo."

This was the day Mama had visited. I figured she and Granddaddy had probably started driving back to Fort Worth by now.

Then all across the room came a falling off of voices, a slowing of forks, a billowing hush, and I felt a form behind me, something sturdier than a shadow, large.

"My God," Arlene said.

"Who the hell is *that*?" my roommate Mike said.

I knew before I turned, and then I turned in my chair.

My God. Granddaddy.

He saw me across the big room the way he could see us in the old days, down that long dining room table—dirty fingernails, a dot of toad blood, a devilish thought. Those old hawkish eyes could see right through anybody.

I wanted to crumple. I felt weak all the way down. But I stood somehow, and there I was in all my prodigal nakedness, having so thoroughly failed to measure up.

He was as towering and craggy as ever, snow-peaked, suited in that Sunday charcoal best of his and walking in like he owned the world, a large chunk of which he did.

"Stephen," he said to me from across the room, and his God-big voice brought that whole big room to silence. He came marching toward me in ten-gallon steps.

I found a proper smile and put out my hand to shake his, all automatically, a rote reaction learned from decades of formality. I remembered when Daddy came home from the hospital on the train and Granddaddy was there to meet him, standing off to the side. They shook hands.

"Stephen," he said again, but lower, a softened tone that I had never heard before. He spoke my name with the tenderness of a prayer.

I was instantly disarmed. His face was open and his eyes were broken and his arms came out and bent around me. He pulled me in under his old oak shade, pressing my face into his fading silk tie.

"My boy," he said. I could feel his old heart thumping against my ear. "My dearest boy."

PART

Home Again
1993–1995

24

NOT EXACTLY AT TWO, BUT CLOSE, GRANDDADDY SCUFFLED IN ON slippered feet. Miss Godwin, crooked and white-headed and not much less enfeebled than her charge, shuffled in at his side. They held each other up in a mutual leaning.

It was November 29, 1993—Granddaddy's ninety-ninth birthday. The ancient grandfather clock in the foyer hadn't been wound in years, so nothing tolled his arrival except a couple of digital beeps from wristwatches at the table. And that had been ten minutes ago.

We, a dwindling multitude, were assembled in the dining room. The boys were starving, and had not been unquiet about it. Will and Dylan had stood at the dining room windows, watching, waiting for Granddaddy to make his way from the Little House. After a lot of elbowing and butt-bumping and sniggering, they had raced back to the table when he was sighted.

For Granddaddy, it was a long day's journey into dinner. First, in the Little House, Miss Godwin had to help him get from his bed to the bathroom, then stood by outside the door as he fumbled through his private preparations.

She assisted him with remarkable subtlety. Granddaddy's fierce independence and solid dignity went from strong feelings about free will and free enterprise to the conviction that he could by God button his own buttons, which he couldn't, of course, but which Miss Godwin slyly fixed after he fumbled with each of them, from the top of his shirt downward. She never, ever commented on the errant stubble that his shaky shaving might have missed, but she usually had to help him repair the knot in his tie, straighten his suit coat, fetch his slippers, and guide his feet into them.

He used his walker to get to his front door, then was pushed in his wheelchair down the walk and across the driveway and up the sidewalk to Aunt Jew's old ramp on the front porch of the Big House, where a great heave was necessary. He was determined to walk the rest of the way, so with Miss Godwin at his side and with the secondary assistance of a cane, several of which (minus firearms) rested in Aunt Jew's old umbrella stand in the foyer, he made his semi-grand entrance.

Granddaddy was positioned at the head of the table in a second wheelchair—Aunt Jew's bottomed-out, bent-wheeled old one, which he was determined to get additional use out of. (It still had her crocheted bullet bag tied to its side.) His old chairman-of-the-board chair had become too high and unyielding for him to get into.

He was sunk low. He didn't care. Nor did he appear to be bothered that his Sunday suit was in the process of swallowing his shriveling body. It was the same charcoal gray wool suit that I remembered from the beginning of time, along with that same Calvin Coolidge–era necktie, which had been out and in and out of fashion over its long lifetime.

Granddaddy had lost weight because of his stubborn attempts to feed himself, but it was that same steel will that was keeping him going. Nobody was fooled by the touches of frailty in his appearance—the pink softness of his wrinkly face; the saggy, liver-spotted arms and gobbler neck; the angel-white hair. Those gunmetal blue eyes were as cold and clear and flinty as ever, and one never knew when they might spring awake to the present and take aim. The boys kept their fingernails clean and their ears washed.

His once great voice may have fallen into a shaky rasp, his ramrod frame shrunk into a question mark, his authoritative steps reduced to slippered whispers, but a mighty fortress he remained. He was a shadow of his former self, but that shadow had been so large in our lives that a little trimming of it didn't make much difference. Nobody crossed him, even this newest, MTV generation of Beckwiths.

The boys knew the drill. All of us did. As Granddaddy raised the Confederate butter knife, preparing to clink it against the crystal water goblet, we bowed our tired and gray and tousled heads. But instead of the usual blessing, Granddaddy said, looking to his right, "Dammit, Godwin, I've got to go to the bathroom again."

"Oh no!" Dylan said, exasperated.

"Mama, I'm starving to death!" Will said with a dramatic whine.

Liz leaned over to try to shush him, but it was too late. As the old man pushed up from the table, with his nurse guiding the push, he looked down upon the boys and said, "Look here, dammit. I may be old and I may have no teeth and my bladder may have shrunk to the size of a black-eyed pea, but I've got money, loads of it, and I can decide who gets what." He and Miss Godwin moved behind the boys, heading toward the foyer and the front-hall bathroom. "And unless you young scalawags want to be stricken from my will and sentenced to penury for the rest of your miserable little lives, you will by God respect your elders, which includes me at the head of your list. Is that understood?"

"Yes sir," they said, in huddled voices, neither sure what penury was but both quite sure they didn't want to find out, considering the snarl in Great-Granddaddy's voice.

"Stephen, say the blessing and get these boys something to eat," Granddaddy said as he scuffed out of the dining room.

"Yes sir," I said.

Dylan was at the upper end of ten now and had been living at what my mother called the Beckwith Nursing Home for most of his life. The boy kept them young and they kept him seasoned.

Will was nine. They were best friends, as close as brothers, and saw each other daily. They attended the same private Episcopal school, although Dylan was a grade ahead.

Liz and I had been living in Fort Worth for almost seven years by then, in a suburb not far from the Big House. We had decided to leave Austin after political upheavals in her office interrupted Liz's career.

I had for years been feeling burned out at my newspaper job anyway, so we both decided to quit and make big changes. Liz signed on as a junior partner with a small law firm in Fort Worth. Two years ago she was appointed a municipal judge, and a year later elected as a probate judge. I fumbled around for a couple of years and then became editor of *Lone Star Gardener*, a state-circulated flower and vegetable magazine.

We were busy, of course, but largely unstressed. We'd both quit smoking. The drinking was gone. The bonfire of our early days had become a quiet glow.

It took a while for the flames to damp down. Those first days home from Willow Ridge were rough. Thank God for AA.

They give you these little chips. One month. Three months. Six months. It's like money in the bank.

You go to the meetings once a week, more if you need to. Sometimes I went to more, especially right at first. Two, three a day sometimes.

When you've gone for the designated length of time without a drink, you come forward at the end of the meeting and get your chip to polite applause. They're these little plastic things, something like the pieces in checkers, light as air and ribbed around the edges. They feel good when you hold them in your pocket. You can slide your fingers across the bumpy edge and it feels like something real.

Nine months was the one I wanted. Daddy didn't get that one.

Six months. That's as far as he got. That's the one that was in his pocket.

Some change. His pocketknife. Keys. Billfold. All of that was in the big brown envelope the sheriff sent to the funeral home. And that dark blue plastic chip.

Six months.

Liz went with me to that AA meeting in Austin, in an old house that smelled like ashtrays and cold sweat. Six months. I got the chip. Same as Daddy.

"So how about a martini to celebrate?" she said afterward.

Sick humor. Real sick. I loved her for treating me like a real person again. We laughed and toasted each other with ginger ales. She for surviving with me for that long, me for simply surviving.

But I didn't tell her about the real anniversary, the one I really wanted. One hundred and ninety-one days.

I had gone back to some old letters, figured out from one I got from Daddy in the hospital just what day he went in, counted the days and came out with one hundred and ninety. That's as far as he got. I wanted one more than that.

Day One-Ninety-One came like any other. We were still in Austin. I went to work, came home at midnight, locked the door, let in the dog, like always. I went to the kitchen and got out the Merry Christmas tumbler.

Why not? It was the actual season. I filled it with ice, then water. All water.

I sat on the couch, in the same enormous quiet, Day One-Ninety-One, and listened.

Daddy didn't say anything. In my memories I went to the river and sat beside the shaded water. The evening settled over me. I went up to the porch and Daddy was there. We sat beside each other.

The night came down and we sat there and smoked. He wanted to tell me something—something he'd forgotten to say—but it didn't come out. I remembered the pages of the rehab script crumpled at my feet and went to bed and kept listening, but Daddy couldn't say it.

Year Two. Year Five. Daddy didn't say anything.

We moved back to Fort Worth, softened our lives, went to soccer games, school carnivals, *Star Wars*, Grandma's. I'd go to AA meetings about once a month.

Year Six. Year Eight. He didn't say anything.

Yet no matter how many times I said the Serenity Prayer each day, I still found myself, in the darkest of my nights, running from the center of my dreams. I knew who was there, waiting for me. He was sitting on the front porch.

In the spirit of ecumenism—and with a nod to my discomfort over the patriarchal role—I asked Aunt Kitty to say the blessing. She hardly ever got the chance.

She beamed her ungainly smile and bowed her mouse-brown head and began, in a softened screech, "Now I lay me down to sleep . . ."

I noticed Will, with head bowed, jabbing Dylan to get his attention and then giving out an exaggerated yawn. Dylan did the same. I sent a stern look their way.

" . . . I pray the Lord my soul to take."

"Amen," we said.

"Good night," Will said.

"Sweet dreams," Dylan said.

"Knock it off, guys," I said. "Thank you, Aunt Kitty."

As Vice-Patriarch, I had been made official carver of the meat. Almost immediately I hit a snag. The great hunk of roast beef began sliding all over the china platter as I tried to secure it with the sterling fork.

"You sure that thing is dead?" Granddaddy asked as he came back into the room. "You may have to wrestle it to the ground, boy."

I leaned into it, and soon I got a grip. I began to carve with the sword-sized gleaming knife, and the beef fanned off the side into wrinkled little heaps. I forked it over to the plates, which were passed to me and then were given plops of vegetables, the squash from the cheese-topped casserole dish and mashed potatoes from a heaping bowl. The boys were the first to dive in, long before the plate-passing had finished.

The feast—this unstoppable, unmovable, seventy-five-year Beckwith tradition, which we attached special occasions to such as Granddaddy's birthday—had begun. We still called it Sunday Dinner.

I was at Granddaddy's left, my designated seat since the year of my birth, 1948. Liz was next to me, then Will, Dylan, Odessa, and my mother. Across from her were Aunt Kitty, then Whyvonne, Laura, Ted, Arthur, and Miss Godwin. The old nurse was stationed next to Granddaddy. His old throne of a chair sat empty at the opposing end of the table.

Ted Blivens was the newest member of the family. Years ago he had been the foreman at the farm to the east and south of our place. Since the mid-1970s he had lived in a trailer—something like Bert's—under a jack oak near the property line, in shouting distance of Granddaddy's three-acre garden.

For years, standing at the back fence almost every morning, they talked growing and fertilizing and weather and more weather. Then ten years ago, when the Longleys sold out to the country club developers— Granddaddy had been telling the developers to go to hell for years—Ted and his trailer needed a home.

Judge, Odessa's husband and Granddaddy's chief helpmate, had died a year before, so Granddaddy offered Ted a full-time position on the Beckwith side of the fence. His trailer was moved to the spot where Odessa and Ethylene's worn-out houses had been. Odessa by then had moved into Aunt Jew's old room.

Now he and Granddaddy could talk about the weather on the same side of the fence, which is just about all Ted did anyway, except for a little hoeing and planting and occasional hammering on things.

A lifetime of ranching and horse riding and farming had brought arthritis to his back and legs and hands. The wind and sun had worn his Caucasian surfaces down to a solid, polished brown, with ropes of wrinkles looping across. He got around with a cane, but when he toured the rows of vegetable crops in Granddaddy's garden, he used a hoe to prop himself along, and he could get the stray weed with it at the same time. Usually he kept his Folger's can in reach for tobacco spitting, but when he was in the garden he aimed his spit at grasshoppers.

If there was one thing Ted knew, it was manure. Sheep, chicken, cow, pig—each had its particular nutrients, drying requirements, and smell, and he could sniff his way through the piles and get the right one on the right crop. He always had his sources and got only the best trucked in from surrounding farms.

As Ted liked to say, "It takes a powerful lotta shit to grow a good tomato." Ted knew his shit, his bugs, his tomatoes, and his weather, and had made a believer out of Granddaddy. He was the only person in the world Granddaddy listened to, at least since Judge passed on. They'd sit on the porch of the Little House, in metal lawn chairs that went back to the 1950s, and talk vegetables and a little politics and a lot of weather. I often quoted Ted in my gardening magazine, and he got a kick out of that.

Ted's main job was standing shoulder-to-shoulder with Granddaddy, holding back the tide of late Twentieth Century civilization, and so far they were doing a good job.

So many things had changed. Fort Worth had become a real city, and Ted and Granddaddy stood guard, making sure it stayed across their fence.

When I was a child the road that went past our house just outside the honeysuckle arch had been a country lane, a farm-to-market road that rolled with the raggedy hills and forested bottomlands for five miles before it joined a main thoroughfare deep in the present city. Now it was a four-lane, traffic-lighted thoroughfare through shopping centers and franchise restaurants and more suburbs, and it was almost always congested. It was named Beckwith Boulevard. ("Honor, hell," Granddaddy said at the time. "They're just trying to get an easement from me for a discount.")

Although the boulevard ran right in front of Granddaddy's property and had encroached somewhat, the Big House was set so far back the traffic wasn't noticeable. My mother had put up a new wrought-iron fence with an electric gate, and the honeysuckle had come back and heaped itself over everything, just like the old days. Once you were beyond the electronically coded gate (11-29-94, Granddaddy's birthday), the world was largely unchanged, just as the old man had always commanded it to be.

Granddaddy saw his main threat coming from the Beckwith Hollow Country Club, which now bordered the southern boundary of the property with the par-four hole six and around which some obscenely expensive houses and swimming pools had been built. They were part of a development called Beckwith Hollow Estates.

"The bastards," Granddaddy liked to say. "They took my name and messed up my land."

The problem was golfers. Almost as soon as the course was completed a half dozen years before, the golfers started slicing balls over Granddaddy's fence, then would climb over to retrieve them. He didn't mind so much when they went into the pecan grove, but when the balls landed in Granddaddy's garden, the golfers invariably trampled his tomatoes or beans, not to mention the footprints that were left across the well-hoed furrows.

"Those God damn golfers," Granddaddy railed. "Doesn't a fence mean anything to anybody these days?"

He had some signs made. In bold red capital letters against a silver aluminum background, they stated: "DO NOT, BY GOD, UNDER ANY CIRCUMSTANCE, CROSS THIS FENCE." Ted nailed one to every third fence-post along the back of the property.

After a couple of months Granddaddy realized the signs weren't helping. He and Ted came up with a plan.

They electrified the fence, one-hundred-and-ten volts. They kept the controls on the front porch of the Little House. They'd sit up there in the hot afternoons with their lemonade—lurking, semi-poised.

They'd wait for the most opportune moment, when a guy had one leg straddling the fence. They'd take turns flipping the switch. Usually they got a pretty good-size scream out of the unlucky fellow. Sometimes he'd rip his britches on the barbed wire, and sometimes his head would jerk so much from the jolt that his hat would flip off into the garden.

This was great entertainment to the old men, and sweet victory. Plus they gathered a pretty nice collection of caps. Wore 'em, too.

Golf balls accumulated as well. Granddaddy and Ted used them as ammo on a second front, the war against the squirrels. Ever since Aunt Jew's demise, which brought an end to her squirrel-thinning wheelchair hunts, the varmints had been increasing. They robbed Granddaddy of his peaches, which he found especially galling. They'd take one bite out of a peach and move on to the next. "Wastrels," Granddaddy called them. "Liberals."

Because the city had surrounded him and the firing of rifles was no longer permitted, he had gone to slingshots. Golf balls were the ammo, squirrels the target, and the old men went armed at all times. Although the shaky marksmen never hit any, it did seem to keep the squirrels on edge and reassured Granddaddy that something was being done.

"There's something I'd like to know," Aunt Kitty announced.

"What's that, Kitty?" my mother asked.

With her knife in one hand and her fork in the other, Aunt Kitty looked up blankly, her face gray-edged and deeply lined, and asked, "Which one's Beavis and which one's Butt-head?"

This brought a commotion of giggles and guffaws from the boys, which included a flare-up of freckles and a general reddening. Will was the reddest, with a scrambled mop almost as robustly red as his uncle Endicott's had been. Dylan's hair, in the strawberry blond vicinity, was only slightly less subdued, something like his father's.

The Beckwith estate, without Granddaddy's knowledge, had added cable television several years before, not only because of better reception but mostly because Aunt Kitty could tune in reruns of *Gunsmoke*. Watching westerns—especially *Gunsmoke*, but she would settle for *Wagon Train* and *The Rifleman* and, of course, *The Lone Ranger*—was still Aunt Kitty's chief entertainment, besides crocheting pot holders and killing dead flies (the boys had picked up the tradition).

The cable also brought in the most modern of the modern world. Dylan was not supposed to be watching MTV, but he had managed to, including *Beavis and Butt-head*, and had gotten Will to watch it with him whenever Will spent the night, which occurred about once a week. Aunt Kitty watched it with them.

So now she knew all about Beavis and Butt-head, except she couldn't tell one from the other. The boys had twisted the whole thing into a game.

"*He's* Butt-head," Dylan said, pointing at Will.

"No, *he's* Butt-head," Will said, jabbing his little finger into Dylan's gut.

And Odessa said, wagging a bony finger at them and shaking her cottoned head, "If y'all ain't both little butt-heads, then I don't know nothin'."

"That's tellin' 'em, Odessa," Liz said.

"No, no, not the boys," Aunt Kitty said. "I mean on the TV. You know, that one with the crewcut. Which one is *that*?"

"That's Beavis," Will said.

"No, Butt-head," Dylan said.

"Yep, it's Butt-head all right," Aunt Kitty said. Her eyes were closed and both hands were up. One went out, then the other. Right hand, left hand. "It's got to be Butt-head. He's always on *this* side," and as she pointed, a dollop of gravy fell off her full fork and onto the linen table-cloth.

Granddaddy, roused from a passing reverie, prepared to speak. He began with his customary, guttural rumble, which was his throat-clearing. The expected hush ensued.

He set his fork down, looked over his domain.

"So who's dead and who's alive?" he asked.

There was some tittering in the crowd. What had sounded like an argument between Aunt Kitty and the boys had made Granddaddy think it was Christmas Card Day.

"So where's the God damn list?" he asked. "Let's get this show on the road!" He was ready for a fight.

"Granddaddy," Mama said, "it's not Christmas Card Day, honey. It's your *birthday*."

"Whose birthday?" he wanted to know.

"*Yours!*" This time she shouted.

"Oh? Another God damn birthday? How many is it this time?"

"Ninety-nine!" Dylan shouted at him.

"*Damn* that's old," Granddaddy said.

One moment Granddaddy could be as sharp and present as a hungry hawk, like the old days, then he'd fade again, sometimes into the past and sometimes over a timeless horizon, into the ether, changing into an old, wide-winged eagle drifting across the thermal winds. My mother was always chasing him, shaking him, grabbing for his attention. It was her job.

She was chief financial officer of Beckwith Minerals, which had become more of an investment empire as the oil business weakened into the background of the Texas economy. Dealing with Granddaddy had always been the hardest part of it, and it had gotten worse as he aged—losing things, forgetting things, wandering across his garden in a steady state of grumpiness.

From the middle 1970s onward, in consultation with Granddaddy, Mama shifted the extra income from the family's oil interests into the stock market, investing in a handful of solid and well-known companies such as Coca-Cola, Exxon, and Merck. Later she gambled on a few unknowns, such as one that had something to do with that new-fangled computer business. "I just like the name of the company," she told me at the time. "Everything is so hard-edged these days. I just couldn't pass up a company with the word *soft* in its name."

She did very little trading; all buying, no selling; many of her stock certificates she kept with her clipping-stuffed recipe book in a kitchen drawer next to the silverware, while others Granddaddy had taken for "safekeeping" into the Little House, to one of a half dozen file cabinets. Sometimes they served as bookmarks for his *Montaigne's Essays* or *Gulliver's Travels*.

None of us had a firm idea what it all might be worth. In the kitchen drawer were at least three million dollars worth of certificates. We wouldn't know for sure about the rest of it until we could go into the Little House and sort things out undisturbed. Granddaddy would have to die first.

Since my return to Fort Worth almost a decade earlier, life in the Beckwith household tottered along. The Big House—and everyone in it—decayed with grace and gentility. Any unpleasantness, such as the Twentieth Century, was politely ignored.

That included the relationship of Laura and Whyvonne. Mama called them "friends." Odessa and Miss Godwin clucked with disapproval, but kept their clucking muted. Granddaddy surely must have noticed that Whyvonne was becoming awfully regular as a guest, but he never said a word. Nor did anyone mention anything about John's frequent and sniffling phone calls pleading for money or sweet-hearted Arthur's very private personal life (he was a librarian) or that moths had eaten most of the drapes in the conservatory.

Laura—as solidly athletic and square-faced and gloomy-eyed as she had been since childhood—was a biomedical researcher at Southwestern Medical School in Dallas, and Whyvonne was the women's track coach at a Dallas university. Both were doctors—Laura had her M.D., plus a Ph.D. in biochemistry, and Whyvonne had a Ph.D. in kinesiology.

They had renewed their friendship three years ago, when their careers brought them separately to Dallas, and their relationship had become a deep and lasting love. They lived on wooded acreage north of the city that was the re-created Eden of their girlhood, without bothersome brothers and absent fathers and all the petticoated rules of society.

With her rah-rah, back-slapping, towel-popping personality, Aunt Whyvonne was the boys' favorite. She raced them to the pecan grove after every Sunday Dinner and played whatever sport was in season.

Granddaddy was struggling to stab a piece of birthday beef Miss Godwin had cut up for him. The wobble in his hands kept causing him to clink emptily against the plate.

"God *dammit*," he said.

Finally he speared a chunk, but on the way to his mouth it fell off his fork, rolled across his napkin-bibbed chest (he looked just like Aunt Kitty in that respect) and, leaving a trail of gravy, plopped into the waiting mouth of one of the dogs who patrolled the underside of the table at all meals.

"God *dammit!*"

The lucky dog was Tricky, one of four who had insinuated themselves into the household after being dumped as puppies at the front gate. They were a mix of shepherds in a quilt of colors, brown and black and white. The others were Hickory, Dickory, and Doc.

Three of them surrounded Granddaddy's wheelchair. One was stationed at Aunt Kitty's chair. There would be occasional forays over to the boys, who could be talked into a handout or two.

As the meal wound down, Odessa and Arthur and Mama slipped out of the room. In a few minutes they were back, carrying in a sheet cake the size of a coffee table. It was covered with a forest fire of candles. As they moved into the room, they flipped off the light switch and began the song. The day was cloudy, and the lack of chandelier light was enough to give the cake a shimmering presence. Everyone began to sing.

Miss Godwin moved the dishes out of the way as they set the cake in front of Granddaddy. He grinned as the cluttered chorus came to an end: " . . . Hap-py birth-day to you."

And we were all ready when Granddaddy came out with the traditional quip, which he had been trotting out at every one of his birthdays for the last thirty years.

"Did anybody remember to call the fire department?" he asked.

With that everybody reached under their chairs and brought out the red plastic firemen's hats Mama had bought at the toy store. We were all in on the surprise. Liz got up from her chair and brought over the hats for Odessa, Arthur, and my mother. The boys, Aunt Kitty, and Ted put on their own, and Miss Godwin slipped one on Granddaddy, then pulled up his chinstrap. I had one on, as did Laura and Whyvonne.

Then the whole brigade bunched up around the old man, leaning into him, as Whyvonne stepped back to get the picture.

Granddaddy's face—with its hills and dales of wrinkles—folded into a wide and crooked smile. It was the last photograph we had of him.

25

CHRISTMAS CARD DAY. NOBODY HAD BEEN ABLE TO GET RID OF IT, NOT
even Granddaddy. Tradition kept its taloned grip on the family.

Actually it grew, sucking into its vortex of guilt and history all who
came near the Big House on the first Sunday of December. Soon after
Granddaddy's grand birthday, it rolled around again.

Liz was doing her family cards there now, plus cards to her courthouse pals. Will licked stamps, Dylan stamped on return addresses, and
both boys were being drawn in to the swampy, mucky soul of the Southern family through tales of lust and avarice and bourbon and ancient,
squirrel-shooting aunts. I was family historian now, a job I had inherited
from Aunt Jew. I did my best to keep up.

Whyvonne, who had become a regular for Christmas Card Day, sent
cards to every member of her track team. Ted included gardening updates
with his cards to his nieces and nephews. Mama felt obligated to send
shelled pecans to all the new neighbors in the country club estates. Miss
Godwin sent cards to all her fellow Sunday school classmates, as did
Odessa. Granddaddy groused and grumbled, signing a few cards with a
slashing wobble.

Arthur, who had become Keeper of the Death Box after he had
volunteered to set up the master list of Christmas card recipients on his
home computer, put each person's relatives on Excel spreadsheets, separated under subcategories such as Shelled and Unshelled.

Aunt Willa remained on the list. She was put under a special category: DECEASED, Possibly.

She got Unshelled. Granddaddy still wouldn't budge.

"Here's a sweet little old man in Fort Worth, Texas, who has just turned a hundred," Granddaddy said mockingly one January morning in the parlor, just after Willard Scott had exited his maps of windblown fronts and swirling jet streams. "The bastard. I'm not going to give him the satisfaction."

A week later—two months after his ninety-ninth birthday—Granddaddy developed a cough, which got steadily worse, which of course he refused to do anything about. Whether it had anything to do with Willard Scott, we weren't sure.

A general, deep weariness overtook him and forced him to his bed in the Little House. It was pneumonia.

Granddaddy was a fallen horse. The struggle was monumental. He'd lean up from the pillows on a shaky elbow, tightening the strings in his baggy neck, and then fall back with a whinny. He moaned and bellowed and snorted, and Mama and Miss Godwin brought him this and that, and tried to make him comfortable, but couldn't please him.

"God dammit, Godwin, where's my cane?"

"Will somebody come take this God damn tray away?"

"Hey, in there, I've got to go to the bathroom, dammit!"

By the fourth day the bellowing stopped.

I took time off from the magazine and came to the house twice a day—once in the early afternoon and again a little after midnight. I stayed at his bedside until dawn each night, giving Miss Godwin and my mother a rest.

At each of my visits Granddaddy's old pajamas seemed bigger as his body faded into itself. His hands were brown-mottled moths, fluttery and timid, and his closed eyes became latticed bulges as his face receded. The tide of his life was retreating.

I was there at the doctor's last visit. Granddaddy was sleeping on his side and the doctor was able to listen with his stethoscope, front and back. Granddaddy, except for his rattled, sighing breaths, didn't stir.

"The congestion's bad, just as you had described it," the doctor told my mother. "It won't be long."

"How long?" I asked.

Granddaddy, facing away, spoke toward the wall in a reedy, breathless grumble: "Longer than . . . you God damn . . . think."

But it wasn't.

On Sunday night, toward midnight, I came again. Ted was on the porch of the Little House, in his usual metal yard chair next to Grand-daddy's empty one. Behind him was a card table with a half-finished checkers game on it, plus an electrical control box with wires that led ominously out across the garden, toward the back fence. He was sunk into his red-checked flannel jacket, his hands deep in the pockets.

"Hidy, Stephen."

I walked up the porch steps. "Hidy, Ted. Kinda cold out here, isn't it?"

"Kinda."

"Been in to see Granddaddy?"

"Yep. Oncet."

"I guess he's about the same."

"Yep."

"Is he saying anything?"

"Nope."

"It doesn't look good, Ted."

"Nope."

I touched him on the shoulder as I went in.

"You sure you're all right out here, Ted?"

"Fine."

"You don't want to come in? Warm up a little? Get some coffee, maybe?"

"No thankya."

Ted never looked over at me. He stared away and down.

Mama was sitting at Granddaddy's little kitchen table, bobbing a bag of tea in a cup of steaming water.

"Hi, honey. Want some? There's plenty of hot water."

"Sure."

She started to get up, but I stopped her. "I'll get it, Mama."

She had recently turned seventy, and the changes were coming fast. The swirls of gray in her hair had become deep currents approaching white, and a shallower gray was leaving its banks and had spread through the rest. That same kind of gray seemed to have reached her hazel eyes, and her eyelids dipped and drooped with a kind of weight.

I took off my overcoat and draped it over the back of the second kitchen chair. I found a mug in the cabinet, put a tea bag in, and poured the water over it. "Any change?" I asked toward the kitchen wall.

"Not much, honey."

"Has he said anything?"

"Not a word. Miss Godwin's in there."

I left the tea to steep and went across the kitchen to the bedroom doorway. The lamp was low. Granddaddy had been rolled over to his side, facing me, and Miss Godwin was putting a new sheet down behind him. She didn't look up.

The old sheet was halfway under him, and I could see the wetness on it. Granddaddy was naked—his fresh pajamas were folded on the bedside table, ready to be put on him. The lessened light took away most of the pain of seeing him that way. I could see a bony arm and its drape of gray skin, a leg not much different from the arm, and the xylophoned chest thatched with white hair.

Granddaddy's face, without his teeth it, was a pitted prune. His sparse hair was fevered damp and plastered in odd swirls over his head. His eyes were closed satchels and his eyebrows had wilted. His laboring breath fluttered through his loosened lips. I had to turn away.

"MR. BECKWITH? IS EVERYTHING OKAY NOW?"

Miss Godwin had finished with her chores, put the new pajamas on him, and gotten him warmly under the covers. She pierced the Little House and half the estate with her voice, but he didn't respond.

As she came into the kitchen with an armload of soiled laundry, Mama stood up.

"Can you tell anything, Anna?"

"No change, Mrs. Beckwith. Maybe worse, a little. That congestion."

"Hello, Miss Godwin," I said.

"Stephen," she acknowledged.

"His breathing is so labored," Mama said.

"The death rattle," Miss Godwin said. "I've heard it before. Miss Jewel, she sounded like that."

Miss Godwin was every bit of seventy herself, but none of the efficiency in her voice or conduct appeared to have been compromised. All those years of contention with Granddaddy didn't show in her treatment of him. Her Christianity was as businesslike as the rest of her. He was another task.

"We'll go now, I guess," my mother said. "And Stephen, you come get us if you need anything."

"I will, Mama."

She came up to me and nuzzled a kiss against my bearded cheek, then she and Miss Godwin moved through the front door.

From the front porch I heard her say, "Ted honey? Aren't you cold out here? Don't you want to come inside? Stephen can fix you some hot tea."

"Nome," he said. "I reckon I'll be just fine out here."

She closed the front door, but I could still hear her. "Suit yourself," she said.

I took my tea into the bedroom and sat in my customary place, in the rocker beside his bed. I settled into the quiet.

Granddaddy's bedroom was the center of his kingdom. From this room had come the ideas and commandments that had created and accumulated and enforced an empire.

He surrounded himself with what pleased him most, work and words. A half dozen glass-fronted, overflowing bookcases lined the walls, and between them were as many metal file cabinets, scratched and worn. Across from his bed was his mahogany rolltop desk, big as a buffalo, and next to it, a library table.

Over every surface—desk and table and cabinet-top—were open files and unanswered letters, geologic maps and company quarterly reports, ledger books and seed catalogues. Scattered books helped anchor the loose pages to the surfaces. There was an Underwood typewriter and a hand-cranked adding machine.

On the nightstand next to his bed was a precarious pile of his favorite books, all of them ancient and weathered, smelling of damp dust and pipe smoke. The room gave off the sweet, musty scent of an old and well-used library.

Heat flowed from the central unit and, across the room, an illusion of heat from the gas fireplace. No wood was in it, just the blue and pink flames from the gas jet. Granddaddy hadn't bothered with real wood, ever, and usually was too cheap to turn on the gas except on rare cold days. It was in the midthirties outside, but that wasn't enough to qualify as a fireplace day. Now, however, he was too ill to protest.

The dim light from the lamp at the bedside, the flicker of gas flames across the room, and the background light from the kitchen behind us created small heaps of comfort. Granddaddy's breaths were long, thin sighs, occasionally rippling with little coughs. My chair creaked when I rocked, a sort of breath itself, which came in rhythm with Granddaddy's. The air outside was quiet.

I could see a weakening in him from the night before, and from the night before that. A week ago we were talking. Friday, when the doctor came, was the last time he spoke. He hadn't opened his eyes in two days.

And the breathing. It had gone from a gruff cough and a grumbled wheeze to something as thin as tissue. Then an hour into my night with him it went to a startling quietness. I got up from the rocker and reached over to touch his hand, which was on his chest.

The slow pulse in the corded vein rumbled warmly against my fingers. Below his hand I could feel the slight rise of breath in his chest, no more than a stirring, a twitch, a hesitancy. Then the easier collapse of an exhale, and another little climb to gain another breath.

The vein rolled loose from the little bit of pressure, and I let go, sliding my fingers across the fan of bones at the top of his hand. It was a furrowed garden, splotched with brown like newly upturned earth.

I came back from the kitchen with more tea. It was one-thirty.

Granddaddy had become restless, and all of it was in his hands. They trembled. His breathing trembled. A part of a voice, perhaps speaking to a dream, came from his unparted lips.

I set my tea down and went to him. I touched the papered bones of his hands. The trembling continued.

"Granddaddy? Are you all right?"

I noticed how alien my voice sounded in the hollow room where nothing but breath had been present for hours. My voice was raspy, half into sleep. He didn't respond.

I reached for my Book of Common Prayer, which I had brought from home and had placed on the nightstand beside me. I'd brought it for my own comfort and to see if maybe something from it might soothe him.

Liz and I, with reluctance and skepticism, had been going back to church because of Will. We wanted him to have a moral foundation— something solid to rebel against, at least—and I had chosen the church of my upbringing, the Episcopal. We didn't mean for it to, but faith took hold in us, gradually, gracefully.

I opened the book to the psalms.

I lift up my eyes to the hills; from where is my help to come?

I continued, but the agitation in Granddaddy's hands got worse. The mumbling became an almost moan.

Then I realized my mistake. I set aside my book and got the one from lower in the bedside stack, the shopworn Book of Common Prayer that had been at Granddaddy's bedside since his Virginia childhood. Its language was Elizabethan, unrevised for centuries. I opened it to the same place.

I will lift up mine eyes unto the hills; from whence cometh my help?

My help cometh even from the Lord, who hath made heaven and earth.

Granddaddy's hand went still. He held down his breath as if he were trying to listen.

The Lord himself is thy keeper; the Lord is thy defense upon thy right hand . . .

I read to the end. Granddaddy was quiet.

By three in the morning Granddaddy's breathing was feathered. I stopped rocking and leaned forward.

Granddaddy, my mind said.

His breathing was hardly there.

"Granddaddy?" My voice was only the breath of a word. I stood and bent and touched his dented wrist again and pressed my thumb into his spongy vein.

A pulse whispered back. A stir. He stirred.

His eyes opened, blinking, empty of seeing.

"William?" he said, a dry breath of a word. "William?"

He sighed, and the sighing was a folding, a closing of breath, the way a morning glory swirls shut at the end of a day. I continued to hold his hand, pressing into the vein, and I heard, down, down, the river going still. As easy as that, emptying.

I settled Granddaddy's hand over the other and pulled the covers up under his chin. I pushed back my tears with my hand.

It was time to go wake my mother. I stood. Beyond the door, in his chair on the porch, I could hear Ted snoring.

26

A mighty fortress is our God,
a bulwark never failing;
our helper he amid the flood
of mortal ills prevailing.

FOR ONE LAST TIME, GRANDDADDY LED THE WAY.

First came the acolytes with candles and a sterling crucifix, then the priest, reading prayers in a tolling cadence deep into the pillared heights of the church, yet Granddaddy's presence prevailed. His huge casket, of forged hardwood, bulled its way down the red-carpeted aisle of the cathedral-size Episcopal church of our youth. The pallbearers—grandchildren of some of the oilmen whom Granddaddy had partnered with in the old days and all of whom he had outlived—bore it with deference.

Granddaddy was enclosed in a casket of burnished walnut, with brass handles, at a price he would have thrown a fit about. "The damn thing costs as much as my last new car," he would have said, but Mama let Aunt Kitty pick it out from the funeral home's inventory, saying, "Well, what the hell, Granddaddy may haunt us for what we're paying, but if this is what Kitty wants, let's go ahead and do it."

We brought nothing into this world, and it is certain we can carry nothing out, the priest read as he moved down the aisle.

"That's for damn sure," I heard Granddaddy say in a private whisper to me. "And that's precisely my point about that damn casket. You could have bought a hundred shares of IBM for what that thing costs. What's wrong with plywood?"

We followed the casket in an uncertain procession.

240

My mother, holding hands with Aunt Kitty, was first among the family filing in. They were the leaders among the survivors—none of Granddaddy's siblings survived him, and only Kitty and my uncle Harrison remained among his children.

Next were Liz and me, with Will between us. Then Laura with Whyvonne, Arthur, and John and Dylan. Miss Godwin walked with Odessa, and Ted brought up the rear. That was the immediate family. Uncle Harrison led a secondary delegation of twenty or so cousins and their spouses.

The church was full—family friends, church friends, business acquaintances, and second and third cousins, once removed, twice removed, and, as Granddaddy used to say, some of them not removed enough. Everyone presented themselves with great dignity and dark finery.

Except John. The day before he had borrowed some money from Whyvonne—God knows he was good for it, with what he was inheriting—and had gone out and bought a bottle of bourbon, the family drug of choice.

All evening he drank it secretly in the back bathroom next to the conservatory, slipping the bottle out of a linen closet, as the family reminisced with cousins in the parlor.

John was supposed to be clean. He was going through a Methadone program—Methadone and I don't know what all—through an outpatient facility in New Orleans.

He had gone from coke to smack in the last few years, and it had finally broken him body and soul. But it did seem like he was rebuilding: his pasty coloring had gotten a touch of blush to it; his clouded eyes showed a little blue light; his washed-out hair had gotten some of its blond sheen back.

By midnight he was back to cadaver status. I had to help him up the stairs to his old room.

Mama could hardly get him up the next day. We pushed him through his morning preparations. He was bent and floppy and gray-green beside me in the funeral home limousine.

"Oh God," he said. "God, Stephen, get 'em to stop."

"What?"

"I'm gonna throw up!"

"Oh shit."

I tapped on the Plexiglas window and told the driver we had to stop. He flashed his headlights to the hearse driver, who flashed to the two motorcycle cops in front. We pulled off to the curb on Beckwith Boulevard, and John dashed over to a bus stop bench, leaned behind it and let loose. There were fifty cars behind us, lights on, idling. Dylan, next to Will on the seat opposite me, watched his father in sullen silence.

"God this is embarrassing!" Arthur said with a flourishing sigh.

"Why don't you just get over your cheap, tired self," Liz said as she hopped out and went over to help John back to the car.

Mama was one limousine back with Odessa and Aunt Kitty, Whyvonne and Laura. I wondered what she was thinking.

For man walketh in a vain shadow, and disquieteth himself in vain; he heapeth up riches, and cannot tell who shall gather them.

The priest—the rector emeritus—godly, sober, and arrayed in black—was of the old school, the Granddaddy school of ancient language and original sin and two-dollar haircuts. He moved from the prayers to psalms, filling the time it took this long family to get into the reserved pews up front. John was uncertain and slow.

"You can get somebody sent on his way to the Great Beyond in less than twenty minutes flat," Granddaddy once said, bragging on the efficient use of language in the burial service of the Anglican church, and if it hadn't been for the large family and its long procession, it could have been done in even less time.

We were late, of course, getting there. Not only was the procession held up at the bus stop, but earlier, just as people were gathering at the Big House for the parade of cars to the church, Aunt Kitty spotted a rare January fly on the dining room table, next to some of the funeral cookies.

She couldn't bear to give it free rein in the house while we were gone. We waited while she went for the flyswatter.

WHAM! And we were off.

I noticed Dylan wink at Will and point to the bulge of the bottle of dead flies in his pocket.

• • •

After several prayerful rebukes and a modicum of hope, we recessed out of the church, following the casket. The final walk with Granddaddy was accompanied by the organ-bellowing, buttress-shaking "Mighty Fortress."

And that was it. No eulogy, no fuss, not even any flowers except at the cemetery. Just as Granddaddy would have wanted it.

27

HARRY AND LARRY LEVY—GRANDDADDY HAD ALWAYS REFERRED TO them as the dueling Jews—were his attorney and his CPA. Don't ask me which was which. I'm not sure Granddaddy knew. He called them both "Levy."

They were humped and wizened, heaped in wrinkles, chimp-eared, suspicious. They shared an office, secretaries, clerical help, and a mutual aversion to each other. Granddaddy had been their major client for more than fifty years.

"Whaduz he mean here, seven grand for legal expenses?" the accountant would say, looking down at the year's debit column of Beckwith Minerals, questioning each item. "That Gott damn Levy. Don't let that bastard get away with it, Beckwith."

"See if you can get him down, Levy," Granddaddy would say.

"You goys, you don't know Gott damn nothing, I tell you. We have to look out for you. Hell, yes, I'll get that bastard to come down."

And that would start another row. Levy & Levy & Associates, at 600 Commerce Street, was a war zone. Granddaddy called the firm Levy vs. Levy.

The legal Levy would fire back about unnecessary tax expenses incurred because of Granddaddy's shortsighted accountant. Around and back they'd go, bickering, pointing out flaws in the other's work, demanding price reductions from the other. The overall result was a discount, which pleased Granddaddy.

We had lots of visits from the Levy brothers after Granddaddy's death. They'd come on Sunday mornings, spend the day out in the Little House looking for certain papers, and invariably stay for Sunday Dinner.

"What's with this oil trust, Levy? That trust should have been separate from the estate. And we could have done a charitable remainder."

"Horsefeathers, Levy! What in Gott's name do you know about it anyway? Stick to your Gott damn numbers, Gott dammit!"

It took them three months to get to the bottom line on the estate. When it was time, Mama gathered us together—another Sunday Dinner—to hear the Levy brothers' final word.

"It's devastating, if you ask me," Levy No. 1 said. We were still at the roast beef stage of dinner. They each had stacks of papers next to their plates.

"And what might that be?" asked Levy No. 2.

"Taxes, Gott dammit. Estate taxes. What the Gott damn attorney let the Gott damn government take."

"What did . . ." My mother was trying to reach in for some answers. They ignored her.

"You expect miracles, Levy? You want us all to go to Gott damn jail?"

"I want these poor people to have something to show for Beckwith's years of toil, that's what I want, Gott dammit! And something to show for these Gott damn attorney's fees, Gott dammit!"

Mama tried again. "So that means . . ."

"You could have sheltered these assets, Gott dammit! Municipal bonds! And what about these Gott damn long-term capital gains?"

They were sitting across the table from each other, menacingly shaking papers at each other, shouting, dribbling gravy.

"GENTLEMEN!" Mama said with a feminine boom, a Granddaddy flourish. "THAT'S ENOUGH!"

They paused and sat back with separate grumbles. But Levy No. 1 refused to desist.

"If Beckwith could see this," he said, "if he had a bit of life left in him, this would Gott damn kill him! Seven million in taxes!"

"Oh my God," Mama said.

"But there will be a bit left over," said Levy No. 2.

"I should hope so!" said Levy No. 1. "The attorney leaves a Gott damn pittance!"

"How much?" John asked. He'd been back in his drug rehab program and on the wagon for several months. Part of his color and a handful of brain cells had re-enlivened.

Levy No. 1 paged through a stapled set of papers, down, down through rows of numbers. Page 7. Page 22. Where was it?

"Here it is, Gott dammit," he said. "Yes, this is the final number, I believe." He squinched his brow and took his blunt forefinger across the page. "Thirty-eight-nine-eighteen, et cetera, et cetera, and change."

"Thirty-eight *what*?" John asked.

"Thirty-eight million, Gott dammit! That's all that's left!"

"Oh . . . my . . . God," John said.

"That doesn't include the land and the house, of course," Levy No. 1 said. "That's the oil properties and the liquid assets."

"My God," I said. "How much more?"

"The developers have offered another seventeen. Prime property, this is. We've just concluded the negotiations. You'll net ten if you decide to sell."

"*Million*?" Arthur asked. He'd perked up, too. We all had.

"Yes."

"So altogether almost fifty million after taxes," Mama said. "It's a little more than I thought."

"Are we rich, Grandma?" Dylan asked.

Whyvonne summed it up. "You ain't shittin', bro!"

"Hell, sell, but wait till I'm gone," Granddaddy had told my mother a couple of years before his death as they considered another, fatter offer from the developers. "This land and I have served our purpose."

We had another family meeting several weeks later and decided to accept the offer from the developers. With a unanimous vote from the family, my mother sold our fifty acres of ancient trees and fondest memories to the Beckwith Hollow Development Corporation. She kept the Big House and one acre that surrounded it.

She didn't want the house. For almost thirty years—since my father's death—it had been too much for her to handle, and for the last ten she had let the needed repairs pile up. Odessa and Miss Godwin were too old to help her clean it; it would have taken two maids and a full-time maintenance man to keep it going, which is what they'd had in the past.

So Mama first looked at the possibility of donating the house to a charitable institution and having it moved. However, after some bids by several house movers, it was decided that, although it could probably be cut into pieces and reassembled elsewhere, the cost would be prohibitive, especially the continuing maintenance. For that reason, several charities reluctantly turned her down.

In that same family meeting we voted to tear down the house.

Late that spring of 1994, after what was our last Sunday Dinner in the Big House, Whyvonne stood and suggested we have one last football game out in the grove, like the old days. It had been years since we'd all participated.

Dylan and Will were made captains, and they got to choose up sides. Will went with loyalty, picking his mother, his uncle Arthur, and me. Dylan, slightly older and that much wiser, went for quality—Aunt Laura and Aunt Whyvonne.

"Just like always, dogdowns are three points," Laura said. "Agreed?"

"Agreed," I said, "but these dogs aren't trained."

"Yeah, but we'll give y'all all four of 'em," Whyvonne said. And she added, with that sneer of athletic superiority she'd had since childhood, "Y'all are gonna need all the help you can get."

She was right. Will was quarterback, Liz was linebacker, and I was the center, the rest of the front line, and the wide receiver. Arthur was supposed to be taking care of the right side, but he usually hopped out of the way when Whyvonne came barreling through. He would have made a better cheerleader.

Just as I expected, the dogs weren't much help. Hickory, Dickory, Doc, and Tricky had not been properly coached, as we had been careful to do in the old days with Wilson and Woody. Then, one or the other of the collies could be counted on to take a quarterback sneak in his teeth and run it in for a dogdown. You just had to convince them to run the right way. Endy used hotdogs.

Before the end of the first half the other side had more than a hundred points, and we had three, thanks to a recovered fumble from Hickory, with Liz and me chasing him in the right direction to our goal trees.

Will kept calling plays that sent the ball my way. I kept getting smashed into the spongy, shady ground, sometimes by Laura but most often by Whyvonne. As always, she played for blood.

I remember lying on my back after another Whyvonne tackle, breathless, exhausted, and Will came over to help me up.

"Let me tell you something, Will," I said, "some wisdom from your old man that I want you to remember for the rest of your life."

"What's that, Dad," he said.

"When you're choosing up sides, always go with the lesbians first."

I had to be there to see that old behemoth fall, and so did Mama, but not the others. They said they were too busy.

By then it was summer. The property had been marked off with red-ribboned stakes, showing where the streets and houses would be. At least a dozen trees were going to have to go, and those awaiting the bulldozer were girdled with the same plastic ribbon.

Two weeks before, we had conducted a giant auction of the furnishings in the house, including things like the enormous chandelier, the pocket doors into the parlor, and even the wooden flooring. Everything sold easily.

Mama let us pick a few things for ourselves. I kept my old bed and Endy's, for Will and his guests, plus the piano. Arthur was an antiques nut and gathered up a number of small things for his condo. Laura and Whyvonne got the last of the saddlery from the shed.

John never showed up. He had departed a day after the meeting with the Levys, flushed with anger. Granddaddy had put John's inheritance into a life estate; to get anything except a monthly allowance, John would have to beg Levy No. 2 for it, and all Levy No. 2 had allowed him on that first day was enough for a bus ticket back to New Orleans. We hadn't heard from him since.

About the only thing Mama kept was the big leaded-glass front door. That was going to be the centerpiece of the house she was designing, which was going to be built on the same spot. She wanted everything else new and clean—air-conditioning that worked, heat that didn't thunder through the house, and no more stairs to climb. She wanted a kitchen that was easy to get around in and enough bedrooms for Kitty and Odessa.

Miss Godwin had moved in with a sister in Dallas, and Ted, who suffered a slight stroke after Granddaddy's death, was placed in a nursing home. Granddaddy had left them each a tidy sum.

Mama's bedroom was going to be in the back of the house, with the same view she used to have from her upstairs bedroom porch. Her memories lived there, she said.

"Dammit!" shouted Jerry of Mac and Jerry's Home Wreckers. He and Mac were each at the controls of a bulldozer. They had estimated six hours to bring the Big House to rubble. After almost ten, nothing much had fallen except the Little House.

The plan was to wrap chains around the pillars and pull them down. That, they surmised, would be enough to destabilize the structure and allow it to collapse under its own weight.

Mama and I watched from lawn chairs out in the front yard. One column came out from the middle, then another, crashing to the lawn and bouncing in a cloud of plaster dust. When Jerry extracted the last column and the hulk of the house was still standing, he hurled his expletive at Granddaddy's mighty fortress. He shut off his dozer and went over to consult with Mac, and they decided to come back the next day. Mama and I returned, too.

They brought reinforcements—a half dozen men and a third, bigger bulldozer. Next morning the three heavy machines lined up on one side of the house and rammed it again and again.

The diesel smoke fumed, the dust rose, and the house came down a corner at a time. My room, the back porch, the conservatory, the kitchen. The dining room, the foyer, the other conservatory, the front parlor. A century of diapers and fried chicken, confused aunts and toiling maids, love and despair, Montaigne and bullet holes.

Mama took my hand as the last wall came down. We left before the dump trucks moved in.

28

It had been a year and a month since Granddaddy's death. The property was almost unrecognizable now, with streets and skeletal houses. Mama's new house was just about finished. She and Odessa and Aunt Kitty were living in a rental house nearby.

Granddaddy's estate had been mostly settled and Liz and I got a boatload of money, plus the monthly proceeds from a trust made up of the oil and gas holdings. Will's college was paid for. Our retirement was financed—in fact, we were talking about early retirement, but neither Liz nor I thought we should quit our jobs. Because of my mother's age, but I think mostly because I was married to a smart woman, Granddaddy had named me trustee for the family business and other entities, such as Aunt Kitty's trust. Because of the Levys' age, I was co-trustee for Odessa's and John's life estates. I had a lot to learn and plenty of work. I had become the reluctant patriarch.

We were considering buying the river place from my brothers and sister and building a weekend getaway there. None of them cared about it. If Liz and Will decided they didn't like it, or if I decided the memories were too much, then the family would sell it. So on a late winter day early in 1995, with Liz and Will and Dylan, I went home to the river.

• • •

I hadn't realized how much of a going down the highway was, beginning at the high bluff of the last red-rocky hill. Suddenly, spreading down and out, is the Brazos River valley and fifty miles of vista. In front is the scrubby hillside and the winding highway, and beyond is a wide floor of farmland. At the far edge is a twisting of trees that hides the river.

We drove on by Dorthy's. Everything was the same—the dusty driveway and asbestos siding, greased-over windows and the 's, which had to be hanging on by a mere filament after all these years. A couple of pickups and a car were in front. Beer-drinkers. Regulars, probably. It was late afternoon.

"There it is," I said to Liz. "Sportsman's Inn. Remember?"

"Yeah, I remember." She was on the passenger side, speaking toward the window. "You see it, Will? Dorthy's?"

"Yeah," he said from the back seat. "Aren't we gonna stop?"

"It's kinda late," I said. "We need what's left of the daylight to get the tents and everything set up. We'll come back tomorrow for lunch."

He sighed back into the seat.

Dylan was next to him, absorbed in a hand-held video game. He didn't look up.

Soon the station wagon was rushing by the clickity air of the bridge. I looked out between the concrete slats and over the railing. The water was a little high but a good blue, moving well.

I was already driving slow and I got slower, curved once and moved left across the road to the shoulder and the gate to our place. I stopped the car and got out.

It had been almost thirty years. When Al and I had come down on that last day, I had gotten the gate because I knew it best. I opened it this time, too.

The rutted road curved and tended down, a half mile of it, through the ranch and to our little of piece of land on the river. First was the open brushland and then the shadowing live oaks, and in ten minutes of dust we were there.

Now I wanted the cabin to be torn up, burned down, collapsed, but it was there — the tattered roof and sagging porch, all of it leaning to one knee back on the other side.

The broken heart of it all. I had to look away.

"I'm glad we brought the tents," Liz said as we got out of the car. She had been keeping her eyes on me, watching me watch my past.

"I bet that place is full of snakes," Will said.

"Maybe ghosts," Dylan said.

I kept very quiet.

It took an hour to get our camp set up. There were lots more little trees than there had been before, so the clearing at the side of the house that I remembered had to be cleared again with hatchets. We'd been camping plenty of times at state parks, so Liz and I had a routine, holding the poles for each other and driving in the stakes and setting out the cooking stuff and unrolling the sleeping bags. We had two tents, one for the boys and one for Liz and me. They got theirs pitched far enough away so we all had some privacy.

As soon as we got things set up, I went down to the high bank. I always liked to watch the water in the last of the light. Almost always the wind died, as it had now, and the river was its own movement without a ruffle of air. You could see the quiet, bending strength of it. Every ripple was a muscle moving.

I wore a jacket but hardly needed it. Spring was waiting in the wings of the air.

The boys ran down to the water, threw some rocks, then went down the bank, yelling they were going to look for snakes. I yelled back I thought they had a pretty good chance of finding one, so I don't think they looked too hard.

When the boys got back I sent them to get the firewood. About the time we finished our sandwiches, the night came down. We got the fire going just in time to keep the chill away a little.

"Are you all right, Stephen?" Liz asked.

"Sure," I said. "Yeah."

The boys were in their tent, back to the video game with flashlights. Liz and I were sitting just outside our tent in front of the fire, letting it die. Beyond, to the left, was the cabin, leaning, worn, dreary.

Liz touched my arm. "Stephen, I'm cold. I'm gonna go get in my sleeping bag and read."

"Okay."

"Aren't you cold?"

"I'm all right. I'm gonna sit out here for a little longer."

"You sure you're all right?"

"Yeah."

Our little fire was enough to make nervous shadows on the leaning side of the cabin. I watched for a while.

I was cold. The shivering was coming in and going deeper. And so were the memories.

I had the flashlight. It wasn't very far. Liz didn't need to know.

In a minute I was there. One step up and I was on the little porch. The boards felt all right under me, solid enough.

My chair was over there. Daddy's here.

I went over to the door and pushed on it and that's all there was to it. The musty dark came open. The last door at the end of dreams, the door I never opened.

Al said don't go. Wait, Stephen. Wait! But I went in and Al was right behind me. He was trying to hold me back, but we couldn't hold each other back because we were pulled forward the way you are drawn to the drop of a canyon.

The flashlight. Everything. This time I had to see everything.

Inside it was the same, except bent down in the back, the leaning wall, but the nails were still there for hanging stuff on and the board that was the shelf; the air would have been twice as dusty damp if one of the windows hadn't been broken.

I had to make the flashlight go over to the cots. They were stringy and moldy and sagging, almost in the same place.

Oh God, Al.

Stephen. God.

"Daddy?"

He was there. One leg, that one leg with the cuff too high and a patch of gray skin and a blunted river of blood.

I went in with my flashlight. I had to see it all this time.

My breathing, strapped in; my heart, bounding; a taste of blood churned through my stomach.

Right there, lying there. Daddy?

I looked: a circle of bare floor, a gauze of dust.

I knelt. I touched the empty place.

29

"OH, STEPHEN."

The lantern was still on inside the tent. She could guess where I'd been.

"I'm all right."

"Shit, Stephen."

Tears were all over my face and in my beard, too many to push away with the back of my hand. I was so cold, deep-down shivery and out of breath, panicked for breath, knotted, reaching hard around myself for warmth. Liz came over and held me.

"You went into the cabin, didn't you?"

"Yeah."

She reached across the tent and opened my sleeping bag for me while I was getting my shoes off. I was working for breath.

"Shit, Stephen."

"I had to." I scooted down under the covers. "Lizzie, I had to."

She got into the sleeping bag with me. She wrapped her legs around me and put her face next to mine and worked with her soft hand to get the tears away.

"I had to see it," I said.

She turned the lantern down to a softened glow.

"I know," she whispered.

"He needed me, Liz. He's been waiting."

I put my head down onto the crook of her arm.

Slowly, a breath at a time, the constriction around my chest was starting to come loose. I worked to get my breath calm. She held me and we were quiet.

The river turned below us, below the high bank; I could hear it lapping. The boys were quiet across the way.

Lizzie opened my flannel shirt. She reached around and held me to her. She brought me close.

My breathing was coming back, pulling through me like warm waves.

Her face came down to my chest and she kissed me. I touched her hair.

I was breathing. I could breathe again.

30

"HERE, FART-FACE, LET ME DO IT," DYLAN SAID, GRABBING THE JAR FROM his cousin.

"Hey, I just about got it," Will said. He reached in. "Lemme have it, Dylan."

"Y'all better be careful with that," I said. "I'm warning you, that stuff is potent."

We were standing on the bank, just below our tents. Liz was fixing breakfast and I was trying to get the poles baited. The boys were supposed to be helping.

Last year, when I was helping Mama clean out the Big House, we came upon a whole case of Bert's Bloodbait #2 in the basement. Daddy must have bought it sometime before Bert died, stocking up, and then forgot about it.

I was overjoyed. Bert's legacy was alive.

I brought the stuff with us. I told the boys the story of Bert's semiannual concoctions, the roadside ingredients, the gathering of buzzards. I warned them of the toxic possibilities when the first jar was opened—it had had more than three decades to accumulate fumes. They weren't listening, of course.

Dylan was doubled over, squeezing the jar into his gut and turning the lid. Will was bent over beside him, trying to get it back. Their faces were inches away when the grand opening occurred. It might as well have been a canister of Mace.

The bouquet spewed out—it was enough to cripple a criminal. Their eyes puckered, their lips watered, their nostrils sweated.

"Holy SHIT!" Dylan yelled. He dropped the jar and ran. Will ran after him, down the bank, down and around the turn in the river and out of sight.

An hour later they returned. When they found out I'd just caught a two-pound catfish and had let two good bites get away, the boys were ready to try fishing with the bloodbait.

After breakfast we went back to the river. I showed them how to handle the stuff. The secret, I said as I baited the hooks, was to keep the jar at arm's length and to turn your head away when you first open it. Hold your breath. Pull out a fingertip's worth, roll it into a ball, and pinch it on the hook. Cast it. Breathe. Immediately wash your hands in the river, wipe them on your pants, and do not have any contact with civilization until you and your clothes have been washed through a double spin cycle. Bleach wouldn't hurt.

In less than an hour we caught three more channel cats, each around two pounds. The boys were hooked on Bert's Bloodbait #2.

By midmorning the action slacked off, and the boys broke away and wandered down the cow path along the river, to the outward bend and the little sandbar.

I watched them. Will had found an easy gait—taking wide, wandering steps, pausing to peer at the clouds and to let the wind come into him. He was learning already. This was the art of the river.

I watched the warming wind at work in his red-scattered hair, ruffling across his T-shirt. I saw him stop at the water and reach for a river rock, a perfect silver dollar of a rock, and skip it across the rippled water. Five skips. I had taught him well.

I remembered my good days here, summer days, when I was his age. I remembered coming to just that spot and farther, down the bank and around the curve from the cabin, where the water gets shallow. I would take off my clothes and put them in a pile.

I'd walk into the warm and tugging water. The sandy silt hugged my toes.

Deeper and deeper—ankles, thighs —and I'd let go and go free, swimming in an unsplashing dog paddle.

I remember the water lapping just under my nose, and with each inhalation came the deep-water smells of old wet wood and broken leaves and washed-away fish, the cattle and the deer drinking upstream, the snakes who lived there and the turtles too.

Brazos de Dios, the Arms of God. Embraced. I remembered. Daddy took my hand and brought me here and opened this whole ragged little world for me—its dusty weeds and patchy shade and rolling water. He loved it, he wanted me to love it, and I did.

Last night I was lying in the tent beneath the layered darkness, in the arms of my love, years deep in dreams. And in those dreams I was lying in my bed in that wide-open bedroom, ruffled in the windy night. I was ten years old.

I heard the front door. It was Daddy. I heard his steps on the stairs, up and slowly up.

They weren't broken this time. His footsteps were firm and easy, coming across the landing, the hall, and into my room.

I kept my eyes closed. I didn't want to ruin it. I'd been waiting for so long.

He came to me and bent. He placed his warm palm on my forehead and brushed back my swirled hair.

"Stephen," he whispered. "Stephen, good night."

By late morning the boys were back. I was still fishing.

"Y'all wanna go meet Dorthy?" I asked.

"Maybe," Will said.

"Nah," Dylan said. "I think I'll hang around here."

"That's fine," I said. "Just me and you, Will?"

"Sure."

Through Dorthy's Christmas cards I'd been following the news of the river community. Things had changed, but not much.

Dorthy had sold Sportsman's Inn a year ago, but it stayed in the family, in a way. She sold it to her "new" waitress, Eileen, but not before Eileen had worked for Dorthy for ten years and got to know all the regulars by heart, who liked what brand of beer and how to cheer up the loneliest of old souls, and especially how to make that chicken-fried steak to golden perfection, taught by osmosis through Dorthy by that original artist herself, Miz Abernathy. The gravy had to have just the right amount of greasy scrapings from the pan, and a dab of cigarette ashes didn't hurt.

Once Eileen mastered all the traditions and "passed mustard," as Dorthy put it, Dorthy sold her the place including the trailer out back and bought herself a new double-wide and set it up at Bert's old place. But she hung around at Sportsman's Inn most afternoons and evenings, drinking beer with the regulars, catching up on the gossip and helping Eileen out in the kitchen. It wasn't much of a retirement.

Dorthy would be at her trailer at this time of day, I told Will as I brought in the poles. We could walk. I told him it was best to walk.

We stayed on the road but our walking had a meander in it. Will took his cowboy boots and socks off, but I told him he needed to bring them along because of all the little rocks on Bert's Road.

Our road had pillows of dust on it, silky fine, and it was important that the bare feet know it. In places the dust was so deep he could slip his foot up to his ankle. It was like fitting your feet into feathers. I remembered.

Every turn in the road was new weather and a special view. At the beginning was the live oak cave where the overhang of green—winter and summer—permanently darkened the air and softened the wind. It was a place of whispers. The redbirds liked the thick of it, and their chirps had a jungle echo.

Then, at the outer edge of the live oaks, we went higher. To our right was a steep hillside covered in big, rusty rocks with crusts of gray-green lichen. Looking north you could see the highway bridge, and to the south you could see where the river bends, where it curves into our little cove of shade. We stopped here. I pointed it all out to Will.

"I want us to have a cabin here," I said. "I want this to be our land and we'll start coming here."

"A lot, Daddy?"

"Sure. Lots of weekends. A bunch in the summers."

"And a new house?"

"Yeah, Will. Where the old cabin is. We'll tear it down and build a big new house, maybe a log cabin, and all along the back of it we'll have the longest porch in the history of mankind."

"We could sit up there and watch our fishing poles, couldn't we?"

"Sure. The easiest fishing in the world. That's what my father always said."

"Mom said you might be too sad to want to come here very much. Because of your dad."

"Yeah. It's sad. I get real sad sometimes, Will. But I'll be all right."

"With a new house and everything."

"Yeah. I think it's gonna be all right."

The road turned outward into the sun, and the dust on the road thinned out. Mesquites, brushy post oaks, and hard green cedars dotted the slope above us. There were clumps of weeds and a hint of early wild-flowers. This was where the cattle fed, but today they were somewhere else.

We turned back again into a new shelter of trees. This time the bridge was hidden behind the hill. The dust was good again here, but the shade was shallower and the birds were quiet. We turned out a second time into the open range, climbing. In twenty minutes we were at our gate.

I'd already explained to Will the system I'd perfected when I was a kid. He wanted to try it. So before opening the gate I waited, leaning against it as Will sat on the road and slipped on his socks and boots. Then I unlatched it where the orange-rusted pipes came together, and the boy climbed on. I stepped clear and let him ride the gate down and away. It stopped with a lurch as soon as it cleared the second rut. A small rush and a pretty good jolt. You'd better have a grip.

I went on through. Will pulled the gate back and latched it. I watched. It would be bad if the cattle got loose.

We crossed the asphalt highway. It wasn't hot enough for the tar surface to cook, so our shoes didn't get sticky. In a minute we were on the other side and moved onto Bert's Road.

It was Dorthy's Road now, I suppose, but I couldn't get used to the change. Most of it, all the way to the trailer, was in the open, running through the same kind of weed-spotted, rolling land as at the end of our road.

The dust was thin and there were lots of little sharp rocks. Nobody walked on Bert's Road barefooted more than once.

Bert's three hills added up to a chore of a walk. There wasn't much to break up the monotony until the second one. At the top of it we could see, to the left, another hill that grew to the tree-topped place where we had buried Bert so many years ago. I wondered if the dynamite scars had healed.

Like the old days, the second hill was the end of boredom. That's when the first sound and smell of us roused the dog on sentry duty and got the uproar started.

Every Christmas letter from Dorthy contained a reference to "those damn dogs." After she gave them all away at the funeral, enough dogs escaped from their new owners to return to Bert's trailer and recolonize with the help of the few natives she had kept. Now she had about the same number of dogs as in the original herd.

She left Bert's old rust-streaked heap of a trailer where it had always been, and we could see it now. She had turned it into a giant doghouse. She kept the dog food in the back bedroom, behind locked doors, and turned one corner of the kitchen into a birthing room. She took off the front and back doors and gave the dogs and cats the run of the rest of it. She even left the old brown couch for them to sleep on.

So the dogs still had plenty of shade underneath the trailer, plus a place to go when it got cold. They pretty much stayed at their trailer and left Dorthy alone at her new one just up the hill, which I could see now, shining like tin foil in the sun. She had a big black satellite dish in the front.

At the first sharp bark, a great dusty commotion began in front of Bert's trailer and under it, barks and half howls and more barks, collecting, and then focusing, and finally moving our way. If Dorthy's count of thirty-one dogs was correct (as of her most recent Christmas letter), that added up to one hundred and twenty-four paws, which was enough to create thunder when they hit the earth and began moving toward us.

I watched Dorthy come out of her trailer as soon as the first warning barks were issued, and Will and I waved. She was in a stringy, florid housecoat, imitation Hawaiian. I could see she had put on a few well-packed pounds, but the wide dress hid most of it. She had a cigarette in one hand and a coffee mug in another. Her charcoal-flecked white hair was dented on one side.

"Stevie, is that you?" she yelled out.

"Hey, Dorthy!" I shouted back.

"That your boy?"

"That's him!"

"Looks just like his piture! So how's my favorite little sumbidge?"

"Does she mean me?" Will whispered.

"That's you, Will."

"Fine!" he answered.

Already I could hardly hear her. The barks and yelps and bayings of the dogs, caught up in the hills and bounding across the air, had become a canine "Hallelujah Chorus." By now the tone of the dogs had changed from guarded semi-growlings to boisterousness. Dorthy's kind words to us had tamed them instantly.

"Get ready!" I yelled to Will. I took his shoulder in my arm.

"I'm ready!" Will shouted.

I had told him, I had warned him, and here they came.

He wasn't ready. Nobody could prepare himself for this. I never could.

In less than a minute this cavalry of dogs surmounted the last hill between us, kicking up a chugging of dust. We stood still in the middle of the road. I brought my boy in tight to me, for mutual support, and then it all washed over us, tongues and tails and yips of joy.

I let go. About all you could do was let go and fall back into it, this rolling sea of fur, this grand outpouring of dogs. Will began to pet as many as he could, but he was soon toppled, and about all I could see of him as he went down was a grand smile and a swirl of dusty red hair.

"What a long damn time it's been!" Dorthy shouted over the wagging pandemonium, coming up behind the dogs, both arms wide open. "Come give the old lady a hug!"

Kay Haddaway

RICHARD HADDAWAY is a third-generation Texan whose father and grandfather were independent oilmen. He grew up in Fort Worth among an odd lot of literate eccentrics. In addition to his degree in journalism from the University of Texas at Austin, he is also proud of his certifications from the Bradley School of Bartending and the J.P. Elwood School of Taxidermy. A longtime newspaperman, Haddaway worked at the *Fort Worth Star-Telegram* for more than twenty years in various capacities—as a copy editor, travel editor, and columnist. Currently he is fiction editor of *Boys' Life* magazine. He lives with his wife, Kay, a CPA, in Fort Worth. They have one grown son, James.